THE MOURNER

After a degree in law and a stint as a journalist, Susan Wilkins embarked on a career in television drama. She has written numerous scripts for shows ranging from *Casualty* and *Heartbeat* to *Coronation Street* and *EastEnders*. She created and wrote the London-based detective drama *South of the Border* of which the BBC made two series. *The Informant* was her first novel.

Also by Susan Wilkins

The Informant

THE MOURNER

SUSAN WILKINS

PAN BOOKS

First published 2015 by Pan Books
an imprint of Pan Macmillan, a division of Macmillan Publishers Limited
Pan Macmillan, 20 New Wharf Road, London N1 9RR
Basingstoke and Oxford
Associated companies throughout the world
www.panmacmillan.com

ISBN 978-1-4472-4144-7

1 3 5 7 9 8 6 4 2

A CIP catalogue record for this book is available from the British Library.

Typeset by Ellipsis Digital Limited, Glasgow
Printed and bound by CPI Group (UK) Ltd, Croydon, CR0 4YY

For Sue Kenyon

PROLOGUE

Rain. Rain bouncing off flagstones, tumbling in torrents along the gutters. The storm made her put off leaving for nearly an hour. She didn't want to brave it, hated getting wet and windblown, but as with many a good instinct it fell victim to reason. It was close on midnight, so she had to get home. As she stepped out of Portcullis House onto the pavement the sheeting rain engulfed her. Within seconds her rimless glasses were awash. She pulled them off, slipped them into the pocket of her raincoat. At least she had a raincoat, but no umbrella; some intern had nicked hers from the office. The Embankment was quiet – a few cars and a night bus ploughing through the deluge. Two lads scampered across the road to catch it, T-shirts plastered to their torsos.

Helen wiped her face with her palm, peered myopically down the road – not a cab in sight. She stepped back under the loggia fronting the building. London was supposed to be a city of drab skies and drizzle, not monsoon downpours steaming off the pavement, not in June. But freak weather was the new normal. Apparently the jet stream had moved south. The 'new normal': that was a phrase that appealed to the politician in Helen Warner. She'd used it in her election campaign and in her maiden speech. It rolled off the tongue, providing a neat encapsulation of the times, regardless of whether you were going for a negative or positive spin. You could apply it to anything: corporate corruption, cuts in public services, food banks, the weather . . .

Was there a taxi rank round the corner in Parliament Square? She wasn't sure. But on a night like this, cabs would be gold dust. Helen concluded her best bet would be to walk south over Westminster Bridge. With luck, she might pick up an empty cab heading back into town. If not she might make the last tube from Waterloo. Mind made up, she tightened her belt, clutched her briefcase to her chest and crossed the road towards the bridge, head down, strands of blonde hair stuck to her face.

Her by-election victory had caused a modest ripple, even though most people couldn't be bothered to vote. It was a safe Labour seat but she'd added a few hundred to the majority. The leadership was relieved; she was young, telegenic and handled the combustible ethnic tribes of her northern constituency with tact and charm. Being a lawyer had become frustrating. Now that she'd found her true calling she worked late most nights on the causes that were her passion. Old hands in the party had warned against too much idealism, but she was determined not to drown in the cynical swill of Westminster politics. Still, she was canny. Whether delivering a sound bite for the cameras on College Green or baiting the Tories at PMQs, she was broadcasting one clear message: Helen Warner is a contender.

She skirted the base of Boadicea's statue. The galloping hooves of the horses drawing the ancient queen's chariot reared above her head as she leant forward into the driving rain. Across the river a blue mist shimmered off the old County Hall and round the wheel of the Eye. She was halfway across the bridge when a black cab emerged from the murk heading towards her on the other side of the road. Its yellow light was on. Throwing up her arm and waving furiously she stepped off the kerb to cross. What she didn't see was a solitary cyclist coming up behind her, pedalling hard. For an instant it seemed inevitable they would collide, but he swerved deftly to avoid her. She got a glimpse of angry eyes under a tight hood.

Holding up her hand in apology she cried out, 'Sorry!'

Her voice was washed away in the downpour. As she reached the far pavement the taxi drew up beside her. She grasped the door handle and pulled down but it wouldn't budge. She tugged at it a couple of times; the driver jumped out of his seat and trotted round the front of the cab. He was a stocky bloke, powerfully built.

She submerged her irritation in a smile. 'God, what an awful night. Your door appears to be stuck.'

No reply, no reaction – he just kept coming straight at her. A hand flew up towards her face and she caught a glimpse of what looked like a wedge of wet wipes before the sweet-smelling odour of chloroform hit her. As the chemical zapped her lungs, she heaved and gasped for air. Then the limbic brain kicked in. Staggering, she swung her briefcase, catching him squarely in the groin. He buckled and fell back.

Suddenly both arms were pinioned at her sides. It was the cyclist. He was behind her. His grip remorseless, he slammed her against the side of the cab. As he held her, the driver ground the toxic wipes into her face. She struggled and kicked. The cyclist grasped her head and smashed it hard against the door. Her legs finally gave way and her body went limp, head lolling forward. The cyclist caught her under the arms.

The taxi driver, still bent double, exhaled and mumbled, 'Vicious bitch!'

His accomplice glared at him, glancing quickly around. 'Let's just get it done!'

Shoving the wipes in his trouser pocket, the driver grabbed her feet. She was a lightweight. It took hardly any effort for the two men to hoist her up, swing her over the parapet and toss her into the river. The tide was high, the river swollen with floodwater. She hit the swirling torrent midstream, her raincoat billowing up briefly as she was swept under the bridge. In less than twenty seconds the current had dragged her under and she was gone.

1

Nicci Armstrong opened her eyes. Early morning sun leaked through a chink in the curtains, streaked across the duvet, warming and hopeful. She locked on to it, luxuriating in the blissful emptiness of bright white light. And for an instant it held her, suspended her in sweet oblivion. Then she remembered: Sophie was dead. Her child was dead. Buried not burned, with full Catholic ritual, Tim had insisted. Nicci had stood at the graveside, tearless and numb, in a borrowed black coat.

Now she couldn't stop it, her brain clicked into playback mode: the call on her mobile, using her warrant card to get past the young plod on the police cordon. Sophie lying across the kerb, one arm twisted behind, her fine fair hair in the gutter, dipping in a puddle of dark arterial blood. One paramedic stood over her, filling in his chit, the other was unfolding a blanket onto a stretcher. But where was the urgency? Why weren't they saving her? As Nicci lurched forward, the burly arms of a traffic cop ensnared her. She didn't remember screaming, although they told her later that she did.

In the many vodka-soaked nights that followed, she searched obsessively through the paperwork for clues. Printed in splodgy biro at the top of the RTA report: 'DOA', dead on arrival at A&E. But had they even tried to revive her? CPR, the paramedic was trained in it, but Nicci had seen him with her own eyes, standing there so calmly with his clipboard, filling in the form.

Nicci threw back the duvet and willed herself out of bed. The questions would always be there, questions but no answers firing across her synapses, following the same well-worn loop. She stepped into the shower. Often she found that just standing under the warm cascade of water and fixing her gaze on the white tiled wall helped clear her head. She discovered, with practice, she could simply let her mind rest on the snowy emptiness of the tiles; eventually the nagging cacophony would fade and she could get on with her day.

The flat was in Newington Green, newly built, open-plan sitting-room-cum-kitchen, one bedroom and a small balcony that overlooked a gated yard filled with bins and a couple of bikes. Nicci had installed a glass-topped table, flat-packed from IKEA, two chairs, a bed plus a luxurious deep-seated sofa from Heals. The sofa was second hand, a present from her old neighbour, Maggie, who'd insisted it was absolutely no use to her any more – Nicci was doing her a favour taking it.

The sofa was the one item of opulence in the bare flat. It dominated the wall facing the balcony, its plush velveteen fabric a chocolate brown island in a sea of bleached blonde wood. Nicci would sink into its soft cushioned folds, curl up and stare out of the window at the ever-changing sky. After the booze, the rows, the recriminations, she'd sold the old place; she couldn't bear to stay there, and this was the solitary cell she'd retreated to. She'd tried therapy, pills – it was all crap. The loop just kept playing in her head. Now she wasn't even sure she wanted to lose it; it was all she had left. It connected her to Sophie.

As she emerged from the bathroom her mobile vibrated and jerked on the kitchen counter. She keyed in the PIN, a text popped up. It was from Blake: *Check out news feeds – Warner case.*

Nicci opened her iPad and the home page brought up the BBC's website. She carried it over to the sofa, settled herself in a corner and scanned the screen. Under 'Breaking News' the third headline to flash up read: *Coroner's Inquest to open in Warner case.*

She clicked on it. The pixelated image dissolved momentarily and rearranged itself. Now the face of Helen Warner dominated the page, on the podium, in mid-flow, at the last Labour Party Conference. Nicci stared at the screen for a few seconds, then picked up her phone, texted back: *So?*

The kitchen was hardly more than a run of cabinets plus a hob, a sink and a microwave set along one wall. But it was serviceable. Nicci got up, filled the kettle and placed a green teabag in a small ceramic pot. Keep yourself fit and healthy she'd been told. People wanted to be kind; instead they'd inundated her with stupid advice. Every acquaintance had a helpful strategy to offer. Bereavement, she discovered, put you at the mercy of everyone's half-baked ideas.

While she waited for the kettle to boil she scrolled idly through the dozen or so emails in her inbox, mostly targeted sales pitches for goods or services she didn't want. But there, as every other morning, she found a cheerful missive from her mother. It ran to nearly half a page: the dog had needed a visit to the vet; he was beginning to feel his age, poor old boy. But the lawn was doing much better this year; having it aerated and treated may have cost a bob or two, but Dad had come to the conclusion it was probably worthwhile. As Nicci continued to skim through her mother's desperate efforts at contact, her phone buzzed.

Blake again: *Partners coming in. could do with yr input. 10:30.* The message ended with a smiley face.

Nicci poured boiling water over the green teabag, watched it turn the colour of pale piss. She sighed, stared at the tea and decided she'd pick up a takeaway coffee en route. Three shots; she had a feeling she was going to need it.

Since moving in Nicci had realized how fortunate it was that her flat was at the rear of the building. The front entrance opened directly on to the bustle of Green Lanes. As she stepped out of the door to the block a posse of schoolgirls barged by, loudly joshing each other. Nicci had to duck back into the doorway to avoid the burning tip of a cigarette arcing in her direction as one of the girls flung her arms akimbo. '. . . Then he goes, "You minger!" So I goes, "Fuck you!" 'n grabs his fucking phone and chucks it under a bus!'

Screeches of laughter greeted this revelation as the girls sailed on. Nicci paused to savour the passing whiff of nicotine and wondered how long it would take before she succumbed. She'd never been a smoker before . . . But then she'd never been a lot of things. The last year had turned her into a person she hardly knew. She recognized the face in the mirror but the blank grey eyes belonged to a stranger.

The day was bright but overcast, a temperamental summer day, the grey flagstones still slick with overnight rain. Nicci crossed the road, passed the Turkish bakery, made an effort to ignore the newsagents and the fine array of cigarettes they kept behind their counter. She headed for the 73 stop, where a queue snaked out under the shelter. Why did Blake always do this – whistle her up, demanding her presence at short notice? He insisted on trying to operate as they'd always done, as if nothing had changed. But of course everything was different.

The bus queue was orderly but sullen; it was a clammy London morning of crawling traffic, kamikaze cyclists, lorries parked in bus lanes and a general taint of diesel and carbon monoxide on everyone's lips.

Nicci recognized the old lady ahead of her in the line; they lived on the same floor. Somewhere in her eighties, she leaned heavily on her stick and her arthritic knuckles clutched the handle of a shopping trolley. She gave Nicci a smile. Nicci returned it with a curt nod. She wasn't about to become the Good Samaritan, the kindly neighbour prepared to fetch and carry for every OAP in need of support from the non-existent community around her.

But the old lady wasn't easily rebuffed. 'Settling in?' Nicci nodded in acknowledgement. 'You look out over the back, don't you? Much less noisy. I face on to Albion Road. You hear the traffic all night.'

Nicci turned away, glancing across the main square of Newington Green to where a bendy bus was inching its way round a parked van.

The old lady followed her gaze, her look turning baleful. 'Now whoever thought those bloody things were a good idea wants their heads examining! Look at 'em, always getting stuck. Course they're bringing in a new version of the old Routemaster. But who's gonna pay for that, eh?'

Nicci reached into her pocket, her fingers closing on her last tab of nicotine chewing gum. It wasn't much of a breakfast, but she could feel her annoyance and needed something to quell the impatience rising inside her, so she pulled out the gum and popped it in her mouth.

The old lady's battered shopping trolley had shifted and come to rest half on, half off the kerb. As she tried to haul it back on the pavement, three youths came loping by, avoiding the bus queue by walking in the road. The first was a gangling lad and he caught the edge of the trolley with his foot. The trolley toppled sideways into the gutter, sending the old lady tottering as she tried to hold on to it. Reflexively Nicci grabbed her arm and steadied her.

The old lady was shaken but she wasn't fazed. 'You wanna look where you're going, boy!'

The youth wheeled round to face her. He was possibly fifteen. The crotch of his jeans hung almost to his knees, his hoodie was regulation issue for every young urban male in the globalized world. 'And you wanna shut your mouth, bitch.'

He emphasized the point by depositing a large gob of spit on the pavement in front of the old lady and Nicci.

Rewarded by a smirk from his two companions, he hiked his jeans, rearranged his package and was about to move on when Nicci stepped forward. Before he realized what was happening she was in his face, hardly an inch from the end of his nose.

Her gaze was steady, a hard slate-grey stare, but a deep well of icy rage lurked beneath the surface. She scanned his face calmly: his soft tawny skin pitted with a few spots, the beginnings of a downy beard. He really was quite a handsome lad.

'I think you owe this lady an apology.' Nicci's tone was even, unhurried.

The lad reeled, took an involuntary step back. Then he laughed. 'Fuck off, bitch!' He turned to his companions for reassurance. 'Can you believe this fucking bitch?'

Nicci took another step towards him. Again their faces were inches apart. 'I'm serious.'

The boy's eyes flickered, he couldn't hold Nicci's steely gaze. But he couldn't back off. His shoulders jerked, he lurched back, pulling a knife from his jeans' pocket. He flicked it open to reveal a narrow stiletto blade about four inches long.

He waved it at Nicci. 'Yeah, then suck on this, you stupid motherfucker!'

Nicci gave the knife a dispassionate glance and smiled. She felt perfectly calm except for the rage. It was curled in her lower belly, an alien creature biding its time. 'What's that supposed to be? Your weapon? A little penknife to match the size of your little dick?'

The boy lifted the blade, his hand shaking as he pointed it at Nicci. 'Ain't no fucking penknife, it's a shiv – and sharp enough to stick it to you, bitch!'

Nicci's smile widened. But her eyes continued to bore into him. The creature inside liked this. It was what it craved. Now the anger was surfacing, shimmering around her like an aura. 'Okay, so let's see you try. I haven't broken anyone's arm in a while. This could be fun.'

The boy hesitated. His mates were watching. The whole bus queue was watching. His chin quivered. 'I ain't kidding.'

'Neither am I. I usually go for a clean break of the ulna – that's your lower arm. You'll hear it snap. It'll probably end up protruding from the skin, so there'll be blood.'

The boy stared at her, his face a mix of fear and incredulity. One of his mates hovered in the background. 'She's a fucking cop, man. Gotta be. Or some fucking anti-terrorist shit. They have guns.'

'You a cop?' The boy seemed almost hopeful.

Nicci allowed herself a small smile but her eyes continued to drill into his, willing him to make the move. She wanted it. The creature inside wanted it – wanted to hurt him, break him, make him bleed.

Sensing this, the boy lowered the blade, started to turn away. 'Fuck this shit, I'm outta here.'

As he turned, Nicci grasped his shoulder and spun him round. 'Not so fast. First you apologize.'

The boy was reddening now, any scrap of self-respect he had left was in the gutter with the old lady's shopping trolley.

He glared at Nicci, shame and resentment making him braver. 'I don't do no apologies. You wanna fucking nick me, nick me.'

Nicci laughed derisively. Suddenly her hand was on his chest and she shoved him back against the side of the bus shelter. He had nowhere to run. He looked petrified, his soft caramel eyes glistening with the suggestion of a tear. Nicci watched him for a moment. Then she took a deep breath and reined herself in. This was totally wrong, she knew that – he was only a kid.

With a shake of her head she changed tack: 'You don't do apologies? You have got to be the stupidest little fuck I've met for some time. So instead of turning to this lady and saying I'm sorry I kicked your trolley, you'd rather be nicked? Well, I have to tell you, sunshine, all our young offender units are fit to bursting at the moment. So they'd have to find a place for you in adult nick. And once the nonces set eyes on a fresh little virgin like you, they'll have a field day.' Nicci pulled her phone out of her pocket. 'But if that's what you want . . .'

The boy's shoulders sagged, he wiped his nose with the back of his fist. Nicci keyed in a couple of random numbers then hesitated. She had him completely, she knew that. She lowered the phone. 'What's your name?'

He swallowed, his voice a croak. 'Leon.'

Nicci gestured towards the old lady. 'Say sorry, Leon, then you can get off to school.'

Leon turned to the old lady, but he couldn't meet her eye. He stared at her feet and mumbled, 'Sorry.'

She responded with a nod. Leon turned on his heel and fled across the road; his mates strolled after him, trying to maintain some semblance of cool.

The old lady was beaming from ear to ear. 'Well, I've never seen the like of that! Not even in the old days.'

She started to clap. The rest of the queue joined in.

An old Jamaican gent doffed his trilby to Nicci. 'Respect to you, Officer.'

Nicci found herself marooned in a sea of well-wishers. She drew in a weary breath; a solid lump of embarrassment had settled in her gut. How the hell did this stuff happen? Yet again it had crept up on her, ambushed her, this fury she couldn't contain. But for the most part it skulked in the shadows, always there, biding its time, waiting for its chance.

And once again she had let it ambush her.

2

Kaz Phelps was the last person off the Glasgow train at Euston. A cleaner was already trundling through the carriages dragging his clear bin bag when she finally managed to collect her chaotic thoughts and her backpack and step down onto the platform. She hadn't been in London since they'd driven her down from Scotland for her brother's trial; she'd been totally cocooned then, escorted everywhere, securely accommodated in an anonymous hotel.

Joey Phelps had been sentenced to life with a thirty-year tariff. The look he'd given her from the dock remained etched in her brain. As she'd delivered the testimony that helped put him away, his eyes never left her face. They contained a chill beyond hatred, but she also knew he was making her a promise: she'd betrayed him, sold her own brother down the river and, no matter how long it took, one day he'd get even. But it wouldn't be today, or even tomorrow – or at least, that's what she got up each morning and told herself.

In her new life under the witness protection scheme Kaz hadn't paid much attention to the outside world. As Clare O'Keeffe she lived in a bubble insulated from the past. Her new carapace kept her safe but separate. She coped by keeping busy. So far as the world was concerned, Clare was just another art student with a family as ordinary, humdrum and boring as everyone else's. Her carefully constructed history was bland – a faked record from a sprawling London comp, an imaginary gap year, which had ballooned into an extended period working abroad. She was a mature student, older and cooler than the rest. And she didn't do any social media crap because . . . well, it was crap.

Mostly she enjoyed her new persona. It allowed her to skim through her days without addressing any deeper feelings and it was certainly easier than being Kaz Phelps, a convicted felon serving out her sentence on licence. To keep the probation service onside and ensure that she was meeting the conditions of her licence she was required to pay regular visits to the Criminal Justice Social Work office in Glasgow; her cover story was that she was seeing a drugs counsellor. In the eyes of her student mates this made her uber-cool.

She worked hard and obsessively at her art, socialized little and deliberately ignored all forms of news. So Helen Warner had been dead a full month before Kaz saw her picture flash across a television screen in the coffee shop where she worked part-time. The sound was always muted and she had to follow the scrolling caption to learn that a police investigation had concluded that the newly elected MP had committed suicide. Kaz pounced on the nearest student and demanded to use his laptop to check the story online. Reeling in disbelief, she ran most of the way back to her flat, buried her face in the folds of her duvet and howled. Then after a tortured night, wired on grief and caffeine, she packed a bag and caught the early morning train to London.

Standing on the empty platform Kaz felt desolate and alone. To say she hadn't thought this through was an understatement. She had no plan. Misery and shock had simply engulfed her. The love she felt for Helen Warner was the beacon that guided her; it had got her through jail time, off the booze and drugs, through despair and the years of waiting. It had even survived Helen's rejection of her. And the notion that Helen had taken her own life – jumped in the River Thames was what it said on the Net – well, Kaz simply didn't believe it. She wouldn't believe it.

Over a year had gone by since they'd seen each other – their only contact had been one postcard from Helen she'd ignored – but the news Helen was dead had twisted Kaz's insides into a knot of searing pain. Even apart and estranged, her ex-lover had remained a vital presence, the one person Kaz was still unconsciously trying to impress. And suicide? It was too unbelievable to accept. Something had happened to Helen and Kaz would find out. No matter what it took or how much it cost her, she'd get to the truth.

3

The taxi edged towards yet another set of temporary lights on Rosebery Avenue. It had been crawling since the Angel. Nicci peered out of the window at a tangle of blue corrugated plastic pipes sticking out of an abandoned-looking hole in the road. The red-and-white crash barrier had collapsed against a mound of mud. They seemed to be digging up half of London; all the cast-iron Victorian water mains were giving up the ghost at the same time.

Nicci checked her watch and leant forward towards the driver. 'You can let me out here. I'll walk the rest.'

He pulled in to the kerb. 'Sorry, love.'

She handed him a tenner; the 73 would've been cheaper, but the cab had offered her the quickest escape from the old lady and her new-found fans in the bus queue.

Turning into Gray's Inn Road she had only a few hundred yards to walk. The offices of SBA Security occupied the fourth floor of a recently refurbished pre-war office block. The interior of the building had been gutted, the facade clad with mirrored glass to create the impression of a new build. The entrance hall was now a lofty atrium filled with slick modern art and a small coffee franchise.

In daylight hours a double-shot espresso was Nicci's drug of choice. Catching the aroma she hesitated, but only for a moment. She was running late and Blake had always been a stickler for punctuality. She swiped through the security barrier and headed for the lifts.

Nicci had been a newly minted detective constable, barely out of uniform, when she first encountered Simon Blake. It was in the wake of the Stephen Lawrence Inquiry and the Met was desperately trying to clean up its act. Blake was then an experienced DCI who'd served his time in all the heavy squads – serious crimes, homicide, robbery. But as the culture in the Met was forced to change, Blake was a man who'd found his moment. At Bramshill he was exactly what they were looking for: he had a degree, an MSc in Criminology; he knew how to get results but didn't look like a meathead in a suit. Rapid promotion to Chief Superintendent followed as he headed up several high-profile murder investigations. And Nicci had become a fixture on his team.

In the last bitter days of their marriage Tim had taken to insisting that Blake had always had a thing for Nicci. How else had she made DS so fast when he was stuck at DC? What Tim didn't understand was that Blake was a player; he read the mood of the times and saw immediately that mentoring and promoting smart young women officers would set him apart from the old guard. Unlike some colleagues, he wasn't looking for any kind of sexual pay-off in return. If he stayed after work for a drink, it was only ever a swift half. Then he took the train home to Surrey, to Heather and his three boys.

When Nicci went on maternity leave to have Sophie, Blake had been poised for promotion to Commander. After that it was all a question of luck and timing – he was the right age, all he had to do was play the game and wait for his chance at one of the top slots. But that was nine years ago now, before both their worlds turned upside down.

Nicci stepped out of the lift and into SBA's spacious reception area with its oversized ferns and two huge undulating leather sofas. There, seated behind a glass desk, was the ever-immaculate Alicia.

She glanced at Nicci over her narrow red-framed glasses, raised a long, decorated nail and pointed. 'He wants you to go straight in.'

Nicci skirted round various workstations and headed for the large corner office. It could've been an upmarket lawyers, a successful IT company or a hedge fund. Around a dozen people were scattered across the large open-plan office – suits, ties, state-of-the-art computer hardware and a general atmosphere of quiet industry. Simon Blake Associates had been up and running for nearly six months. Their main remit was security, in whatever form the client required. They also provided a broad range of private investigative services from simple process-serving to preparing defence briefs for a growing number of law firms. Professional, trustworthy, discreet – that was the brand Blake was attempting to build, backed by high-tech surveillance and a rapidly developing expertise in computer forensics and fraud.

Blake had left the Met a very angry man. His career had stalled when he found himself the fall guy in a power struggle between the Commissioner and the Mayor. He'd had operational oversight of the Territorial Support Group and on his watch a couple of gung-ho officers beat up a climate-change campaigner on a demo, fractured her skull and put her on life support. She was eighteen, female, middle class and white, so the media went to town. Scalps were duly called for and the Commissioner's priority was to save his own. Blake took the rap and was moved sideways to a non-job in community liaison. Promises were made – his loyalty would be rewarded.

But Blake knew it was bullshit. He was tainted. So he abandoned any prospect of a full pension and walked.

A year down the road he was more than glad that he had. The end of his career as a public servant gave him a new lease of life. At fifty he was heading up his own business with equity partners who knew better than to interfere. Crafty politicians, unscrupulous colleagues and the baying media pack were all things of the past. SBA operated mostly under the radar and he was his own boss. And whereas the recession had sent many enterprises to the wall, the security sector was booming. Blake let his wife keep the Prius. He finally bought himself that Aston Martin DB9 and he didn't have to justify it to anyone.

Nicci paused at the heavy plate-glass door to the office. Blake was leaning back in his chair, mid-sentence, his hands outspread to emphasize a point. She caught his eye and he immediately waved her in.

Seated on the sofa facing the desk was a small woman clutching a coffee cup. Blake got to his feet.

Nicci mumbled an apology. 'Traffic.'

Blake's smile was only a tad sceptical. He waved a hand, indicating his guest: 'This is Julia Hadley – Helen Warner was her partner. My colleague Nicci Armstrong.'

Julia looked to be in her mid thirties, around Nicci's own age, it was hard to tell. Her clothes were expensive and slightly arty but her mousy hair was scraped back in a severe bun. Her cheeks were a little too pink, the darkly etched shadows under her eyes betraying a slew of sleepless nights.

Nicci stepped forward and offered her hand. 'I'm very sorry for your loss.'

Julia responded awkwardly. Her hand was decked out with

rings and was slightly clammy. But she met Nicci's gaze and nodded acknowledgement.

Blake returned to his chair as Nicci settled at the far end of the sofa, making sure not to crowd Julia Hadley.

Blake leant on his desk, placed his fingertips together pensively. 'Well, Ms Hadley and I have just been discussing the police investigation into Helen's death. They certainly pulled out all the stops and, on the face of it, everything was done that ought to have been done. Now the matter has been passed back to the Coroner.'

Julia Hadley turned abruptly towards Nicci, her eyes glassy with the glint of a tear. 'She didn't kill herself . . . I don't care what anyone says, what the police think. There's absolutely no way.'

Nicci nodded, more as a gesture of reassurance than agreement.

Blake glanced at the notes in front of him. 'The police seem to be relying heavily on the Facebook posting, which appears to be a suicide note—'

Julia Hadley erupted at this, her frustration flooding out. 'It's total rubbish! On Facebook? Doesn't even sound like her. And she was always leaving her phone lying about. She's lost two in the time we've been together.'

Nicci's eyes met Blake's. 'The suicide note was posted from her phone?'

Blake nodded.

Julia jutted her chin, her eyes darting from Blake to Nicci. 'Anyone could've got their hands on it. Anyone.'

Nicci nodded sympathetically. Julia could contain her grief but not her anger. That was a feeling Nicci knew only too well; trying to hold it all together and failing. Julia's raw pain reminded her of her own. She glanced at Blake to check that he was happy for her to pick up the baton, then asked, 'What about CCTV?'

Julia huffed. 'Yeah and that's another thing – where the bloody hell is the CCTV? She left the building just past midnight—'

'The building being . . . ?'

'Portcullis House. On the corner by Westminster Bridge. That's where her office is. She'd only been elected in January. She . . . she was so . . .' Julia sniffed and swallowed. 'It's what she'd always wanted, a career in politics. And she had to fight for it. Well, because of us. She wasn't going to lie. And some people are still quite prejudiced.'

Julia's eyes softened, for a second she was lost in memory. Blake and Nicci exchanged a covert look as they waited for Julia to drag herself back.

Rubbing her nose delicately with the tip of her index finger, she went on: 'She often went back to the office to work after the House rose. Sometimes she didn't leave until late – it wasn't unusual.'

Nicci nodded. 'And did anyone see her or speak to her?'

'A colleague saw her at the coffee machine about ten.' Julia sighed.

'But nothing later than that?'

Julia flung a challenging look at her interrogators. 'That doesn't mean she was planning to kill herself! She was working, that's all.'

Blake made a note on his pad then looked up. 'So . . . according to the security scanners she left the building at twelve seventeen. Then we have a gap of forty-eight hours until her body was found washed up at low tide down the river near Tilbury.'

Julia winced at this, the terrible end of the story. She took a breath, transferring her gaze to the expanse of sky through the window behind Blake as she forced herself to plough on: 'After she left the building there are no pictures. No record of which way she went. We're talking about the middle of Westminster, only yards from the Houses of Parliament, but that night half the CCTV cameras were on the blink! It's ridiculous.' Julia turned to Nicci, palms outstretched. 'It doesn't make sense. Unless of course it was deliberate.'

Nicci returned her gaze. When there was no sensible explanation, try conspiracy; she'd been there too. 'No pictures at all?'

'Well, the camera on the doorway picked her up.'

'But that's the last digital image of her?'

Julia tossed her head impatiently. Sensing that an explosion was imminent, Nicci reached out and gently put a hand on her shoulder. 'I know you must've been over this too many times already, and no one seems to be listening. But the detail matters. We need to build up as accurate a picture as possible of what we do know.'

Julia bowed her head. 'I'm sorry . . . I . . .'

'You don't have to be sorry.' Nicci waited for her to look up, met her eye. 'Seriously, you don't. So, no CCTV?'

Blake watched the interchange with the ghost of a smile. This was why he'd wanted Nicci here. There was something in her manner, a sincerity you couldn't fake. She'd been the best interviewer in the squad.

'The police supposedly looked into it,' Julia sniffed. 'It was very wet that night. They reckon some cables linking the network round Parliament Square, the bridge and the Embankment got waterlogged. And they were digging up the road.'

'That's London for you.' Nicci tried a smile.

Julia just glared back. 'I know. And I've heard it all. Cock-up, not conspiracy. The experts have spoken. And they may well be right. But there is one thing I do know for certain, Ms Armstrong. My partner did not jump in the river of her own accord. Helen did not commit suicide.'

Julia Hadley's eyes flickered as she spoke her lover's name for the first time. For a moment they all sat in silence. Then Julia reached for her bag and began rummaging until she found a crumpled tissue.

Blake and Nicci exchanged a look. In the Met their relationship had been very different. He'd been the big boss, she'd been just one of many officers on the team. Now they were operating in a different universe. The team had been reduced to a double act and they were both still getting used to it.

Blake cleared his throat. 'Well, Ms Hadley, the first thing I have to tell you is that we can offer no guarantees.' He glanced at his notes. 'The investigation into your partner's death appears to have been thorough . . .' His voice took on a regretful tone. 'And of course there's the issue of the suicide note.'

Julia couldn't contain herself. She leapt to her feet. Nicci hadn't realized just how small she was, how frail and birdlike, only a few inches over five feet.

She folded her arms defiantly across her chest and marched over to the window, then turned to face them. 'A suicide note on fucking Facebook! If you'd known Helen you'd know just how risible that is. Okay, she did Twitter, had loads of followers on that. But that was part of the job. She had no time for social media outside of work. So whoever set this up didn't even know her.'

Blake nodded. Julia remained, shoulders hunched, glaring

at him. Nicci watched in silence for a moment. She didn't want to add to this woman's pain, but they needed to dig, to get beyond the told and re-told story.

Keeping her voice calm and neutral, she inclined her head. 'What did the note say and why are you so sure Helen didn't write it?'

Julia spun to face her. 'It said that . . . that she felt she'd let everyone down and she couldn't stand that . . . Then it . . .' She clenched her jaw and swallowed hard. 'It asked people to forgive her. Forgive her for what? It's nonsense. Bloody nonsense!' With this the dam inside finally burst and tears coursed down Julia's cheeks.

Nicci got up from her chair, picked up a box of tissues from Blake's desk and offered them to her. 'What time was the posting? Was it after she left Portcullis House?'

Julia pulled a tissue from the box and blew her nose. 'About fifteen minutes later. The police said it was sent from her phone.'

Nicci pondered this. 'And the weather that night? You said the CCTV network was waterlogged?'

Julia wiped her face with the tissue. 'It was pouring. Torrential rain.'

Nicci turned to Blake. 'Well, if I was in an emotional state and I was going to commit suicide, I'd write my note in the office, then I'd go out and do it. I wouldn't try and compose it in the pouring rain on a mobile phone.'

'Could've been an impulsive decision.' Blake was playing devil's advocate; he knew Nicci had a point.

'It could.' Nicci's tone was dismissive. 'It's also possible someone could've cloned her SIM, killed her, posted the note.'

They both looked at Julia, who'd been following their exchange with a tense frown.

Blake pursed his lips. 'Did the police ever suggest that possibility, Ms Hadley?'

Julia shook her head, her lips narrowing into a tight smile. She balled up the tissues and tossed them in the bin. 'Fiona Calder was right. She said you'd be the best people for the job.'

Blake's jaw slackened, Nicci shot him a glance.

He paused for a second to conceal his surprise. 'You discussed coming here with the Assistant Commissioner?'

'Helen's father organized a private meeting with the Commissioner.' She let out a bitter laugh. 'It was all bullshit. Fiona Calder sat in on the meeting. The Commissioner obviously felt the need for a female presence. I think they were all scared I'd make a scene.'

Nicci caught her eye. 'And did you?'

Julia shook her head ruefully. 'What would've been the point? Afterwards, she escorted us out. She took me aside, asked if I was okay. Then she said if we weren't satisfied perhaps we should hire a private investigator.'

Blake could no longer contain his astonishment. 'She actually said that to you?'

Julia nodded. 'Then she mentioned your firm. Said you were former police officers, not some cowboy outfit. She said you'd be thorough and trustworthy.'

Blake and Nicci could only look at each other, both equally dumbfounded.

Julia gave a puzzled shrug. 'That's why I'm here. I thought you knew that.'

4

Kaz wandered across the station concourse and out on to Euston Road. She had to admit that in her new life north of the border she'd missed all this, though it was hard to say what this was. She was London-born but like many a cockney had grown up in Essex. Down south was home, the place she belonged. The light, the pace, the rhythms were unique. The streets were full of hustle and frequent hassle; people could be abrupt, disinterested. Still, in London she always felt free, it was a city of infinite possibilities. Endless waves of immigrants and refugees meant it belonged to no particular tribe and yet to every tribe. The global mega-rich bought up the best property because if all else failed and they needed a bolt-hole, London would save them.

Kaz wandered through Bloomsbury in the vague direction of the West End. She was adrift, but back on home turf, which carried her footsteps forward. She had nowhere to stay, thirty quid in her pocket, a maxed-out credit card and very little of her student loan left in the bank. She'd lost the flat Joey had bought her; it had been seized, part of civil proceedings to recover assets derived from his criminal enterprises. Not that she wanted it, but the money might've come in handy.

At first, living frugally hadn't bothered her. She was free and that was the main thing. She worked part-time and in her second year won a modest scholarship. But making ends meet had got harder. These days she lived on pasta and home-made soup.

And art supplies were bloody expensive. She much preferred working in oils to cheaper acrylics and on proper canvas, big canvases, which she stretched herself. But her furious work rate devoured materials. She'd taken to shoplifting oil paints – as did half the students in her year, but Kaz was far better at it. She knew about security cameras and blind spots, which shop assistants to avoid: stuff she'd learned as a kid, much as other kids learnt to ride a bike. Her mother, Ellie, had been an accomplished hoister back in the day; she'd shove Joey in the pushchair and Kaz would trail along at her side – following instructions, providing cover or filching the odd item, learning dexterity and speed.

Soon Kaz found herself selling surplus paint she'd nicked to other students. She didn't rip them off, only took a small profit, which helped keep her head above water. She didn't regard this as particularly criminal and the risk was negligible. It was no more than common sense to use the talents you had to get by.

Kaz stopped in Russell Square, found a bench in a patch of dappled sunlight and took out her phone. She scrolled through the address book until she found the number she was looking for. Yasmin had been her cellmate for the last year she'd been inside. They'd exchanged a few texts, but Kaz had been heading north into the witness protection scheme by the time Yasmin got out. Kaz didn't even know if the number was current, they hadn't been in touch for nearly a year. She let it ring, expecting it to be dead or disconnected.

After three rings a voice came on the line. 'Yeah?'

'Yasmin?'

'Who the fuck dis?' The tone was matter-of-fact rather than hostile.

Kaz smiled to herself – that sultry nicotine voice and its weariness. 'It's Kaz – Kaz Phelps.'

The line was silent for an instant then a dry chuckle erupted. 'The fuck it is! Where you bin, girl?'

'Long story. You still in Walthamstow?'

'Nah, I'm in the fucking Bahamas lying on a beach. Wot you think?' Yasmin chortled, a deep-throated, filthy laugh that immediately brought the image of her old friend into Kaz's mind.

Kaz grinned to herself. 'Listen, babes, I know I haven't been in touch but—'

'How's that little brother of yours? You living in clover, girl?'

'Not exactly. And Joey's in the nick. Doing life.'

Yasmin gave a low whistle. 'Sorry to hear.'

'That's why I'm calling, Yas. I know it's cheeky, but I've been up north. Now I'm back I need a place to stay. Only for a couple of days. Wondered if you could help me out?'

Kaz steeled herself for the brush-off, the vague excuses. Calling Yasmin was a long shot and the measure of her desperation. But what she heard was the rumbling laugh. 'Sounds like I'm doing better than you. You get your arse over here, I'll text you the address.'

'Thanks, babes. I really appreciate this.'

'Hey, no probs.'

Kaz hoicked the backpack on to her shoulders and crossed the square to the tube station. She took the Piccadilly line to Finsbury Park and changed to the Victoria. When the train finally emerged into daylight she gazed out at the endless

Victorian brick terraces and fifties council blocks of north-east London. This was territory her brother had coveted – rich pickings, but also riven with gangs. Kaz suspected there'd been some bloody battles, more than she knew about. There were plenty who'd established a lucrative business in these parts and who weren't about to give ground to some upstart from Essex. As Kaz rode to the end of the line, her gaze surfing through patches of sunlight, it struck her how little she actually knew about her brother, how much she'd ignored. Now he was out of her life, safely behind bars, but forgetting the past was impossible. He was still Joey. She thought about him every day and the guilt at having been the one who got him put away gnawed at her.

She emerged from Walthamstow Central, once a country station but long since swallowed up by urban sprawl, and followed the map on her phone to a neat road of bay-fronted, Edwardian terraced houses. There was residents-only parking, rows of wheelie bins and shouts of laughter from the playground of a nearby primary school. The address Yasmin had sent was number 27. Kaz stopped outside the house. The front window was obscured by thick lace curtains, the door freshly painted in black gloss. She rang the bell.

A key turned in the heavy deadlock, the door opened and Yasmin screeched, flapped her hands and swept Kaz into a hug. Kaz dumped her backpack near the door and was invited to follow her old friend down the hall.

Yasmin glanced over her shoulder, face wreathed in smiles. 'I can't believe you, girl! You look like a fucking charity shop. And the hair? Dyke cut – not cool. We gotta do some serious shopping.'

She herself was wearing a tight business suit, the jacket

tailored to the waist, emphasizing her figure, with a low-cut silk blouse exposing several inches of cleavage.

Yasmin cocked her head and grinned as she pushed the door to the sitting room open with the tips of her long manicured nails. 'Now tell me what you think, babes. Have I done all right or what?'

The room Kaz stepped into took full advantage of the period features of the house. It was an Edwardian parlour hung with plush velvet curtains. There was a red chaise longue, several armchairs and, in a glass-shelved alcove, a row of champagne glasses. Yasmin was bursting with pride.

She looked happier than Kaz had ever seen her. 'Done all the design myself. So whad'you think?'

Kaz didn't know what to think. 'Yeah, it's . . .'

Her gaze rested on a gilt-framed sepia photo of a regal Victorian lady in a corset holding a riding crop. She searched her brain for a suitable compliment and came up empty. It was sumptuous all right. The attention to detail was impressive and none of the furnishings were cheap. Still, there was no mistaking what it was. This space that Yasmin had so lovingly created was an upmarket brothel.

5

Nicci finally got her coffee hit courtesy of Alicia. She collected a pint-sized mug with the slogan 'Keep Calm Then Fuck Them Up', a birthday gift from her colleagues, and carried it back into Blake's office. He was staring out at the dead-eyed reflective windows opposite as he rhythmically jangled the coins in his trouser pocket.

Nicci watched him for a moment. 'Sure you don't want anything?'

He shook his head, ran his fingers across his close-cropped balding scalp. 'A very senior officer in the Metropolitan Police Service tells Warner's partner to hire a private investigator? Why would she stick her neck out like that?'

'You could try asking her.'

Blake turned away from the window.

He might be a businessman now, but more than twenty years as a serving officer had left its mark, shaped his sympathies. 'If this ever got out, Calder would be finished. They'd have her job.'

Nicci perched on the edge of the sofa, tipped a sachet of sugar into her steaming black coffee and gave it a stir. 'She must think the investigation's flawed.'

'Maybe, but would you put your career on the line for it?'

Nicci sipped her coffee; it was hot and sweet, another

newly acquired habit. She took a moment to savour it before answering.

'Okay, say she knows something. Maybe it's just a whiff, the hint of some kind of political skulduggery. That's a mine-field for the Met. So what does she do? You've got a bunch of neurotic politicians at City Hall and a hemmed-in Com-missioner. They go through the motions, tick all the boxes, but their first instinct is going to be to put a lid on it.'

Glancing at Blake she wondered if he was even listening. She was stating the obvious; he'd have already thought all this and more in the time it took him to escort Julia Hadley to the lift.

Blake rubbed an index finger over his clean-shaven chin. 'I doubt it.'

'You doubt they've put a lid on it?'

'Obviously they have. I doubt Calder's got a conscience. Wasn't that your next point?'

Nicci grinned. 'Yeah.'

This was vintage Blake – streets ahead and making sure you knew it. He had an arrogance that had not always served him well. In his Met days he'd worked to keep it under wraps, but Nicci had noticed his attitude had become looser of late, especially with her.

He drew a sharp breath through his nostrils. 'Knowing Calder, she's got an agenda.'

'So what we going to do? Say no?'

Nicci knew it was a silly question. Blake loved a walk on the wild side and there were aspects of the new business, par-ticularly the highly lucrative computer forensics, which he found decidedly tame. She recognized the glint in his eye: he was moving into overdrive.

He drummed his fingers on the desktop, sucked his teeth.

'What we're going to do is go back to square one. I want to delve into every aspect of Helen Warner's life, including all the stuff her partner, her family, her friends, her esteemed political colleagues and the papers don't know. Pascale and Liam can do the background brief. And I want Eddie in on this too.'

Nicci grimaced. 'Eddie? Oh please, Simon, no . . .'

'He's a very resourceful bloke. Don't be so judgemental.'

Realizing it was an argument she was never going to win, Nicci picked up her mug, got to her feet. 'We shouldn't touch this with a bargepole, you know that, don't you?'

Blake feigned innocence. 'Just some preliminary research, get the lie of the land. Then we'll make a decision.'

Nicci gave him a sceptical look. 'I have a couple of defence briefs I should be working on.'

'When are the court dates?' He started to flick through the pages of his notebook.

'End of September.'

'They can wait.'

'Okay.' Her hand was on the handle of the plate-glass door when Blake caught her eye. There was more.

He hesitated, but only for a second. 'First I want you to go and see Fiona Calder.'

Nicci let go of the door, stared right back at him. This was beyond the call. 'Me? No way.'

'Come on, she likes you, Nic. After the Phelps case you certainly earned her respect . . . and, well . . . obviously there's the other stuff . . .'

The other stuff. The death of her child. At least he had the decency to look slightly shame-faced, but Nicci still hated it; the assumption he could use her.

She gave him the look, the icy stare. 'It'll take me two weeks just to get past her PA.'

'Text her. You must still have her private number.'

Nicci wasn't about to budge. She stood with her ridiculous mug in her hand and waited. Blake flicked through some papers, checked his watch, but eventually he met her eye.

'C'mon, Nic, you know the deal. The business we're in now, we use what we have. 'Cause that's all that we have. That's why we're called private investigators. We've no backup, no legal authority. Nothing but our brains and our contacts.'

'And so I should use the fact that . . . that she gave me support . . .' Nicci's voice faltered. She swallowed hard and turned away. She was damned if she'd cry.

Blake watched her, conscious he was being tough, pushing her. But he also knew she'd hate it even more if she thought he was going soft on her. 'Needs must, Nic. She's never going to talk to me. I really wouldn't have a hope in hell of getting past her PA.'

Nicci kept her voice low: 'You're a fucking bastard and you can fuck off!'

Blake gave her an apologetic shrug. In the past she'd have never spoken to him in such a manner. But they weren't serving officers any more – no 'sir' and 'ma'am', no chain of command. This was a different world; everyone was freelance. He needed her and they both knew it.

Blake opened his palms in a placatory gesture. 'At least think about it.'

'No!'

'Could hold the key to this investigation.'

'Fuck off.'

Nicci grabbed the plate-glass door and hauled it open. Blake watched her go with a wry expression on his face; he was glad to see her showing some spirit. Six months ago he hadn't even been sure she'd survive. She'd been a broken reed but he'd offered her a job anyway. It wasn't altruism, it was self-interest. At least that's what he told himself. In a competitive market, he needed to build a reputation on results and he wasn't likely to find many ex-coppers out there of the calibre of Nicci Armstrong.

As usual, her instincts were spot on and she was right about the case. A sensible man would say no. In terms of time and aggravation, there'd be little profit in it. But profits weren't everything. Blake still needed a reason to get up in the morning. Going up against those smug bastards sitting it out for their pensions – that appealed to him.

A private smile flitted across his face as he pressed the intercom on his desk. 'Alicia, is Eddie about? Can you track him down for me?'

6

Kaz sat at the kitchen table, hands cupped round a mug of tea. The kitchen was long and narrow, at the back of the house with a side door onto the garden. She watched as Yasmin, standing in the open doorway, had a quiet word with one of her girls. The girl wore an ivory, antique lace negligee over a tightly laced bustier, forcing her small breasts into tiny mounds and reducing her waist to hardly more than a hand-span. The girl listened attentively to Yasmin's instructions. Her pale face was surrounded by a frizzy halo of auburn hair. She had an air of childish innocence. Kaz judged her to be fifteen at most.

Yasmin patted the girl's arm. She shot a nervous glance in Kaz's direction then disappeared down the garden. Out of the back window Kaz could see a low, prefabricated structure with a half-glazed door and a couple of obscured windows. It looked like some kind of site office. The girl opened the door and stepped inside.

Yasmin joined Kaz at the kitchen table. 'All fixed. The girls can bunk up, so you'll have your own little room. It ain't big, but it's clean.'

Kaz shifted in her chair, she wasn't sure how she felt about all this.

She'd come expecting a sofa to kip on, not a knocking

shop full of underage prozzies. 'Look, I don't wanna put you out, Yas.'

Yasmin smiled. She reached over for the clutch bag propped up on the windowsill and brought out a pack of Menthol Superkings. 'N't a problem, babes. Rooms in the house are strictly for business. But we cosy enough down there. Got a shower, three bedrooms, Sky and Wi-Fi. Trust me, them whores are spoilt rotten.'

She offered the cigarettes to Kaz, who shook her head. 'Still off the ciggies? Good for you.'

Kaz wasn't feeling particularly good. She was batting away memories of her own teenage years servicing the sexual needs of a drunken father. 'So how the fuck d'you get into all this?'

Yasmin pulled a brushed chrome Zippo from her bag, lit a cigarette and inhaled deeply. 'You was my inspiration, girl. Don't take no shit from no one, that's what you was always saying. I got out, I thought, Fuck this! I ain't going back to him. I don't need no scumbag pimp.'

'Yeah, but this must've cost a packet. Where'd you get the money?'

Yasmin tapped the side of her nose, looking smug. 'You ain't the only one learnt stuff inside. I done courses too.'

Kaz sipped her tea. 'I don't recall a course on how to run a whorehouse.'

'I done computer skills, found stuff on the Net – how to write a business plan. And that's what I done when I got out. Made a plan and went to see the man.'

'The man?'

'Mr Kemal – old john of mine. Got loads of interests round here: taxis, property, chain of kebab shops. Now I'm a businesswoman and he's my investor.'

'And he leaves you alone?'

'He likes the money I bring in. He got clients he wants to impress, then I hire a hotel suite, arrange a private party for them. Classy stuff. You in need of cash, babes? I can set up a few sessions for you.'

Kaz gave her old mate a sidelong look. Yasmin held up her palms. 'Strictly hostess work, you don't even need to fuck 'em if you don't want. Some of them are big tippers.'

'Thanks, but no thanks.'

Yasmin shrugged. 'Only trying to help.'

'I'm a student. Being poor is part of the deal. I don't mind it.'

'I worked with a girl once, she was a student. We done a lesbo double-act. She turned tricks her whole way through college. Now she's a doctor, an ortha-whad'you-call-it, ortha-something surgeon.'

'Yeah, right.' Kaz chuckled.

Yasmin put on a show of wide-eyed innocence. 'I ain't lying, babes. Her name's Shilpa. Still sends me a Christmas card every year. Reckon if I ever need a new hip, she'll fix me up.'

Yasmin cackled with laughter and Kaz joined in. In spite of the venue, it felt such a relief being in Yasmin's company and not having to pretend.

'So what's going on with you, girl?' Yasmin reached across the table and put her hand over Kaz's. ''Cause I gotta say, without meaning to cause offence, you look like shit.'

Realizing that the laughter had somehow turned to tears, Kaz swiped beneath her eyes with both index fingers. Yasmin blew a long plume of smoke up at the ceiling and waited. Then she got up, tore a piece of kitchen paper from a roll on the counter and handed it to Kaz.

Kaz wiped her nose and sighed deeply. 'Remember my lawyer?'

Yasmin sucked her teeth. 'Well that bitch was always gonna cause you grief. So what happened? Once you was on the outside she didn't want to play no more?'

'She had a partner.'

'Really? Wow, that's a surprise.'

'She did me a lot of good, Yas.'

Yasmin slapped her hand on the table. 'She was playing with you, girl. Bitches like that, it turns them on, hanging with the bad girls. She made you her pet, but you still a jail-bird. What you think was gonna happen? She takes you home to meet Mummy and Daddy and all her posh friends?'

The tears were coursing down Kaz's cheeks and they didn't seem to want to stop. Seeing this, Yasmin huffed, put a hand on her hip and straightened the bodice of her jacket. 'Now you making me feel bad.' Kaz's tears dripped onto the tabletop and started to form a small puddle. Yasmin tore off two fresh sheets of kitchen roll. 'You give me the address, I'll go round there and slap her myself!'

Kaz took the kitchen paper. She mopped her face, but still the tears kept coming. Swallowing hard, she managed to meet Yasmin's eye. 'She's dead, Yas. A month ago. I only just found out. Says on the Net she committed suicide.'

Yasmin's eyes widened. 'Fuck me!'

'She didn't commit suicide. No fucking way.'

'Then why they saying that?'

'I don't know. I don't fucking know!'

Yasmin put a hand on her shoulder. 'Oh, babes, maybe you just didn't know her as well as you think. We all got stuff inside we don't show. Maybe she had troubles you didn't know about . . .'

Kaz blew her nose hard. 'She was really clever, y'know. Got elected to Parliament. Back in January. She was always full of big ideas, stuff she wanted to do. She wasn't afraid to upset people.'

Realization spread over Yasmin's face, she gawped at Kaz in disbelief. 'What? You mean the MP that jumped in the river? That was her? I saw it on the telly. Ages ago. How come you only just found out?'

'I dunno.' Kaz balled up the kitchen paper in her hand. 'I don't watch much telly.'

'It's been everywhere. There were even pictures of her with some bint in *Hello!* magazine.' Yasmin sounded impressed. 'I never realized that was her.'

'You probably never saw her.'

'One time I did. In the visitors' pen.' Yasmin gave a rueful smile. 'Really had a thing for her, din't you?'

Kaz became absorbed with unravelling and refolding the soggy kitchen paper. 'Yeah. I did.'

A mobile phone on the kitchen counter trilled with an incoming text. Yasmin picked it up, opened the text, scanned it and huffed. 'Aww, that's all I fucking need!'

Kaz began to get up. 'Listen, babes, I don't want to put you out. I can find somewhere else to crash . . .'

Yasmin clicked the phone off, tossed it on the counter. 'The fuck you will. It's nothing. Just a bit of business, that's all.'

'I don't want to be in the way—'

Yasmin put a hand on her hip, thrust her shoulder forward and glared at Kaz. 'You got a problem staying in a whorehouse?'

Kaz pulled a serious face. 'No. But I ain't doing no lesbo double-act to pay the rent, okay.'

Yasmin tilted her head coyly. 'Nah? Don't you fancy me no more? You used to. I know I ain't her, but we had some sweet times, din't we?' Her wistful smile turned into a smirk. 'Remember when we charged that screw to watch?'

Kaz grimaced. 'Oh no, he was gross! I don't wanna think about him.'

Overcome by giggles, Yasmin wrapped her fingers around an imaginary cock and jerked her hand up and down. 'He was staring and pumping away at his limp little dick! Took him ages to get off. Remember?'

They both started to crack up.

Yasmin grabbed Kaz's arm, pulled her to her feet and enveloped her in a hug. 'You stay here long as you like, 'til you get your head straight. 'Cause I know you, Kaz Phelps, you're gonna go digging into this mess, n't you? And all you'll find, girl, is grief.'

'I just want to know what happened to Helen.'

'You won't never know that. Not for sure.'

'We'll see.' Kaz managed a thin smile. 'You're a good mate, Yas.'

'Too fucking right, I am. And you still fancy me a bit – admit it.'

'Yeah.' Kaz grinned. 'It's 'cause you're so fucking vain.'

7

The Investigations Department at SBA Security was stuck in a corner and occupied the smallest amount of floor space. Blake oversaw its caseload himself. But as his de facto number two in the unit, Nicci had the pick of workstations. None of this desk-sharing crap, which was the latest cost-cutting wheeze in the Met. Accordingly she'd secured herself a snug spot, back to the wall, panoramic view out of the window.

She dumped her mug, flopped down in the high-backed leather chair, scooted it away from the desk, put her feet up and took out her phone. She scrolled through the contacts list; Blake was of course right, she still had Fiona Calder's number. She stared at it. The other thing he was probably right about too was Fiona Calder's intervention; whatever she was up to would certainly throw light on the conundrum of Helen Warner's death.

Seated at the adjacent workstation, Pascale threw a questioning glance her way. Nicci was not known for her regular office hours.

'He must've got you out of bed.'

Nicci huffed, took a slug of coffee. 'Not quite.'

Grinning, Pascale returned to her keyboard. She hailed from the Ivory Coast by way of Paris, spoke five languages fluently and was the best researcher Nicci had ever worked with. She and Liam were the permanent back office presence in Investigations. Beyond that, Blake tended to rely on a freelance pool of former police officers, either retired or semi-retired. Liam, who was in his twenties, dubbed them the old codgers. But with the workflow changing from week to week Blake needed flexibility as well as reliability. He wasn't about to pay anyone to sit around twiddling their thumbs.

The core business was security. For that he had Rory and Hugo, a former army major and a captain, both of whom had seen active service in Iraq and Afghanistan. Large, square-jawed, posh public schoolboys, they were frighteningly fit and, although unrelated, could be mistaken for twins. A regular flow of beefy ex-squaddies in dark off-the-peg suits passed through the office en route to jobs as bodyguards and bouncers. At the end of a dire office party Nicci had got pretty bladdered and ended up snogging either Hugo or Rory; she was never quite sure which and so had subsequently taken to ignoring both of them.

The other side of the room and spiritually on a different planet were the techies. These were all IT professionals specializing in the burgeoning arena of cybercrime. No one else in the firm really understood what they did, Blake included, but he had persuaded his financial backers to invest in a shedload of state-of-the-art computer kit on the basis that this was where the future lay. The techies moved around in their own little bubble, huddling together occasionally for bursts of excitement as if part of a game to which no one else was privy. Nicci watched them from time to time, always busy like worker bees.

The section head was Bharat, a timid and painfully polite young man. Nicci had made a point of making friends with him. He loved to explain; given encouragement, his confidence soared. She was canny enough to play the girly listener.

In return, she got the lowdown on the latest gadgets, the best new apps and all the technical help she needed.

Nicci put the phone on the desktop and swivelled it round in a circle with her index finger. Telling Blake to fuck off had certainly afforded her a degree of satisfaction, but the detective in her was as keen as he was to find out why Fiona Calder had stuck her neck out.

From what they'd been told, it sounded as if the Met had conducted an over-hasty investigation into the MP's death, batting it firmly back to the Coroner. Yet Julia Hadley was adamant that it wasn't suicide. Although it was quite possible, even likely that Julia was blinded by grief, Nicci's intuition backed her judgement. That left two possibilities: accident or murder. Occasionally people drowned in the Thames, usually as a result of boating accidents. There was the odd swimmer who underestimated the strength of the current, the occasional drunk who misjudged their footing, but Helen Warner clearly didn't fit into these categories. Post-mortem and toxicology reports would be presented at the Coroner's inquest, and Nicci was pondering what these might contain when, out of the corner of her eye, she caught sight of Eddie Lunt barrelling across the room towards her.

Eddie was barely medium height but carried plenty of extra inches round his girth. His ginger hair was neatly buzz-cut and he wore a carefully sculpted beard and moustache. Always smiling, his features were cherubic. Yet Nicci thought of him more as a malevolent pixie.

He'd started his career going through celebrities' dustbins and built up a nice little trade selling celebrity gossip to the tabloids. Then ambition and technology got the better of him when an old lag of his acquaintance showed him how to hack voicemail. Eddie found himself in on the ground floor of this particular racket. Soon he had wires on over a hundred people ranging from D-list reality TV stars to the great and the good. As scoop followed scoop, the gossip mags, celebrity columnists and newspaper editors were queuing up to use his services.

When the shit hit the fan and the scam was busted, Eddie was one of the first to be hung out to dry. He pleaded guilty to illegally intercepting phone messages and served six months in jail. However, Eddie Lunt was never a bloke to waste an experience. He spent his time inside building up a raft of underworld contacts and mastering a few new tricks, and emerged from prison with his legendary optimism intact.

Hoisting his jeans from under his paunch, Eddie rested one expensively leather-jacketed elbow on the side of Nicci's workstation. 'All right, Nicola?'

This earned him a baleful look. Only her mother called her that and even then she didn't like it.

'Just been in with the guvnor. The Warner case! That's a turn-up, innit. Simon says I'm on the team. Says you asked for me specially.'

'He's winding you up, Eddie.' She gave him a regal smile. 'I hate you as much as I ever did.'

Eddie shrugged, a man totally beyond offence. 'No worries. Rumour has it the honourable member was a bit of a party girl. Probably liked a toot. So is that an angle you wanna play?'

Nicci folded her arms and turned her chair to face him. 'Eddie, let me explain something to you. A woman has died. Possibly in suspicious circumstances. Our job is to find out what happened to her. What we're looking for here is the truth. Not an angle. Not a story. We want to establish who was involved and the actual events that took place. Does that make any sense to you?'

Eddie nodded, grin still in place, like a schoolboy faced with a grumpy teacher who for some strange reason wouldn't accede to his charms. 'I know a few dealers on the Westminster beat. Posh boys, very discreet. Supply you anything. Top-notch gear. You want me to find out if Helen Warner was on anyone's radar?'

'Excellent idea.' Anything to get rid of him.

Eddie beamed. 'No worries. I'll keep you posted.'

The phone on Nicci's desk vibrated with an incoming text, drawing a speculative glance from Eddie. 'Boyfriend on your case, is he?'

Nicci picked up the phone and fixed him with her iciest stare. 'You ever, *ever* touch my phone or any of my stuff, I will hack off your balls with the bluntest instrument I can find. Do I make myself clear?'

'Fair enough.' He shrugged and lumbered off towards his own desk, where he unwrapped a sub the size of a baguette and started to devour it in canine gulps.

Exchanging a disdainful glance with Pascale, Nicci clicked on to the newly arrived text. It was from Blake and read *please*, followed by a smiley face with heart-shaped eyes.

Nicci ran her hand through her hair and sighed. She knew she was snookered. She could continue to kick off, go home, open a bottle of vodka. But where would that get her?

Fiona Calder had been a more than decent boss. When the investigation into career criminal and psychopath Joey Phelps looked set to go pear-shaped, Calder had personally stepped in and overseen his arrest. Instead of claiming all the credit, she'd happily acknowledged Nicci's contribution, letting her know she could expect to make DI when the next vacancy came up. But Sophie's death had put paid to all that. In the mayhem that ensued Calder had tried to support her, but the Met had policies and policies ruled. The second time she was found to be drunk and incapable on duty the Met's disciplinary system kicked in. She was processed, counselled, and still the result was a foregone conclusion – retirement on medical grounds.

Nicci didn't regard herself as an alcoholic or even a problem drinker. She drank when she needed to numb the pain. In the circumstances, she regarded it as a reasonable strategy.

Casting another glance across the room at Eddie, she pocketed her phone and got up. 'Pascale, can I bum a ciggie?'

'Thought you'd stopped again.'

'Stop, start – y'know how it is.'

Pascale rooted in her capacious bag, brought out a packet of lights and tossed it to Nicci.

'No, I only want one.' She slipped a single cigarette out before returning the packet. Holding the filter delicately between thumb and forefinger, she headed for the lifts.

When she stepped out of the main doors she saw that the building's miscreant band of smokers and skivers were sunning themselves against a wall. She accepted a light, pulled down a lungful of smoke and held it. It made her feel like a defiant teenager again. It also made her feel sick. She exhaled, managed a couple more puffs, then dropped the cigarette on the pavement and ground it aggressively under her heel.

Why did nothing ever bring relief? Why was she alive and Sophie dead? Why couldn't she have been lucky and led an ordinary, blameless existence, like her parents, like her sister? She'd tried her best, worked hard to be a decent police officer. Why had she been singled out to wade through shit?

As the anger blossomed, bringing a tension to her chest and diaphragm, she pulled out her phone and keyed in the PIN. Swiping through her contacts, she found the number again. She didn't owe this woman a single thing. She certainly didn't owe the Met anything. Use, be used, it was the same merry-go-round for everyone. Calder had a choice, she could tell her to fuck off. Nicci allowed the resentment and self-pity to build to a crescendo, and once she was sure she didn't give a flying fuck for anyone, she stroked her thumb over the number and watched the screen turn to a black void before informing her that she was calling Fiona Calder.

8

Kaz hadn't realized how tired she was. The journey down from Scotland, combined with the heartache of Helen's death, had taken its toll. The little cabin-like room in Yasmin's pre-fabricated shed was as neat and cosy as she'd promised, and Kaz slept for a couple of hours until the afternoon sun came blazing between the venetian blinds and woke her.

She could hear whispered voices through the thin partition wall. There were three girls, all teenagers; Yasmin had introduced them. Two were from Belarus, their skin pale and translucent. The other girl was a Somali refugee. Ebony and ivory: Yasmin reckoned that was her brand and a definite hit with the punters. They were all illegal and had been supplied by a cousin of Mr Kemal. Yasmin explained she had other girls who worked on a freelance basis, but they tended to be older and have families.

Kaz struggled to sit up. Her neck was stiff and her head ached. She coughed; her chest felt tight and sore with the first hint of an infection. Hanna, the auburn-haired waif that she'd first seen in the kitchen, put her head round the door.

Her eyes were a pallid green and extremely wary. 'You want coffee?' The soft voice carried a marked accent.

'Yeah, cheers.'

'Espresso? Cappuccino? Latte? We got machine.'

'All mod cons, eh?' Kaz grinned. 'I'll have a latte.'

The girl scanned Kaz's face; she seemed to be searching for clues. 'Yasmin good boss, very good boss.'

Kaz met her gaze with a direct look. 'You don't have to say that, y'know. Just 'cause I'm her mate.'

The girl shrugged, but there was defiance in the green eyes. 'I don't say lies.'

'Good for you.' Kaz grimaced and twisted her neck to ease the tension. 'Don't suppose you got any painkillers?'

The girl nodded and disappeared. Kaz could hear a snatch of conversation in an incomprehensible tongue and a stifled giggle. She glanced at her watch: nearly three o'clock.

At half four she was supposed to start her shift at the coffee shop, which she'd completely spaced out. She could deal with that by calling in sick. But in three days' time she had her monthly scheduled appointment with her probation officer; if she didn't show up for that then they would definitely know she was off the grid. Kaz thought about this and decided she didn't care.

Hanna returned with a glass of water and a blister pack of ibuprofen. She handed them to Kaz.

'Cheers.' Kaz swallowed two tablets and drank the water.

Hanna stood and watched. There was curiosity in her face behind the unwavering vigilance. She didn't seem in any hurry to leave.

Kaz looked up at her. 'Been here long, have you?'

'Six month, I think. Yasmin very good boss.'

'You said that already.'

The girl pursed her lips.

Kaz handed her the empty glass. 'Six months? You learnt English pretty quick.'

'My father was schoolteacher. He teach me since I'm ten.'

'He know you're here?'

'He dead. He get sick, sell his apartment, give money to my sister and me and tell us to go.'

'So you came here with your sister?'

'No. We go to Germany. On autobahn we work the truck-stop. My sister get stabbed. Turkish boy, he help me, bring me to England. Now I work to pay him back.'

'How much you owe him?'

The girl tilted her head and pondered. 'Dunno. Maybe ten thousand euro?'

Kaz gave a low whistle. 'Expensive help.'

Hanna frowned, her chin quivering, but when she answered her tone was matter-of-fact: 'Better than dead from some fucking truck driver on autobahn.' She nodded to reassure herself. 'I make coffee.'

Kaz watched her slide out through the narrow door. She was hardly more than a kid, yet she had the look of a survivor. Kaz had encountered plenty of teenage hookers in prison; most of them had serious drug habits, but Hanna was clear-eyed and alert. She seemed intent on gathering information, learning as much as she could as fast as she could. Kaz wished she'd been that smart at Hanna's age.

Relaxing back into the soft pillows she let her eyes close. She was drifting off when the shed door slammed, followed by raised voices and sobbing. Kaz sat up and listened. The crying became louder. She got up to investigate.

The short corridor outside her narrow cubbyhole led to a larger room furnished with a television and a sofa. Hanna and Volha were seated on either side of Saafi, the Somali girl. Blood was dripping from her nose to the floor and Hanna was attempting to staunch the flow with a towel. Saafi brushed it away; she was hysterical, her body rigid with pain and fear. She held her shaking hands out in front of her – the knuckle of her right hand was contorted and bleeding. Her wrists were fastened together with a pair of handcuffs.

Kaz stared in disbelief. 'What the fuck's going on?'

Hanna shot her a quick glance. 'Tevfik, Mr Kemal's son. He come with a friend. They both drunk.'

Kaz shook her head. 'Haven't you got any security?'

'Yasmin take care of it.'

'What, a couple of drunken thugs – on her own?'

Hanna flashed her a warning look. 'Yasmin take care of it.'

Kaz wasn't so sure. Yasmin knew her business, that was clear enough. But this didn't feel like a normal occurrence to Kaz.

She took a step closer, stooped to Saafi's level. 'What happened exactly?'

The girl's eyes were brimming with tears. 'Tevfik angry.'

'With you? Why?'

Saafi was calming down, the sobs subsiding and her shoulders drooping. Her nose was clearly broken and it bled copiously into the towel. Kaz remained where she was, hands on hips, waiting for an answer.

Finally Saafi mumbled, 'I dunno.'

'This is fucking ridiculous! I'm gonna go and see if Yasmin needs any help.'

Hanna sprung to her feet. 'No! Yasmin take care of it. She don't like you interfere.'

'What you so scared of? If Yasmin's taken care of it, then there won't be no problem, will there?'

Kaz didn't wait for a response. She pushed past Hanna and stepped out of the door. Her feet were bare and she was still wearing the jeans and a skimpy vest she'd slept in. The gravel on the rough path bit into the soles of her feet, so she skipped over onto the grass to avoid it.

The back door was open. Kaz paused on the threshold and listened. Muffled voices could be heard in the front parlour, then there was a thunderous crash of breaking glass. One of the shelves in the alcove maybe? Kaz didn't hesitate. She strode through the kitchen and down the hall.

The door to the parlour was ajar and Kaz decided that surprise was her best weapon, so she kicked it open. The door flew back on its hinges and three faces turned immediately towards her. Yasmin was backed into a corner, arms across her chest, hugging herself protectively, a split lip oozing blood.

In the centre of the room a young man stood with a bottle of vodka in his hand and an angry scowl on his face. He wasn't very tall and he wasn't very old. No more than twenty, Kaz reckoned. Another boy lounged in a chair – he was completely wasted, eyelids drooping.

Taking advantage of their confusion, she marched into the room, stopping only inches from the young man's face. 'I'm guessing you're Tevfik. So what the fuck you think you're playing at?'

The young man rolled back on his heels. Kaz was at least three inches taller.

He staggered to regain his balance then he laughed. 'What the fuck?'

Kaz rested her hands on her hips and eyeballed him. 'My question exactly. What the fuck?'

Tevfik laughed again, turned towards Yasmin. 'Who's this bitch? I ain't seen her before.'

'She's just a mate. She's got nothing to do with this.' Yasmin's voice was steady, but Kaz could see she was trembling.

His smile turned to a sneer. 'Then why's the bitch in my face? She's asking for a smack, don't she know that?'

Kaz stepped forward. 'Yeah? Fancy trying it, you pint-sized streak of piss?'

'It's okay, babes.' Yasmin reached out and put a gently restraining hand on Kaz's arm. 'I can handle this.'

It didn't look that way to Kaz, but registering the pleading desperation in Yasmin's eyes, she backed off.

Tevfik grinned and swayed a little. He was compact but his tight T-shirt revealed enough pecs and biceps to suggest he could pack a punch. He turned towards the fireplace and hurled the vodka bottle straight at it. The bottle exploded, spraying glass and vodka across the carpet.

He flopped into the chair with a satisfied smirk. 'What's your name, bitch?'

Yasmin caught Kaz's eye, then turned to Tevfik. 'I told you, Tev, she's just a mate.'

'She your special friend, is she? Most of you whores is queer. But a bit of dyke action, I could go for that. You girls can put on a little show for us, then I'll fuck you both.'

Kaz gave a dry laugh. 'In your dreams, dipshit.'

Yasmin moved cautiously forward. 'Come on, Tev, I'll get the girls. They'll put on a show for you. Something really hot. I got new toys upstairs you ain't even seen.'

He ran his hand through his close-cropped dark hair and fixed Yasmin with a petulant stare. 'Nah, I want her and you, right here on the fucking floor. Right now.'

'She's not in the business. I told you she's just a mate who's visiting.'

A leer spread across the young man's face. 'She's in my father's whorehouse. That makes her my father's whore. And you don't wanna upset the boss, do you, Yas? So get me another drink and let's see you get naked.'

He licked his lips. Yasmin shot a nervous glance at Kaz.

Kaz read the shame and embarrassment in her look. All this talk of being a businesswoman, being her own boss – it had all sounded a bit too good to be true. She was still a prostitute, controlled by a pimp; nothing had really changed. Still, Kaz felt for her friend, didn't want to see her humiliated in front of this tosser.

'Okay, you want a show, you wanna fuck us . . . let's see if you've even got the tackle to manage it.'

The young man spluttered. 'What you talking about, you stupid bitch?'

'Your dick. I wanna see it. Inspect it. Get it out. Show us.'

'Fuck off. You'll see it soon enough.'

'See, that's what I thought.' Kaz nodded sagely. 'Girls do like to gossip. Know what they say about you, Tevfik? They've seen a lot of dicks in this place, but yours is undoubtedly the smallest.' Kaz crooked her little finger. 'Bit bent too. Got a kink in it, like old whatsit – Bill what's-his-face, the American president.'

Tevfik was out of his chair with remarkable speed considering how drunk he was. He bunched his fist and threw an impressive right hook, which passed within a whisker of Kaz's chin. Having stepped dextrously aside to dodge the blow, she kneed him hard in the groin, grabbed a china figurine from the table and cracked him over the head. He went down in a heap at Yasmin's feet. His friend opened one eye, farted and returned to his drunken stupor.

Yasmin stared down in horror at Tevfik's inert form. 'Babes! Aww, you've fucking done it now! You think he's dead?'

'No. Though I wish he was.'

A look of panic spread across Yasmin's face. 'You gotta grab your stuff and get out of here. Mr Kemal's gonna go apeshit.'

'So all this businesswoman stuff is just window-dressing, is it?' Kaz shook her head sorrowfully.

Yasmin turned on her, furious. 'You don't fucking judge me! It's all right for you – you get out the nick, you got family waiting. You're all set up. Me, I come out to fucking nothing! If it weren't for Mr Kemal, I'd be living on benefits and turning tricks on the street.'

'I don't judge you, Yas.' Kaz threw up her hands in surrender. 'What was I supposed to do – stand by and let this little turd beat you up? I don't care whose fucking son he is.'

Yasmin's shoulders were hunched with tension as she turned away. 'I had it under control. You shouldn't have interfered.'

'Well, I'm sorry.'

Taking out her phone, Yasmin clicked it on to check the time. 'Awww, fuck me! They're gonna be here any minute.'

'Who is?'

'I phoned Mr Kemal's office fifteen minutes ago. He knows what Tevfik's like when he's had a skinful. They're sending someone over to sort him out.'

'Then he'll understand.'

'No, he won't understand. He can smack the boy about all he wants, but no one else lays a hand on his precious son. It's a question of honour with this lot. Don't you know nothing?'

Kaz glanced around for inspiration. 'We could say there was some other punters here and a fight broke out. He ain't gonna want to admit to being dropped by a woman.'

A low moan rose from the body at their feet and Tevfik rolled onto his back.

'Not dead then,' Kaz sniffed.

Yasmin scowled. 'Help me sit him up.'

The two women leant over him, took an arm each and

heaved him into a sitting position. He started to splutter and choke; Yasmin pushed his head forward as he vomited down the front of himself and over Kaz's bare feet. The stench of bile and booze rose up fiercely and hit Kaz.

She let go of his shoulder. 'Fucking hell!'

He flopped sideways against Yasmin's leg. The doorbell rang. A look of pain and resignation spread across Yasmin's face.

Seeing the panic in her friend's eyes, Kaz grabbed her arm. 'Listen, I'm gonna take the rap for this. He came at me, I hit him, it's my fault. I'll tell them the truth.'

Yasmin stared at her with a mixture of admiration and anguish. 'Babes, they gonna kill you.'

9

Nicci took the tube to St James's Park and found herself facing the austere steel-and-glass tower that was New Scotland Yard. As a young cop this had been it, this was where she'd aspired to be. Now, according to the media, the Yard was going to be sold off – cuts dressed up as reorganization and reform. The bean counters and the politicians had won. The job had changed. Maybe she shouldn't be sorry any more that they'd booted her out.

She wondered how Fiona Calder viewed the 'reforms'. Knowing Calder, she'd emerge unscathed. She'd always been a survivor, blessed with friends in the right places. Calder was one of the few senior women officers who seemed able to surf the macho culture and remain unaffected by it. She would never have called herself a feminist – that was far too radical a term for a woman like Calder – but Nicci couldn't imagine that she'd ever been bullied. She had a natural authority despite her small stature; exuding charm she remained slightly mysterious. All that was known of her private life was that she had a husband who did something in Whitehall and no children.

The young officer sent to escort Nicci wore an immaculately laundered blue shirt and a silk tie; he looked expensive and ambitious. There was no small talk. He led her briskly to the Assistant Commissioner's office suite, offered her a chair and disappeared. Nicci sat for nearly fifteen minutes, resting her gaze on the scudding cirrocumulus clouds passing the broad eighth-floor window. The day had turned out finer than expected. Shafts of sunshine were even breaking through.

It was almost four o'clock when the door to the inner office opened and two burly men in badly fitting suits emerged, clutching briefcases and files. Nicci realized how out of touch she was with the place. Back in the day, they would've been from the Home Office, but these two didn't look polished enough. Now the power was with City Hall and MOPAC. Whoever they were, they seemed extremely pleased with themselves.

The younger of the two had a huge neck bulging over a tight shirt collar. He turned to Calder with a smug smile. 'The main thing is, we don't want the media getting wind of it yet.'

Calder smiled serenely, 'Of course not.'

As they began a stately progress to the outer door, Calder caught Nicci's eye and smiled.

The fat man stopped. 'When the time comes, we'll feed them a hint on Twitter, let them ferret it out for themselves. Then they'll be more likely to pick it up and run with it.'

He seemed to be enjoying his own ingenuity.

Calder waited a second or two then offered her hand to shake. 'I'll send you my notes on the briefing paper by Friday.'

The fat man nodded, oblivious to the fact he was being dismissed.

As they disappeared into the corridor Calder turned to Nicci and raised a cynical eyebrow at her departing guests. 'Sorry to keep you, Nicci. I must say, you're looking really well. Come on in.'

Nicci followed the Assistant Commissioner into the inner office.

'Did anyone offer you a coffee?'

'I'm fine. Trying to kick the caffeine habit.'

Calder settled herself in the black leather desk chair, Nicci took the seat opposite, all too aware that she was being closely scrutinized. Fiona Calder was at least four inches shorter, a petite figure but a huge presence.

'Thank you for seeing me at such short notice, ma'am.'

The Assistant Commissioner shot her an amused glance. 'I think we can skip the formality.'

'Old habits, I guess.' Nicci shrugged.

Fiona smiled, swivelled her chair slightly. 'Well, I've just been informed that old habits need to change. Reform is the order of the day. Though personally I don't see that chasing villains from behind a desk in Sainsbury's is really going to improve matters.'

Nicci laughed. 'They're not serious?'

'Oh, indeed they are. And we've all got to get onside or be shipped out. Too many chiefs, not enough Indians, that's the thinking.'

'I'm glad I'm out of it.'

Fiona studied the younger woman's face. There was warmth as well as regret in her eyes. 'Are you? I was very relieved when you called. I did write, but you never replied.'

'I'm sorry about that . . . I just . . . things got a bit . . .'

'Well, you're here now. That's the main thing.'

They exchanged awkward smiles. She'd made it into the inner sanctum, but Nicci found herself at a loss. This was crazy. How the hell was she supposed to broach the subject of Helen Warner's death? She was here under false pretences, exploiting her former boss's goodwill, and that didn't feel right.

Sensing the younger woman's discomfort, Calder adopted

a maternal tone. 'One of the reasons I'm glad you're here is that I wanted you to know that I tried to stop them forcing you out, I really did. The whole thing was nonsense.'

Nicci's mind whirled back to the hearing. It had been an all-male medical panel, two hats and a shrink. The shrink smiled a lot but his weasel words still reverberated through her. She had trusted him with her naked grief and he'd turned it against her. She'd been honest about the booze and the pills; he'd used that to find her unfit for duty.

How many alchies had she worked with over the years? How many stressed-out depressives, who couldn't investigate their way out of a paper bag? But they weren't forced to retire on medical grounds. They weren't labelled as mental health cases.

Fiona Calder noticed the colour heighten in Nicci's cheeks. She wanted to reach out, offer comfort, but she was by nature a cautious woman and very conscious of the importance of proper boundaries. So she waited for Nicci to collect herself.

'I get the boot, my ex-husband gets promoted.' Nicci retreated behind a cynical laugh.

'Life isn't always fair—'

'That's an understatement.'

'Tim's a good officer. But not a patch on you.'

'Did you tell the panel that?'

Fiona tilted her head to one side and smiled. 'I understand your resentment. It's natural.' She took a considered breath. Nicci's phone call had come out of the blue and certainly taken her by surprise. Her habit was to take the time to consider every move, only sometimes that wasn't possible. 'You've had a raw deal. Grief affects people differently, it takes time to process. I don't think the panel took that into account.' She hesitated then decided. She'd be going out on a limb, but

Nicci was worth it. 'So what I am prepared to do is go back to them now and insist they look at your case again.'

Nicci blinked several times. Had she heard correctly? She could feel a constriction in her throat; was she about to cry? She swallowed hard. 'I don't know what to say. I never thought . . . I didn't come here expecting . . .'

'I know you didn't. But the reality is we're desperately short of good officers, particularly women officers, with your sort of experience. The Met invested a lot of time and money in you. Now you're back on your feet, makes sense we should recoup our investment.'

Nicci shook her head in disbelief. 'The medical panel ruled me unfit for duty. Period. No "Come back later and we'll see how you are". And as I recall, I was rather rude to them.'

Fiona opened a folder on her desk. 'I pulled up their report from the archives. Says here you called the psychiatrist a two-bit effing jobsworth who hadn't a clue about policing. That's just the edited highlights. Several other more graphic expletives were used too,' she finished with a grin.

Nicci returned the smile ruefully. 'The point is, they were right. I was unfit for duty.' She shifted in her chair; she was having difficulty holding Calder's gaze, so she let her eyes drift towards the window and the patches of blue beyond. 'Look, I still drink too much. I haven't thrown myself into therapy and seen the light. Nothing that much has changed really. I'm still a mess.'

Fiona Calder watched Nicci intently for a moment then leant her head back and sighed. 'Everyone has tragedies in their lives. And some are truly terrible. But we're human beings. We have to find ways to go on. And we all have to find our own way.'

'Yeah, well I'm still looking.'

'All the more reason to get back to what you do best.'

Lost for words, Nicci crossed her legs and focused on the photographs and commendations lining the wall to the Assistant Commissioner's left. She'd only been in the room a few minutes and already everything was starting to unravel. She'd dreamt, usually after a heavy drinking bout, of being reinstated, of apologies, getting her warrant card back, her record expunged. What she'd never believed was that it would actually happen, that she'd walk into the Assistant Commissioner's office and be thrown a lifeline. Until now, Blake had been the only one willing to help her. He'd been her saviour. He'd seen her at her worst and still offered her a job.

Calder leant forward, resting her elbows on the desk, and fixed Nicci with a kindly eye. 'What happened to you was . . . Well, I don't know that anyone ever gets over the death of a child.' She paused for a moment, drew in a sharp breath. 'And obviously there are no guarantees. You'd have to be reassessed, the panel would need some persuading. But it's an opportunity to get your career back. Surely that's worth a try?'

'I don't want a career.' Nicci surprised herself with the vehemence of her reply.

Fiona merely raised an eyebrow. 'As I recall, you were pretty ambitious.'

'And look where that got me.' Now the words came tumbling out. Nicci couldn't seem to stop them. 'If I hadn't been so concerned about my fucking career, I'd've been at the school gate to meet her, instead of leaving her to . . . to . . .'

Nicci fought the tears welling in the corners of her eyes. This was not what she'd intended and it certainly wasn't what she wanted. She swallowed hard, made a supreme effort to rein in her emotions, reminding herself that she had a job to do, she wasn't here for sympathy.

'It was an accident, Nicci. It wasn't your fault.' Fiona smiled with gentle concern.

Nicci could only shake her head, she didn't trust herself to speak. Coming here had been a mistake; she should've stuck to her guns with Blake, made him do his own dirty work. She'd had enough prodding and poking from family, friends, everyone who felt the need to ply her with their opinions and advice. But she reminded herself it was Blake she was angry with, not Fiona Calder. For about thirty seconds that thought held her in check, until Calder made another effort to empathize.

'You must've been through hell and back in the last year.'

'What you going to tell me next? "What doesn't kill you makes you stronger?" Believe me, I've heard that and every other cliché in the book and it makes fuck all difference!'

'I'm sorry. I don't mean to sound patronizing.'

Suddenly feeling penned in, Nicci got up from her chair and moved to the window. She drummed her fingers on the sill, oblivious to the panoramic view. 'No, no, you're fine. It's not you. I'm just . . . look, I know you're trying to help me, but the panel got it right, ma'am. They were on the money, still are. I am unfit. That's why I ignored your letter.' Nerves had left her mouth dry and her palms clammy. It was time to come clean and spit it out. 'You know why I finally came here today? Blake sent me.'

It took the Assistant Commissioner a couple of seconds to pick up this thread. 'You mean Simon Blake?'

'I'm working for him now.'

Fiona Calder looked genuinely taken aback. 'You're working for Simon Blake? What? As a private investigator?'

'I thought you might know that.'

Fiona's brow furrowed. 'Well I didn't. How on earth did that come about?'

Nicci shifted her gaze to the window again, she couldn't meet the Assistant Commissioner's eye. 'Blake offered me a job. The GP wouldn't sign me off any more and I was running out of money.'

'Why on earth didn't you come to me then?'

'The point is, Blake's world suits me fine. I work when I want, and when I want to stay at home and drink myself into oblivion, that's what I do.'

Fiona got up from the desk and took a tentative step towards Nicci. 'You should see someone. It doesn't have to be some Met-approved shrink. I have a friend who's a psychotherapist. She's brilliant, hugely experienced and—'

Nicci raised a warning palm and backed away. She had to remember why she was here, she needed to put space between them. Now that they were both on their feet Nicci found that the height advantage bolstered her confidence. 'Aren't you wondering why Blake sent me? Surely you want to know?'

Fiona shook her head sadly. Then returned to the desk and sat down, her eyes never leaving Nicci's face. Remaining perfectly still, she waited.

Furious with herself, Nicci turned to stare out of the window again. She'd fucked this up royally. Well, Blake had nobody but himself to blame.

Finally the Assistant Commissioner spoke, her tone detached and professional. 'Okay, so tell me. Why did ex-Commander Blake send you?'

She was streets ahead already. Nicci knew without even looking. Still she turned to face her directly; Calder had tried to help, she deserved a straight answer.

'You know why. The Warner case.'

Fiona sighed, rubbed her forefinger over the crease between her brows as if to ease away the pain. Then she closed the folder on her desk. 'I had no involvement in that.'

Nicci felt like a complete scumbag, but there was no going back. 'You pointed Julia Hadley in our direction. Why?'

'Whose idea was this? Yours or Blake's?' Calder fixed her with a steely glare. 'I hope it was Blake's.'

'Does it matter?'

'And I was stupid enough to think you'd come here for my help.' An acid tone had crept into Calder's voice. Nicci could feel the weight of her disappointment.

'I have.'

'Don't think you can play me, Nicci.'

The look that accompanied Calder's words was blistering; it had cowed murderers, politicians and every species of villain in between. Nicci could see the tension rippling through Calder's jaw. She wished she'd just explode and throw her out. At least then it would be over.

But in the next instant the anger evaporated. Calder's eyes glistened with the hint of a tear and she spoke very quietly. 'It never crossed my mind for one moment that you of all people would end up working for an outfit like Simon Blake's.'

Nicci felt her cheeks redden. Calder's disillusionment with her was palpable and it filled her with shame. She wanted to apologize, somehow explain, but before she could speak the Assistant Commissioner turned away with a weary shake of the head.

'You'd better go.' It was an order, not a request.

Nicci hit the first coffee shop she found on Victoria Street. It took all her willpower not to make it the first pub. The encounter with the Assistant Commissioner had left her feeling shitty enough; she knew if she fuelled that with booze she would be on a downward spiral. She settled instead for a double-shot espresso.

The place was in a late-afternoon slump – a student tapping away on his laptop, a gloomy young woman texting as the toddler strapped in the stroller beside her grizzled and whined.

Nicci glanced at the child, as she always did, then turned away. Every child reminded her. She found herself a window seat, started to pile up the dirty crocks and wipe the table with a paper napkin. A boy emerged from behind the counter, clearly reading her actions as a reproach. He dumped the cups and saucers on an adjacent table, sprayed hers with cleaning fluid and smeared it across the surface with a cloth. Nicci thanked him and he nodded curtly. She settled in her seat and gazed out at the slow stream of buses, taxis and cars floating past the window.

What had Fiona Calder meant when she said it had never crossed her mind that Nicci would end up working for an outfit like Blake's? And why did that idea upset her so much?

Nicci sipped her coffee for a couple of minutes, then pulled out her phone and speed-dialled Blake's number.

He answered on the second ring. 'Nic?'

'I'm taking a guess, but I'd say we've been set up.'

There was silence on the other end of the line. Nicci listened to his breathing.

'Yeah, I did wonder about that. Any hints as to their agenda?'

'Nope. As soon as she rumbled me, I was out the door.'

His tone was diffident. 'Okay, well I'll see you back at the office.'

'Don't you think it might be sensible to pass on this one?'

'Why?'

'Simon, it's a can of worms.'

'That's a bit dramatic. It's just another investigation.'

He was trying for nonchalant, but failing. She could sense his excitement. This was exactly the kind of opportunity he'd been waiting for – controversial, a headline-grabber – and he didn't care about the risk.

'So we're still going ahead?'

She heard a dry chuckle at the other end of the line. 'Hell yes!'

10

Kaz propped Tevfik against the chaise longue while Yasmin answered the door. He raised his hand slowly and wiped it across his mouth. Opening his eyes, he looked up at Kaz. At first his expression was blank and confused, but then he started to remember. His fingers went to the back of his head and came away smeared with blood.

His face crumpled into an angry scowl. 'Fucking bitch!'

A large, middle-aged man appeared in the parlour doorway. His dark hair was grizzled and greying, his face lined. But there wasn't an ounce of flab on him. He was solid muscle. Looking down at Tevfik with a mixture of weariness and disgust, he spoke in Turkish, but the sharp anger in his tone needed no translation.

Tevfik hung his head, raised a pleading hand and launched into a gabbled explanation. Yasmin had slipped into the room behind the newcomer, with two serious-looking minders bringing up the rear. Tevfik pleaded and whined, pointing at Kaz.

The man's gaze travelled in her direction, then he shot a glance at Yasmin. 'Who's she?'

Kaz stepped forward and met his eye. 'I'm Karen Phelps and I can speak for myself. Are you Mr Kemal?'

The man scrutinized her for a moment, nodded. 'Sadik Kemal.'

Yasmin edged forward. 'Mr Kemal's brother.'

Kaz sighed. 'Okay. You wanna know what really happened here or are you just gonna take his word for it?'

Tevfik tried to scrabble to his feet. 'Fucking whore tried to kill me, that's what happened.'

'Don't look much like a whore to me.' Sadik cast an appraising eye over Kaz. 'Too scruffy.'

Yasmin was at his elbow. 'She's a mate, a student. We met inside. She just came to visit. This is all a big misunderstanding, Sadik, I swear.'

Sadik's lip curled with what might have been amusement. 'You met inside? Now she's a student? What kind of fucking student does time?'

Kaz folded her arms. 'They call it the rehabilitation of offenders. Government policy, if you wanna know. And I'm a fine art student at Glasgow School of Art.' Kaz pulled a small wallet from her jeans pocket and slipped out her plastic student ID card. She kept her thumb over the name, but showed Sadik the mugshot.

He glanced at it, shook his head and laughed. 'Fuck me! So, Miss Student, what you doing, starting a fight in a whorehouse?'

'I didn't start it. I just finished it. Your nephew was drunk and breaking the place up. You're a businessman, this is cutting into your profit margin. So, in a way, I've saved you some money.'

Sadik rested his fists in the pockets of his leather jacket and directed a baleful stare at Tevfik. 'If you can't drink like a man, then don't drink. Drink Coke or milk, like a child. Now go get in the car.' One of the minders stepped forward and helped Tevfik to his feet, while the other dragged his mate from the chair.

Tevfik shrugged the minder off and glared at his uncle. 'You just gonna let this go? You let these bitches laugh at me? Baba would not let this go. I'm gonna talk to Baba.'

Sadik growled at the minder. '*Onu alin!*'

The minder grasped the boy's arm and dragged him out of the room.

Sadik turned to Yasmin. 'Clean this place up.'

A look of relief spread over her face. 'Thanks, Sadik. We'll be up and running again before tonight, I promise.'

'You better be. I got some business associates flying in. You do something special for them.' He licked his lips and leered. 'And for me, eh?'

Yasmin nodded her head enthusiastically. Kaz watched her and mourned. The confident businesswoman had morphed into a girly hooker, deferential and totally compliant. Kaz knew enough about her mate's past to know how hard it was for her to escape this world. But was Yasmin really so delighted at the prospect of giving head to an ageing gangster, whose pleasure was to humiliate her? She doubted it.

Sadik turned his attention to Kaz. 'Okay, Miss Student. You come and take a little ride with us.'

Yasmin's face froze. Fear consumed her. Desperate to avoid meeting Kaz's eye, she busied herself picking up shards of glass from the floor and table.

Kaz stood her ground. 'No. I don't think so.'

'You don't think so?' Sadik seemed amused. 'You got a lot of balls, I'll give you that. But, sadly, as my nephew said, there are still some matters here we need to resolve.'

Kaz glanced around her. Should she run? Not really a viable option. Even getting past Sadik to the door would be near impossible. She put her hands on her hips and feigned nonchalance. 'I think before you make any rash decisions you need to know what you're getting into here.'

His mouth twisted into a smile but the eyes were hooded and cold. 'Yeah?'

'Yeah. I was just on the phone to my brother.'

'Your brother?' Sadik smirked. 'And why should I fear this brother of yours?'

Kaz shrugged. 'Well, it wouldn't be him personally who came after you, because he's currently in the nick for murdering two police officers. You know how it is though, the family business goes on.'

There was a flicker in the hooded eyes. 'What you say your name was?'

'Phelps. Kaz Phelps. My brother's Joey Phelps. I disappear, it'll take our people a couple of hours to pick up your trail. Joey's got a temper. Anything happens to me, he'll wipe you out. You really wanna start World War Three 'cause your nephew can't hold his drink?'

'Joey Phelps, eh?' Sadik nodded thoughtfully, pursed his lips, eyes boring into Kaz. He turned to Yasmin. 'She telling the truth?'

Yasmin's hands were full of large broken chunks of glass that rattled with the trembling of her fingers. 'Y-yeah, Joey's her brother.'

Sadik's gaze came back to rest on Kaz. 'Maybe I sell you back to him.'

Kaz met his look with her own penetrating stare. She knew that in a game of bluff the essential thing was to remain casual, unconcerned even. She kept her tone neutral. 'You could try it.'

The Turk folded his arms. Kaz's gaze didn't waiver. Was he buying the story? The switch to defensive body language suggested he might be. But she knew that playing it out was still extremely risky. She waited, willing herself to stay calm.

Sadik tilted his head to one side. 'I got a relative in Basildon, my wife's brother. He say Sean Phelps is running things now. That right?'

Kaz blinked, the only indication of her surprise. Was it a trick question? There was no way of telling.

'As I said, the family business goes on. My cousin runs the Essex end of it.'

Suddenly furious, Sadik jabbed an index finger in Kaz's direction. 'You tell your fucking cousin from me to stay in fucking Essex! He think he can come up here, start taking over our turf. I know what he's been doing. I don't care how many fucking scumbag Ruskies he got – I don't roll over for no one. You tell him that. I see you here again I send you back to fucking Sean in twenty fucking pieces. You got that?'

He continued to eyeball her for about ten seconds to ensure the message had sunk in. Then he turned on his heel and walked out. The front door slammed behind him.

Kaz and Yasmin stared at each other open-mouthed. Yasmin collapsed into an armchair. 'Awww fuck me. For sure he was gonna do you, babes. I told you what they was like.'

Kaz took a deep breath and raked both hands through her hair. She realized that her heart was pounding in her chest. 'I need a drink of water.'

She picked her way through the broken glass and headed down the hall to the kitchen. Yasmin followed. Lifting a mug from the draining board Kaz filled it from the tap. She drank half of it standing then slumped in a chair.

Yasmin scrabbled in her bag, brought out a packet of cigarettes. Her hands were shaking so much it was all she could do to light it. 'When he sent Tevfik to the car I thought he was gonna let it go. But I told you what they was like. Didn't I? I told you.'

Kaz glared at her. 'If you know what they're fucking like, then why work for them? All this businesswoman bullshit! Is this what you want your life to be? Living in fear of pricks like him.' She drained her mug and slammed it down on the table.

Yasmin drew deeply on her cigarette, her eyes brimming with tears. 'You don't understand, I—'

'Yeah I do. You'd rather suck dick than stack shelves in Tescos. You think it's easier. Maybe it is.'

'I'm sorry, babes. I'm so . . . sorry . . .'

Dumping the cigarette in an ashtray Yasmin buried her face in her hands. Kaz watched her for a moment. Yasmin had always played it so cool, pretended to be streetwise and tough, but this was the reality. Her spirit had been broken a long time ago.

Kaz sighed then reached out and patted her friend's arm. 'Look, it's okay. I'm sorry. This is not your fault. But I need to get my stuff and get out of here before they change their minds.'

Yasmin dried her eyes on her sleeve and nodded. 'Yeah. You gonna call your cousin, tell him about this? Get some protection.'

'I'll have a job.' Kaz got up from the table. 'Sean's been dead for two years.'

11

Fiona Calder sat at her desk, fingers interlaced, staring into space. The Warner case: Nicci's bland description made it sound like just another investigation. She wondered if she'd been too harsh, but the news that Nicci was now working for Simon Blake had completely wrong-footed her. Nicci was an officer, a very good officer, who'd suffered a terrible tragedy. She deserved help and support to get back on her feet. However, the death of Helen Warner was another matter entirely. It had presented the Met with the most serious challenge the service had encountered, certainly during Calder's time in the job. But who was equipped to deal with it? No one.

The Commissioner was a decent enough man – slightly old school and ramrod-backed – which was why the politicians had chosen him. For them it was all about media image. They treated policing as a brand and he was their Captain Birdseye. Unfortunately his entire career had been spent in the regions. In the capital it was a different game and he really didn't get it. He thought he could run the MPS, as he insisted on calling it, like an old-fashioned chief constable, steady hand on the tiller, the occasional rallying speech to the troops. When it came to the web of lies and transgressions, the secret alliances that underpinned the organization, he was clueless.

Calder had joined the Met at nineteen. She'd grown up in

Enfield in a modest Thirties semi; for her, becoming a copper had been an escape from the typing pool. Her parents were proud as punch of their only daughter. She'd endured the years in uniform and being called a plonk, but she never let the culture get to her. In her experience, most of her male colleagues were simple, predictable and easy to manipulate. And being a small woman had worked to her advantage: the decent blokes were protective and the bullies underestimated her. She watched and listened and learnt, rising rapidly through the ranks at a time when promoting women had become a political necessity. Her entire career had been spent in London and when it came to the Met she understood the beast better than most; she shared its scars, felt its fears and was privy to its nasty little secrets.

London was a capital city of the twenty-first century, rich and poor cheek by jowl, and, as the divide widened, the nature of policing was being tested to the limits. She knew the public's perception of crime rarely fitted the facts. Most people's sense of safety was an individual matter, depending on personal psychology as much as experience. And the media was always ready to ramp up the drama.

Telling Julia Hadley to hire a private investigator – had that been a mistake? Calder rarely acted on impulse. She'd wanted to do the right thing and had judged it safe at the time. Now she realized she'd been naive. The nucleus of power never stayed still, it was always shifting. And in an organization like the Met it was impossible for her to be on the inside track. Women could never be included in the cabal. But as an outsider it was easier to watch and predict, or so she thought. Warner's death was just the tip of the iceberg. The whole process of government could be undermined, that was her real fear, and there was no telling where it would all end.

Calder's mind flitted back to Nicci and the Phelps case. After Joey Phelps' arrest, the IPCC had carried out a thorough review. Nicci was one of the few officers who came out of it smelling of roses. She was smart, hardworking and thorough, and it was obvious to all concerned that she'd played a pivotal role in taking down a very dangerous villain.

But that was before. Before a three-ton truck with dodgy brakes had wiped out her little girl.

What was Nicci capable of now? Calder had no way of knowing. And were they about to end up on opposite sides? Calder had few qualms about using Simon Blake; he'd made his choice when he boarded the private security gravy train. But Nicci?

Calder snapped out of her reverie. She was an assistant commissioner in the Metropolitan Police Service and she was standing on the edge of a precipice; this was no time for sentimentality. She picked up her phone and summoned her staff officer. Two minutes later the young man in the blue shirt and the silk tie stepped into the room.

'Put your thinking cap on, Jamie. Who do we know on the tabloids, middle-ranking, but good at whipping up a nice bit of moral outrage?'

Jamie pondered, rubbed his chin. '*Mail* or the *Express*?'

'Either.' Calder swivelled her chair to gaze out of the window. 'Okay, you can dress it up a bit, but here's the gist. We're shocked – no, extremely shocked – to learn that a firm of private investigators is looking into the tragic suicide of Helen Warner. And we're particularly concerned that her grief-stricken family is being exploited by individuals whose sole motivation is private profit.' She spun the chair back to face him. 'And making a name for themselves.'

Jamie was scribbling a note. 'A source at Scotland Yard?'

'Senior source . . . but I want plenty of distance from this.'

'I'll feed it through the Press Office, make sure they can't track it back.'

Calder smiled her assent. She thought of Nicci again, but only fleetingly. There were far bigger issues at stake. She was on dangerous ground and she knew it. But if she didn't act, who would?

12

Joey Phelps lay on his back on the hospital-style gurney staring up at the bright strip light, which traversed most of the low ceiling. There wasn't much pain, just a dull ache. He fingered the dressing; the wound was still oozing, but not much. Had any vital organs been hit? He was hoping not. Still, he didn't feel that confident any more. Stupid to trust anyone, let alone some knob who wanted to be a raghead. It was all starting to feel like a huge mistake.

He'd been in the prison system nearly two years, including time served on remand in Belmarsh. After his triple murder conviction he was sent north to Full Sutton in Yorkshire, which was judged to be a safe enough distance from his old sphere of influence. However, whilst there, leave to appeal against his sentence was refused. Joey was a brooding mass of anger and resentment; his high-priced lawyers had failed him and the reality of long-term incarceration was setting in.

So he singled out one of the jail's kingpins, a Mancunian drug baron, hard as nails, and beat him to a pulp. To avoid all hell breaking loose Joey was shipped out immediately and landed in the DSPD unit at Frankland. He looked around him, saw he was surrounded by a bunch of complete wackos, and that was when it dawned on him he needed to get a grip and change tack.

Dr Fishburn, the psychiatrist assigned to him, was young

and ambitious. Joey knew instinctively how to play him. He hooked Fishburn with his troubled gangster act and allowed the young doctor to tease out graphic tales of childhood abuse suffered at the hands of his father. These had the advantage of a ring of veracity because by and large they were true. He embellished the picture with details of his early teenage sexual liaison with his older sister. Then he let the doctor shepherd him through several cathartic outbursts, during which he gave a passable performance of grief and shame.

In reality Joey felt nothing; he never had. Emotions didn't bother him. In the back of his mind secret thoughts about Kaz lurked, but he kept them tucked well away. There were scores to settle on a number of fronts, but that would have to wait.

On the psychiatrist's recommendation, Joey was returned to the wing. He spent as much time as possible working out in the gym or playing sport. It soaked up his unruly energy and calmed his ire. He spent time in the prison library too; googled Fishburn and read his blog – pretentious crap mainly. He signed up for an alcohol and drug abuse programme, not because he had a problem but because he knew it was another way to get the system working to his advantage. In group-therapy sessions he quickly learnt to play the contrition game. It wasn't hard to figure out the kind of bullshit the shrink and the offender management team wanted to hear. They lapped it up.

While all these things helped Joey to survive from day to day, the prospect of serving a thirty-year tariff still hung over him. If he dwelt on it too much he could end up thinking he'd be better off dead. Lifers did top themselves; there were plenty of stories circulating and they gave him the creeps. To counter this he began to create a fantasy of himself as a PoW.

He remembered the old war movies he'd watched on the box as a kid. Him and Kaz curled up in front of the big old Phillips telly. Steve McQueen was his favourite, trying to jump a barbed-wire fence on his motorcycle, the Krauts trying to machine-gun him, but he never lost his cool. Joey even persuaded a tame screw to smuggle him in a pair of aviator shades so he'd look the part.

Giving free rein to his imagination, Joey moved mentally into a dream world where there was just no way he'd be spending the bulk of his adult life in jail. This in turn cheered him up, lightened his mood; he found the days passing more easily and fury at his situation abating. The prison authorities were really no different to the Krauts and Joey's task was to outwit them. It was like any computer game he'd ever played: he was the hero and heroes always came out on top.

Joey's opportunity came much sooner than he expected when the governor and his senior offender manager had a discussion about Dr Fishburn. They were concerned that the young psychiatrist was too keen to build a reputation and, as a result, rather naive in his dealings with certain inmates – Joey Phelps in particular. In their mind, Joey was a straightforward psychopath. As a precaution they decided to transfer him to Whitemoor Prison in Cambridgeshire.

Joey arrived at Whitemoor to find the cell next door occupied by a nineteen-year-old Brummie lad who'd taken a machete to a rival in a gang feud. The lad fancied himself as a jihadist so he'd changed his name to Mohammed and converted to Islam. Joey immediately saw the potential and within a week of meeting they'd struck a deal.

The pecking order amongst the Muslims on the inside was pretty strict. You had to have 'gone over' to training camps in Pakistan or Afghanistan to be taken seriously. But the small clique who ruled the roost had all fought against Assad in Syria; they were respected and feared. Mohammed was of Caribbean parentage, had no radical cleric to vouch for him and was finding the Qu'ran hard going. As far as his Muslim brothers were concerned he was a bit of a chancer, who'd yet to prove his credentials as a true believer. Then Joey walked into his cell and offered him the opportunity to change all that.

Joey played the role of white, racist bigot to a tee. When Mohammed knifed him in a fight on the landing, witnessed by a dozen onlookers, everyone assumed it was the real deal. Mohammed looked like an avenging angel as he was hauled off the hapless Joey and marched to the cooler, with chants of 'Allahu Akbar!' ringing out from his admiring brethren. It was music to his ears.

The problem for Joey was that Mohammed's zeal for authenticity had got the better of him. It was after five o'clock and the day shift had clocked off when Joey was stretchered into the Healthcare Centre. The stab wound was in his mid torso but Mohammed had been a bit too keen and the blade had penetrated deeper than intended. Joey fingered the gash. There wasn't much blood; he felt more like he'd been punched. But he was sweating profusely. Then without warning bile rose in his throat and he puked. He realized he must be in shock.

The night nurse had just come on duty. She took one look at him and summoned the on-call doctor. Dr Papadakis was Greek and had only been in the UK for a month. His English was barely passable, but with the nurse's help, he carried out an examination. It was difficult to judge the depth of the wound and, given its location, to determine whether any major organs had been damaged. Papadakis pondered his options, he had a wife and three kids in Athens and he needed to keep this job. The private company who provided the on-call service had made its policy clear when they recruited him: no mistakes, no come-backs, always err on the side of caution.

A discussion was in progress between the nurse and one of the prison officers, much of which he didn't understand. The prison officer wasn't happy; he seemed to regard the patient with some suspicion, but that wasn't Papadakis's problem.

He looked down at the young man. Whatever crime he'd committed certainly didn't show in his face. His eyes were blue, his look almost angelic as he lay there trying to tough it out. Yet there was a rising sense of panic. Clearly in shock, his expression suggested the pain was getting worse, which could mean internal bleeding. Dr Papadakis decided it was an emergency and issued his instructions.

At about ten past six a couple of paramedics turned up and Joey was transferred to their stretcher. Papadakis offered him pain relief, but Joey refused.

The prison officer was due to go off shift, but when he phoned the office he was told that the night shift were short-handed and he would have to accompany Joey to the hospital. His name was Travers, he'd seen it all, been in three riots and faced down every sort of villain. He matched Joey in size, but his belly sagged over his belt and his forty-a-day habit had put pay to any claim to fitness.

He stared down at Joey with a gimlet eye as he snapped on the cuffs to shackle them together. 'Right, Phelps. Medic says you're going to hospital. But don't let that give you no ideas.'

Joey lounged back on the pillow with a weak smile. 'If you

lot was doing your job and keeping them fucking ragheads in order, I wouldn't be laying here bleeding like a stuck pig.'

Travers' lips curled into a sarcastic grin. 'Oh, poor you.' He turned to the paramedics. 'Can we get this bloody show on the road. I got a darts match at half eight.'

As the trolley was wheeled out into the yard towards the waiting ambulance, Joey let the fingers of his free hand stray to the side seam of his jogging pants. Out of sight under the blanket, he started to pull at the loose thread with thumb and index finger.

The trolley was lifted and slotted into the back of the vehicle, then the doors slammed shut. Travers sat down on the side bench, his left hand cuffed to Joey's right. With his other hand Joey continued to tug at the thread, and as the stitching unravelled he could feel the razor-sharp blade of the home-made shiv come free from the material and drop into his hand.

Joey turned his face towards Travers, who was twisted sideways, peering through to the front cab. His chin was elevated exposing the side of his neck. Joey could see small patches of grey stubble that he'd missed when shaving.

The vehicle was moving slowly. As soon as it cleared the prison gates it picked up speed and the siren started to wail. Joey liked the sound; as if it were riding to the rescue. It was just the adrenaline pump he needed. The discomfort from his wound was minimal, a battlefield scratch any true soldier would ignore. He took a deep breath and identified the jugular vein as it emerged from below the jawline and travelled down the neck. His grip tightened on the narrow handle of the weapon.

Travers didn't even see the blow coming. The lethal blade plunged into his neck three inches below the ear. He gasped in shock as a spurt of arterial blood arced sideways and hit the wall of the ambulance. Eyeballs frozen with incredulity, he slumped sideways.

As Joey rammed the shaft home he looked into the prison officer's eyes and saw the void open up. His heart soared. For him, it was the perfect moment. Raw power – nothing matched its potency. The warrior had risen, reclaimed his authority. And Joey knew his days as a PoW were over.

13

Nicci spent half an hour sitting in the coffee shop in Victoria Street, staring out of the window and churning over her meeting with Calder. The reason she'd gone there had become irrelevant. She'd been offered a way back, a chance to return to the only job she'd ever wanted and she'd turned it down flat. Maybe she was actually mad. Somehow the sorrow and booze had warped the neural pathways in her brain or had turned her biochemistry toxic. She'd come out of Calder's office feeling ashamed of how she'd behaved, especially after the kindness the woman had shown her.

When she finally walked back to Victoria to pick up the tube, she discovered that there'd been an 'incident' at Bond Street and the whole Central Line eastbound was down. As she didn't fancy the pushing and shoving necessary to get on a bus she started to walk.

London had been her city since she explored it as an eighteen-year-old student at UCL. The first in her family to make it to uni, moving to the capital had left her exhilarated but broke. So she learnt the city on foot, mile upon mile of grey flagstone pavements flecked with rock-hard gum accretions clinging to the pathways like some exotic lichen. When she joined the Met on the graduate entry scheme she was the only trainee at West End Central who knew the patch.

It was six thirty by the time Nicci made it back to the

office; she had a faint hope of checking in with Blake then going home. She pictured her flat, a bottle of wine on the table and the relief of solitude.

There was a meeting in progress in what they rather grandly called the board room; in fact it was an office of comparable size to Blake's, furnished with a large oval table and half a dozen cheap IKEA chairs. Blake was seated at the end of the table, Eddie was at his elbow like an attentive hound, Pascale and Liam were there with piles of papers in front of them. Nicci sighed – they'd obviously been having a busy afternoon.

Easing open the plate-glass door, she caught Eddie in full flow: '—point is, boss, once you start digging . . .'

Blake heard her enter and looked up. Eddie, sensitive to every shift in his master's attention, broke off. Conscious of being watched, Nicci slipped into a chair and cracked open one of the bottles of water on the table.

Finally she allowed Blake to catch her eye. 'Eddie's come up with quite a promising lead.'

Nicci took a long slug from the bottle. 'Yeah?'

Blake gave Eddie the nod.

'It's just this bloke I know, media adviser at Labour HQ. I used to feed him stuff when he was on the red-tops, so he owes me a favour or two. Now he reckons—'

Nicci fixed Eddie with a resentful glare. It helped to find someone to dump on. 'Let me guess: she was shagging a senior member of the Shadow Cabinet. No, better still, a senior member of the Shadow Cabinet's wife. She thought it was a) true love, wife chucked her, went back to the old man, she topped herself in despair, or b) wife chucked her, she got the hump, decided to sell her story to the *Sun* and the forces of darkness moved in on her.'

Nicci took another long draught of water and wiped her mouth on the back of her hand. Eddie glanced at Blake for guidance, but he was just smiling. He knew why she was kicking off and in anyone else it would've annoyed him. But this was Nicci. He closed the file in front of him and checked his watch. 'Maybe we should call it a day. Thanks, everyone. It's been really useful.'

Pascale and Liam gathered up their papers, grateful to escape.

Reluctant to be excluded, Eddie hovered. 'Anyone fancy a bevy?'

Blake was focused on Nicci; he didn't even give Eddie a look. 'Not for me. We'll pick this up in the morning.'

Once Eddie had shuffled out Blake threaded his fingers together, waiting for Nicci to speak. Ignoring him, she continued to drink.

He gave her a quizzical look. 'So what's your plan? Go home and swap that for a bottle of vodka?'

'Not that keen on vodka.' She crinkled her nose.

'What can I say?' He tilted back in his chair, but his expression remained laid back. 'I'm sorry we had to do it this way.'

Nicci almost snorted on her water. 'No you're not!'

'Did she give you a hard time?'

'Not really. She thought I'd gone there for her help.'

Blake rubbed his chin with his thumb. He was scanning her face. 'Don't feel bad, Nic. She's playing us, we just played her back. That's all.'

Nicci met his gaze but didn't reply.

He got up, slid his hands in his trouser pockets. 'What did she actually say?'

'She said she'd had no involvement with the case.'

'See, she's lying too.'

Nicci shot him an acid glance. 'Oh, well that's all right then.'

Blake jangled his change, the only sign of his frustration, then his brow wrinkled with concern. 'Y'know, if you're not up for this, you only have to say.'

'Then what you gonna do? Rely on some sleazebag who owes Eddie Lunt a favour?'

This drew a wry smile of acknowledgement from Blake. 'You're right. I do need you. I just . . . well, you know, I worry.'

'Don't.' Nicci flashed him a resentful look. He knew exactly how to push her buttons. 'I do best when I've got distractions. Plenty of stuff to do and to think about.'

'Well, this certainly fits the bill.' He picked up his expensive tailored jacket from the back of the chair. 'You didn't want to hear Eddie's contribution, so what's your theory then?'

'Haven't really got one. But I think the partner's right: definitely not suicide. She wasn't the type. Accident? Unlikely.'

Blake nodded. His face was solemn, but there was a glint in his eye. 'Murder then. Some trouble taken to make it look like suicide, so could be a professional hit. That takes us to who – and may also explain why the Met don't want to touch it.'

Nicci plonked the plastic bottle down on the table and carefully screwed the top on. 'Is that why you can't resist this?'

Blake had the gleeful expression of a small boy who'd just been given permission to ride the big dipper, but he maintained the nonchalant tone. 'Well you've got to admit, it's marginally more interesting than investigating some boring company takeover or preparing a defence brief for some guilty-as-hell villain with only half a brain.'

Nicci couldn't help but smile. 'I'm telling Heather on you! Poor woman thinks you've settled for the easy life and the easy money. But you still want to get down and dirty with the big boys, don't you?'

'Do I?'

Blake gave her a look of wide-eyed innocence, but Nicci pressed on: 'Calder's worried, the whole pack of them are running scared. You've got to ask yourself why, Simon.'

He checked his watch. 'I never was much good at the politics.'

Nicci knew him well enough to realize the calm indifference was a sham. 'You were just too egotistical to play the game.'

'And you're not?' He gave her a provocative glance. 'C'mon, Nic, you could've used your visit to Calder to negotiate a way back in for yourself. Why didn't you?'

'Don't try and be smart. You're just avoiding the question. This case could put you out of business.'

He eased the jacket on, settled it on his shoulders and adjusted his tie. 'Okay, let's look at that. This is exactly the kind of case you need to make a reputation.'

'Yeah, but a reputation for what?'

Blake's gaze drifted towards the window. 'It's all going to be up for grabs. The way policing's going in this country, they'll outsource as much as they can get away with. Homicide, the investigation of serious crimes, fraud – most Chief Constables are going to end up buying it in just so they can keep the public happy and maintain a few uniforms on the beat.'

'You really think it'll come to that?'

Blake laughed. 'Don't you think some policy wonks in Whitehall aren't already drawing up the plans? It's not just going to be back office and support services.'

'I don't think the voters'll accept it.'

He widened his eyes as if surprised by her naivety. 'I think the world is changing very fast. I plan to be ahead of the game. Then those smug bastards at the Yard'll be queuing up begging me for a job.'

Now they were down to the nitty-gritty.

Nicci got up and followed him into the outer office. 'So it's all about payback?'

'Depends if payback's what you want.'

Nicci ran her fingers through her hair. What she wanted was peace, an escape from the recriminations that shadowed every waking hour and skittered through her dreams, but that didn't feel as if it was coming any time soon. 'How the fuck do I know what I want?'

Blake paused and considered her for a moment. 'You know Eddie's asked me for share options.'

'Cheeky sod. I hope you told him where to get off.'

'I did. But if you were to ask me the same question, I'd call the accountants and put the wheels in motion. You need to think about the future, Nic. Where d'you think you're going to be in ten years' time?'

Nicci stared at him for a moment and laughed. 'I don't even know where I'll be in a week's time.'

'Then take the share options. They could turn into serious money. What have you got to lose? We sink or swim together. Could be exciting times for us both.' He gave her a wistful smile. 'Who knows? Could maybe even help you get your life back.'

14

Kaz left the house in Walthamstow by the back door. She climbed over the fence into the garden behind and found a way out through an alley that led into another street. Sadik Kemal seemed to have bought her story, but she wasn't taking any chances. She ducked through the side turnings with her hood up and jumped on a bus that was headed into town. The top deck was almost empty, she sat at the back and stared out of the window. Kids were playing football on Hackney Marshes, shouting and laughing, people were walking their dogs and enjoying some evening sunshine.

It made Kaz feel even more wretched and alone. Some homecoming; she'd only arrived in London a few hours ago and already a man she didn't even know had wanted to kill her. She considered her options; there weren't that many. At least it was summer; a night sleeping on the streets probably wouldn't be too bad. A student hostel would be better, if she could find one. Then again, it was still high season for tourists, so the likelihood was they'd be full.

The bus trundled through Dalston making frequent stops and as it turned into Kingsland Road, Kaz realized they were heading towards Liverpool Street. She got off in Bishopsgate and rode the escalator down into the main station concourse; she allowed herself to be carried along with the crowd. She had no fixed notion of where she was going, but somewhere in the back of her mind was an unconscious longing, a desire to go home. She bought a coffee and sat on a step watching the legion of homeward-bound Essex commuters marching past her.

The last time she'd seen her mother had been at Joey's trial. Ellie had sat in the public gallery, supported by Brian, her late husband's dogsbody and now Ellie's live-in lover. When Kaz gave her evidence, Ellie had got up and walked out. All contact had been severed with her family when she went on the witness protection scheme. It seemed pretty unlikely they'd have anything to say to each other if they were to meet now.

Ellie had been a far from perfect parent and any affection she did have had always been reserved for her son. Kaz had known this as soon as her little brother was born. Ellie may have omitted to feed him and change him, but her attention, when she wasn't drugged up to the eyeballs, had always been focused on Joey.

Having sat staring into space for nearly an hour, Kaz came to a decision, bought a ticket from the machine and boarded the Billericay train. She had no idea whether Ellie and Brian were still living at the old place. They'd be unlikely to welcome her, but with Helen dead she had a visceral need to retreat, find a familiar bolthole. Only then could she get her thoughts straight and make a plan.

She didn't have enough money for a cab so she took a bus from Billericay station. She walked the last mile or so. The house looked benign and glowing in the fading summer light. Russian vine was tumbling over the walls and there were several varieties of clematis. A 'For Sale' board was nailed to the gatepost. The housing on the entryphone had been removed and its circuit board hung down, attached by a single wire.

The electronic gate was ajar. Kaz stood looking at her old home, different and yet the same; clearly they were moving or maybe they'd already gone.

As she walked across the gravel drive she could see a faint glow leaching through the dark dining room from the kitchen at the rear. It was the only visible light in the dusky interior. Kaz hesitated. She felt apprehensive, though she couldn't say why. She didn't want to ring the doorbell and risk having to offer some explanation for her presence to strangers.

She skirted round the side of the house. The wrought-iron gate leading to the back garden stood open. Kaz peered round the corner. The patio, overshadowed by the back of the house, was almost in darkness, but she could make out the silhouette of a man. He wasn't tall – slight in build and holding a bottle of beer in his hand. He stepped into a patch of light pooling out from the kitchen and Kaz recognized Brian.

'Well, come on then, you two! We gotta celebrate.' He raised the bottle and laughed.

A much larger figure stepped out of the house, but his face remained obscured and he had his back to Kaz. He too held a bottle, which he raised and chinked against Brian's. Kaz felt a jolt of fear and nausea rise from her stomach to her throat. As he put the bottle to his lips, his face caught the light. The cheeks were now bearded but Kaz knew there could be no mistake; it was definitely Joey.

15

It was nearly dark when Nicci Armstrong got off the bus in Newington Green. The aroma of meat and fat wafting from the kebab shop on the corner reminded her that all she'd had to eat was a BLT at about one o'clock. She considered the run of fast-food establishments all trying to entice her with their wares and opted for a curry. Curry went with beer and if she stuck to beer instead of opening a bottle of wine she had a better chance of not getting completely pissed.

After Blake left she'd spent some time in the office trawling the Net; the Warner case had attracted wide and diverse coverage. Pascale had already sifted the reams of data and Nicci settled for transferring a selection of the researcher's files to her iPad, which she stuffed in her backpack. When she finally put the key into her own front door it was close to nine o'clock.

She was unloading the takeaway from a plastic carrier onto the kitchen counter when she heard a soft tapping. It puzzled her at first, but further investigation revealed that someone was knocking on the door to the flat. Access to the building was controlled by an entryphone system with a buzzer; no one had ever got past that to the actual door before. Nicci peered suspiciously through the spy-hole. It took her a second to recognize the old lady from the bus stop and she appeared to be carrying something.

Nicci's first impulse was to creep away, pretend there was no one home. But the old lady must've heard her come in. If Nicci ignored her she'd probably only come back later, so getting rid of her quickly now was probably the best option. Nicci opened the door.

The old lady beamed and held out a plate with two cup-cakes on it; one was slathered in pink icing, the other green. 'My granddaughter always brings me cakes when she pops in. They're from that fancy new bakery on Upper Street. I just wanted to say thank you, officer. You lot have a hard enough job and you could've just minded your own business this morning.'

Nicci stared at the cakes, searching in vain for a way to refuse the gift. But the old lady's plate-carrying hand was shaking as she leant heavily on her stick.

Nicci smiled and took them. 'Thanks. But look, I'm not actually a police officer. Used to be, not any more.'

The old lady shrugged. 'You certainly gave that young hooligan what for. Ethel Huxtable. I'm over there, number five. I seen you come and go a few times since you moved in. But people aren't neighbourly nowadays, not like they used to be. Different world, I suppose.'

Ethel's eyes were watery but totally blue, the gaze clear and steady. Suddenly Nicci felt chastened. The figure before her might be stooped and wrinkled and embarrassingly old, but underneath she was still fearless.

Nicci held out her hand. 'Nicci Armstrong. Pleased to meet you, Ethel.'

Ethel rested her bony hand in Nicci's. Though the skin was papery and baby soft, she had a firm grip. 'I won't keep you. Smells like an Indian. I love a good curry, but they don't much like me any more.'

Nicci smiled. Ethel turned and began a slow progress back across the hall. In addition to Nicci's there were three other flats on the same floor. Nicci watched Ethel fumble with her key and disappear behind the door of number five.

Nicci's own grandmother had died of a heart attack at eighty-six; at the time it had seemed a tragedy. The family all gathered, sad but restrained. Tim hadn't wanted Sophie to attend the funeral – she was only four and he thought it inappropriate. But Nicci knew that the little girl had a strong bond with 'Big Nana'; she needed to understand what had happened, be part of the family ritual. There was a bit of a row and Tim gave in. Later, when it came to arranging his daughter's own funeral, he was implacable. He insisted on controlling every detail, his rage excluding Nicci totally. He would have banned her from the proceedings entirely if he could have.

Nicci placed the pink and green cupcakes on the table. Sophie would've definitely gone for the pink one. She wasn't a particularly girly girl, but Huggy, her favourite bear since she was a toddler, had been pink with white ears and paws. This had caused Nicci problems, because he was always getting grubby. Then her mum had read the label and pointed out that he was machine washable. After that Huggy had a monthly bath, watched by a fascinated Sophie, on the strict understanding that although swimming in the washing machine was fun for bears, little girls shouldn't try to emulate it in any way.

Nicci opened the fridge: there were two cans of beer left. She considered them for about three seconds then reached for a bottle of Pinot Grigio. Unscrewing the top, she poured herself a large glass and stripped the cardboard lids off the takeaway. Should she transfer the rice and chicken tikka marsala onto a plate? It was easier not to bother. She got a fork from the drawer and started to eat standing up.

Pascale had been collating information from the Net all day and she'd made a summary of her discoveries so far. Nicci propped her iPad on the kitchen counter and scrolled through the pages as she ate.

There was some background on Helen Warner – her by-election victory, her earlier legal career, plus quotes from a couple of articles on being an out lesbian in politics. Nicci scanned the photographs and only then did it dawn on her that they'd actually met. She should've remembered. Warner had been Kaz Phelps' lawyer. She'd been present once at an interview, she'd even called Nicci the night DS Bradley was murdered by Joey Phelps. Nicci racked her brains, trying to recall whether she'd run into Warner after that. By the time Kaz Phelps agreed to give evidence against her brother, she had a different lawyer, a bloke. Why had she parted company with Helen Warner? Nicci couldn't remember, too much had happened since then, though she wasn't sure she'd ever known.

Rolling through the images of Helen Warner culled from newspapers, gossip magazines and the Net, Nicci noticed they all looked remarkably alike. Her public face was a broad, tele-genic smile; in an odd way, she looked more American than English, the style and presentation hinting at some transat-lantic political charm school. Nicci searched in vain for any telltale signs of drunkenness or any scenes that might suggest a drug-induced loss of inhibitions. But the pictures revealed nothing more than an attractive woman, who knew how to pose.

She flicked the cover back over the screen and was dump-ing the foil cartons from her takeaway in the bin, when a door in the outer hall was slammed with some force. This was rapidly followed by a female voice, high-pitched and angry. Nicci couldn't make out the exact words. She stood stock-still for a moment and listened. She'd heard noise and commotion out in the hall before. The sound insulation in the flats was generally good, but the occupants of number six opposite had a tendency to row and this sometimes spilled out into the communal hallway. Nicci's policy was to ignore it; her door was locked, her solitary cell secure. She had no need and certainly no desire to involve herself in other people's messy lives.

She had poured herself another large glass of wine and was about to settle on the sofa, when the pounding began. A fist, she imagined, was being applied heavily and rhythmically to the door of number six.

Now the voice was clearer and louder. 'Bastard! Yer fucking bastard!' There was more hammering, then a deeper thud – the door being booted, followed by the low grizzle of a child crying.

It was the sound of the child that forced Nicci to go and look. She wandered down the hall, glass in hand, and peered through the spy-hole. She'd never spoken to her neighbours at number six. Once or twice she'd passed the woman on the stairs, exchanged a nod. Through the fisheye lens of the spy-hole she saw a skinny girl in a vest top and jeans, squatting with her back to the wall, cradling a baby. The baby was about nine months with a mop of black hair, its mouth was open, dribbling tears and snot, and it was howling.

Nicci sipped her wine and watched. There was nothing to be done. She'd attended enough domestics in her time to know the futility of outside intervention. The baby's cries were piteous and the young woman's face pained and tense as she tried in vain to comfort the child.

Then another figure inched into view across the lens of the spy-hole. Nicci could hear voices and a thin, bony hand reached down to the girl's shoulder. It was Ethel Huxtable.

Nicci's view through the spy-hole was severely distorted. But she saw Ethel raise her stick and heard its hard and insistent rap upon the door. For the second time in one evening Nicci found herself shamed by the feisty old lady. She took the chain off, unbolted her door and opened it. Hardly a second later the door to number six also opened. Framed in the doorway, a large scowling figure towered over Ethel by more than a foot. He was about thirty, head shaved to black stubble, muscled shoulders under a khaki vest.

Ethel wagged an accusing finger at him. 'You should be ashamed of yourself. Look at the state of them.'

The young woman crouched, clutching the baby to her, rocking it and silently weeping. The man's eyes rested on her for a moment and Nicci thought she saw him blink away a tear.

But Ethel wasn't finished. 'What kind of man treats his wife and kiddie like this? I'll tell you what kind – a bully and a coward.'

He rocked back on his heels, his gaze seeming to float over Ethel's head to the lights set in the ceiling above; Nicci realized he was drunk or high or both. He put a hand on the door-frame to steady himself then he made an effort to focus on Ethel. Nicci's muscles tensed as she readied herself to step in.

But his tone was surprisingly mild. 'You don't know nothing about it.'

A vacant smile flicked briefly across his face, then he turned and disappeared back into the flat. The young woman scrambled to her feet, pushed past Ethel and scurried in after him with the baby. The door slammed.

Nicci stepped forward and took the old lady's arm. 'What are you playing at, Ethel? You could get yourself in serious bother. He's off his face.'

Ethel smiled serenely. 'How were the cakes? Nice treat?'

'I'm not joking.' Nicci shepherded the old lady back towards her own door. 'You could get hurt.'

'Oh, him and me have had words before. They're always rowing – baby's left to scream its little lungs out.'

Nicci shook her head ruefully. 'You don't ever back down, do you?'

Ethel gave her a wrinkly grin. 'My dad was a boxer. Learnt it in the army during the first war. He taught all us kids to stick up for ourselves. Boys and girls alike, he made no distinction. His code was simple: you don't go picking a fight, but if it comes to you . . .'

As she pushed the door to number five open, Nicci smiled. 'How old are you, Ethel?'

'That's a very personal question.'

Nicci laughed. 'Okay, I'm thirty-five.'

Ethel gave her an appraising look. 'Bit scruffy, bit skinny and you drink far too much. Is that why you're not married with kids of your own?'

Nicci stopped in her tracks; she wasn't expecting this kind of directness. But before she could react, Ethel squeezed her hand. 'Take no notice of me. Gobby and rude, that's what my Eric used to say. I'm eighty-nine, as it happens. Ninety in March. The family are planning a do. You can come if you like.'

It was impossible to take offence. Ethel knew that being old had few privileges and she was determined to take full advantage of those she did have. Her blue eyes betrayed a definite sparkle and Nicci suspected that a bit of aggro with the neighbours had provided her with much better entertainment and stimulation than an evening dozing in front of the telly.

Once she'd ensured that Ethel was safe behind her own front door, Nicci returned to the flat. She glanced around, noticing just how spartan and impersonal a space it was. The bottle of Pinot Grigio sat open on the kitchen counter – less than a third of it was left. On an average night Nicci would get through a bottle and a half, sometimes two. Ethel was right, she did drink too much. But how did the old girl know? Was that really how she came across: the single female wino getting quietly sozzled behind closed doors, oblivious to the fact she'd let herself go a bit?

Nicci put a stopper in the wine and returned it to the fridge. She sat down at the table, opened the iPad, called up a fresh page and started to make her own summary of the main points of the case so far.

16

Kaz retreated rapidly into the shadows, acutely aware of the scrunching of her feet on the gravel path. The temptation was to just turn tail and run, but then they might hear her. It was Joey, she was sure it was Joey. Except Joey was in jail.

As Kaz tiptoed her way along the side of the house chaotic thoughts cascaded through her head. Sean was dead, of course he was, she'd pulled the trigger herself. Still the Turk had insisted he was back running the business. Joey was banged up, she'd given evidence at his trial, now there he was in her parents' back garden, clinking beer bottles with Brian. For an instant Kaz wondered if she was going mad. None of it made sense.

She turned the corner to the front of the house and was suddenly caught in a phalanx of headlights. The first car pulled up inches from her, a large van following it through the open gate. Doors flew open, she was grabbed and spread-eagled on the bonnet. Only then did she realize it was a police car. They held her fast as she watched armed cops swarm from the van and round the house. A tubular steel ram brought the oak front door off in a single blow. The cops poured into the house. There were shouts of 'Armed Police!' and she heard her mother scream.

A uniformed officer clicked a pair of speedcuffs on her wrists. A third vehicle pulled up on the drive and DCI Cheryl

Stoneham climbed out of the back. Kaz stared at her, then recognition dawned. It was the cop who'd interviewed her and Joey in Southend, though she'd put on quite a bit of weight.

Stoneham glanced in Kaz's direction with a baffled frown, then she strolled over. 'Well, you're the last person I expected to find here.'

Kaz gave her a tepid smile; she was in shock, heart pounding. It was simply easier to say nothing.

The sergeant from the armed response team came out of the house, cradling his MP5.

He walked up to Stoneham and shook his head. 'Just the two of them. It's all fields out the back, so he could've done a runner. I've sent some of the lads over there to take a look.'

Stoneham sighed. 'Thanks, Martin.' She turned to Kaz. 'Let's go inside, shall we, and see what's what.'

Kaz's wrists were pinioned behind her. One of the uniformed cops put a hand on her arm and shepherded her into the house behind Stoneham. It hadn't changed much since her last visit, except armed police were noisily searching upstairs and one of them was standing guard in the hall. Kaz followed Stoneham into the kitchen. Ellie was seated at the large pine table with her face in her hands. Brian sat opposite staring at a half-drunk bottle of beer. A wine glass lay shattered on the tile floor close to the table leg.

Flanked by two uniforms and concealed by the DCI's bulk, Kaz was not immediately visible to her mother.

Ellie opened her mouth and gave vent. 'What the fuck is this about? You bust in here, mob-handed! You got no fuckin' right!'

Stoneham moved forward towards the table. 'We know he's been here, Mrs Phelps. ANPR cameras tracked him in a stolen car all the way down the A12. The car's parked just up the road.'

'I dunno what the fuck you're talking—' Ellie's eye alighted on her daughter and the words evaporated. She stared at Kaz as if she'd seen a ghost, then venom erupted from some previously hidden reserve as she hissed, 'I might've known you was behind this.'

Kaz just stood there, pale, handcuffed, and let her mother's hatred wash over her.

Stoneham watched the two of them with interest. She gave the uniformed officer a nod. 'Take the cuffs off.'

The officer complied. Kaz rubbed her wrists. Ellie's eyes didn't leave her daughter's face – accusing, blaming, despising. Kaz tried in vain to hold her gaze. The pain was familiar, it had always been there, but now it was turning into a Gordian knot in Kaz's stomach. She gritted her teeth; no matter what, she wouldn't cry. Her feelings wouldn't betray her.

Stoneham scanned them both thoughtfully. The sergeant from the armed response team stepped through the sliding door to the garden.

'Found this down the garden, boss.' He held up a plastic evidence bag containing a beer bottle. 'Looks like it'd only just been tossed. Beer's still frothy.'

Stoneham shot a glance at the matching bottle on the table in front of Brian.

She smiled. 'We're going to find his prints on it, aren't we? So you may as well tell us the truth.'

Ellie folded her arms defiantly. 'I don't know what you're on about. If you're talking about my son Joey, he's in the nick. Where you lot and his lying scumbag of a sister put him. I ain't got nothing else to say.'

Kaz looked at her mother's implacable face. Did she really believe that her boy could do no wrong? Was such wilful blindness natural to all mothers or only women with Ellie's drug-fucked psyche?

Across the table, Brian sat staring at Kaz, his face twisted in a malevolent sneer. The late Terry Phelps' whipping boy, a little ferret of a man who'd wheedled his way into the boss's shoes and bed. Could he have taken over the business, him and Ellie? Someone was certainly using her cousin Sean's scary reputation as a cover to keep the competition at bay. But did Brian and Ellie even know that Sean was dead? Kaz's brain was reeling; none of it made sense.

She realized how stupid she'd been to even think of returning to this place.

Turning, she faced Stoneham. 'Joey was here moments before you arrived. They was having a drink out the back.'

Ellie flew out of her seat, sending the chair toppling backwards. As she lunged at Kaz, Stoneham's DS caught her round the wrist.

He held her firmly but Ellie fixed her daughter with a glacial stare. 'When I got pregnant with you, yer Nan wanted me to have an abortion. I wish I'd taken her advice.'

17

Kaz was driven to the police station in Basildon for questioning. She made a simple statement; all she could say was that she'd gone home and seen Joey. Then she waited. It was well after midnight when Stoneham appeared. Joey was on home turf and he'd gone to ground without a trace. Kaz wasn't surprised. The field at the back of their parents' house abutted on to woodland. It had been their childhood playground and was an ideal place for someone who knew the ground to lose his pursuers.

Stoneham was tired and frustrated. She came in with a box of doughnuts, which she offered to Kaz. Ellie and Brian had been charged with harbouring, they'd refused to talk and within an hour a solicitor had appeared to demand bail.

Stoneham devoured her second chocolate glazed doughnut, dabbed the crumbs from her lips with a tissue and gave Kaz a weary smile. 'You're free to go. However, I can hold you in protective custody until morning. Then we can get an officer from witness protection to pick you up. Have you got anywhere to go?'

'Not really.'

'He killed a prison officer, y'know. Sliced open the jugular.'

Kaz could only nod dumbly. She felt numb and exhausted. 'Will you get him?'

'Doing our level best. He got in a knife fight, escaped en route to hospital. Looks like it was all planned.'

'Was he hurt?' Kaz didn't want to ask the question, but she couldn't help herself.

Stoneham sighed. 'As I say, it was a put-up job, so doubtful. But I've had it from a chiz that your cousin Sean's picked up the reins again in the last couple of months. My guess is, he'll try and get Joey out the country.'

Kaz's thoughts were a jumble, her head ached. Sean again, resurrected from the dead. She met Stoneham's gaze. 'That doesn't make a lot of sense to me. Joey and Sean never really got on. Last I heard, Sean was in Spain. I don't think he'd come back.'

Stoneham eyed the box of doughnuts with longing. 'When Joey went down, perhaps he saw his opportunity.'

'I doubt he'd help Joey.'

'Well, someone is. Any ideas?'

Kaz knew she was skating on very thin ice. Stoneham was a sharp, intuitive cop – could she smell Kaz's guilt? Someone was using Sean's identity, his reputation. But how many people even knew he was dead, let alone that Kaz was the one who killed him?

Her brain was too fuddled with weariness to think. Less than twenty-four hours ago she'd boarded a train in Glasgow, now she wished she'd stayed put. She needed to sleep, just close her eyes and rest. The prospect of spending another night of her life locked in a cell didn't appeal – there'd been too many of those already – but one thing was certain: with Joey on the loose, it was the safest place for her to be.

18

Nicci was in the office by eight the next morning and had the place to herself until eight thirty when Alicia arrived. The worker bees of cyber-security drifted in shortly after; Bharat, in bicycle helmet and backpack, greeted her with friendly surprise. When Pascale and Liam put in an appearance just after nine fifteen, they were both somewhat embarrassed and awkward. Nicci assumed this was because they'd been caught out for bad timekeeping. She assured them she couldn't give a toss.

Pascale quickly settled at her desk, booting up her computer while Liam, avoiding everyone's eye, rushed off on some errand. Nicci looked up from her screen, read Pascale's tension, observed the retreating Liam's panic and the penny dropped.

Pascale, sitting bolt upright in her chair, pretended to be far too intent on checking emails to be aware that Nicci was watching her.

'Are you two . . . ?' Nicci wasn't sure how to put it; she lifted her hand and gave a questioning wave.

Pascale mumbled something to herself in French – Nicci couldn't make out if it was a curse or a prayer – then turned to face her. 'Are you going to tell Simon? Because . . . well you know his views. When he found out that temp was involved with Hugo, he sacked her straight away.'

Nicci frowned. 'What? What temp?'

'And if it comes out, then Liam must tell his fiancée, and we're not sure we're ready for all that yet.'

'Liam has a fiancée?' Nicci became aware of the slackness of her own jaw. 'He's hardly a grown-up.'

'Engaged for two years. I feel so bad, Nicci, really I do. I never meant it to happen.' Tears were gathering in the corners of Pascale's eyes.

Nicci realized that there was a whole world here she wasn't part of. Ever since she'd taken the job she'd absented herself. She came and went, did the work required of her and ignored all the people around her. In the same way she'd ignored Ethel Huxtable and her rowing neighbours.

She leant back in her chair and let this sink in. What had happened to her? She lived in a bubble, isolated and alone. She tried to remember the last time she'd visited her parents or her sister. Friends? Since Sophie's death there'd been no social life, she'd cut herself off from everyone. Help had been proffered, she'd been invited out to dinners, on trips, but she'd refused it all and gradually people had given up.

She became aware that Pascale was watching her nervously shredding a tissue. Nicci could readily see how Pascale's exotic mix of West African beauty and Parisian chic had floored the hapless Liam.

Painting on a smile, she clicked onto one of the documents on her screen. 'Look, I've made a list of people who figured in various ways in Helen Warner's life. I'm forwarding it. I want as much detail as you can dig up on each one.'

Pascale scrunched the tissue into a ball. 'You mean, you're not going to . . .' A solitary tear coursed down her cheek. Nicci glanced at her, she felt awkward; she didn't want to get sucked into Pascale's Gallic melodrama.

She attached the list to an email and pressed send. 'Your private life is none of my business. Though, if you take my advice, I wouldn't let Eddie get wind.'

Pascale reached out and grasped Nicci's hand. 'I won't forget this.'

Nicci could feel the warmth and slight dampness of Pascale's palm and the intimacy spooked her. However business-like and efficient Pascale seemed on the surface, underneath she was still very French. But what did that make Nicci? An emotionally constipated Brit? When had she turned into this aloof, uncaring individual? The old Nicci would have responded with a hug.

She drew her hand away on the pretext of checking her watch. 'I need to . . . er . . .' Nicci's eyes darted round the office in search of inspiration and alighted on Eddie Lunt, at the coffee station, tipping sachets of sugar into a pint mug. 'I need to have a word with Eddie.'

Nicci got up and made her escape. She walked briskly across the room towards Eddie. As she bore down on him, he looked up, blinking in surprise. She was feeling rather foolish, annoyed that such a small incident could so confound her. She wasn't a cold person. Tactile contact had never bothered her in the past. She'd had a child, for chrissake: sticky hands and bodily fluids came with the territory.

Meeting Eddie's eye, she desperately tried to regain her composure. 'Eddie, I need a word.'

He beamed and put down the mug. ''Course. What can I do yer for?'

Nicci sighed as she hurriedly dredged her memory. 'This contact of yours . . . in the Labour Party? Is he reliable?'

Eddie looked relieved. Her fierce manner had suggested he

was in for a bollocking. He knew Nicci didn't like him, though he wasn't sure why.

'Ray? Yeah, I'd say he's reliable. Has been in the past.'

Still floundering, Nicci folded her arms: 'I've seen your notes, but . . . could you just—'

'Yeah, no probs. Well, story is, the party wants a new policy initiative on drugs. Something to put clear water between them and the other lot. Hollister's very keen on this.' Nicci's gaze had drifted off, she was miles away. He tilted his head. 'Robert Hollister? Shadow Home Secretary?'

Nicci shot him a combative look. 'Fuck off, Eddie, I know who Hollister is.'

Eddie grinned. 'They been doing a bit of private polling and the thought is they might take a punt on some degree of legalization. Plays well with younger voters.'

Nicci forced herself to show interest. 'How does this involve Helen Warner?'

'New back-bencher, bit of a radical, legal background, good on telly, ideal person to fly a kite.'

'So she was arguing for the legalization of drugs?'

'Yeah. She done a couple of talk shows. Visited some youth projects, got down with the kids, y'know the sort of thing.'

'I don't see how that would get her killed.'

'My point exactly, Nic!' Eddie beamed, his pixie face crumpling with glee as he warmed to his subject. 'And this is what old Ray told me. Helen Warner, she was one of these types who thinks she's gonna change the world. Hundred and fifty years ago she'd've been a female missionary paddling up the Zambezi in a bloody canoe. She weren't satisfied with doing a bit of PR at the leadership's behest. She wanted to get stuck in, save Central America from the drugs trade. So she goes on a private fact-finding mission – Mexico, Guatemala,

Honduras, El Salvador. According to Ray, she met some pretty interesting people on both sides of the law.'

'What are we saying here? She pissed off some Latin American drug cartel and got murdered for her pains? That's a bit fantastic. Why would they care about a British MP?'

'Ordinarily they wouldn't. But, as I say, her job was to fly a kite. What if they thought the next British government was seriously contemplating legalization, which would mean a sizeable cut in profits for them? Portugal, Spain, Italy, they're into decriminalization. Maybe they decided to send a message?'

'A message?' Nicci pursed her lips. 'Oh, come on, Eddie, sounds like a bad action movie.'

Unfazed, Eddie shrugged and changed tack: 'I agree. But you see there is another angle here if you dig a bit deeper. Haven't told Simon yet. Let me show you.'

Without waiting for a reply Eddie strolled across the room to a corner desk. Nicci huffed, he simply expected her to follow. His desk was a chaotic jumble of papers and post-its and discarded sweet wrappers. Nicci had never ventured into his territory before and now she knew why.

He scooted a chair over from an adjacent workstation and turned it round for her. 'Take a pew, boss.'

'Don't call me boss. Simon's the boss.'

'Fair enough.'

They both sat down and Eddie woke his computer. He clicked through several documents until he produced a montage of pictures of Helen Warner.

'Yeah? So?' Nicci was getting impatient.

'Mostly pap shots. These guys stake out the top clubs, restaurants, see what blows their way.'

'I know how the paparazzi work.'

'Yeah, but take a look at this.' Eddie ran the cursor across the screen, past Helen Warner, to a partially obscured face behind her left shoulder. 'Recognize him?'

Nicci peered at the screen. 'Okay, it's Hollister.'

'Right on the money.' Eddie grinned and clicked his way through several more pictures. 'Have a look at these. All taken outside a top London eatery.'

Nicci frowned. She hated the way he said 'eatery', as if he were some trendy food critic. She gritted her teeth. 'Just explain. I haven't got time for twenty questions.'

'Take a closer look.' Eddie gave her a puckish grin. 'Hand on the arm?'

'Meaning what?'

'Rumour has it, she was gonna be his new PPS.'

Nicci shrugged. 'All the more reason for them to go out to dinner.'

His expression was doleful, though she got the feeling he was privately amused at her naivety. 'That's the charitable way to look at it. Thing is, Robert Hollister has a rep. He's shagged his way through most of the female flesh in his own party, not to mention a few on the other side too.'

'Oh for fuck's sake, Eddie, she was a lesbian.'

'A pretty tasty one too. And who's to say she didn't swing both ways?'

Nicci gave him her blankest stare. No way was she about to be drawn into his world of smut and innuendo.

'Hollister's the golden boy.' Eddie blinked at her as if it was all so obvious. 'Shadow Home Sec, in line for leader if the current one buggers it up. Warner was a girl who clearly wanted to get on.'

'Girl? She was in her middle thirties,' Nicci snapped in irritation. 'About the same age as me. That makes her a woman.'

Eddie accepted the rebuke with a nod. 'Yeah, all right, a woman who wanted to get on. That's what I'm saying. All the drugs stuff, her trips south of the border – she was doing it for him.'

'Not everything is about sex, Eddie.' Try as she might, Nicci couldn't understand what Blake saw in this guy. 'And anyway, so what? The voters couldn't give a stuff about politicians' sex lives. He's more likely to win votes for his infidelities. So even if they were having an affair, it's hardly a motive for murder. Not in this day and age.'

Eddie rubbed his close-cropped head, reflecting on this. 'All I'm doing is gathering facts – strikes me he was giving her one. Is that relevant to her death? Who knows?'

'He was "giving her one"?' Nicci imagined hitting him, picking up the lamp from the desk and smashing his stupid face in. 'That's not a fact! All you're doing is taking a photograph and overloading it with ill-informed supposition. Helen Warner was openly gay, had a civil partner and was about the most unlikely person in Westminster to trade sexual favours for advancement.'

He beamed and scratched his bearded chin. 'Maybe you're right.' His endless good humour really was cloying. 'You're the detective, Nic, not me.'

She glared at him. Blake called her Nic. He was entitled to such familiarity. Eddie Lunt wasn't.

'Are you taking the fucking piss?'

His bushy brows flew up with innocent incredulity. 'Nah, course not. My job's just to dig up as much info as possible. And it's all grist to the mill, that's what my old news editor used to say.'

Nicci glared at him in disbelief. Did he really think she'd buy his bullshit? Probably, since he was still beaming at her, his pixie features exuding benevolence. How the hell had her life come to this? Working with an ex-con and chancer like Eddie Lunt, when Fiona Calder had offered her the opportunity to be a real police officer again.

Turning on her heel, she stalked off. Blake had got it totally wrong. She'd worked with some moronic cops in her time, but Eddie Lunt was a fucking liability.

19

Kaz was woken with a mug of tea, an occurrence that had certainly never happened before when she'd been in a police cell. Stoneham had gone off duty, one of her DS's appeared and said they were still trying to get in touch with witness protection. But Kaz had already made up her mind, she wasn't hanging about. She told the officer she planned to head straight back up north. They gave her a lift to Basildon station. Jumping on the first train, she lost herself in the crush of morning commuters bound for Fenchurch Street and the City.

Her night in the cells had offered some time for reflection. How the hell had Joey escaped from jail? It was ludicrous. She'd turned her back on everything and everyone to help send him down and still the prison authorities couldn't keep him under lock and key. In the dark recesses of her mind there was ripple of admiration. And fear.

It had taken a while for the shock to subside. The bunk was hard, the plastic mattress stuck to her damp cheek. In the early hours she'd finally managed to corral her scattered thoughts. Joey was on the run and his main concern would be not to get caught. Getting out of the country had to be his priority. He had funds salted away in offshore accounts and contacts in mainland Europe. Coming after her would be the last thing on his mind.

Nevertheless Kaz had to be careful. Being secretive, lying, hiding, these things were all second nature. The problem was she was broke, an impecunious student living on credit. She didn't even have the price of a hotel room.

As she stood, crammed up against the door of the train watching the flat estuary marshlands scudding by, she thought about Helen, her lover, her saviour. She'd have done anything to break into Helen's world. Impressing Helen, winning Helen had been the obsession that carried her through the long years of jail time. But Helen was gone. Her body washed up like a sack of rubbish on the banks of the Thames. Even the thought of it was piercing. What the fuck had happened to her? Could she have killed herself? Maybe it was just some bizarre accident. Kaz didn't believe either of those things. She knew too much of how the world worked, of the kind of people who were out there.

When the train finally pulled into Fenchurch Street she let the flow of commuters carry her out of the station and into the City streets beyond. She wandered through the side turnings and found herself in Leadenhall Street. A queue snaking out of the door of a sandwich bar reminded her that she hadn't eaten since the afternoon before. She walked on, selected a coffee shop with tables stretching back into the dark interior. She ordered coffee and a bacon roll, counting out her small change and finding she had just enough to pay.

Taking a table at the back she sipped her coffee and waited for the food to arrive. It was mid-morning and the place was bustling. She'd placed herself strategically to watch all the comings and goings: office workers, shop workers, a couple of builders in heavy boots from a nearby site collecting take-aways. There were three people serving, young and harassed,

119

they didn't stop. Kaz waited nearly ten minutes for her bacon roll to arrive with apologies. She smiled at the scrawny kid who delivered it and let it all wash over her. She was getting the lie of the land.

The bacon was salty, the roll crisp. She savoured every mouthful, wiped her fingers on the napkin and considered her next move. The adjacent tables were closely packed to accommodate as many customers as possible. Kaz's immediate neighbour was a young woman texting on her phone; as the phone dinged with a reply, her frown deepened. She wasn't having a good morning. On the other side of her was a lad, probably a student, tapping lethargically on his laptop and yawning. Beyond him three lairy blokes sat round a table having an animated conversation. They were in their thirties, suited and booted, collars unbuttoned, loosened ties.

Kaz sat back and tuned in. The one facing her was chubby with close-cropped hair and a red face.

He opened his palms, laughing, as he addressed his companions: 'I mean, fuck me, wha'd she expect?'

The man facing away from Kaz lounged back in his chair, rubbing his shiny, bald pate. 'She expected ding-dong wedding bells. It's what most of 'em expect.'

'Not me, mate!' Red face shuddered emphatically. 'I'm not going down that road. If it don't work out, then you're stuffed. Half of everything, every bonus you get for the next twenty years. A live-in shag's one thing. But marriage? I'm a feminist, me. Everyone equal, pay your own bills.'

They all guffawed and rocked back in their seats. Kaz got up, slipped her backpack on one shoulder and edged her way between the tables. Pushing a chair aside she used it as an excuse to dip her hand down and scoop up the leather briefcase sitting on the floor next to Baldy. The move was swift and deft. Holding the briefcase in front of her, she headed for the door without a backward glance.

20

Nicci took the tube to Clapham South, skirted the southern tip of the Common and set off along Nightingale Lane. Julia Hadley's postal address was Wandsworth rather than Clapham and, turning right off the main road, Nicci soon found herself in a leafy enclave of smart Edwardian family homes, known locally as "twixt the commons". Julia had advised her not to drive; parking was strictly residential permit holders only and the roads she walked down had a liberal smattering of late model Audis, Mercs and four-by-fours.

The house turned out to be a tastefully restored semi with the original art nouveau stained-glass in the front door. Nicci rang the brass bell and let her gaze wander over the black-and-white tiled path and the neat privet hedge. She knew from Julia Hadley's appearance that she leant towards the arty, so the house probably reflected her taste more than her late partner's.

Nicci had to ring the doorbell again before a bleary-eyed Julia appeared. She was swathed in a purple bathrobe and full of profuse apologies; their appointment was for eleven, somehow she'd overslept. Nicci followed her along the hallway and into a light, airy kitchen, glancing in the adjacent rooms as she went. The decor was expensive with original features and retro touches balanced against decidedly modern furniture. More Julia than Helen? It was hard to tell.

The kitchen was built around two large slabs of granite set at right angles. Julia invited Nicci to take a stool at one of them as she busied herself with the coffee machine. As Julia shuffled from sink to cupboard, her fluffy purple mules slapping the polished ceramic floor, Nicci watched her.

The shoulders seemed permanently hunched, the bags under her eyes were worse than at their previous meeting, but through some effort of supreme will she chattered on. 'My cleaning lady usually comes in on a Tuesday, but her youngest broke his arm. So that's why the place is in such a mess.'

Nicci glanced around; there was a newspaper on the table, a plate, a mug and two empty wine bottles on the draining board.

'I don't think anyone'd call it messy.'

She hadn't expected this comment to be controversial but it sent a jolt through Julia Hadley. 'Helen was very particular. She liked everything to be neat and tidy.'

Julia's palm flew to her mouth to suppress the tears. 'Some days I . . . I wake up and for a moment I think I can hear her moving about.'

Nicci knew just what she meant. It was why she'd moved. In the old place she'd end up going from room to room, feeling her daughter's presence, hearing noises, opening a bedroom door and expecting to find Sophie there. She took a deep breath. It was tempting to tell Julia Hadley that she too knew all about loss, but that wouldn't be professional. As a police officer she'd learnt to compartmentalize her feelings. You didn't take the job home; equally, you kept your private life and personal pain separate from the job. Too much empathy could be dangerous, it clouded the judgement.

Adjusting her position on the high leather stool, Nicci smiled and changed tack. 'Such a lovely house. I've never had much of an eye for design, colours, that sort of thing. My mother despairs of me.'

Julia pulled a tissue from the pocket of her robe and blew her nose. 'My first job after university, I worked for a design magazine.'

'It shows. What do you do now?'

'I set up a small PR consultancy with a couple of friends. Most of our clients are in the arts.'

The distraction seemed to be working; Julia was more composed. Nicci continued to shepherd the conversation along: 'That's very brave – starting your own business.'

'I see no point in working for someone else if you can be your own boss.' Julia tossed her head and Nicci got a glimpse of the grit behind the grief. Julia Hadley was a business-woman in her own right, not just Helen's partner.

'A couple of different things have come up that it'd be useful to talk about.' Opening her bag, Nicci took out a note-book and one of Eddie Lunt's pap shots, though she kept it concealed. 'If you feel up to it, of course.'

Whatever emotions were washing through her, Julia had got a grip. She gave Nicci a tight smile. 'No problem. Fire away.'

'I gather Helen was taking a political interest in the legal-ization of drugs.'

'Well, you were in the police, weren't you?' Julia huffed. 'You know it makes sense.'

Nicci gave no reply; she wasn't getting into that. 'And she went on some kind of fact-finding mission to Latin America?'

'It's what back-benchers do. Pick a controversial topic in the hope it'll get them noticed.'

'So Helen did this off her own bat?'

'Yeah. But as a lawyer she was pretty clued up on the subject. She'd defended plenty of drug mules. The harm comes from organized crime, not ordinary people snorting a couple of lines on a Saturday night.'

'Is that what you and Helen did?' It was a risky follow-up, but Nicci knew she had to push it to get anything useful.

Julia merely shot her a cynical glance. 'You really are an ex-cop, aren't you?'

'Sorry.' Nicci smiled. 'I'm not being judgemental, just trying to build up a picture.'

Julia drew the folds of the bathrobe around her for protection. 'Helen didn't do drugs at all. She hardly drank. She hated losing control. I've smoked dope since I was at uni. Helen never joined me. She was a curious mixture of puritan and liberal. She didn't judge anyone else. But she sure as hell judged herself.'

Julia started to suck the thumbnail of her left hand. Nicci noted the tension, the jitteriness in her glance. Was she using cannabis now, to medicate her grief? Nicci suspected something stronger.

Mirroring Julia's behaviour, Nicci examined her own thumbnail, then glanced directly at her, as if a random thought had just occurred to her. 'Robert Hollister? A contact at Labour Party HQ has suggested that Helen was in line to be his PPS.'

'Well, she hadn't mentioned that to me. But I wouldn't be at all surprised.'

'Why not?'

'It was Robert who encouraged Helen to run for Parliament. The Hollisters are old family friends. Robert was a student of Charles' at Oxford. Charles Warner is Helen's father.' Julia blinked a couple of times. 'He's seventy-two – this has really hit him hard.' She swallowed, her chin quivered. 'Poor old Charles.'

Nicci nodded and waited. Julia glanced at her then turned away. She seemed at a loss.

A tense frown had gathered between her brows, she tried to ease it away with a finger. 'Do you want to see her room?'

An abrupt change of subject – Nicci wondered why. She scanned Julia but found no clue. Was Helen's connection with Robert Hollister an issue? The way Julia had responded to his name didn't suggest that. What seemed more likely was that she was simply finding it painful, having to explain her dead partner's life to a stranger.

She followed Julia upstairs to a large bay-windowed room at the front of the house. There was a Victorian chandelier hanging from the elaborately moulded ceiling, but the rest of the room was white and minimalist with a glass desk under the window and a low leather and chrome Barcelona chair.

Julia Hadley sat down on the bed and ran her fingers over the delicately woven threads of the pure white duvet. 'She also had a study at the back of the house. The police took that apart. But Helen spent more time here, she needed her own space.'

Nicci walked over to the window. The curtains were pale peach but heavy and opulent, she could imagine how cosy it made the room when they were closed at night.

It was a room to envy, the opposite of her own bleak, cur- tainless cell. 'This was a sort of sanctuary then?'

Julia seemed about to speak, then hesitated. Nicci could see that she was struggling. With her feelings, her conscience? Hard to tell. Nicci waited.

Finally Julia looked up at her, her fingers plucking nerv- ously at the fabric of the duvet. 'There's something I need to show you. Something I didn't show the police.' She got up. 'I won't be a minute.'

Nicci watched her leave the room. A bit of a rocky start? This was always going to be a slow process, but if they were to get anywhere she had to dig deep, and Julia Hadley's resistance was already apparent.

She ran her own fingers over the pristine duvet. Partners, but they had separate rooms. Should she read any significance into that? And could Eddie possibly be right – had something been going on with Robert Hollister? Nicci wanted to resist that notion, mostly out of distaste for Eddie. She was still pondering these questions when Julia returned.

She held out a Nokia smartphone. 'My old phone. I use this and a BlackBerry.' She tapped in the PIN. 'I keep this for personal calls. My firm pays for the BlackBerry.'

Clicking on Helen's name, Julia scrolled to the last text and offered the phone to Nicci. 'I got this from Helen about five o'clock on the day she—' The look on Julia's face was pure sorrow.

Nicci took the phone and read:

Hey babe – don't think badly of me. I never wanted to hurt you. Politics, what a shit-show! I really thought I understood the game and was smart enough to play it. How dumb am I? Love you always xx

Nicci read the message through twice. She was aware of Julia's eyes upon her and the tension pulsing off her. 'What do you think she means?'

'I've no idea.'

Nicci didn't believe that for one moment. 'Had she done something to hurt you?'

'No. Of course not.' Julia's eyes were glassy with tears.

'So are you reading this as a possible suicide note? Is that why you didn't show it to the police?'

'No! It's confusing . . . I don't know what to think. I just can't believe that Helen would kill herself.'

'Is it that you don't want to believe?'

'No!'

Julia plumped down on the bed, sending ripples across the soft, undulating duvet. Nicci was keeping herself firmly behind the professional facade, but her heart went out to Julia, locked in misery. She wondered about the hidden nooks and crannies, the places we keep the agonizing thoughts we try to hide even from ourselves. We all have them, she knew that. And now she was getting a glimpse of Julia's. Nicci turned back to the text, scanned it once again and pondered. What was Helen trying to say to her partner on the day she died? Maybe the police investigation had got to the truth after all. Perhaps Helen Warner did commit suicide.

21

Kaz stepped out of the coffee shop and set off at a brisk pace. She didn't run, but she didn't hang about. And she didn't look back. It was a long time since she'd done any serious thieving, but she hadn't forgotten the basics. She turned left down Gracechurch Street. Spying the red circle and blue bar of the tube roundel, she headed for Monument station. As she dipped into the entrance she allowed herself a brief backward glance. Just a rolling sea of faces, no one focused on her, no pursuit. So she hadn't lost the touch.

She bought the cheapest ticket and boarded a westbound Circle line train. The late morning lull meant she found a corner seat with ease. Only then did she open the briefcase. It was good-quality leather, undoubtedly Italian, a zipped compartment at the back, the larger front pouch secured with buckled straps. She unfastened these and looked inside – a laptop in a carrying sleeve, two phones, a hard-backed notebook, a couple of cheap gel pens and a Mars bar. There were a series of leather pockets sewn into the inside wall. Kaz checked through them: an out-of-date lottery ticket, two different coffee franchise loyalty cards and a foil-wrapped condom. She sighed. Not a bad haul if you had the means to fence the goods. But what she'd been hoping for was a wallet and cash.

She pulled open the zip on the rear compartment and

found an Oyster card in a plastic holder. At least that was something of immediate use. Tucked behind it was a five-pound note.

Disappointed, she sat back in her seat and stared out of the black window into the rumbling tunnel beyond. What she needed was a plan or at least some notion of what to do next. She'd hoped the briefcase would furnish her with the means to get a cheap hotel room. A safe bolthole where she would have time to think. Clearly, laying her hands on some cash would require some serious pickpocketing, and she wasn't sure she was up to that.

Scooting her fingers one last time round the fabric lining of the briefcase she came across a small lump. Further investigation revealed another tiny pocket. She pulled the Velcro apart and felt inside: a plastic pouch. Glancing down into the bag, she turned it over to examine the contents: three blue capsules. Medicinal or recreational? Hard to tell. She smiled wryly to herself, time was she'd have popped them anyway. But now? Since she got news of Helen's death, the possibility of chemical release had been niggling at the fringes of consciousness. Just a little something to take the edge off, whispered the monkey brain. Who would know? Who would care? Kaz gave the monkey a mental slap and refastened the briefcase. She took a deep breath. Now more than ever she needed her wits at their sharpest.

The train rattled on westwards, passing through Embankment and Westminster. Kaz thought about her Glasgow life. Her new identity under the witness protection scheme was starting to seem more attractive by the minute. Yet she'd always felt she was lacking something. She'd moved through her new life in a bubble, insulating herself from contact and emotion. She had acquaintances but no friends. Much as she enjoyed the classes and had thrown herself into the work, it somehow never really engaged her at a deeper level. Nothing did. The only thing that dug right down, that she felt in her gut, was her passion for Helen. Helen, who'd played her and rejected her, Helen, who was dead.

At Sloane Square a trio of posh girls loaded down with shopping bags plonked down opposite her. They seemed oblivious to their surroundings, occupying the space as of right, their boisterous conversation dominating the carriage. Kaz felt envious, not so much of the money as the ease. She wondered if she could ever achieve that sense of entitlement. What would she have to do? She thought of the blue pills in the briefcase. Maybe they'd do the trick.

The girls got up to alight at South Kensington. Kaz let her gaze skim over the moving letters of the station sign and she had the glimmering of an idea. There was one person who'd always been in her corner, who hadn't dismissed her as some useless slag. Mike Dawson had taught her life drawing and his recommendation had secured her a place at a top college, Glasgow School of Art. At the time of Joey's trial, he'd sent her a postcard wishing her luck in his elaborate spidery handwriting. He was an odd bloke, mostly unreadable. Still, he was the one person in her life who'd gone out of his way to be kind to her, though he had nothing to gain by it.

She pulled out her phone and rapidly scrolled through the contacts list. There he was: Mike Dawson, Onslow Square, South Kensington. She glanced at the open carriage door: she had about fifteen seconds to decide.

22

Nicci sat facing Julia Hadley across the granite counter of her swish kitchen. They had cups of coffee in front of them, but Julia was ignoring hers. The phone with Helen's text sat on the polished surface between them.

Nicci gave her a sympathetic smile. 'Okay, I'll give you my opinion. Guilt, certainly. And contrition. Does that mean she'd decided to take her own life? It's a possibility – but only one possibility.'

Julia raised her eyes, they were moist, over-bright. 'Are you just saying that to make me feel better?'

'No, that's not my job. You've hired us to discover the truth.' Nicci shifted, moving her foot to rebalance on the high stool. She could sense the tautness in Julia, the instinct to hold back pulling against her desire to tell. 'That's probably going to include things you don't want to look at.'

The probe had gone in. Julia clutched her arms about her tightly, trying to hold herself together.

Nicci watched the interior struggle. 'Someone gets murdered, that's an extreme thing. About the most extreme thing. Aspects of their life come to light, secrets, deceptions. It's a nightmare for those left.'

Julia shot her a resentful glance then her whole body slumped; the internal dam had burst. 'Okay, if you want to know, I think she was having an affair. Possibly the papers or some website had got hold of it. Maybe that's what the text was about: she thought it was going to break.'

Nicci simply nodded in the hope she'd go on. Instead Julia started to cry, quietly, discretely. Picking up the box of tissues on the worktop, Nicci slid it in Julia's direction. 'Do you know who?'

Julia shook her head briskly and dabbed her eyes; she didn't know, she refused to know.

As Nicci continued to wait, questions skittered through her brain. Was Eddie Lunt right? Had Helen been sleeping with Robert Hollister? Nicci resisted the notion, but the detective in her couldn't ignore it. 'Are we talking a man or a woman?'

Julia's eyes crinkled into something approaching amusement and she looked up suddenly. 'Helen was a lesbian!'

Nicci shrugged. 'Some people are a hundred per cent one thing or the other, but in my experience that's not true of everyone. Maybe Helen was closer to the middle of the spectrum than you'd like to think.'

Julia stared then gave a short, sour laugh. 'Because she was beautiful? She couldn't really be gay because she was beautiful? That's a very clichéd view, very male too. Also you're the detective, answer me this – if you were an ambitious politician and bisexual, would you opt for the lesbian tag? It's not the smartest career move, is it?' Julia plucked another tissue from the box and blew her nose. Annoyance fizzed off her then she sighed. 'Sorry. I don't mean to be rude.'

'Rude's fine.' Nicci painted on a smile. 'I want to know what you really think.' She put her hand on the counter between them, reaching out but not touching. 'Listen, Julia, we need to come to an understanding. Or rather, you need to make a decision.'

Julia concentrated on wiping her bloodshot eyes. She was reining herself in.

Sensing the polite shutdown, Nicci tapped the counter, waiting until Julia's gaze rose to meet hers. 'Either you trust us, or you don't trust us. It's a choice. I need to know your suspicions, if you have any. I need to know the things you're confused about. I need to know the tiny things that don't seem important. So, basically everything.'

A sigh rippled through Julia's frame. 'The thing is . . . if Helen was actually murdered, I just feel . . . well, who can you trust? The police investigated. You should be able to trust the police, shouldn't you? But their whole approach, it was never right.'

'They just went through the motions?'

'Yeah. Exactly.'

'And you're asking yourself why? Why didn't they want to look at this? It's a scary thought.'

Julia leant against the back of her stool, gazing over Nicci's shoulder. 'Helen used to say I was blinkered, lived in a bubble – nice house, nice car, good job – a middle-class bubble. I expect people to be polite to me in shops. I expect tradesmen to be reliable.'

Nicci smiled. 'Don't we all.'

Julia turned to meet her eye. 'As a lawyer, Helen'd dealt with all types. The dregs, you might say. All I know are my family, my colleagues, friends I went to school and uni with, and they're all decent people. That's the assumption you make, isn't it? Well, it's the assumption I make. Helen didn't, maybe you don't.'

Nicci gave her a rueful smile. 'There are individuals out there capable of any atrocity you can imagine. But it's true, mostly we don't meet them.'

'You mean people like me don't meet them.' Julia sniffed.
'I'm stupid and privileged and naive. That's what Helen
thought. But when it came to appearances – and politics is all
about that – I fitted the bill. That's why she asked me to be
her civil partner, she knew I wouldn't embarrass her.'

Nicci tilted her head. 'You sound quite bitter.'

Julia swept her palm across her forehead as if to brush
aside the pain. 'Oh, I knew what I was getting into. I think she
did love me, in her way. It was just never enough.'

'But you loved her?'

Julia hunched her shoulders and stared down at her
hands, cradling the left knuckle in the right palm. 'Yes. She
was it for me. The one and only. I'd've done anything to make
it work.'

'So you put up with the affairs?'

'I only really know about one. But who can tell, there were
probably others. She had this client – she was completely
obsessed with her. Then when she proposed to me she told
me in a roundabout way that it was over, she was putting the
past behind her, focusing on her political career. But Helen
was always secretive. Lawyers make the best liars you know.'

Nicci grinned. 'Oh yeah, I do know.'

A wounded smile crept over Julia's features. 'A couple of
months ago she told me she had to go to Edinburgh for a
conference. Then I saw a bill on her desk, a hotel in Glasgow.
Later I asked her why she'd gone there instead, just an innocent enquiry. She completely denied it, insisted I'd misread
the bill. Why would she deny going to Glasgow?'

Nicci scooted her tongue across her upper lip. Glasgow.
This was getting interesting. 'You think this was the same
client?'

'Her – someone else? I don't know.'

'The client you're thinking of, have you got a name?'

Julia clearly had, but hesitated; saying it would make it real and part of her resisted. 'It could be Karen. Helen used to visit her in prison. Sometimes she talked about that and there was always a . . . a certain tone in her voice.'

'Have you got a surname?'

'She might've mentioned it ages ago. But I don't remember.' She caught Nicci's eye. 'Really I don't. Couldn't we get hold of a client list from her old firm?'

Nicci nodded, even though such an enquiry was unnecessary. She already knew the client Julia was talking about. It had to be Kaz Phelps.

23

Kaz wandered along the north side of Onslow Square. A magnificent Victorian terrace of stucco and brick, it rose to four storeys and oozed money. Every porticoed door was freshly painted, every iron railing topped with impressive spikes. Kaz was puzzled; how come a down-at-heel art teacher like Mike Dawson lived on millionaire's row? She tracked the numbers along the street until she came to his basement flat. A short flight of stone steps led down to the front door. She hesitated. It was tempting to simply turn tail, but then the door opened.

The first thing she heard was his hacking cough, painfully phlegmy, then he emerged, wearing an old hoodie and clutching a hessian shopping bag. His claw-like hand grasped the balustrade as he started a slow ascent up the steps.

Kaz peered down at him through the railings. 'Hello, Mike.'

As his eyes slowly rose to meet hers she felt a wave of trepidation sweep over her. It was fear; not of harm or danger – that sort of fear was commonplace in her life. She could handle that. What she feared was his indifference. Maybe he wouldn't even remember her.

His eyes wrinkled against the sunlight, but his gaze was as piercing as ever. Recognition dawned. 'Karen?' He broke into a huge grin. 'Karen Phelps! Well I never! I was thinking about you just this morning, wondering how you were getting along.'

Kaz felt elated but shy. 'Since I was in London, thought I'd look you up.'

'Well I'd have been jolly offended if you hadn't.' He flapped his hand, beckoning. 'Come on, come inside and I'll put the kettle on.'

Kaz went down the steps and followed her old teacher into the flat. Although it was a basement, the interior was surprisingly large and light. A huge open-plan room stretched from the front of the property to the back with a conservatory and floor-to-ceiling sliding glass doors onto the rear garden. The space comprised sitting room, dining area and kitchen rolled into one, plus in the corner at the back Mike had a large studio easel with a half-painted canvas on it. Several more paintings were propped against the wall.

Mike beamed at her. There was a moment of awkwardness as Kaz stood there wondering if she should give him a hug. Somehow that didn't really feel appropriate with Mike.

He rubbed his hands together with glee. 'Make yourself at home.' He bustled into the kitchen area and began filling the kettle, raising his voice to be heard above the noise of the tap. 'I want to hear all about Glasgow. And I hope you've got a sketchbook to show me.'

Kaz deposited her backpack and the stolen briefcase near the door then wandered over to the easel. 'I don't think I've ever seen any of your stuff before. Mind if I look?'

'Be my guest. I don't paint that much nowadays, I don't really have the energy. Plus I'm lazy, I'd rather just sit in the garden and soak up the sun.'

Kaz studied the half-painted work on the easel. A monumental figure, possibly female, was emerging from the white expanse of canvas – a bit like a Henry Moore sculpture, although tortured and slightly contorted.

She smiled. 'I like it. Unusual.'

Mike was taking floral ceramic mugs from the cupboard and arranging them on a tray. 'No it's not. It's totally derivative. Francis Bacon did it first and he did it far better. But I've got a dealer who does very well selling to the Chinese. They'll buy anything vaguely European, especially if they think it's a bit rude. And now I'm retired, I have to do something.'

'When did you retire?'

'Last Christmas. Had a few health problems.'

Kaz waited for him to elaborate, but he didn't and it seemed intrusive to ask.

Having filled the teapot with boiling water, he put it on the tray and carried it over to the low, carved oak coffee table that sat between two massive sofas. Kaz watched him as he moved; he'd always looked ancient to her and now he was much thinner, his hunched shoulders rising up towards his ears like angel wings. He'd coughed several times since she arrived, a rumbling eruption deep in his lungs; it didn't sound good.

As he eased himself down on to one of the sofas with obvious relief, Kaz positioned herself on the sofa opposite.

'I'll be mother then, shall I?' He gave her his lopsided grin. 'Milk?'

'Yeah, milk no sugar, thanks.' She smiled back at him, remembering her first impression of Mike Dawson. With his dark eyes, vulpine features and long wispy grey hair, she'd thought he was a dead ringer for Rasputin and scarier-looking than any of the many villains she'd encountered in her life. Yet he'd turned out to be the kindest, straightest bloke she'd ever met.

What the hell – it wasn't as if she had anything to lose. 'I've got a problem, Mike.'

'I rather thought that might be the case.' Seeing the look of confusion on her face he inclined his head. 'I saw the television news this morning. I gather your brother has murdered a prisoner officer and escaped from jail.'

'Yeah. That's one part of the problem.'

'There's more?' His manner was direct as always, but gentle. There was no judgement.

Impulse overrode caution and Kaz decided to just go for it. 'About a month ago the police pulled my ex-lover's body out of the Thames. I only just found out. They're saying she committed suicide, but I don't believe it. I think she was murdered. That's why I'm down here. I need to find out what happened to her. Oh, and I need a place to stay.'

Mike ran a long, paint-rimmed fingernail over his stubbly chin as he absorbed the information. He nodded his head slowly a couple of times then smiled. 'Well, I think I've got some chocolate digestives somewhere. Strikes me we've got some serious thinking to do, so we'll need them.'

24

Joey wandered through narrow avenues of dense foliage, sweat dribbling down his face and neck. The midday sun blazed down on him, hot but diffused by the heavy plastic sheeting which formed the garden centre's makeshift roof. The feathered fronds of exotic palms brushed his shoulder as he passed. Water puddled around the bases of the plant pots, moisture and heat combining to create a humid fug.

It felt a bit like the steam room in the exclusive gym and racquet club near London Bridge where he'd been a member before his incarceration. He'd fitted right in among the bankers and lawyers, even winning a grand off some hedge fund manager he'd thrashed on the squash court. It was the world he'd aspired to, one where he belonged. But somehow it had all gone pear-shaped.

The assiduousness of the police pursuit had surprised him. Turning up mob-handed at his mum's place seemed a bit unnecessary. Plenty of convicted felons went on the lam and hardly rated a mention in the media. But maybe they weren't serial killers. This was the label Joey had ended up with: psychopathic serial killer.

The tabloids had reported his conviction with relish, crowing over the long sentence. Now they were slamming the prison authorities for his escape. He'd been dubbed the 'angel of death', mainly because it fitted with a pap shot they'd dug up of him with an old girlfriend. She was a soap actress he'd hung out with briefly. But then Joey's liaisons were only ever brief. The picture had been taken at some swanky party; piercing blue eyes, gorgeous grin, he looked far more of a star than the anorexic waif clinging to his arm. Joey loved this photo and had even obtained a copy of the original from the photographer, which he'd hung on the wall of his cell.

As to the tag 'psychopathic serial killer', he'd become comfortable with that too. People had died at his hand, he made no bones about that. Most of them deserved it. Maybe there'd been one or two who didn't. But in any soldier's career there was bound to be some collateral damage.

The term psychopath carried negative connotations and when his offender manager had first used it to describe him, Joey had been tempted to give the moron a slap. Back then, he'd only been aware of the adverse implications of the term. It was only after he'd done some research, got stuck into the real neuroscience, that he found he really did fit the profile, and what's more it confirmed what he'd always believed: he was indeed special, his brain was wired differently. And that was a huge advantage.

Arguably, psychopathy was an evolutionary step forward. The rapid fight-or-flight response had been a lifesaver for primitive man, when survival meant legging it from bears and woolly mammoths and the like. But there weren't many woolly mammoths lurking round the corner in the modern world. Fear and anxiety were debilitating emotions, they paralysed you, stopped you from thinking rationally. Those rare individuals who never lost their nerve, who could always be ruthless and decisive – individuals like Joey – would always have the edge.

Joey had just been unlucky in his parents. Terry Phelps

had been a criminal because he was too stupid to get what he wanted by other means. This had been apparent to Joey even as a kid. But his father's way had become his way, and that was the root of his problems. If he'd had a proper education and a father who'd supported him instead of beating the shit out of him, he'd have never landed in jail. He'd have been a CEO or a City trader or a commando in the SAS, and when he took out some scumbag he'd have been doing it for Queen and country and they'd have given him a fucking medal.

Joey mused on these things as he wandered and waited. His picture was all over the papers and on the telly, but he wasn't that worried about being recognized. Since he'd been inside he'd let his hair grow and once he'd started to plan his escape he stopped shaving. Now with a shaggy blond mane and a thick reddish beard, he looked nothing like his mug shot.

Finding a shady nook with a rustic wooden bench he settled himself on it. An elderly couple towing a trolley took him for one of the garden centre staff and asked directions to the rhododendra. He gave them a sunny smile and pointed randomly. They pootled off.

When the police had come crashing through his mum's front door he'd got over the back fence nimbly enough. In the dark woods behind the house he soon lost his pursuers. He'd managed to progress at a steady jog. The stab wound in his side had continued to ooze a little, but with the adrenaline pumping he felt very little pain.

When he'd emerged from the woods onto an unmade farm track, it was still light enough to recognize familiar land-marks. He'd stopped to catch his breath and rest his palm on the trunk of the big old oak where he and Kaz had once tried to build a treehouse. Their imagination had far exceeded their skill and the rickety boards they'd used to create a platform between the spreading branches had collapsed under their weight and resulted in him falling about ten feet and breaking his collarbone. As always, Kaz had sorted it, filching a couple of notes from their mother's purse and then bundling him into a taxi to Basildon A&E. When he'd returned home with his arm in a sling, Ellie had assumed he'd been fighting and had given him a clout.

The farm had once been a hive of activity, with a small dairy herd and chickens and geese scampering round the yard. When he passed through last night, there hadn't been a creature in sight and the land had given way to acres of oilseed rape. The red-brick Victorian farmhouse had been sold off as an executive home, and Joey had paused to cast a longing eye over the brand-new Audi four-by-four parked on the jet-washed cobbled drive. Unfortunately it was securely locked and alarmed, so any attempt to boost it would be sure to attract attention. He'd settled instead for a kid's BMX bike that he found propped against a wall.

After pedalling through the back lanes he'd finally come out onto the A127, then ridden a few miles along the cycle path in the direction of Southend. Breaking into the garden centre had been a piece of piss. He'd spent the remaining hours of darkness curled up under the cover of an empty hot tub. Waking at first light, he got himself a drink from a standpipe and searched out a quiet corner where he could hide away until his mother showed up.

Ellie had never been a reliable parent, but she was fiercely loyal. The stroke that had torpedoed Joey's father had also served to set her free. Slowly she'd weaned herself off the diet of booze and pills that had sustained her through her long marriage to a domineering bully. With Terry wheelchair bound and incapable of speech, she'd taken up with Brian, moving him into the house and the marital bed. By the time Terry was finally dead and buried, she'd reinvented herself as matriarch of the clan. Joey indulged her fantasy – after all, she was his mum – and paid the bills. But he never made the mistake of listening to her nonsense. She'd suggested the garden centre as a rendezvous; he probably shouldn't have listened to that either, but there'd been no time for debate with the Old Bill piling out of their cars and trying to break down the front door.

With hindsight, it had been a stupid mistake to go back. The only reason he'd done so was to retrieve a laptop, a clean smartphone with a removable battery and some cash hidden in a secret compartment behind a tiled conduit in one of the en suite bathrooms. They'd been stashed there long before his arrest as one of several precautionary measures he'd taken to ensure he had an escape route in place, should he ever need it. The alternative would have been to rely on Ellie and Brian to evade surveillance and get the stuff to him, but knowing them they'd have ended up leading the police right to him. So he'd taken the risk. He had to – he needed that laptop. It contained all his contacts and access to his offshore accounts. At least it was still safely tucked away in its hiding place, and even if the worst happened and the police did get hold of it, everything was well encrypted so it wouldn't be the end of the world.

Without a watch or phone he could only guess the time. The sun was overhead and scorching. He'd always been a bit of a sun-worshipper, but the mugginess in the garden centre was really getting to him and the wound in his side had started to throb. Where the hell was Ellie? Suddenly overcome with dizziness and feeling sick, he struggled to his feet. If he could just get out of this fucking heat. He took a step forward, stumbled, the concrete floor flew up to smack him in the face and for the first time in his life Joey Phelps fainted.

25

Nicci got back to the office at lunchtime. She'd already spoken to Pascale en route. As she skirted round the work-stations and headed for her desk, Pascale swivelled her chair, caught Nicci's eye. 'Nobody will talk. Mention the witness protection scheme and there's an omertà.'

'Okay, let's see if we can by-pass them.' Nicci dumped her bag down. 'She's at Glasgow School of Art, I think. When I went up to see her before her brother's trial the name she said she was using was Clare O'Keeffe. Might be true.'

Pascale turned back to her keyboard and started to tap away. Nicci was just logging on to her own computer when she sensed someone approaching. She glanced up to see Liam, looking sheepish, hands shovelled in the pockets of his chinos.

'Want a coffee, boss?'

'What's up with you? Hasn't she told you I'm not ratting you out?'

'Just trying to be nice.' He grinned.

'And you are nice, Liam.' Nicci gave him a mocking smile. 'I'll have an espresso, good and strong.'

He clipped his forehead in mock salute. 'Coming up.'

She watched him head for the coffee station. She meant it; Liam was nice. He was also young and unscathed, a situation she envied. Happy-go-lucky seemed his natural state. She scanned the room – quiet, industrious. People were getting on with the job and Nicci realized that having puzzles to solve, inquiries to pursue, had made her feel more composed. Her synapses were nattering with questions and theories. What she'd told Blake hadn't been a lie – she felt much better when she was busy.

Her mind skipped back to Julia Hadley, a woman obsessed with solving the murder of a lover who was unfaithful. Maybe it wasn't just Helen's killer Julia wanted found; maybe what she really wanted to know was why her love hadn't been enough.

Nicci pulled the spiral-bound notebook out of her bag, got up and headed for Blake's office. He was on the phone, but waved her in. She perched on the arm of his sofa and waited for him to end the call.

He clicked the handset off and slotted it back in its cradle. 'Well, you certainly rattled Fiona Calder's cage. Tomorrow's *Mail* is running a column on profit-hungry private investigators preying on grieving families. They're not naming us specifically, 'cause they know I'd sue, but it's all over the web that it's the Warner case and we're the outfit in the frame.'

Nicci raised her eyebrows. 'Interesting.'

'It's more than that.' Blake got up from his chair. He was buzzing. 'Means you can stop feeling bad about the sorry cow. She's a serving police officer, Nic. She knows who's behind the Warner murder and she's playing games with it. I think she's using us as a diversion, giving the media something to chew on.'

Nicci frowned as she considered this. 'That's just supposition.'

'Well, what is she up to then? The murder of a politician by persons unknown, who the Met have decided to protect?

Goes to the heart of the democratic process. We don't assassinate our leaders or throw them in jail, we just vote for the other lot. It's what makes us civilized.'

Turning the notebook over in her hand, Nicci ran her fingers along the wire binding. 'Assassination? That's a bit strong. Helen Warner was a backbench MP and a very junior member of the opposition. She had no power.'

'Then why go to such lengths to cover up her death?'

'It's easier.' She puffed out her cheeks.

'This is not about easy.' Blake ran his palm over his greying, neatly razored scalp. 'I used to have a lot of time for Calder – she's smart. Whatever she's up to, it's far more complicated than that.'

Nicci crossed one knee over the other and pondered. 'Okay, whose interests was Warner threatening?'

'That's what we need to find out.'

'You're not going along with Eddie's theory?' She gave him a sidelong look. 'Some drug cartel? I mean, really?'

'It's a possibility. At this stage we can't rule anything out.'

'Come on, Simon, I love a good conspiracy theory too. But remember what you used to say to us back on the squad: violent crime, murder, is ninety-nine per cent cock-up. People reacting viciously to situations they can't control.'

'Yeah, that's true enough. But what about the one per cent, eh? Professional hit with a political motive? That's a totally different kettle of fish. We're going to have an interesting time with this.'

'Maybe a bit too interesting.'

'I told you when I hired you that it wouldn't be boring. I'm keeping my promise.' He grinned at her mischievously.

'Yeah, and why did you hire me? 'Cause I've got to say, it's never made a lot of sense.' It was a flip remark, tossed back at him in the spirit of banter.

His gaze met hers, but only for an instant. He was a big bloke, tough, no prisoners, a rugby player in his college days. Yet the look in his eyes was momentarily tender, almost wistful. It was neither professional nor paternal and she only got a glimpse, still it sent a shockwave through her. Blake was a married man, happily married as far as she knew. He certainly wasn't one of these middle-aged creeps whose eyes strayed to your tits every time they talked to you.

He coughed and folded his arms. 'You were a bloody good copper, Armstrong. And even with your brain in a sling you're still more use to me than most of the retired clowns out there. So . . .' He transferred his hands to his hips, he was back in boss mode. 'Let's show them who the real detectives are, shall we?'

Nicci smiled. Whatever that look had meant – and she wasn't even sure if it was desire or simply empathy at her loss – it was gone. Maybe she'd imagined it. Now they were back on an even keel. There was a job to do. And it was becoming clear that job had shifted from difficult to downright dangerous.

26

Kaz licked chocolate off her fingertips, she was on her third biscuit and watching Mike in amazement. He had a sheet of paper on the table in front of him and was mapping it all out in graphic form with squiggles and notes connected by arrows. In a circle at the top he'd written 'Inquest?' He'd used an iPad to track back through the BBC's website and the most recent postings on the Warner case, then he'd pulled up a page for the Inner South London Coroner's Court.

Now he was on the phone pretending to be a plummy-sounding journalist as he put the Coroner's officer straight. 'Yah, obviously I know it was adjourned. But until when? This is information which should be in the public domain. Oh, really? You really want me to write that in my newspaper? Okay, so just tell me when?' His spidery pen skipped across the paper and he smiled with satisfaction. 'Yes, thank you for your help. Indeed, I will bear that in mind when I write the article.'

Mike clicked the phone off and gave Kaz his lopsided grin. 'Ten a.m. tomorrow, Southwark Coroner's Court. Looks like there'll be a lot of press interest, that's why they're being bloody awkward. And we'll have to be there early to get in.'

Kaz furrowed her brow. 'So you mean anyone can just go and listen?'

Mike nodded. 'Oh yeah. They're obliged to notify family,

friends – anyone who has an interest. But it's a public hearing. You just turn up and queue.'

'How d'you know all this stuff?'

'What can I tell you?' Mike shrugged. 'I'm an interesting old fart, who's led a colourful life.'

Kaz grinned. 'Yeah and the rest.'

Mike returned the smile then his expression turned serious. 'The Coroner'll hear all the evidence. That means the police will have to explain why they think it's suicide. He'll probably ask for evidence from family and friends about her state of mind. And there'll be the results of the post-mortem. You sure you're up for all that?'

Kaz nodded, but the feeling in her gut was heavy and molten. 'I just wanna know.'

'What if the Coroner agrees with the police?'

'You think he will?'

Mike smoothed the stubble on his chin with index finger and thumb. 'I honestly don't know. But think about it, Karen. The death of an MP? They're going to dot all the i's and cross all the t's, aren't they?'

'I suppose.' Kaz stared at him. His craggy features and bloodshot eyes were curiously reassuring, they gave him the air of some ancient wizard. 'It just don't make any sense. Why would she do that?'

'Did you love her a lot?' Mike delivered the question in a delicate, detached tone, like a doctor asking about some embarrassing complaint.

Kaz drew in a breath. This was all hurting far more than she expected. 'Yeah. But it was messy. She didn't want to be with me.'

Mike reached over, patted her hand. 'Okay, here's the really difficult question. Did you actually know her? Being in love is not the best vehicle for insight into someone else's heart. It reflects your state of mind not theirs.'

'You saying she might've been really depressed and suicidal and I wouldn't even have known it?'

Mike tilted his head apologetically. It struck Kaz that he was probably right. She tensed her jaw to stop the tears. It didn't work. Mike watched her cry for several moments, a thick crease between his heavy brows. Then he got up, went over to the kitchen counter and picked up a tea towel. He returned with it and dropped it in Kaz's lap. 'Here, use this. I don't believe in paper tissues – save the planet and all that.'

Kaz wiped her eyes with a corner of the red-and-white checked towel. She watched him collecting up the mugs, scooting biscuit crumbs off the table. She'd trusted him and he hadn't judged her. He was on her side and he was prepared to help, just as he'd done before. To Kaz it didn't make sense. Why would anyone behave like that? Perhaps Mike was simply a good person. Kaz hadn't encountered too much kindness in her life. It felt strange and therefore suspect.

She was mulling this over when a chirpy electronic jingle floated across the room from the vicinity of the front door. They both turned towards the unfamiliar sound. Kaz's stomach lurched – it was coming from the stolen briefcase.

Mike gave her an equable smile as he rinsed the mugs. 'I think your phone's ringing.'

27

Eddie Lunt was resting his eyes and his stomach after a very good lunch. The food was some kind of Thai-chinky-noodley whatever; the reason it was good was that Eddie hadn't paid for it. Denzil, a contact of his at one of the UK's largest mobile phone companies, had picked up the tab. Reason was Denzil had aspirations to move across into the security sector. He'd wanted Eddie's advice. Eddie wanted Denzil to stay put, where he was far more useful. So Eddie had suggested a deal, involving a cash retainer; Denzil would in effect be in the security business, except no one else would know about it.

Eddie was pondering the best way to sell this unorthodox arrangement to Simon. In his snug corner of the office he knew he was out of all the important sightlines, so he could just kick back in his chair and take his ease. He was feeling relatively happy with his efforts to date. Denzil could turn out to be a valuable asset. Plus he'd already unearthed a couple of useful leads in the Warner case and he knew Simon appreciated his contribution.

The abrupt spinning of the chair took him completely by surprise. His feet twisted off the desk, he lost his centre of gravity and toppled sideways. He landed in a heap on the floor with the chair on top of him. It was only then that he saw Nicci Armstrong standing over him, arms folded.

Nicci was an odd fish and no mistake. An ex-DS, Simon

really rated her. But she had a bitch of a temper and for some inexplicable reason Eddie often found himself on the receiving end. As he scrabbled to his feet and struggled to right the chair, she simply stood there looking peevish. She made no apology. When he was finally upright again, she drew in a sharp, impatient breath.

'Labour Party. This contact of yours, I want to talk to him myself, dig a bit deeper into Warner's political background. ASAP. Think you can manage that?'

'Yeah, no probs—'

Eddie didn't say more, there didn't seem much point since she was already walking away. He rubbed his shoulder; he'd hit the deck with a hefty thump and would probably have a bruise. Yet he felt no malice. His whole life he'd been slapped about more than he would've liked. It came of being a small bloke with a mild disposition. People bullied him because they could. Ma always said he was too good-natured by half and she was probably right. Eddie opened his desk drawer and took out a supersize bar of Dairy Milk; he'd been saving it for teatime but he reckoned it might help. He'd read an article in the *Metro* as he travelled in on the tube – new American research had provided overwhelming confirmation of the healing properties of chocolate.

Nicci Armstrong returned to her desk. She'd been having a reasonably okay day, but then as usual Eddie had sent her into one. He was a lazy sod, no two ways about it; why Simon kept him on the payroll was a mystery.

She swivelled her chair and caught Pascale's eye. 'Any luck?'

'Sounds like you were right about the name.' Pascale glanced up from her screen. 'They've got a Clare O'Keeffe just finished the second year on the Fine Art BA. They've promised to send me a mug shot. Problem is, it's the holidays. I'm working on an address. But maybe a mobile number would be more useful?'

'Yeah, that'd be great.' Just talking to Pascale made Nicci feel better. She was smart, efficient – the opposite of Eddie in every way.

Opening her notebook, Nicci discovered the pap shot of Helen flanked by Robert Hollister still tucked in the back. She considered it for a second: an old family friend who'd sponsored Warner's move into politics. Okay, maybe he was a serial shagger, but that didn't mean his relationship with Helen was anything but professional. She opened her file drawer and dumped the photo in an empty sleeve.

Kaz Phelps and her involvement with Helen Warner, that was a far more promising lead. If Helen had gone to Glasgow in secret, presumably to see Kaz, then there was a chance Kaz was also privy to aspects of Helen Warner's life that Julia knew nothing about. Lovers and secrets often went together. The problem was going to be tracking Phelps down. Nicci was pondering what Phelp's reaction would have been to the news of Warner's death when she noticed Eddie Lunt weaving across the room towards her.

'What's the problem now, Eddie?' she sighed.

Resting a hand on Nicci's desk to steady himself, he skimmed a finger across his damp brow. His chubby cheeks were ashen beneath the neat sculpted beard. 'It's old Ray. At the Labour Party. My contact, y'know you wanted to talk to him. Seems he's topped himself. Went under a tube train at Bond Street yesterday teatime. A wife and three little kiddies.' Eddie shook his head in sorrow and disbelief. 'I only spoke to him a few hours before. I can't believe it. I'm gutted.'

28

Mike Dawson's back garden was compact but lushly planted with a colourful array of flowers, shrubs and trees. At the end with the sunniest aspect a small bower had been created, shaded by a wooden trellis overhung with clematis. Kaz perched on a sun lounger and stared at the smartphone in her hand.

Fortunately, by the time she'd recovered from the shock and crossed the room to the stolen briefcase, the phone had stopped ringing. She'd told Mike it wasn't important, but he'd given her an indulgent smile and suggested she go into the garden, where she'd have privacy and a better signal.

She turned the phone over in her hand. Presumably it was PIN-protected, so if any message had been left she'd be unable to access it. All the same, she wondered who was calling Baldy. If indeed the call had been for him. Stolen phones were a liability, a piece of piss to trace nowadays. She should've dumped it straight away. Hanging onto it had been a stupid mistake; clearly she'd lost the habit of thinking like a professional.

The sliding doors onto the garden were wide open and Kaz could see Mike busily making sandwiches in the kitchen. He didn't seem to eat much himself, but he was intent on being a good host. While she had no qualms about nicking from Baldy – he was fair game – she felt like she was abusing

Mike's generosity by bringing the stolen briefcase into his flat, and that did not sit well with her. Now she just wanted to get shot of it. The problem was how?

She glanced around the garden at the high walls of crumbling brick held together by a dense web of creeping foliage. Chucking stolen goods over into a neighbour's garden? Not really an option. Kaz was racking her brains for a way out when the phone pulsed in her hand. She'd turned the ringer off as soon as she'd retrieved it from the briefcase. Now the screen was flashing with an unknown caller.

Kaz hesitated. Part of her knew it was stupid, but there was a perverse curiosity too; she clicked the button to answer. 'Hello?'

The voice on the other end was male, languid and posh. Baldy? She didn't think so – he was more Essex. 'Onslow Square, South Ken? Very salubrious. So I presume you're doing this for kicks rather than money? Am I right?'

Kaz's stomach turned a somersault, what the fuck? She'd been tracked. The phone! Why the fuck hadn't she dumped it? Any twelve-year-old dipper would've had more sense. She felt like a complete moron. She took a breath, told herself to get a grip.

She raised her voice half an octave, nerves adding a girly quiver: 'Yeah, I guess.'

'Well, I don't think Mummy and Daddy are going to be too happy when we come knocking at the door, are they?'

Kaz waited for a moment, sniffed. The suggestion of a tear would certainly help. 'Are you the police?'

'The police?' He chuckled. 'Seriously? Okay, listen carefully, here's the deal. Briefcase and its entire contents will be returned. No questions, no recriminations. Otherwise it'll be knock-knock and Mr Plod will be involved. We can pinpoint your location to within twenty-five metres, so I'm looking at two, maybe three properties. Have you still got the briefcase?'

'Yeah.'

'Good girl. And do you want to sort this out sensibly?'

'Yeah.'

'Okay, come out of the front door and wait on the pavement, you'll be met.'

'You mean like ... now?' Kaz sounded like a munchkin even to herself; she wondered if she was overdoing it, but he didn't seem to notice.

'Is that a problem?'

'I don't want my mum to see? She might ask what I'm doing.'

'She might. But you'll think of something, won't you, because you're a cunning little bitch. If you're not outside in five minutes, this is going to get far worse. Do we understand each other?'

Kaz sniffed again, reduced her voice to a teary whisper. 'Yeah.'

He hung up.

She stood there, holding the phone, mind racing. What the fuck was in the briefcase? Half an hour on the tube, a short walk, she'd been at Mike's – maybe a little over an hour. So, less than two hours since she'd lifted it and in that time some bunch of security tossers had tracked the phone, pinpointed her location down to the street. It was probably the laptop they were after; it must contain sensitive data of some description. She thought back to Baldy; she'd just taken him for an overpaid city boy – the suit, the obnoxious attitude – not exactly the sort of guy you'd trust with secrets.

Mike was standing in the doorway, a plate of sandwiches in one hand.

'Don't know if you're still hungry after all those biscuits?'

She had only seconds to make up her mind. The truth or a lie? But what lie? Her brain flipped to autopilot; all she had to do was spin a yarn, maybe something about Joey.

'What's up?' Mike was scanning her face, his artist's eye missing nothing.

If she told him the truth he'd know what a slag she really was. He'd probably boot her out – and he'd be right to do so. The shame of it was already seeping through her. She had to force herself to meet his gaze. His eyes were so dark it was unnerving. And he was no fool.

She forced a smile. 'That briefcase isn't mine. Nicked it from a bloke in a coffee shop. I was looking for cash to get somewhere to stay, before I thought of coming here. But he's obviously got some security outfit on the case. They've tracked the phone.' She got up from the lounger. 'Look, I'll just get my stuff and go. I'm sorry.'

Mike put the plate of sandwiches down on the wrought-iron garden table. 'What's in the bag that's so valuable?'

'Not sure. I'm guessing the laptop.'

'Probably.' Mike scratched the stubble on his chin as he considered this. He seemed surprisingly relaxed about the whole thing.

Kaz took a step towards him. 'I'm really sorry. I never meant to involve you in stupid stuff like this.'

'But I am involved. You're my friend. So I'm involved.' He spoke as if it were blindingly obvious, as if he were affronted that she would suggest otherwise.

She shook her head. 'I don't get it. This is my problem. I don't want to get you in trouble.'

Mike's sharp features softened into a grin. 'I've spent my whole life getting into trouble. I regard it as an artistic duty.'

'What, you'll help me 'cause that's what artists do?' Kaz gave him a puzzled frown.

He slid his hands in his pockets and laughed. 'No, Karen. Artists paint, draw, create things! Maybe it's not artistic duty, more the duty of every human being to reach out. Give help when they can.' He raised a bony hand to encompass both flat and garden. 'This place belonged to my wife. I lost her five years ago. She had a stroke. I woke up in bed one morning, she was beside me as usual, but she was dead.' He smiled but the pain was obvious. 'It was . . . the worst thing I've ever experienced. We got married in 1963 – her family insisted. They were very proper and very rich. Her father was a slum landlord, came over here from Estonia in the twenties, made himself more English than the English. But was he a hero or a villain? Who are any of us to judge the lives of others? Walk down this very respectable street, you'll find every kind of individual from a Saudi princess, who treats her pooch better than her maid, to a German multi-millionaire, who wants to give his fortune away but his kids won't let him.' Mike fixed her with a kindly smile. 'I've met some criminals in my time, most of whom never went to jail, but I don't think you're one of them.'

'I feel as if I disappointed you.' Kaz shifted from one foot to the other.

'Presumably the backpack's yours? Is there a sketchbook in it?'

Another one of his odd questions. Kaz frowned. 'Yeah.'

He gave her the lopsided grin. 'Then you haven't disappointed me.'

Kaz felt the phone vibrate in her hand. She turned it over,

glanced at Mike. 'Probably them again. They gave me five minutes to get outside on the pavement with the briefcase.'

Mike considered this. 'That means they don't know which house. These tracking devices can only give them a rough location. And there are three flats in this building alone. Also, how legal is any of this?'

'That's why they're trying to get me outside.'

A glint came into Mike's eye. 'Okay, I've got an idea . . .'

29

Simon Blake had his hands in his pockets, feet planted squarely behind his desk chair. A frown creased his brow as he listened to Nicci summarize what they'd been able to discover about the circumstances surrounding the death of Eddie's contact.

'Hardly any reporting of it, just another suicide on the underground. Police were called, uniform dealt with it.'

Blake jangled the change in his pocket, glanced at Eddie. 'You knew him, Eddie, what do you make of it?'

Eddie was sitting hunched up on the sofa, cradling the mug of tea Pascale had made for him. Nicci couldn't make up her mind whether he was genuinely upset or whether it was all just part of his schtick. Either way, he still annoyed the hell out of her.

'Known him ten years or more.' There was a tremor in Eddie's voice. 'He was . . . well y'know, a nice bloke. It don't seem to me the sort of thing he'd've done. He loved them kiddies, well, and his wife. Youngest was only three. He wouldn't do something like this to them. He just wouldn't.' Eddie blinked away a tear. 'Ray was a grafter, done the job, went home to the family. I never knew him involved in any hanky-panky.'

Blake glanced at Nicci. 'What's your take on it, Nic?'

Nicci shrugged. She found Eddie's sentimentality saccharine, but was she letting annoyance cloud her judgement? She turned to him, frowning. 'You said you met him in a pub round the corner from the Labour Party.' He nodded. 'Crowded?'

'Pretty busy.' Eddie's chin was quivering. He made an effort to compose himself and went on: 'It was four-ish. Plenty of people knocking off, in for a bevy before the train.'

Nicci returned to Blake. 'Conversation could've easily been overheard or even monitored.'

'And an hour later he's dead. Coincidence or conspiracy?' Blake shot her a mischievous look. 'When we talked after lunch you were resisting the conspiracy route.'

'No I wasn't. I was just doing what you taught me, boss, keeping an open mind.'

'And now?'

'Now?' She drew in a sharp breath, pondered the question. 'Okay, Labour MP supposedly kills herself? Doesn't seem the type. Party official is questioned about her death. Another suicide. I don't know . . . I don't know what to think.'

She turned away from both men, found herself some space in the corner of the room.

'Gut reaction?' Blake wasn't about to let her off the hook.

Nicci flicked her head, more shudder than shake. 'Not enough information.'

'Right then.' Blake drummed his fingers on his desk then clicked the mouse to wake his computer. 'Let's see who we've got with contacts in the transport police.' He scrolled through his address book. 'Here we go. Ken Sturridge, retired superintendent in the BTP. We've used him before. I'll get him to do some digging. Might be able to get a look at some CCTV.'

'Five o'clock on the Central Line?' Nicci reminded him. 'Pretty crowded.'

'BTP should've got some witness statements at the very least.' Blake looked up from his computer and frowned. 'Who did you speak to?'

'Transport for London. But their press office has already given the suicide story to the media. It must look clear-cut.'

'The Met are convinced Helen Warner committed suicide. That's why I asked you for your gut reaction. You start putting the incidentals together, what do you get? Just a coincidence? Two unrelated suicides?'

'No. Something's going on. No idea what, but it feels connected.'

'I agree.' Blake had a glint in his eye as he picked up the phone. 'Let's say for the sake of argument a professional hitman was sent after this friend of Eddie's. Crowded tube platform isn't ideal, but it's an easy way to make murder look like suicide.'

'Bloody hell.'

Caught up in the excitement of the case, Blake and Nicci had forgotten Eddie was still in the room. They both turned to look at him.

'Poor old Ray.' He blinked at them, shook his head. 'Poor old Ray.'

30

Mike Dawson mounted the steps from his basement flat to the street, an old beany hat pulled low over his eyes. He took his time, carrying his hessian shopping bag in his hand. When he made it to street level he paused to glance up and down the road. There were a few cars in the residents' parking bays, but plenty of spaces. Crossing the road with an easy gait, he stopped in front of the iron railings separating the street from the private gardens at the centre of the square. He inverted his shopping bag and out tumbled the leather briefcase. He stooped to pick it up out of the gutter and made an elaborate show of swinging it back and forth several times, building up momentum. He then lobbed it over the railings into the shrubbery beyond.

Retrieving his shopping bag he set off up the street at a leisurely pace. He'd walked no more than ten metres when two men leapt out of a silver Ford Focus and raced towards him, shoving him none too gently against the side of the car. Both were in their twenties, solidly built, with close-cropped hair and bland faces.

The taller of the two placed a restraining hand on Mike's chest. 'Not so fast, granddad.'

Mike opened his mouth, sucked in a lungful and hollered. 'Help! Help! I'm being mugged! Call the police!'

The men seemed taken aback. Mike managed to bat one

with his shopping bag, but then the taller one pinned him firmly against the car. Seeing his colleague glancing nervously up and down the street, he hissed, 'Just get it!'

While the other man sprinted across the road and vaulted the railings, the taller one tightened his grip on Mike. Mike started to wheeze and cough. Then from nowhere Kaz appeared. She was holding up her phone and filming them.

'Let him go, you bastard! I'm calling the police!'

The tall man swivelled in her direction. He looked surprised, but he continued to grasp Mike firmly by the throat.

She danced around just out of his reach, keeping the phone's camera firmly focused on him. 'I'm warning you, let him go! Let him go.'

Mike wriggled to free himself. He was stronger than he looked and his captor struggled to maintain a grip. It lasted only seconds, Kaz filming the tussle.

Further up the street, two builders in hard hats emerged from the open door of a property undergoing renovation. Kaz saw them and began waving her free hand.

'Help! Help! Call the police! These blokes are mugging an old man!'

The builders didn't hesitate. They came thundering down the street. The tall one shot a look across the road to where his companion was climbing back over the railings, the briefcase in his hand.

He jabbed an index finger in Mike's face. 'This isn't fucking over, granddad!'

Mike regarded him coolly. 'Oh yes it is, sunshine. Or within five minutes our little home movie and your vehicle licence plate is going to be all over the web. And that's not what the corporate clients want to see, is it? Bad for business. Now take your stuff and fuck off! Case closed.'

The man's confidence wavered. Mike was glaring at him, the two beefy builders were closing fast. With a grunt of frustration he jumped into the Ford Focus, started the engine, rammed it into first, accelerated hard, braked to pick up his mate then roared off.

Kaz filmed the retreating car thwacking over speed bumps until it reached the end of the street and disappeared. She and Mike grinned at each other. She was beginning to feel that being back in London wasn't such a mistake after all.

31

Kaz and Mike celebrated their victory over the dark forces of corporate capitalism in a ritzy patisserie in Kensington largely patronized by Chinese tourists. Kaz had a millefeuille, which she'd never tried before. Mike sipped camomile tea and smiled at her attempts to eat it elegantly with a fork. She gave up in the end and used her fingers.

They chuckled over the details of their escapade and agreed that the timely appearance of the builders was pure luck.

Finally, when Kaz had licked all the cream from her fingers, she rocked back in her seat and fixed him with a direct look. 'Ain't you ever gonna say it then?'

'Say what?'

'If I hadn't nicked it in the first place . . . well, you know what I mean.'

'No, I don't. Explain.'

'It was a stupid move. Stupid stupid stupid!'

Mike coughed then laughed. 'You know the old saying, either stop thieving or become a better thief.'

'Point taken.' Kaz grinned. 'Anyway, it's not why I came down here.'

'No, it's not. We need to focus on the inquest.'

Kaz saw that his eyes were pitch-black and over-bright, with dark shadows beneath. His brow was slick with perspiration. She wondered if he was in pain. She'd seen him sneak a couple of pills from a bottle he carried in his pocket and swallow them with his tea. She came to a decision.

'Y'know, you've helped me enough. And having a place to stay, well that would be brilliant. But you don't have to carry on with this.'

'I don't have anything better to do right now. There are enough bad paintings in the world, I don't need to add to their number.' He flashed her that lopsided grin again.

'I know you said you lost your wife, don't you have any kids?'

He hesitated, but only for a second. 'One son. Adrian.'

'Where's he?'

'Lives in Hong Kong.'

The last thing she wanted was to upset him, and she could tell from his tone of voice and the sad look on his face that he wanted her to drop it, but she persisted. 'Mike, you helped me, I wanna help you. Don't you think it's time to call him?'

Mike eyeballed her defiantly. Had she over-stepped the mark?

Then he shook his head, picked up the delicate porcelain cup and took a sip. 'Last time I saw him is when he came to his mother's funeral, all buttoned up and angry, black tie, black suit.'

Kaz waited for him to say more but he didn't. His dark eyes rested on the lip of the cup. She scooted the remaining crumbs round her plate.

He set the cup down in its saucer. 'Can I get you some more tea?'

'No thanks.'

Had she ever met a better person than Mike? Kaz didn't think so. He had an open-hearted generosity that was rare. So what was wrong with his twat of a son?

She caught Mike's eye. 'He should've grown up in our house.'

'Perhaps he thinks he did.' His lips started to form a rueful smile but then a bout of coughing seized him. Once it subsided, he drew a ragged breath, composed himself. 'So, what's the plan?'

Kaz hesitated. She really wanted his help. He was sharp, knew how to sort things out. Not in the way villains did, always on the back-foot, always suspicious. Mike had a vast array of proper knowledge and what he didn't know he knew how to find out. Still, she felt reluctant to involve him. It wouldn't be fair.

Sitting back in his chair Mike monitored her inner struggle with a melancholy eye.

He took a wheezy breath. 'Listen, Karen, you've done me the courtesy of being honest with me, so I think I should reciprocate.'

'You don't have to talk about it.'

Lacing his skeletal fingers he leant forward. 'I'm ill – well, obviously.' He seemed to ruminate on this then sighed. 'Nothing to be done about that. There's little I can tell you about my son. He was close to his mother. As I said before, she came from a wealthy family. Her father paid for his schooling. I think Adrian regards me as a layabout and a scrounger.'

'Maybe he should take one of your classes, then he'd know what a brilliant teacher you are.'

Mike shrugged. 'He sees art as just another commodity. His grandfather and uncle encouraged him to go into the commercial world.'

Kaz gave a dry laugh. 'What is he – a banker?'

'A lawyer. Mergers and acquisitions. He doesn't discuss his life with me. When he needs advice, he goes to his uncle.'

The chin beneath his stubbly beard quivered a little but he disguised it by lifting the teacup to his lips. Kaz imagined bottling Adrian. They sat in silence until the waitress came to take Kaz's plate.

Mike smiled at Kaz. 'More cake?'

She shook her head. 'Does he know you're ill?'

'No. And I don't plan to tell him. I've made my arrangements. There's a hospice I like. They'll provide care at home, then as an in-patient. But I've got a few months probably before it comes to that.' A mischievous glint crept into his eyes. 'Today was fun. Outwitting those two knuckleheads. Bucked me up no end.'

'Some good's come of it then.' Kaz laughed.

He nodded. 'Yes. Did you ever read much poetry at school?'

She gave him a sheepish look. 'I never went to school that often.'

'I suppose not.' His vulpine features creased into a broad smile. '"Do not go gentle into that good night" – you ever hear that line?'

Kaz shook her head.

'Dylan Thomas. Welsh poet, drank a lot. I've been thinking lately about the best way to die. Should you rage or simply accept the inevitable with grace?'

'Depends if you get time to think about it. Having time to be scared, that wouldn't be good.'

He scratched his beard. 'And are you wondering if your Helen had time to be scared?'

A spasm of agony erupted inside Kaz. It hit her like a punch in the gut. Her balled fist flew to her mouth, a reflex to hold it all in.

'I'm sorry.' Mike's brow furrowed with concern. 'I didn't mean to be quite so direct.'

'It's okay.' Kaz swallowed hard. 'Fact is, it's what I think about all the time. Ever since I found out. How? How did it happen exactly? When she hit the water, was she conscious? The fear? Lungs filling up, not being able to breathe . . .'

He reached over and covered her hand with his bony talons.

Her tear-filled eyes met his. 'She didn't kill herself, Mike. I know she didn't. Some bastard did this to her.'

He nodded in sympathy rather than agreement. 'We need to know the truth, whatever the truth is.'

'Do you think that's possible?'

He raised his eyebrows. 'You never know until you try.'

'You've got enough on your plate. I feel like I'm using you.'

As he hunched his shoulders the angel wings seemed to rise towards his ears. 'Maybe we're using each other. I don't think it's a bad arrangement. Do you?'

32

He wasn't a drinker, nor did he care much for socializing with clients. To Simon Blake, business was business, that's what the office was for. When forced to entertain investors he always tried to make it lunch. He'd made his wife a promise: leaving the Met meant no more long hours and ridiculous shifts, he'd be home at six thirty to sit down to a proper family meal. This was his life now and generally it worked – except when it came to dealing with Duncan Linton.

Linton was the man who'd made it all possible – a City grandee with deep pockets, he'd taken a thirty per cent stake in Simon Blake Associates. Once he came on board the sniffy banks changed their tune, other equity investors took a punt and suddenly Blake wasn't just another ex-copper scrabbling around for backers, he was a player in the security business.

Tall and patrician, with a shock of white hair, Linton had the manner and vowels of a man born to wealth and privilege; his wife Elspeth had a title and connections to half the landed aristocracy.

After their first meeting Blake found himself disliking Linton's languid upper-class confidence. Then he did a bit of digging and found it was all just a front.

Far from being born with a silver spoon, Linton had started out a lowly private in the army, working his way up to sergeant. He then anglicized his Polish name, set up a small investment firm, sweet-talked a few well-heeled clients and with the immigrant's drive to succeed spent the next forty years making himself and his investors seriously rich. A multi-millionaire and fixture on *The Sunday Times* Rich List, he was a man who knew exactly how the world worked. But he'd learnt from the bottom up and that made all the difference to Blake. So what if he felt the need to pretend to be posh? Everyone had their foibles. Blake had decided not to hold it against him.

Linton was almost seventy but he remained a restless spirit; he had to keep moving. He preferred cars and jets and hotels, hated sitting in offices. He held meetings in restaurants, usually over dinner, often with the head chef fawning at his elbow. So when Blake got the summons at five thirty he had to tell Heather he'd be home late. He was dining with Duncan Linton. She knew he had no choice.

The restaurant, tucked away in a side street in Chelsea, was one of Linton's regular haunts. Blake had been there several times and assumed Linton probably owned a piece of it. Collecting bits and bobs that pleased him – restaurants, racehorses – was something of a hobby with him. It didn't really matter whether they made a profit; he liked to eat, he liked to go to the races, so he allowed himself these small indulgences. He joked that it was his modest equivalent of an oligarch buying a football club.

The food was traditional British with a twist and even a steak-and-chips man like Blake had to admit it was pretty good. Arriving early, Blake positioned himself at the end of the bar so he could watch Linton make his entrance. It was always worth it.

Linton was a showman; his presence filled a room. He entered like royalty: no fuss, nothing loud or flamboyant, yet with the expectation that everything would immediately revolve around him. And it did. It was a neat trick and one that Blake admired. It created an aura of natural authority, making it easy to believe that your savings, your pension fund, your very last penny, would be safe in his wise and capable hands. Blake had realized early on this was his patron's special talent.

Linton made a stately progress from the reception area to the bar with the maître d' bustling ahead, shooing his path clear. The executive chef emerged from the kitchen wreathed in smiles. Linton shook his hand, asked what he'd recommend today. There was a brief exchange about the finer points of pan-frying duck.

Finally Linton's eye alighted on Blake and he smiled warmly as if he'd just spied a favourite courtier. 'There you are, dear boy! Glad you could make it.'

Blake offered his hand to shake; he was prepared to play Duncan Linton's game, but only up to a point. 'You're looking very fit, Duncan.'

'Oh, Elspeth has found me a personal trainer. I think it's a load of nonsense, but it keeps her happy.'

'Well, I'm glad she's keeping you on the straight and narrow.'

There was no sarcasm in Blake's tone, although there could've been. Eddie Lunt's inquiries had turned up a twenty-five-year-old Bulgarian model who Linton kept in a small mews house in Fitzrovia. It had disappointed but not surprised Blake to discover that the man he'd come to admire was something of a cliché in his private life.

The maître d' escorted them to a quiet corner table and Blake saw it was laid for three diners. He'd been given no hint that someone else would be joining them. Two waiters pulled out their chairs and they settled at the table. The business of napkins and menus and the appearance of the sommelier precluded any discussion. Linton didn't offer any information and Blake wasn't about to ask.

Linton drew a pair of half-moon spectacles from his inside pocket to peruse the wine list. The sommelier hovered. 'A bottle of Cristal to start, Juan. Then I think something a little spicy . . .'

A discussion ensued on varieties of Spanish Grenache. Blake tuned out, he drank wine only when he had to. His gaze skated across the room and it was then he noticed a horribly familiar face heading towards them.

Blake hoped it was a coincidence. Was he really coming their way? Rumour had it that once the IPCC had finished with former Detective Chief Superintendent Alan Turnbull he'd slunk away to take up a lucrative consulting job in Abu Dhabi. The man approaching their table with an assured smirk on his face certainly had a golden tan.

He thrust out his hand in Blake's direction. 'Good to see you again, sir.'

Blake had little option but to accept the handshake.

Linton peered at the two former police officers over his glasses. 'Of course I'm sure you two know each other. How was your flight, Alan?'

'Some kind of nonsense with baggage handlers – which is why I'm late. And for which I apologize.'

The waiter drew back the third chair and Alan Turnbull sat down.

Blake knew that Linton was watching him and he wasn't about to make himself any sort of hostage to fortune. So he smiled politely at Turnbull. 'How are you, Alan? I hear you've been abroad.'

Turnbull leaned back in his chair. 'Great place, the Emirates. I've thoroughly enjoyed my time out there.'

The two men regarded each other warily. They were refugees from the same organization, but as far as Blake was concerned that was where any similarity ended. Turnbull had been chucked out for gross misconduct. He'd set up his former colleagues, betrayed his bosses' trust and the general opinion was that he'd gotten off lightly – he should've gone to jail. But given his connections with the Mayor's office and the potential for yet another ugly scandal, it had all been swept under the carpet.

Still Blake couldn't resist the temptation to rattle his cage just a little. 'I'm out of touch with the Yard since I left. Didn't you used to work for Fiona Calder? How is she? She always really impressed me, even before she became Assistant Commissioner.'

The permatan bathed Turnbull's features in an eerie glow. Aware he was being baited, he gave a wry smile. 'Sadly the Assistant Commissioner and I didn't see eye to eye in the end.'

Blake feigned surprise. 'Really? That's a pity.'

Linton was watching the joust with interest. He held up his menu. 'Well, gentlemen, shall we order? Then we can get down to business.'

They made their choices in turn and Linton relayed them formally to the waiter. Apparently in no hurry, he folded his spectacles and returned them to his pocket. Blake found his expression unreadable. It was his party and there was nothing to do but wait.

Linton rearranged the thick damask napkin in his lap and turned to Blake. 'Of course you know, Simon, that Alan and I have been working closely on developing contacts out in the

Gulf.' Blake knew no such thing and he was pretty sure that Linton was aware of that. 'The security sector out there has been growing at a phenomenal rate, well, ever since Iraq.' Linton steepled his fingers. 'And I've been thinking that it's time we expanded SBA's international dimension.'

Blake now had a shrewd idea of where this was headed and he was determined to stop it in its tracks. 'I agree entirely, Duncan. And that's why I've been talking to a couple of ex-Special Forces officers who served with Rory McLaren.' He glanced at Turnbull. 'Rory works for me. Former intelligence officer, speaks a reasonable amount of Arabic.'

Linton nodded sagely, but he wasn't to be deflected. 'One of the things we've discovered – and Alan can back me up on this – is that with all the political unrest in the region, the sheikhs have come to the conclusion that employing civilians, like former police officers, creates a better, more liberal impression. Foreign squaddies tend to alienate the local populace.'

'Depends on what you're employing them to do.' Blake met Turnbull's sardonic gaze defiantly, but realized the smug bastard had the drop on him. This was all a set-up.

The sommelier approached with a bottle of champagne in an ice bucket. Linton peered at it, gave a nod, then turned his attention back to the conversation, a smile spreading across his face as if a completely new idea had just dawned on him. 'I think we're all agreed that SBA has terrific potential both in the UK and abroad. Which is why I think that you could do with some help, Simon, to facilitate our expansion plans. And now that Alan is back in London I think he'd make the perfect number two for you.'

'It's an interesting suggestion, Duncan.' Blake had seen the bullet coming but could find no way to dodge it. 'But I don't really know that we'd have enough to keep him occupied at present.'

Turnbull smiled. 'I can understand your reluctance, Simon. SBA's your baby. But in the next couple of years a lot of current policing functions will be contracted out. You can't hope to win that kind of business as a one-man band. You need to start thinking strategically and on a broader canvas. That's where I can help.'

Blake had held his ire in check so far, but Turnbull's bare-faced cheek was nothing short of an insult. What, was he supposed to sit back and let his firm be shanghaied?

'I thought we were talking internationally. Your experience in Abu Dhabi, brown-nosing a few rich sheikhs, isn't going to help you negotiate with our new police and crime commissioners, is it?'

Linton smiled, but his gaze was hard. 'Actually, Simon, it is. This isn't the Met any more; we're in the security business and the bottom line is providing client satisfaction at the right price. Alan understands that. After all we are in business primarily to make a profit.'

'I gather he understood that even before the Met chucked him out for gross misconduct. You really think, with a reputation like his, anyone is going to listen to him? He'd be a fucking liability.'

Blake regretted this as soon as it was out of his mouth. He saw the smug glances traded between Linton and Turnbull. They knew they had him on the back foot. Cursing his own stupidity, Blake reined himself in.

The sommelier placed three glasses on the table and began to slowly fill them with champagne. All three watched the pale amber liquid cascade from bottle to flute. Once the delicate operation was complete, Linton turned the stem of his glass between thumb and index finger – that initial effervescence always made him smile. It reminded him how far he'd come, who he was.

'It's your business, Simon, obviously.' His tone was steely. 'But it's still in its infancy and I need to protect my investment. You do understand that.'

Blake looked glumly at the champagne, over-priced, over-rated piss. He hated it. 'Of course, Duncan, but—'

Linton raised an admonitory finger. 'All I ask, Simon, is that you take my advice. The past has no relevance here. I think you two'll make a brilliant team. Now, let's drink a toast to SBA and its future as one of the UK's leading security operators.' Linton's unremitting gaze met Blake's and he smiled. 'Presumably that is what you want?'

33

Nicci Armstrong didn't do regular office hours, it was one of the few perks of her new lifestyle – or that's what she told herself. She came in when she felt like it and often she was the last to leave. She preferred working late. After the cleaners were gone she could kick back and watch the city skyline fade to black. It also made it easier to forget she had nothing to go home for. She tended to miss meals. Living on a diet of sandwiches and takeaways didn't seem to be doing her any harm. Her jeans were looser, a definite benefit. Cooking she'd always regarded as a chore, one of the obligations of family life. Still, she'd always fed her child well and had been proud that Sophie liked her vegetables and was never a fussy eater.

She was mulling over the developments of the day and doodling in the margin of her notebook, the same serpentine pattern over and over; it helped her focus. Two possible murders dressed up as suicide. But were they related? And the second one, the bloke on the tube, was it even murder? Were they reading too much into the coincidence? You could argue yourself round in circles, which was exactly what she'd been doing for the last hour. In front of her were three lists. The first – known facts – was very short. The second consisted of lines of inquiry to be pursued. The third, questions to be answered, took up a full page.

She rubbed her eyes and was considering wrapping things

up for the evening when she heard the lift doors open. A moment later Rory McLaren appeared with one of his part-time operatives in tow, a tall, muscular young man with a sullen expression. From the sound of it, Rory wasn't too happy either.

'I don't care if it's a fucking rug-rat on a leash. She's the client, if she wants you to walk her fucking dog, you do it.'

'I'm a bodyguard, not a fucking dog-walker.'

Rory jabbed an index finger in the man's chest. 'You work for me, you're what I fucking say you are.'

As he turned away in disgust, the young man bleated, 'Why can't the fucking maid do it?'

'Oh, and you're going to do the maid's job, are you?' Rory turned to glare at him. 'You're going to clean the bog and serve the fucking tea?'

He was striding across the room towards his workstation when he noticed Nicci watching them with some amusement. She gave him a nod. He simply glared back at her, embarrassed that she'd heard him swearing. It was a kneejerk reaction and old-fashioned nowadays, but he'd been brought up never to use bad language in front of women.

Nicci got up from her desk and eased her shoulders into a scuffed leather jacket. She was taking her time and Rory knew why. Fucking ex-cops – he had no problem peppering his thoughts with expletives – they liked to play games, to torment you. He'd been in desert sandstorms, trekked over mountains, survived some of the toughest terrain on the planet and still got the job done. He was in Baghdad the day Saddam fell, in Helmand he'd flushed the Taliban out of rat-holes. But his life back then seemed simple compared to now. These days his job encompassed whatever the client wanted it to. No matter how ludicrous their expectations he was supposed to deliver; no mean feat when his team consisted of a handful of washed-up squaddies and gormless part-timers who ran moaning to him because they'd been asked to walk a dog.

Nicci meandered across the room, around the desks. She knew Rory didn't like her, and for some reason on this particular evening that left her feeling sad. In the Met she hadn't got on with all her colleagues; still, there'd been a camaraderie, a sense of common purpose. That wasn't the case here.

Rory was maybe ten years older than her, hair greying at the temples, superfit and always tense. He eyed her suspiciously as she walked towards him. His boy hovered.

'Clients, eh?' Nicci commiserated. 'They always want more.'

Rory nodded stiffly. 'Indeed.'

She waited, realizing she wanted more too. When it wasn't forthcoming, she turned away with a shrug. 'See you tomorrow then.'

'Right.'

As Nicci walked away towards the lifts a thought flitted across her mind – she started to imagine having sex with Rory. It was a random notion that seemed to pop up from nowhere. It felt odd. He was nothing special. She couldn't remember the last time she'd had any vaguely erotic feelings. Nor could she remember the last time she'd had sex. After the divorce, her life had revolved around Sophie. And since Sophie's death grief had simply engulfed her. This was all rather curious.

She boarded the bus in Rosebery Avenue, regarding her fellow passengers with a speculative eye. She watched a lad with a bulky sportsbag take a seat in front of her. He was way too young – and cocksure with it; when he saw her checking him out he gave her a teasing smile. She turned and stared out of the window, but inside she was smiling.

As the bus trundled on to the Angel then up through Islington, Nicci allowed herself to savour this new sensation. Something had shifted inside her – there was an ease, a lassitude. Was it pleasure? Whatever it was, it had nothing to do with bug-up-his-arse Rory or the boy on the bus. It was about her. It struck her how frozen she'd become, how far she'd retreated and switched off. She hadn't even been that aware of it. But tonight she felt lighter. Did she need to analyse it, or maybe just enjoy the feeling?

The bus slowed to a crawl then joined a queue of stationary vehicles. Nicci peered out into the soft, summer dusk. Up ahead the familiar blue-flashing lights were visible, probably some kind of traffic incident. It wasn't far to her stop so she decided to walk.

She stepped off the bus and noticed the young man following suit. Coincidence or conspiracy? She found she was smiling yet again, and there was a definite buoyancy in her stride as she set off down the road.

On the fringe of Newington Green the reason for the hold-up became more apparent. There were four police cars and an ambulance in attendance. Uniforms were rushing about, directing traffic and taping off a stretch of pavement. As she got closer Nicci saw it was the area just outside her building.

A couple of WPCs were trying to disperse a smattering of curious onlookers who'd gathered on the other side of the street. Nicci skirted round them to get a better look. Outside the entrance to her block of flats, two paramedics were standing over a figure lying prone on the pavement. They looked uncomfortable, unsure what to do. A uniform ran over to them, issued some instruction. Nicci had witnessed enough of these kinds of scenes to know that the person on the ground was dead. And violence was probably involved.

She turned to someone in the crowd. 'What happened?'

A girl in a baseball cap answered without making eye contact. 'Old lady that lives in the block. Word is she was stabbed.'

Nicci's gut went into a spasm of dread. She flew across the road. One of the WPCs tried to grab her but Nicci spun herself free. 'I live in the block. I might know her.'

'No, you can't go over there!'

Nicci sidestepped the officer and a second uniform who moved in to assist. She made it to the paramedics before they managed to catch up with her. And as they pulled her away she got a look.

The old lady's head was resting on a folded coat, the face waxy pale, mouth slack. Her frail limbs were splayed out, there was a smear of blood on the pavement – if she was stabbed it must've been in the back.

A single glance confirmed Nicci's worst fear: it was Ethel Huxtable.

34

Tim Armstrong didn't like working nights, especially with his wife expecting, but having been newly promoted he tended to get more than his fair share of the unpopular shifts. As on-call DI for the Homicide Assessment Team he knew the boss's eye was on him and he needed to prove he was up to the mark. So instead of sending one of his DCs to take a preliminary look, he'd decided to come in person.

The Hackney DS who'd called it in regarded the death as suspicious. A very elderly lady had been found dead in the street. There was blood and a rent in the clothing, which raised the possibility that it was a stabbing.

Tim parked his car across the road behind the ambulance; it was only then that it occurred to him he knew the building. He stopped on the kerb, stared up at the block in the gathering dusk. Then it came to him: this was where Nicci had moved to after they'd sold the house. The realization balled into a knot of anger in his belly. He should've stayed in the bloody office! The last thing he needed, particularly now, was an encounter with his ex-wife.

Unfortunately, before he could gather his thoughts, a uniform confronted him and he had no choice but to show his warrant card and allow himself to be ushered through the cordon to where a couple of young DCs from the borough were standing around trying to look as if they had a purpose. He eyeballed the nearest, asked to be brought up to speed.

Oriental, petite and nervous, she held her notebook in a shaky hand. 'Call came in at eight oh-five, sir. Paramedics arrived first. Several people had tried to help her.'

'Help her how exactly? Do we think she was attacked?'

The young DC looked blank, glanced at her companion for support. She was new to all this but then so was Tim, they were both taking that big step up. The difference was, he was in charge now.

He gave her a patient smile that was designed to calm both their nerves. 'Okay, old lady collapsed on the pavement – could be natural causes – why are we suspicious?'

She seemed puzzled by the question. 'The DS said.'

'Any witnesses to what happened?'

'Not sure, sir.'

Tim glanced at the other DC, who looked even younger, like a skinny teenager with low-grade acne and a floppy fringe. 'Do you know?'

'No, sir,' he stammered, reddening. 'DS just said to wait here.'

Tim could quite see why. They'd had a brief exchange on the phone. Brisk and straightforward, the Hackney DS sounded like an officer who knew his business.

Tim drew in a breath. 'Well where is the DS now?'

'He's in the building, sir,' the first DC spoke up, drawing confidence from the fact her colleague seemed even more clueless. 'Talking to a witness.'

Tim nodded. 'Okay, start with the first people on the scene. Detailed statements. What they saw, what they did and did anyone see a potential assailant? Don't let anyone drift off until you've got their details. Have the uniforms coral them if necessary. Got it?' She nodded vigorously. Tim turned to the other one. 'You got it too?'

The young DC stroked back his unruly fringe. 'Yes, sir.'

Tim paused to survey the scene. The area surrounding the body had been taped off pretty efficiently, entry and exit route established, but that would've been done by the uniforms not the rookie DCs. The HAT car with his own DCs should be arriving soon. They could take over.

He approached the paramedic. 'Was she dead when you arrived?'

He nodded. He was heavy-jowled and carried an air of weary resignation. 'We tried CPR, but she was gone.'

'What d'you think?'

'Heart probably, but there's blood, possibly a puncture wound in the back.'

'You think she was attacked?'

'If she was stabbed, at her age the shock could've brought on a heart attack.'

'How old do you think she was?' Tim gazed down at the body.

The paramedic was checking his watch. 'Pretty old.'

Tim turned away, was he doing this right? He'd followed, he'd watched, but it wasn't the same as being in the driving seat.

Then he remembered and glanced back over his shoulder. 'Oh. Thanks, mate.'

'You're welcome,' the paramedic responded with a surly upward glance.

Tim headed into the building. The downstairs lobby was bare and functional, a grey tiled floor, a steel door on the narrow lift. It was reasonably clean and unscathed, suggesting the outer door was secure. He could hear voices on the landing above so he started up the stairs.

The DS from Hackney CID was called Delgado. Tim had never met him but assumed he must be the tall, lanky bloke who came into view as he mounted the stairs. At first he could see only a suit jacket and the small balding patch on the crown of Delgado's head. Then he caught a glimpse of the woman he was talking to. Sod's fucking law!

Hearing his approach, the DS swivelled round. 'DI Armstrong?' Tim nodded. Delgado grinned, looking back towards the woman. 'That's funny. You two've got the same name.'

Nicci glared at her ex-husband and he glared back. Neither found it in the least bit funny.

35

The side ward contained eight beds, four along one wall, four facing them along the other, with a large window at the end. Joey Phelps was in the bed next to the window and it was the early morning sun filtering through the blinds that finally dragged him back to consciousness.

At first he thought he was handcuffed to the bed. When he tried to lift his right hand to rub his face it snagged. But on further investigation he discovered there was a cannula in the back of his hand connected to a drip and a bag of saline hanging above the bed.

It took several moments for him to get his eyes to focus. His mind was fuddled and jittery. He had no idea where he was and no memory of what had happened to him. When he levered himself up onto his left elbow for a better view, pain shot through his abdomen.

A face appeared, female, smiling. 'Hey hey, you need to relax.' She eased him back down onto the bed.

Mouth claggy and dry, he tried to speak but could only croak. 'What the fuck . . .'

'I'll get you a drink.'

She disappeared, returning moments later to push a straw between his parched lips. He tasted cool, fresh water and sucked hard until he had drained the beaker. As he did, his eyes took in her uniform. A nurse – so was this a hospital ward? His disordered brain skittered round gathering data, trying to make sense of it all. He remembered searing heat, feeling giddy, then nothing.

'How'd I get here?'

'I've only just come on shift, I'd have to look at your notes. But I know they operated last night.'

'Operated?' He knew the word but struggled to apply it to himself.

'The doctor will be round soon and she'll explain everything.'

Time passed, it could've been moments or hours. He drifted off. Trollies clattered, voices glided across the ward. Sometimes he managed to home in on the odd word, but mostly he slept. Dark woods, dank foliage, he was carrying a heavy pack, searching out a path.

Waking with a start he felt cool fingertips on his wrist. A small, elfin girl in blue surgical scrubs was taking his pulse.

She fixed him with a steady gaze. 'Morning. I'm Doctor Chakraborty.' She didn't look old enough to have left school, let alone be medically qualified. 'How are you feeling?'

Joey examined his thoughts. How was he feeling? The fog had lifted. His vision was steady, he was thirsty and more than a little peckish. He watched her studying him. She had alert nut-brown eyes behind rimless glasses and tiny, delicate hands. She seemed benign enough, but he needed to be in control, to get back in the driving seat.

He tilted his head, gave her the quirky, boyish grin. 'So did you save my life? Should I kiss your hand?'

'That won't be necessary.' Her smile was reserved. 'You've had a laparotomy, only a small operation. You were unconscious when you came in and we were concerned that you might have some internal bleeding. But you've been lucky, your abdominal muscles are very strong, they absorbed a lot of the trauma.'

'All them hours in the gym weren't wasted then.'

Apparently oblivious to the blue eyes and the charm, she produced a clipboard. 'I need to take some details. What's your name?'

'John.' It was the first name that popped into his head.

She paused, pen hovering over her notes. 'You were lucid briefly when they brought you in. The doctor who admitted you wrote down Sean.'

Joey rubbed his bristly chin. He'd always hated beards; being unshaven made him feel hot and grubby. 'Well, they call me that back home. In Ireland. Over here I'm John.'

She raised her eyebrows, but that was the only indication of her scepticism. He didn't sound Irish and he was trying to be charming, so the name was probably a lie. He'd been knifed, probably in a fight. But that wasn't her business. Her job was to assess his post-operative condition and report back to her boss before his ward round. They treated at least half a dozen stabbings a week. Their fatality rate was below the national average. As long as it stayed that way, her boss would be happy.

Lowering the clipboard, she fixed him with a direct look. 'It's not the hospital's policy to automatically involve the police.'

'Good.' He grinned. 'It's not my policy either.'

'You must take the antibiotics you'll be given. Take all of them. We've repaired the damage to the muscle and subcutaneous tissue, but there's a danger of infection. Do you have a GP?'

'I move around a lot. You know how it is.'

'We won't be writing to your GP then. You must rest. I'd

like to keep you under observation until the end of the week.'

'I got no problem with that.'

She assumed he was lying. No doubt he'd discharge himself at the first opportunity, this sort always did. 'Perhaps you could give the nurse a name and address for our files. Any worsening pain, any dizziness, come back.'

Joey tried the little-boy-lost look one last time. 'Seriously, Doc, I am grateful. I hear what you say.'

'Then hear this. Stop carrying a knife. People get killed. Next time it could be you.'

She turned on her heel and stalked off: a good woman on a mission to help others. He'd never experienced that motivation but nevertheless he admired her grit. She was not much older than him, she saw straight through the bullshit, yet she soldiered on. Trouble was, she was sharp and soon, maybe on her next break, her attention would stray to a screen somewhere, she'd see his picture flash up and she would recognize him.

He needed to disappear. But as soon as he walked out of the hospital he'd have half of Essex police on his tail. He had no money, no phone and he felt like shit. Still, he wasn't that bothered. One of the great advantages of being a psychopath was that in a situation such as this he had no real anxiety. Problems always had solutions. He would find a way out.

Joey leant back on his pillows, closed his eyes and let his mind float free while he waited for the right idea to come to him.

36

Even though Southwark Coroner's Court was within easy walking distance of Borough station, they took a black cab the whole way; Mike insisted. He explained matter-of-factly that the tube in rush hour was simply a bridge too far for him now. Kaz offered no resistance; she was finding that there was a certain relief in letting him take charge of arrangements.

First thing that morning he'd insisted that she needed to contact her probation officer, saying it would only stir up trouble for herself if she didn't. She'd borrowed Mike's ancient desktop computer and with his help she had composed an email. Her old tutor, she informed them, had invited her to London to submit some work for a special award. She expected to be away a week or so, but would keep them posted. She volunteered Mike's name and phone number so they could verify the story should they so wish. From what she knew of the over-stretched, undermanned Glasgow office, as long as the paperwork added up and their arses were covered, they wouldn't bother.

The narrow side street approaching the court building was jammed solid with traffic. The media pack were busily setting up camp in the car park of the old council block opposite. A few onlookers were hanging over balconies and perching on walls, curiosity piqued by the influx.

Kaz and Mike decided to abandon their cab a dozen yards

up the road. As they got out, a police motorcyclist sailed by waving at other vehicles, instructing them to halt and give way. The black Audi he was escorting cruised past and drew up outside the court.

Mike paid off their cabbie while Kaz watched a surge of bodies sweep across the road to engulf the Audi – reporters, photographers, cameramen balancing their rigs, all jostling for pole position. Before the vehicle had even stopped the front passenger door flew open and a suited minder stepped out to release the back door in one fluid motion.

A man emerged who looked vaguely familiar to Kaz. Sleek, smiling, he blinked at the cameras a couple of times then, as if he'd just remembered where he was, put on a grave face. He ducked back into the car to offer a hand to his companion. She slid across the seat, got out and carefully smoothed down her pencil skirt. Reporters rolled forward, jabbing microphones and questions at the couple.

Unfazed, the man raised his palm for quiet, then addressed the throng. 'Ladies and gentlemen – I know you've got a lot of questions. Indeed, I have myself. And that's why we're here today. Helen Warner was . . .' He paused, swallowed hard and clutched the woman's hand. 'She was a colleague of immeasurable talent. And she was a personal friend. Both my wife and I are devastated by her loss. And we're here today to give our support to Charles and his family in the hope that some light can be shed on this terrible tragedy. Thank you.'

With one last curt nod of the head, he gathered the woman under one arm and, ignoring the barrage of shouted questions that pursued them, shepherded her into the building.

Kaz turned to Mike, who'd joined her on the pavement. 'I sort of recognize him. Who is he? Some politician?'

'Robert Hollister. Or "Rob the Throb" as *Private Eye* calls him. He's popular because he looks a bit like George Clooney's younger brother, or so they reckon.' He sniggered and pulled a face. 'Don't see it myself.'

They joined the slow-moving queue edging towards the building. Kaz slotted her hands in her pockets and stared down at her tatty trainers. Would she even be admitted to the courtroom? Or would some snotty official take one look, hold up a hand and say: *Not you, no business of yours what happened to Helen Warner.* Feeling Mike's bony hand come to rest on her arm, she glanced across at him and received a reassuring smile.

A flustered court usher was allowing people through the door in twos and threes. The line had ground to a halt and bodies were bunching in behind them. It reminded Kaz of life inside: waiting in claustrophobic queues, tuning in to the tension of the inmate behind you, sensing any rise in stress levels that might indicate they were about to kick-off.

Looking for relief she let her gaze rove about and that's when she realized she was being observed. A gaggle of smokers had occupied a patch close to the main entrance; among them was Nicci Armstrong, leaning against the plate-glass window, savouring the last puff and staring right at her. Their eyes met. Nicci raised her eyebrows in greeting, the ghost of a smile hovered on her lips.

She ground her fag underfoot, pushed forward and forced herself into the queue directly behind Kaz. 'I wondered if you might be here.'

Kaz was spared the necessity of replying by the usher, who counted them through the door with a snap of her clicker.

As they debouched into the foyer, Nicci stepped in front of them. There was no avoiding her.

'Didn't realize this was your case.' Kaz suppressed her annoyance.

'Well, it is and it isn't.' Nicci gave a diffident hunch of the shoulders and glanced at Mike.

He stuck out his hand. 'Mike Dawson.'

She accepted the handshake. 'Nice to meet a friend of Clare's.'

'It's okay,' Kaz told her. 'He knows who I am. He's my old art teacher, helped me get into Glasgow.'

'Oh, I see.' Nicci frowned, her pallid face and red-rimmed eyes suggested a serious hangover. She seemed to be having problems focusing.

Kaz turned back to Mike. 'Nicci's one of the cops that sent my brother down.'

'Not a cop any more.' Nicci corrected her. 'And presumably you've seen the papers? Joey broke out.'

'Yeah, I saw.' Kaz shifted restlessly. 'His priority'll be to get out the country. I doubt he'll be coming after me.'

'Still, you need to take care. Witness protection can only do so much.'

She nodded. 'So what you doing here?'

Good question, thought Nicci. What was she doing there? Her senses were dull with pain. She'd been up most of the night. She felt dizzy and nauseous, though it was hard to tell if it was from booze, shock or her ricocheting guilt and despair at the death of Ethel. Trying to convince her former colleagues, and her ex-husband in particular, that she might have a relevant lead on the murder had rapidly turned into a fiasco.

Delgado had been listening to her theory with an open mind. Then Tim had turned up. Nicci knew that losing her temper with him had been plain stupid. Yet the very sight of

him – his coiled resentment, his sarcasm – simply set her off.
Delgado had watched bemused as they tore into one another.
After that, any possibility of rational discussion vaporized.
Nicci had retreated, fuming, to her flat and opened the first of
several bottles.

When her alarm went off at seven she'd had problems
remembering where she was and who she was, let alone that
she still had a job to do.

Attending the Warner inquest was crucial. All the relevant
players would be present, plus she needed to be there for Julia
Hadley. And she had to be there for this – the likelihood that
Karen Phelps would put in an appearance. Blake was supposed to be coming too, but as yet he hadn't turned up.

With some effort she fixed her bloodshot eyes on Kaz and
forced a smile. Making contact was one thing, but which way
would Kaz jump? Would she run for cover? There was only
one way to find out. Nicci could muster neither the energy
nor lucidity to play games.

'I work for a firm of private investigators now. We've been
asked to look into Helen Warner's death – by her partner,
Julia.'

Kaz held Nicci's gaze, her expression neither hostile nor
benign. It had been the same in all their previous encounters:
Nicci had always found it impossible to get past Kaz's inscrutability. When they'd met up in Glasgow, just prior to Joey's
trial, it had been amicable enough. But Nicci knew that Kaz
Phelps had wariness written in her DNA. Persuading her to
reveal the true nature of her relationship with her former
lawyer would not be easy.

'So – she doesn't buy the suicide story either?'

'No. She doesn't.' Nicci watched Kaz absorb this. It was as
if she'd slipped away to some private realm. From the corner

of her eye, Nicci observed the way Mike Dawson's gaze rested softly on his protégé.

'Is she here? Can I meet her?'

Kaz's response stopped Nicci's jitters in their tracks. 'You sure you want that?'

'Yeah. Why wouldn't I?' This was accompanied by a defiant stare. 'I'd like to give her my – whad-you-call-it? – condolences. Yeah, I'd like to do that.'

37

Should she try to intervene? After a day of deliberation Fiona Calder hadn't really managed to come to a firm conclusion. There'd been a death on the tube that had unnerved her. The connection with Helen Warner was tenuous, but there was a connection. Even so she'd begun to wonder if she was simply being paranoid. There was no evidence – but then there was no bloody evidence for any of it.

On the morning of the Warner inquest she'd been at her desk by seven a.m., staring out of the window at the hazy morning sun struggling to break through. The interests of justice and the interests of the Met didn't always coincide. That was a proven historical fact. Maybe she was a fool to worry about these things. Keep your head down, wait and see – that had been her husband's advice. But then Geoffrey was a civil servant, not a cop.

At nine thirty she'd decided to go for the fool's option. She walked into the Commissioner's office and asked for a private word. His mood was peevish. He had a meeting scheduled at ten with some policy wonks from MOPAC. He continued to briskly sign his way through a pile of correspondence, while informing her he could only spare five minutes. She'd put her case simply and concisely.

The death of Helen Warner was continuing to attract a great deal of media coverage. A firm of private investigators had been retained by the family and somehow the press had got hold of the fact – she omitted to mention that she herself had been the source. Now the Met was in danger of appearing slapdash in their investigation. Indeed, the blogosphere was buzzing with speculation and accusation.

The Commissioner huffed, he was not a social media man; he regarded it as a waste of time. It might entertain his grandchildren, but that didn't make it a reliable barometer of the public mood in his opinion.

He raised his fountain pen from the letter in front of him and pointed the blunt end at his Assistant Commissioner. 'Fiona, is this strictly necessary? I will not pander to the press or the politicians. You know that.'

It was a phrase he liked. Calder had heard him utter it on a number of occasions. She also knew it was meaningless. Pimp or pander? Whatever you wanted to call it, getting down and dirty with all the other creatures in the political jungle had certainly become part of the job.

She smiled. She'd taken the precaution of freshening her lipstick and wearing a tailored blouse that set off her figure to its best advantage. These things shouldn't matter, but they did. Ever the pragmatist, she'd become expert over the years at exuding just the right amount of femininity, relying on subtle touches like the undertones of an expensive perfume.

She tilted her head, sighed wistfully. 'Only trying to cover your back, sir.'

The Commissioner snapped the cap on his pen and exhaled. His expression softened. 'I know you are. And I know you're one of the few people around here I can rely on to do that.'

Their eyes met. Calder had often wondered if it was true that all men thought of sex, what was it, every hour at a conservative scientific estimate. What a handicap to be saddled with! It was no wonder half of them couldn't think straight. They were forced to compartmentalize in order to manage rational thought at all. That put them at a huge disadvantage. So much so, she could almost feel sorry for them.

Judging that she had his full attention, she broadened her smile. 'The big question is, what will the Mayor say?'

'Say to what?' His tone was tetchy.

'Did Helen Warner commit suicide? He'll be asked – he'll pass the buck directly to us. Then you'll be asked.'

The Commissioner shrugged. 'I'll just say my officers carried out a thorough investigation.'

'What if it turns out they didn't?'

'What the blazes are you getting at, Fiona? Phil Slattery assured me—'

'That's not the point I'm making, sir. Once the question is out there, you'll be forced to have an opinion. The inquest will throw up a lot of public sympathy for the family. If you say she did kill herself, you'll be the bad guy. If you say you don't know, you're relying on your officers and the coroner, you'll be the weak guy.'

The Commissioner frowned, rubbed the side of his nose. 'Well, what are you suggesting?'

'We need to slow the pace. We won't be rushed. We ask for an adjournment.'

'On what grounds?'

'Toxicology. No one understands it. We say we're still awaiting the results of important tests.'

'Then what?'

'We've got some breathing space. Everyone'll get excited about something else. More time, less flak.'

The Commissioner pondered, slumping back in his chair.

His brow crinkled into a worried frown. 'We do think she committed suicide, don't we?'

Calder kept her response noncommittal. 'I'm sure Phil Slattery's team have been very thorough. But you know as well as I do—'

'Yes, yes.' He flapped his hand, waving away any further argument. 'All right. Phone him. Do it.'

Calder got to her feet. 'Thank you, sir.'

As she walked back to her office she felt lighter. It was hard to say why. She'd kicked the can a few yards down the road. A small achievement in the scheme of things, but it kept the situation fluid. It would apply pressure – and with luck that might lead to someone showing their hand.

38

When the coroner announced to a packed courtroom that the case would be adjourned for three weeks to give the police time to complete their investigation, a groan of disbelief rolled round the room. The coroner himself had been similarly aggrieved when the embarrassed SIO had stood in his office five minutes previously and explained that they needed more time to complete all the toxicology.

Detective Superintendent Phil Slattery had thought he was home and dry until he got the Assistant Commissioner's call. To say he was pissed off was an understatement. She'd been trying to put a spoke in their wheel from the outset. He had it from a reliable source that she was the one who'd suggested to Julia Hadley that she hire a private investigator. And Simon Blake, of all bloody people! It was outrageous.

Slattery was roughly the same age as Fiona Calder and the two of them had come up through the ranks together. But when it came to the positive discrimination game, Calder had played a blinder. And here he was, stuck in the middle-management logjam. Detective Superintendent was probably it for him, but that didn't make him any less of a copper, or any less loyal. The Job, the Met – it had given him and his family a good life. He wasn't about to betray that now.

As the courtroom started to empty he walked over to Charles Warner. Helen's father was still sitting in the front row, hands folded in his lap, staring into space. Robert Hollister was standing next to him, talking into his mobile.

Slattery took a deep breath. 'Mr Warner, I'm really sorry about this, but—'

There was no chance to say more because Hollister was in his face. He clicked his phone off. 'What's going on, Superintendent?'

Charles Warner's watery eyes rose to meet Slattery's. He looked haggard and defeated. He made no attempt to speak, not that Hollister would let anyone else get a word until he'd finished spluttering in righteous indignation.

'This is totally unacceptable!'

'Indeed it is, sir.' Unruffled, Slattery looked Hollister in the eye. They both knew the politician was huffing and puffing because that's what politicians did. There would be a private discussion later, but this was neither the time nor place. They were simply going through the motions for the old man's sake.

Julia Hadley edged along the row and placed her hand on Warner's arm. 'Charles, we've got a taxi for you.'

Hollister shook his head vehemently. 'No no! Charles can come with us. We insist.' He turned and sought out his wife. 'Don't we, darling?'

Paige Hollister was standing slightly apart from her husband, her face blank but composed. She seemed to be sealed in her own private bubble, disconnected from her surroundings.

'Darling?' Hollister's tone carried a hint of petulance. 'We're offering Charles a lift.'

Her soft grey eyes slid slowly round to settle on her husband. 'Absolutely, darling.' Then she remembered to smile.

*

Kaz and Mike had found a seat in the back row. The decision to adjourn puzzled them both. They continued to sit, unsure how to react.

'I don't get it.' Kaz scanned the room. 'Why this farting about? The cops must've known before this that they weren't ready.'

'You would think so.' Mike leant back in his chair.

'So what's going on?'

'Beats me. We could ask your friend the ex-cop.'

A bottleneck had formed at the exit as an impatient knot of bodies tried to make their way out. Kaz thought she caught a glimpse of Nicci but it would've been impossible to reach her. As she gazed around the room, her eye travelled to the front row and the old man being helped to his feet by Robert Hollister. Presumably this was Helen's father. He'd been mentioned by Hollister when he did his spiel for the cameras. But what about the rest of the family? Helen had never talked about them beyond the bare facts: no sisters, maybe two brothers, and her mother was dead.

And what about Julia? Which one was she? Had she been accorded a place in the respectable Warner clan?

Following Mike, Kaz got up and began a slow shuffle along the row towards the exit. They were approaching the doors when she felt a hand on her shoulder. Habit made her flinch and turn, ready to lash out, ready for anything.

A smile and chuckle greeted her. 'Goodness me, Karen – you do look fierce! I didn't mean to startle you.'

It took her a moment to recognize the assured lizard-eyed smirk of Helen's old boss. But Neville Moore wasn't only that; as far as Kaz knew he was still her brother's lawyer. And if Joey had indeed escaped abroad, you could be sure of one thing – he'd be in touch with his brief. Beneath the good humour, Kaz was aware of an underlying tension as he leaned towards her to murmur conspiratorially: 'You're about the last person I expected to bump into here.'

39

The Audi drew away from the kerb leaving Julia Hadley on the pavement. Although her shoulders were slightly hunched, she looked every inch the businesswoman, a practised professional smile holding back the grief.

'What now?' She turned briskly to Nicci.

Nicci took a swig from her plastic bottle of water while she pondered the options. The pain across her forehead had settled into a muted ache. 'Well, there's someone in the Met wants to keep the investigation open, so that's probably a good thing.'

'Not for Charles it isn't. This is killing him.'

'How are you doing?'

'I'm fine.'

That seemed fairly improbable. Nicci had watched Julia bustling round, trying to play the role of dutiful daughter-in-law to the suffering patriarch. Now that he'd been swept off in Robert Hollister's car, she seemed lost, standing there nervously twisting the rings on her left finger.

It was hard to discern what sort of relationship really existed between the dead woman's father and lover. Nicci suspected that, like many ageing parents, Charles Warner had only been granted snapshots of his daughter's life. He was mourning his little girl, the child who'd sat on his knee and whose innocence he could still believe in.

Nicci tossed the water bottle into a bin and checked her phone. She was waiting to hear back from Delgado, the Hackney DS investigating Ethel's murder. All she'd got was a curt text from Blake saying he was busy and would see her back at the office.

Juggling thoughts about Ethel and the Warner case was scrambling her brain. It was also stopping her heading for the nearest pub. Hold it together, just a bit longer, she told herself. She didn't want to let anyone down.

Glancing at Julia, she decided to go for broke: 'There's someone who'd like to meet you.'

'I'm not talking to any more bloody journalists.' Julia scowled.

'Someone who knew Helen.'

Was it Nicci's slight hesitation or maybe her tone of voice? Julia was on it straight away. 'You've found her, haven't you?' A faint flush crept up her cheeks.

'She found me really. I was hoping she might turn up today.' Nicci took a breath. 'So, how do you feel about meeting her?'

It was hard to read the look that slid into Julia's eyes. Nicci realized she had her own mask of inscrutability.

When she finally replied, her tone was firm but detached. 'I'm sure it'll be fine.'

40

Kaz's priority was to escape from Neville Moore before he could prise any information out of her, information that would be relayed straight back to Joey. But the shuffling crowd waiting to squeeze through the narrow exit held them all like a net. And the last thing she wanted was to introduce Mike. Unfortunately both he and Neville Moore shared the same class confidence and manners – they immediately exchanged handshakes and names.

'I'm guessing you're an artist, sir.' The lawyer's eyes flicked back and forth from Mike to Kaz, reading every detail. 'One of Karen's teachers, perhaps?'

Mike fixed him with a beady eye. 'Former teacher. I'm retired.'

Left with little choice, Kaz decided to take the bull by the horns. 'Listen, Neville, I know Joey's gonna be looking for me—'

Moore's palm flew up in front of him. 'Hang on! Let's get one thing clear. Your brother is an escaped convict and I have absolutely no knowledge of his whereabouts.'

If she hadn't been feeling quite so apprehensive, this would have amused Kaz. But she'd had enough experience of lawyers, Helen included, to know how they operated. The weasel words cut no ice with her. She gave him a cynical smile. 'Whatever. But you're still his lawyer?'

211

'I am. And I would urge him to turn himself in. So if you or members of your family have any contact with him—'

'Oh, come on, Neville – I grassed him up. You can't have forgotten that. I've got a new name and a new life under the witness protection scheme. If Joey finds me, I'm dead.'

It was only when Mike grasped her by the elbow that Kaz realized she was shaking.

'I'm certain, Mr Moore, that as a respectable member of the legal profession you would not do anything to compromise Karen's safety.' Mike fixed the lawyer with a penetrating stare.

'Of course I wouldn't,' Moore huffed. 'But I've known Joey Phelps since he was sixteen years old. He's a complicated young man – as I'm sure you know, Karen. He understands the danger and penalties involved in the life he's chosen. And I wouldn't necessarily assume that he's bent on vengeance.'

The courtroom had almost emptied. The three of them remained standing in the aisle.

Kaz gave the lawyer a steely glare. 'Give him a message from me, Neville. We had a deal and he could've stuck to it. He could've stopped the killing. But he didn't. He broke the deal. I got no regrets.'

'As I've already said, I have absolutely no means—'

Kaz stepped forward until she was right in the lawyer's face. 'Bullshit! You think I don't know how it works? Oh, you've got plenty of respectable clients and big posh offices now. But push comes to shove, you're still a villains' brief. Transfers between offshore accounts, contact through intermediaries? There's serious money to be made in that game – and you're not about to say no to that, are you?'

Neville Moore didn't waiver. He met her ferocity with

raised eyebrows and a mild look of scorn. 'Is this what Helen told you, in your more intimate moments?'

'You know fuck all about me and her!'

The lip curled to match his gimlet eye. 'Oh really? It may surprise you to know I enjoyed Helen's confidence on a number of matters.'

'I didn't know it was a competition.'

He took a step back, shaking his head as if to reprimand himself. 'It isn't. Look, I have no wish to quarrel with you. I'm here out of grief and concern for a valued former colleague and friend.'

Kaz met his eye and was nonplussed to see the hint of a tear. The notion that Neville Moore even had feelings came as a surprise. He'd been Helen's boss. He was still Joey's lawyer. He was a pompous prick. Apart from that, she knew nothing about him.

'Strange times, indeed. I never imagined it would come to this.' A haunted look flickered across his features. 'I wish you well, Karen, I really do.'

He gave them a thin smile, turned and headed for the door.

41

As they came out of the court building, Kaz's phone buzzed in her pocket. Having asked to meet Julia, she'd supplied Nicci Armstrong with her number, although she hadn't expected such a swift response. Nicci's text suggested a venue round the corner in Borough Market.

Kaz hesitated. The encounter with Joey's lawyer had unnerved her. She knew the sensible thing to do would be to rip the SIM out of her phone and take the next train back to Glasgow – that was her safe haven. The longer she remained in London, the more she was at risk.

As a convicted criminal she'd been released from prison on licence to serve out the rest of her sentence in the community, but technically she wasn't free. If the authorities in Glasgow weren't fooled by her email and realized she was off the grid, she'd be in breach of her licence and in danger of being recalled. But by far the greater risk, the thing that really scared her, was being tracked down by Joey.

She glanced up from her phone to see Mike watching her.

'The ex-cop,' she explained. 'Wants me to meet Helen's partner in a coffee shop at quarter to eleven.' She checked the digital clock on her phone. 'Twenty-five past now. Whad'you think?'

'I think you've already made up your mind.' He flashed her his lopsided grin. 'So let's go.'

The place was easy enough to find, located in a cobbled lane on the edge of the market. High-ceilinged, walls stripped back to the soft and yellowing London stock brick, with a carved oak counter salvaged from some East End boozer running the length of one side. A sumptuous array of cakes and pastries covered its top.

Kaz scanned the room: no sign of Nicci yet. Then she looked at the counter. She'd avoided breakfast, psyching herself up for the inquest and the ordeal of having to listen to the grisly details of her lover's demise. Now she was ravenous.

Mike peered over her shoulder. 'Chocolate brownie looks good.'

'You want one?'

'You do. I'll just have a camomile tea.' He thrust a tenner in her hand.

'No, Mike!'

He wiggled a finger dismissively at her. 'I need to sit down. Over in the corner, that okay?'

As Mike wound his way round the tables, Kaz ordered a chocolate brownie, a large cappuccino and a tea. She was just picking up her tray from the counter when Nicci Armstrong came through the door, followed by a small, mousy-haired woman in a short, collarless leather jacket. Kaz stopped in her tracks. Was this really Julia?

In her mind she'd formed an image of someone large, blonde and Junoesque, full of posh confidence and lethal on a hockey pitch. How could *this* be the woman Helen Warner had chosen? This tiny person with the snub nose and pinched face of a scared rabbit.

The awkwardness of the moment wasn't lost on Nicci. She painted on a smile. 'Julia Hadley, meet Clare O'Keeffe.'

Kaz stood rigid and tall, holding the tray. 'My real name's Karen.'

'Yeah I know.' A crease gathered between the woman's brows. 'You're really beautiful. But then, I knew you would be.'

Kaz blinked, took a breath. She'd imagined this moment on many a sleepless night. But she'd imagined it with a Sig Sauer in her hand and Julia's blood splattering across the white walls of Helen's tasteful flat.

So this was the lover Helen Warner had preferred, the woman she'd elected to share her life with. It didn't make sense, and yet it made complete sense. Julia Hadley matched the decorous restraint of every other aspect of the lawyer's life.

A fist of pain travelled up from Kaz's belly into her chest, she tasted bile in her throat. She wanted to cut and run, but the sorrow in Julia's eyes mesmerized her.

Feeling tears pricking her lids she thrust the tray into Nicci's hands. 'Could you just grab that, go and sit down with Mike. I'll get some drinks. Coffee? Tea?'

Taken by surprise, Nicci almost dropped the tray before recovering enough to respond. 'Yeah, er – double espresso.'

Julia seemed to be the only calm one. Oblivious to her surrounding, eyes riveted on Kaz, she smiled. 'I'd like a still mineral water. But let me help you.'

42

He was a big-hearted bloke, a firm friend, a reliable colleague – Eddie Lunt appreciated these qualities in himself and it came as a surprise when others didn't perceive them. Nicci Armstrong had a tendency to treat him like shit on her shoe – hard to say why – but it was a fact of life since he'd joined SBA.

The inquest had been adjourned and at half twelve she'd come steaming back into the office and laid into him for having a pre-lunch coffee break.

'Don't you ever stop eating?'

His eyes nearly crossed as he focused on the Jammie Dodger that was en route to his open mouth. The news of Ray's death had been niggling at the back of his mind all morning and when he was upset, he ate. He popped the biscuit in whole then pursued her across the office to her desk, flinching as she hurled her bag at the chair. That wasn't a good sign.

Mouth oozing Dodger and jam, he attempted a smile. 'You got a mo?'

'Fuck off, Eddie, I'm busy.' She pulled out her mobile.

'Only I been—'

'Are you deaf?'

'Only—'

Caught in her unremitting, icy stare, the words froze in his

217

biscuit-filled mouth. Then without warning her expression softened to a frown as a thought arose.

'Actually, Eddie, there is something useful you can do.'

Brushing the crumbs from his lips, he signalled his willingness to assist.

'I want you to go to Glasgow. Know it at all?'

'Yeah, it's in Scotland.'

She drummed her fingers on the desk. Was this his idea of humour? You could never tell with Eddie. She knew only too well she was being a complete bitch. Having a go at him had become a habit, a default setting to relieve her general level of stress and irritation. But she wasn't about to beat herself up – he was after all a scumbag – he deserved it.

The morning had been frustrating in the extreme. Hanging around outside the Coroner's Court her head had been full of Ethel Huxtable. The old lady's body, her waxen face, the blood on the pavement. Delgado had promised to get back to her. But the likelihood was Tim had bent his ear, explained man-to-man that his ex-wife was mental. An alchy, retired on medical grounds for the excellent reason that she no longer knew which way was up. In his shoes, she'd have done the same.

Juggling all this with the Warner case had left her feeling ragged and emotional. She dragged herself back to the matter in hand and focused on Eddie. 'I need you to check something out for me.'

He beamed. 'It's what the man pays me for, Nic.'

The temptation to whack back a sarcastic riposte was overwhelming, but Nicci resisted. 'Okay. Helen Warner went to Glasgow a month before she died. Stayed at Malmaison, we think. The supposition is she went to meet up with Kaz Phelps, a former client. I met Phelps at the inquest this morning. Phelps insists she had no idea Warner was in Glasgow or that she might have been looking for her. Claims she hadn't seen her in over a year.'

'You wanna know if she's telling the truth?'

'Exactly. And if she is, then why did Helen Warner take a secret trip to Glasgow which she felt the need to lie about?'

Eddie folded his arms across his ample paunch as he pondered. 'I got an old mate on the *Herald*, been there years. Knows every concierge in every hotel in the city, probably every pimple on their arses too.'

Nicci gave him an acid smile. 'That'll be useful.'

'If we're talking about evidence, like hanky-panky on hotel CCTV, then yeah, it will.'

Licking her index finger, Nicci held it up. Point to Eddie.

He checked his watch. 'Must be a train an hour. From Euston it's probably just under five hours. I can be up there by teatime. Meanwhile I'll speak to my mate, get him on the case.'

Eddie Lunt in brisk, enthusiastic mode was something she'd never witnessed before. Was he trying to impress? Or could it be genuine excitement at the prospect of a trip to Glasgow? Nicci didn't much care, so long as he cleared off and left her in peace.

'Good. Keep me posted.'

'You'll let Simon know?'

'Yep. And don't rack up the expenses or Simon will be pissed.'

The pixieish grin spread across his chubby face. 'As if.'

She'd turned back to her desk and was checking her phone again so she didn't immediately see what prompted his explosion.

'Awww, fuck me sideways with a fucking bargepole!'

Nicci glanced up and followed the direction of his gaze. At

first all she could see was Simon Blake, standing in the reception area shaking hands with someone. Then the other man turned and she saw the horribly familiar features of former Detective Superintendent Alan Turnbull, once her boss and almost her nemesis.

Nicci stood rooted to the spot; she could feel the blood in her ears surging, the anger rising.

A voice drifted over: Eddie again. 'Looks like even fucking Abu Dhabi didn't want him.'

She took a deep breath, glanced at Eddie in surprise. 'How do you know Turnbull?'

'Fucker nicked me for phone hacking, which on the one hand was fair enough. Except that at the time he was dining out with every editor in Wapping and taking bungs like they was going out of fashion. So I call it a bit of a fucking cheek.'

Nicci didn't respond. She was fixated on the fact that Blake had started to walk across the office towards them, Turnbull following in his wake, glancing from left to right with a smirk on his face.

Eddie slipped sideways round the desks to make his escape. 'I got a train to catch. Good luck.'

As Blake approached, Nicci could see the tension in his face. He stepped aside and waved Turnbull forward with a diffident smile. 'I think you two know each other.'

'Nicci, how are you?' Turnbull loomed over her, his hand outstretched, a lairy grin on his face. 'I must say, one of the bonuses for me of joining SBA is that we'll be working together again.'

43

When she'd first got out of jail, the summertime city had been one of Kaz Phelps's chief pleasures. She'd walked and walked, from the riverside eyrie where her brother Joey had lived, to the mansion block in Bloomsbury that had been Helen's home. The hot pavements and cool gardens – back then she'd observed every detail with a fresh, curious eye. The plane trees in full leaf – she remembered sitting in their generous shade in Russell Square as she got up the courage to go and ring Helen's doorbell.

But her lawyer had ended up with a different doorbell, and she was facing it now. Julia had invited her round so they could talk privately.

In the coffee shop, with Nicci Armstrong playing detective and firing questions at her, she'd found it hard to get the measure of Julia. As well as the lover they had in common, they also shared the belief that there was no way Helen Warner had killed herself. So, at the very least, there was stuff to talk about.

Still, standing on the black-and-white-tiled path, Kaz hesitated. This was probably a mad idea. On the other hand, she was hoping Julia would have answers to some of the many questions that had been running through her mind. Whether she'd share them remained to be seen.

Kaz glanced up the street. It was predictably posh. The

houses were large Edwardian semis, worth possibly a couple of million in London's over-inflated property market.

She tried to imagine Helen coming and going from her new home, exchanging friendly greetings with her equally affluent neighbours. Julia and Helen, two middle-class professional ladies – no one would've called them dykes – living in leafy Wandsworth. A respectable, virtuous, contented couple? Something must have gone awry though, breaching the walls of Helen's refuge, tipping her over the line into the world Kaz knew. How else could her bloated corpse have ended up in the river?

Although she hadn't seen her lover's body, it was the image that had stuck in Kaz's mind. She wondered if Julia shared that too.

She took a deep breath and pressed the doorbell. It was set in a brass surround, which someone obviously took the trouble to polish. A chime sounded within and a few seconds later a figure appeared behind the glass. Kaz guessed that Julia had been waiting.

The door opened and they exchanged tentative smiles. Julia was wearing faded jeans and a loose silk shirt – it was meant to look casual, except the shirt was unbuttoned, revealing a low-cut vest. And she was barefooted, which sent a jolt through Kaz. Helen had padded barefooted through her flat the day they'd slept together; Kaz could still remember her feet on the honeyed wooden floor and how seductive she'd found this first glimpse of naked flesh.

Julia flapped her hand. 'Come in, come in.' She had none of Helen's grace.

Following her into the house and down the hall to the kitchen, Kaz sneaked a look into the sitting room. The sofa was one she remembered from Helen's old place.

On the massive granite-topped counter there was a bowl of olives, a bottle of white wine and two glasses. A nervous tension was burning off Julia.

Kaz could feel it, and she watched Julia's hand tremble as she picked up the bottle. 'My father always says once the sun's over the yard arm – but that's bollocks really if it's not going to get dark until nine o'clock.'

Kaz shook her head. 'I don't drink.'

'Oh well – a cup of tea then?' She put the bottle down.

'Yeah. But don't let me stop you.'

Julia gave an airy wave. 'I can take it or leave it. Brought up with ridiculous middle-class notions of hospitality, I suppose.'

Eyes surfing round the immaculate kitchen – very Helen – Kaz managed a wary smile. 'Oh, my old man served booze any time of the night or day. Mostly whisky, usually straight from the bottle.'

Julia's gaze turned wistful. 'We come from very different places, don't we?'

'Yeah, we do. Which is why I was her client and you was her partner.'

Julia raised her chin; she was ready to be polite, friendly even, but not challenged. 'Helen was quite a socialist. I don't think a person's class was ever an issue with her.'

Kaz chuckled, she couldn't help it. 'You serious?'

The comment wasn't intended to provoke, but Julia bridled. 'Her political commitment was—'

'I'm not talking about that.'

Their eyes met, anger crackling on both sides. *She wanted her, not me* – Kaz wondered if that was yet another thought they shared.

It was Julia who turned away. Cheeks flushed, hand

trembling, she reached for the bottle of wine, unscrewed the top and sloshed a hefty measure into one of the glasses.

She gulped down a large mouthful. 'I'm sorry, I don't mean to – all this has been, so difficult, so painful.'

Kaz sighed, she hadn't come for a row. 'Yeah, I do know that.

Another mouthful. 'I'm sure you do.'

Folding her arms Kaz perched on one of the high leather stools. 'You got any idea at all what could've happened to her?'

Julia shook her head slowly. Her face settled into the mask of sorrow that Kaz had seen in the coffee shop. Her words were slow and deliberate. 'I have no fucking idea. None at all. Not even a theory.' Her gaze zoned in on Kaz. 'I was wondering if you had.'

'All I know is she didn't commit suicide.'

Julia frowned. 'It really wasn't you she went up to Glasgow to visit?'

'Like I told Nicci, she might've come looking, but we never met up. Witness Protection tuck you up pretty tight.'

'I don't understand any of it.'

Picking up an olive from the bowl, Kaz popped it in her mouth. Watching Julia take another absent-minded swig of wine, seeing her eyes grow distant as the booze started to kick in, she felt a pang of nostalgia for that blurring of sharp edges, the sliding away of inhibition.

She needed to get some answers before Julia got totally wasted. 'But you've hired Nicci Armstrong and a bunch of ex-cops. What do they say?'

Julia swirled the wine round her glass then drained it. 'I think they agree it wasn't suicide. Beyond that . . .'

She refilled her glass. Stared into it. 'I just wish she'd left some message for me.'

'If she was murdered, she'd never have had the chance.'

When Julia looked up, there were tears running down her cheeks. She wiped them with the back of her hand. 'Glad you said it, not me.'

Kaz got off the stool. She had the distinct sense she was being played. Julia's small stature was deceptive. She had been talking to police and detectives for weeks – and yet she couldn't bring herself to say Helen was murdered?

She scrutinized the neat, petite woman in front of her. Since they'd met earlier in the coffee shop, Julia had washed her hair, applied some discreet mascara, changed her clothes. Shoeless, she'd made herself smaller. Tanked up on half a bottle of wine she seemed all the more fragile.

Kaz towered over her. 'What exactly d'you think's gonna happen here? We get a bit cosy, we get a bit pissed. And if I have sex with you then I'll open up and tell you all the secrets you think I know about Helen?'

Julia's jaw slackened, she swayed on the balls of her feet, colour rising in her cheeks. 'No, I—'

'Oh come on, Julia. You been rumbled. Wine, olives? Hair all soft and shiny, touch of cleavage?'

Julia took a gulp of wine to steady herself. 'I just – I just want to know why?'

'Why she was killed? Me too.'

'Why you?' The look in Julia's eyes hardened. 'Why did she want you? I built my whole life around her, supported her career.' Her face crumpled into an angry scowl. 'What the fuck is it about you?'

So now they'd got to the nub of it. Julia was glaring at her like an aggrieved toddler. All Kaz could do was exhale and shrug.

And Julia hadn't finished. 'I know you're lying about

Glasgow. You met her at Malmaison, slept with her, didn't you?'

'No—'

'Nicci might buy that, but I don't. I saw the postcard you sent her. "Thanks for a great time, K." Remember that? I found it in her desk drawer.'

'That was from ages ago.'

Julia's fists were clenched, her face streaked with mascara and tears. 'I just want to know the bloody truth!'

Kaz moved away, giving her a wide berth. She hadn't come to upset the poor woman. The fantasy of revenge she'd once had seemed completely absurd now. And she wouldn't have needed a gun to harm Julia. She could've finished her off with her bare hands.

The advantage her height gave her was somehow freeing. Maybe this was the ego-trip blokes experienced when they went out with a small, dainty woman? Bigger did mean more powerful. It fuelled her confidence.

When she'd rung the doorbell she'd felt unsure. Now a chaos of conflicting emotions was cascading through her. Julia's raw pain, her tears, her vulnerability, somehow it was all quite seductive. However much Kaz resisted it, still she felt the pull. She had the power and she wanted to use it.

Julia pulled a tissue from the box on the counter and slowly wiped her face and nose. 'I'll put the kettle on.'

Her voice was cracked and small, she seemed unabashed by her outburst. Kaz watched her. However unconscious it might be, Julia knew how to play the game. A man wouldn't have hesitated. Prey and predator. She was offering herself, trading the only real asset she believed she had. It was an ancient, instinctive ploy.

Kaz stepped across the room and gently put her hand on

Julia's arm. Julia glared then something in her seemed to give way and she slowly inclined her head towards Kaz's shoulder. A gesture of submission or just emotional fatigue?

Kaz lifted her hand and stroked Julia's hair. 'Listen. She wanted you. She married you.'

Julia's head rested on her shoulder, her eyes brimmed with tears. Kaz folded her arms round the narrow frame. She could feel Julia's warmth, her breath. Her hair carried a flowery scent. It felt good to be holding her. What the fuck? Why not?

Julia raised her face to be kissed, letting her eyes close.

Kaz stroked the tip of her little finger along Julia's lower lip. 'Don't close your eyes.'

She blinked, gazed up at Kaz.

A ghost of a smile greeted her. ''Cause I'm not her. She's dead.'

'I know that.'

44

Blake sat behind his desk, fingers steepled, brow furrowed, trying to appear calm and in control. Ranged in front of him were Nicci, Bharat and Rory; insofar as SBA had 'heads of department' they were it.

Taking a breath he leant back in his chair and opened his palms. 'I quite understand your reservations, Nicci, but his role will be mainly strategic.'

Nicci had her hands on her hips and was glowering at him. 'What the fuck does that mean?'

'He's not an ideal choice, I grant you, but we're under pressure from investors and we need to develop a longer term perspective for the business.'

She was fizzing with fury. Rory watched with interest. He and Bharat were bystanders in the argument; it was between the two ex-cops.

Nicci shook her head in disbelief. 'I've worked for Turnbull. I know all about his strategies. He's a user and he's got no scruples. New firm, all set up and ticking over nicely. He's here for your job, Simon. It's a takeover. Can't you see that?'

'Oh come on, Nic,' Blake huffed. Her anger he could handle, it was the disdain in her voice that stung. 'You really think I'm going to let that happen?'

'Then grow some balls and tell the investors no.'

'It's not as simple as that.' He shoved back his chair and stood up. He'd been up most of the night searching for some way to resist Linton's diktat. It had left him feeling beleaguered. What he needed was her help.

She simply glared at him. 'Why not? You think they're just going to pull the plug if you don't kowtow? There's money to be made, they know that.'

Blake turned away to face the window. It was more or less what his wife had said, though she'd been gentler and more deferential to his bruised ego.

The financial world of banks and investors was new territory for him. He'd dealt with plenty of villains over the years, but this lot were something else. Duncan Linton had threatened him and he'd caved in. Setting up his own firm had been a dream and he'd stumbled and panicked at the first fence. He felt ashamed of the way he'd handled things, but he couldn't afford to let his employees see that. Especially Nicci.

He took a deep breath and turned back to face them. 'Okay, I hear your concerns. But the decision's made. He starts tomorrow.' He glanced at the two silent men. 'What about you two? Anything you want to say?'

Bharat shrugged his shoulders; arguments put him on edge, he just wanted to get back to his computers.

Rory had built a career in the army thanks to his ability to manage men and their fears. He could see the tension pulsing off Blake, sense the underlying distress. The boss was out of his depth and scared – that much was obvious. Nicci's tactic, haranguing the guy, was counter-productive. Rory's technique was to bide his time. He flashed Blake an encouraging smile. 'Well, we'll have to see how it goes.'

Nicci glared at him. Trust bloody Rory to be a useless

wimp. Bharat's acquiescence she expected. She stomped out of the room.

Blake gave the remaining two a shrug of masculine complicity. Women, eh?

As they headed out he called after them, 'Thanks, guys.' But his face was pale, his palms sweating.

Rory wandered across the office to Nicci's workstation. She had her feet up on the desk and was scrolling through messages on her phone.

'Are you free this evening? Perhaps you'd join me for dinner.'

Nicci almost dropped the phone in surprise. 'What?'

He was standing with his hands interlaced loosely behind his back – the stance of a soldier at ease, reflecting the habits of a lifetime. 'I think we should talk about all this, don't you?'

'I suppose so, yeah.' She put the phone down, her colour and awkwardness rising. 'But I've got to go over to Hackney – talk to some cops about a murder.'

He drew his own mobile from his trouser pocket. 'Let's exchange numbers and you can text me when you've finished. I'll pick you up.'

'Er, yeah – okay.' She stared at him for a moment. 'Is Bharat coming too?'

Rory glanced up from his mobile, amused. 'Seriously, what would be the point in that?'

45

Kaz held Julia Hadley in her arms and gently rocked her. She'd hated this woman, had lost count of the nights she'd spent imagining revenge scenarios. What she'd never imagined was this. They were in the sitting room on the sofa that had belonged to Helen. Sex had been Julia's chosen weapon. Or maybe it was just the booze that had alchemized her resentment and anger into desire. But Kaz had gone along with it, at least initially.

In the kitchen they'd kissed, shyly, nervously. At first Kaz got a buzz from the fact she was being offered the opportunity to dominate and seduce the woman who'd caused her so much pain. Julia wanted to know what Helen had got from her – well she could certainly show her some of that – or she thought she could.

When it came to it though, it felt cold-blooded, and ripping Julia's clothes off to have full-blown sex on the ceramic-tiled floor seemed ridiculous. Kaz discovered that the sadistic gene, which definitely ran in her family, seemed to have passed her by. There was no pleasure for her in being either emotionally or physically cruel to Julia. So she'd led her into the sitting room, sat her down and cuddled her instead.

Julia had relaxed; her eyes still red-rimmed from crying, she seemed relieved at Kaz's decision.

As Kaz stroked her hair, feeling the quiet inhalation and

exhalation of breath, the weight of Julia's head on her shoulder, she had the first real moment of peace she'd experienced since leaving Glasgow.

Learning of Helen's death, the rage it had invoked, the headlong rush down to London to find the truth – and on top of all that, seeing Joey – it was like being swept up in a whirlwind. She'd found some respite with Mike, his unconditional kindness had soothed her. But she'd been left emotionally wrung-out. What she needed more than anything was time to stop and think.

The email Mike had helped her write might buy her some time with the probation service. But once they started asking questions she'd be at risk of being recalled to jail for breaching her licence. And then there was the spectre of Joey. How the hell had he escaped and where was he now? Ibiza? Almost certainly. He had plenty of contacts out there. He may have even managed to keep the business up and running while he was inside. And he'd soon get access to some of the cash he'd salted away in untraceable offshore accounts.

She wondered how much she should fear him. She'd seen first-hand what he was capable of; it was no exaggeration to say her little brother was a murderer and a psychopath. At one time she'd been the only person he truly cared about, the one person he'd never harm, but the bond forged through their terrible childhood had been severed when she'd testified against him in court. She'd betrayed him, and there was no way Joey would ever forgive her. Sooner or later someone would come for her – or maybe he'd want the pleasure of pulling the trigger himself.

So where did that leave her now? Cradling her ex-lover's lover and wondering which outcome she preferred – ending up dead or back in jail.

Suddenly aware that Julia was watching her, she murmured, 'You okay?'

Julia nodded. 'I feel a bit embarrassed.'

'Why?'

'Emotion and booze, never a good combination.'

Kaz smiled. 'It's a while since I done it. But no, never the smartest move.'

'So what do we do now?'

'Well, now we've got the crap out the way, we could have a proper discussion about all this.'

Julia eased herself free of Kaz's arms and leant back against the sofa. 'Okay. Let's do it.' Her tone was confident; the delicate femme persona had been shed.

'Okay.' Kaz kicked off her shoes and folded her legs under her. 'My view is Helen Warner treated me like shit and probably you as well. But she was clever and fearless, she also helped me turn my life around and she didn't deserve to die. I wanna know who killed her. I wanna know why. And then, whoever they are, I wanna make those fucking bastards pay.'

A hint of a tear glistened in Julia's eye but she smiled. 'I'm beginning to understand why she was in love with you.'

Kaz gave her an arch grin. 'I could say the same.'

Their eyes met. Enemies about to become allies? Kaz was wary. Growing up surrounded by meanness hadn't made her one of life's optimists. She was happy to play along and see how things developed. Trust? Now that was different matter.

And Julia was wearing her own mask, she had her own secrets to protect. Still, there was considerable relief in her gaze. Since the moment she'd received the news of Helen's death she'd felt totally alone. At least now someone else felt as infuriated by official acceptance of the suicide theory as she did.

'So how do we approach this?'

Kaz had been giving it some thought, but she needed more information before she could come up with a strategy. 'Nicci Armstrong was pretty smart when she was a cop. But what d'you know about this outfit she works for now?'

'They're called SBA. The guy that runs it is Simon Blake – he was a commander in the Met. Helen's father managed to get a meeting with the Commissioner to discuss the investigation. They were really cagey about the whole thing. It was the Assistant Commissioner who took me aside afterwards, suggested that I hire a private investigator and recommended Blake.'

'Why d'you think he did that?'

'She, actually. Her name's Fiona Calder. Nicci knows her.'

Kaz got up and took a turn about the room. 'Okay, so what's Nicci done so far?'

'I think she's been going through the evidence. She's asked me loads about Helen.'

'Bugger all basically?'

A look of amusement spread over Julia's features. 'Yeah. Probably.'

Kaz ran her hand through her hair – a gesture that reminded Julia of Helen. 'Then it's time we put the screws on her. Make her realize that this is not just another case and she needs to pull her finger out.'

'You think she'll respond to that?'

'Yeah. Me and her have got some history. I'll have a word, if you like.'

'Yeah, that would be good.' Julia's back was straighter, her whole being seemed lighter. 'And thanks. I mean, I know you're not doing this for me, but . . .'

Kaz's phone started to trill in her jeans pocket.

She gave Julia a smile as she drew it out. 'Wonder what Helen would make of this? The two of us?'

'I think she'd approve. She had a keen sense of irony.'

Glancing down at the phone Kaz tapped in her passcode with both thumbs. A message carrying a video clip popped up. She hit the play button.

As the clip started to play her jaw slackened, composure draining from her features. 'Awww, shit!'

Julia frowned. 'What's the problem?'

Kaz's eyes were riveted to the small screen. A low keening sob was emanating from the handset.

Kaz bunched her other fist. 'Fuck! Fuck! Fuck!'

Puzzled, Julia got up. Fury was erupting in Kaz and she couldn't contain it, couldn't keep still. She let Julia take the phone.

Julia peered at the screen. A woman's face was pressed close to the camera lens, her left eye was puffy and closed up, her swollen cheek oozed blood. A hand was grasping a hank of her hair, pulling the head back slightly to reveal a plastic ligature biting into the flesh of her neck. And the ligature was being slowly tightened. She gasped for breath.

'My God!' Julia gasped in horror. 'What is this? Who is she?'

Kaz was turning in agitated circles, arms clasped round her torso. She was fighting back tears of rage. It took her a moment to respond.

'Her name's Yasmin. She's a friend of mine.'

'They're killing her! We must call the police.'

'The police!' Kaz turned on her. 'They'll be fuck all use. Yasmin's a prostitute. She'll be dead in a skip before they even get a trace on the phone.'

'We've got to do something.' Julia was holding the handset

with rigid fingers as if the pain on the screen was searing her hand. 'I'm calling them.'

They watched Yasmin's eyes open with a start as the ligature was released. She coughed hoarsely. Her fingers flew up to the deep red welt ringing her throat. Muffled laughter could be heard behind her.

Then a male voice: 'So – now y'know where it's at. I wanna word wi'd you, Kaz Phelps. There's a pub in Tottenham. In the High Road. Bricklayers, innit. I wanna see you stood outside, on your own, eight o'clock. I see anyone wi'd you, you keep me waiting, your lil' fuck-buddy here, she's dead meat. You feel me?' He laughed. 'Yeah, I think you do.'

The clip ended, the screen went black. Kaz and Julia stared at each other.

46

Nicci Armstrong took the bus to Hackney. It was packed with kids who'd just got out of school. She watched them joshing each other. Seeing them en masse always made her think of Sophie – this is what she should be doing now: coming home from school with her mates, texting on her phone. Sometimes it felt to Nicci as though her heart had been ripped out. But somehow she was still alive. It seemed the undead came in many guises; mostly they passed unnoticed and didn't have fangs.

DS Delgado had finally responded to her several messages and invited her to come in and talk. The local CID operated from a two-storey office block in a new business park on the edge of Hackney Marshes. The reception area was tiny with no seating. Nicci folded her arms and leant against the scuffed wall.

Delgado emerged from the lifts, greeting her with a polite smile. 'Thought we'd go round the corner for a coffee.'

'I was chucked out on health grounds, not for misconduct.'

This earned her a sardonic glance from the cop. 'Your ex is upstairs, talking to my boss. Didn't think you'd want another encounter.'

Nicci huffed out a sigh. 'Okay. Fair enough.'

They headed out of the door and across the car park of

the adjacent plumber's merchants, Delgado leading the way. Nicci took the opportunity to observe him; same rank as her when she'd left, but their paths had never crossed. He was older – around forty was Nicci's guess – tall, maybe six three or four, rake thin, his dark hair receding at the temples, a small tonsure at the crown.

As soon as they were clear of the building he pulled out a pack of cigarettes. A heavy smoker, the smell of nicotine hung on him like an acrid aftershave. He offered the packet to Nicci. She hesitated then took one; he sparked up his lighter and applied the flame to her cigarette, then his own. This brief ritual was wordless, but the act of sharing eased the awkwardness between them.

Delgado strode on. He walked in loping strides, shoulders hunched, one hand in his trouser pocket, the other carrying the fag up and down to his lips. Nicci wasn't a slow walker, but she found herself having to make an effort to keep up.

When they reached Homerton High Street he stopped outside one of the big coffee chains. 'This okay?'

Nicci nodded, they discarded their cigarette butts and he held open the door.

Once they were finally settled in a corner with their drinks, the cop rested his elbows on the table and opened his palms. 'Well, you know the drill. You tell me what you know. I listen. And I tell you nothing.'

Nicci tipped a sachet of sugar into her double-shot espresso and gave it a stir. 'As I explained last night, Ethel was my neighbour, I didn't know her well. But she and I were involved in an incident at the bus stop.'

The DS took a notebook from his jacket pocket and flicked over the pages. 'With this teenage boy?'

'Leon. No last name. But he must be local.'

Delgado squinted at his handwriting and gave a dry chuckle. 'Nowadays I can't read a bloody thing without my glasses.' He drew a leather spectacle case from his inside pocket. 'You're probably still a bit young for such an affliction.'

Nicci smiled. 'I have others.'

The DS rested the glasses on his nose and peered over them. 'Yeah, I gather.'

'Listen, I don't mind you checking me out. It's what I'd do in your place. But don't just rely on my ex-husband. Please.'

Delgado was scanning his notes; his dark, deep-set eyes and sharp features gave him a foxy air. He didn't look up. 'A colleague of mine knows Bill Mayhew. We had a word.'

Nicci turned the coffee cup in its saucer. That was a stroke of luck. Mayhew was her old DCI, she knew he'd have given her a good rep.

'Haven't seen Bill in a while.' She smiled wistfully. 'But I hope you'll take his word rather than Tim's.'

Delgado laid his notebook on the table, took off the glasses and rested them on top. There were legions of blokes like him in the Job – steady, competent officers, not particularly ambitious, but behind the easy manner was a wary inscrutability. Nicci admired that brand of masculine professionalism: solid, efficient, unemotional. In a tight spot, he'd have your back.

He seemed to be considering his words carefully, but when he spoke the flip tone took Nicci by surprise. 'I hate to think what my ex-wife would say about me. We manage to be civil, y'know, for the kids.'

She smiled, wondering if he'd say more. Her own divorce was still a sour memory – the rows, the anger, the painful compromises. She'd hated it every time Tim had come round to collect Sophie. Much as she'd wanted her daughter to have a proper relationship with him, she still resented it. Resented the trips with the new girlfriend, Sophie's excitement and pleasure at the treats Tim arranged for her.

Delgado was on the other side of the equation – the weekend father, the dispenser of delights. Nicci realized he was scrutinizing her. If he'd talked to Mayhew presumably he knew. She hoped he wouldn't refer to it. Any mention of Sophie at this point would be likely to crack her open. Then he would end up thinking she was an unreliable basket case.

He shook his head sadly. 'My ex-wife thinks I'm a loser. We've got two boys. The youngest was a toddler when I found out she was screwing my best mate. He's a chef. Pretty good one too. Started a chain of tapas restaurants. He's made a mint. They live in the Cotswolds now. Boys have got horses, quad bikes, go to a posh school with a bunch of rich kids.' He grinned. 'They probably think I'm a loser too.'

Nicci felt she was being played. Why was he opening up to her in this way? She hadn't come here to share painful confidences or hear about other peoples' messy lives. It was just irritating. She was there for Ethel Huxtable, to get justice for a feisty old lady who could've given them all a lesson in courage. The rest was bullshit.

She took a sip of coffee, set the cup back on the saucer. 'Was she stabbed?'

'They're doing the PM this afternoon. Then we'll know for certain.'

'But you're working on the assumption?'

'Yeah, I guess.'

'So where are you up to? If Tim's still around, are HAT and the borough running the inquiry jointly? When's the murder team taking over?'

He gave her a pleading look.

'Oh, come on, Delgado . . .'

'Jack.'

'Jack the lad?' She laughed. 'Yeah that figures.'

'My name's actually Joaquin. When we first came over, kids in my class couldn't pronounce it. But they could manage spic. I preferred Jack.'

More personal trivia. Nicci had to contain her annoyance. It was his way of processing her, being sympathetic – because she was an ex-cop with a dead kid – while skilfully avoiding the nitty-gritty.

Fixing him with a piercing stare, she leant forward. 'Come on, Jack, I just want to know what's going on. I'm sure you and your team know what you're doing. But my ex – and I don't say this with any bitterness – is a crap detective.'

'Well, I can tell you what I've been doing. Spent the morning talking to the victim's family. Seems she was quite a character.'

'I know.'

He nodded wistfully. 'They showed me this scrapbook. She was a real firebrand in her youth. Worked as a bus conductor, started campaigning for equal pay and that got her into trade unionism. She was on Hackney Council for years, became an alderman, back when they still had all that.'

None of this surprised Nicci, but it left her with an even greater feeling of stupidity and guilt. 'I wish I'd taken the trouble to talk to her more.'

Delgado sighed, checked his watch. 'Okay, so you think this kid Leon is a possible suspect.'

'It's definitely where I'd start.'

Reaching for his notebook, the DS uncapped his pen. 'Run

through the incident at the bus stop again. I want to make sure I've got an accurate note.'

'We were queuing. Ethel had one of these little shopping trollies on wheels. The boy accidentally kicked it over. Ethel had a go at him. He gave her some lip. I intervened.'

Delgado wrote rapidly in a small, neat hand. 'You intervened? How?'

Nicci found she had to swallow hard, a tight knot of emotion was rising up from her stomach into her chest. It was fear – the fear that her anger, her desire to punish and hurt the boy, had got the old lady killed.

She caught Delgado scanning her, she knew she'd set him wondering. 'The kid got stroppy, pulled a knife.'

'On you or Ethel?'

'On me. I – well, basically I intimidated him into backing off. This was in front of his mates. He certainly lost face. So I think he's got a point to prove.'

The DS's lip curled in amusement. 'I'll bet you're a mean son-of-a-gun when you want to be.'

'If the occasion calls for it.' Was he being patronizing or admiring? You could read it either way.

'Description?'

'Five seven, mixed race, probably fourteen or fifteen.'

Having completed his notes, Delgado glanced at Nicci and smiled. 'Okay, well, we'll look into it.'

Nicci watched him put the notebook and pen in his pocket. He rubbed the dark stubble on his chin, took a sip of coffee. He seemed fidgety, but maybe he was just craving his next cigarette.

They'd reached an impasse. Like any member of the public she'd made her statement, it had been duly noted and that was that. He was as good as his word: he'd listened and told her nothing. The information would be assessed and processed – in due course. But that wasn't good enough for Nicci.

'Look, if this kid decided to knife Ethel, because I pissed him off . . .'

He frowned. 'That's a big if.'

'Trust me, I've got enough grief in my life without carrying the guilt for this too.' Feeling the tears start to well up, she cursed her own weakness.

Delgado watched her struggling to hold it together. Women losing it, it was his Achilles heel. He took a slug of coffee and wiped a smidgeon of froth from his lips with thumb and index finger. Nicci pulled a tissue from her bag and blew her nose. If this had been a deliberate ruse to manipulate him, it would've been brilliant.

As it was she simply felt like shit. 'Sorry.'

'Okay, but this is between us. It gets out, my boss'll have my balls in a wringer.'

Nicci looked up at him, surprised but grateful.

'I'm a sucker, aren't I? An easy mark.'

'If you think this is deliberate—'

'No . . .'

Their eyes met.

'Okay, what the hell.' He shook his head wearily. 'You don't have to feel guilty – we've got a confession. Your ex and my boss are talking to the CPS, see if it'll stand up, before they charge him.'

Nicci stared at him. 'Charge who?'

'Another neighbour of yours – at number six – ex-soldier: Nathan Cosgrove. You know him?'

'By sight, not by name.'

'We took him in for questioning last night. Apparently, he and Ethel had words on several occasions.'

Nicci frowned. 'Yeah, and I saw one of those occasions. She told him off, but he wasn't bothered by it. Have you seen him? He's a big bloke, solid muscle. If he lost it, it'd be fists. He could deck anyone. I don't see him sneaking around and knifing an old lady in the back.'

Delgado laced his fingers. 'Well, DI Armstrong is convinced Cosgrove did it. He had us questioning the guy half the night.'

'Are you serious?' Nicci could feel the tension in her stomach. The fury rising. 'The time I saw Cosgrove he was high as a kite. You put some fucked-up soldier in an interview room all night and make him sweat, what kind of confession is that?'

'It was done by the book. The doctor passed him fit to be questioned.'

Nicci shook her head in disbelief. 'Have you looked into his history? Because his defence brief will. Where did he serve and how long's he been out?'

'Three tours in Helmand.' Delgado pushed his cup aside. 'Came home a couple of months ago.'

'Did you watch him being interviewed?'

'No. My shift ended at ten.'

Nicci raked her fingers through her hair. She knew she had to rein herself in. Blowing her stack at Delgado would get her precisely nowhere. And the fact this shit show was being driven by Tim made her even more furious. It had all the hallmarks of his stupidity and ambition. A quick result before the HAT team had to pass it on? And he gets the credit.

She could see the cop was uncomfortable and getting ready to bail. 'Come on, Jack, think about it.'

'I don't know the details. At the moment my DI is going along with it.'

'That's because it's good politics. Get a result before the murder team's brought in. Makes everyone look good.'

Delgado had his arms folded, his long, lanky limbs drooped off the chair. Nicci could feel the exasperation pulsing off him.

He loosened his tie, the collar was missing a button. 'Once he's charged, it's out of my hands.'

'Is it?'

'You ever worked in the boroughs? You know the caseload they expect us to carry? Especially now.'

Nicci's face was sympathetic but she wasn't about to let him off the hook. 'Just because he's got two arms and two legs doesn't make him okay. A confession obtained overnight from a veteran with possible combat stress? I doubt the CPS'll be happy with that. But the paperwork could take days. Meanwhile any forensics associated with an alternative suspect like Leon will be lost.'

He unfolded his arms and exhaled.

'By then it won't be your problem though, will it?'

Delgado's dark eyes flashed with their own indignation. 'Don't you guilt-trip me, lady.' He wagged a finger at her.

'I'm not.' She stared straight back at him until the hang-dog expression dissolved into a wry grin.

'You're a fucking piece of work, Nicci Armstrong. You know what Mayhew said about you?'

She smiled. 'Probably that I was a fucking piece of work.'

'He said you were the best DS he'd ever worked with, a born detective, and the Met should be pulling out all the stops to get you back in the job.'

Nicci managed a dry laugh. 'That's not about to happen any time soon.'

Delgado stood up, shoved both hands in his trouser pockets. 'Okay, here's the deal. You let me look for Leon. Don't go looking yourself and don't interfere. Stay right out of it. Wait for my call. Agreed?'

'Absolutely.' Nicci beamed. 'Thanks, Jack.'

47

It was five thirty, which gave Kaz two and half hours and the clock was ticking. She swallowed down the bile stinging her throat. The video clip of Yasmin being tortured had nearly made her puke. This was all her fault. Now an acid tension was thrumming through her.

She didn't really have a plan, it was more a crazy idea born of desperation. It required a ton of luck and a car. The voice on the phone was Tevfik Kemal, she was pretty certain of that. But was he acting alone or with the backing of his uncle? Sadik was the one to fear. If this was a freelance piece of revenge from the miserable little scrote, she had the ghost of a chance. However, she doubted Tevfik had the balls to damage an asset like Yasmin without the tacit approval of his father.

The last time she'd driven a car she was seventeen. She had no licence and had never taken a test, but she'd omitted to mention these things to Julia. The Figaro was garaged at the end of the garden in a lock-up, which had access into an old mews running along behind the houses. Julia fitted a Yale key in the wooden door and opened it. The car sat there small and round and pink, like something out of a cartoon.

Kaz glared at it – a motorbike would've been better, she could definitely ride a motorbike – but this? 'Does this bloody thing even go?'

Julia shot her a glance, she was even more jittery than Kaz. 'It's just retro styling, course it goes.'

'I'll take your word for it.'

Julia's face was tense with concern. 'This is madness. You can't deal with these people yourself. We have to go to the police.'

Kaz squeezed down the side of the garage, ran her eye over the stupid little car. 'And say what? Cops won't get within a mile. *These people* are serious villains, don't you get it?'

'All the more reason—' She stopped herself, decided to change tack. 'Okay, let's call Nicci Armstrong. She'll know what to do.'

Kaz ignored the comment. Julia was right about one thing – this was madness. She was Clare O'Keeffe now, an ordinary student living a blameless and untarnished life. The problem was Clare O'Keeffe couldn't help Yasmin. It required a gangster mentality to front up to other gangsters. Joey's sister, Terry Phelps's daughter, *she* had that mindset, she'd grown up with it. It had also landed her in jail.

To deal with the Kemals she had to become that person again, the old Kaz Phelps. After Joey's trial she'd vowed to herself that she'd never go back, never cross that line again into her father's murky violent world. But if she did nothing, her friend would die.

She smiled cynically to herself, the likelihood was she and Yasmin would both be murdered. She'd shamed Tevfik, offended his father's vicious, misogynistic code. They were out to get her. She had a choice – face them now or run. If she ran back to Glasgow her new identity would probably protect her. But what would happen to Yasmin?

She peered through the side window at the dash. It was a

very long time since she'd been behind the wheel. Still, how hard could it be?

Julia was right behind her. 'You sure this friend can help?'

'No. Fuck me, Julia! Are you gonna lend me the car or not?'

'When did you last drive in London?'

Tension and anxiety burnt off Kaz. 'I ain't got time for this.'

'Okay, look, I'll drive you to your friend's.'

'No. I don't want you to get involved.'

'I am involved. Either I come with you, or I call the police.'

Kaz huffed. 'I ain't got time to argue.'

Julia's style of driving could never have been deduced from either her appearance or manner. She navigated through the back streets of South London – Brixton, Camberwell and up to the Blackwall Tunnel – like a rally driver. The manoeuvrability and speed of the little car surprised Kaz. The rush-hour traffic had been a worry, but they got through the tunnel and out on to the A13 without too many hold-ups.

Kaz sat fretfully in the passenger seat wondering if this plan was merely mental or totally deranged. She'd tried calling Glynis a couple of times, but got no reply. The last time they'd met was at Kaz's father's funeral. She could've moved in the meantime. Plus the cops would've taken the place apart when they charged Sean with murdering Glynis's boyfriend, Dave Harper.

As they turned off into Langdon Hills, Julia broke her long silence. 'What if your friend's not home?'

'Well, we try and come up with a way to break in without the neighbours calling the police.'

Julia side-eyed her with disbelief.

Kaz returned the look. 'You asked. And you insisted on coming.'

Knuckles white from gripping the steering wheel, Julia was struggling in vain to get her head round all this. 'Is she a good friend? Will she want to help?'

'She's more of a relative than friend. Used to be married to my cousin Sean.'

'Where's he?'

'Officially in Spain. Unofficially dead.'

Julia lapsed into silence. She'd stepped into Kaz's world and it was alien terrain, a place Helen probably knew about and could've maybe explained. But Helen was lost, leaving Julia floundering in a backwash of grief and confusion. Driving was actually a relief, it gave her a task to focus on.

Kaz was equally uncomfortable. Mention of Sean put her on edge. It sent her thoughts scuttling back to dark memories – the brutal fight as he tried to rape her, the blood puddling out across her beautiful wooden floor after she'd shot him. She'd put all this away, consigned it to the past, to the old life. Still it reminded her that she was capable of handling extreme situations and the icy rage flowing through her veins was her best ally.

She directed Julia along several side roads to the cul-de-sac where Glynis and Sean had lived. But when they pulled up outside the detached chalet bungalow, Kaz got a shock. During her cousin's long years in jail the property had become drab and rundown. Now the crumbling render on the walls had been repaired and painted pink. Mediterranean-style slatted shutters had been added to the windows. The front garden was filled with an array of flowers and a neatly mown lawn. Glynis must've moved.

Kaz cursed under her breath. It'd always been a long shot.

She registered that Julia was looking at her with an anxious gaze. She sighed. 'I reckon she's moved.'

'Maybe the new people have a forwarding address?'

'Nah, that's not gonna help—' But Julia was out of the car and heading up the path. 'Julia!'

By the time Kaz had got out, Julia was ringing the doorbell. The sing-song chime was greeted by the sound of a barking dog. The door opened a crack, held on a security chain.

Kaz stared at the nervous figure peering out and her frown of annoyance dissolved into a smile.

Julia was confidently dishing up some spiel about market research. Kaz joined her on the step.

'Hello, Glyn. I hardly recognize the place. You've given it a facelift.'

Two wide, heavily mascaraed eyes blinked at her.

'Kaz? Blimey! Hang on.'

The door closed and immediately reopened with the chain unhooked.

Glynis was hanging on to the collar of a yapping Staffordshire bull terrier and beaming at her. 'I don't believe it! Come on in.'

Julia hesitated, peering warily at the dog.

'He won't hurt you, love. He just gets overexcited.'

Kaz smiled. 'This is . . . my mate Julia.'

Glynis hauled the dog off and they followed her into the house.

In Kaz's memory, Glynis had been neat, but not what you would call obsessively house proud. Now the interior was immaculate. The polished, pristine hallway led to a sitting room with a conservatory opening out onto the garden.

Glynis shooed the dog out into the garden and closed the

sliding door. 'I'll put the kettle on. Unless you fancy something stronger?'

Kaz's eyes were darting round, processing, assessing just how much the place had changed.

She glanced down the garden, where the bounding dog was chasing a punctured beach-ball. 'This is a bit of a flying visit. We ain't exactly got a lot of time. You've certainly made some changes round here.'

'I got some life insurance money. From Dave.' She shot a sheepish look at Julia. 'Does she know about . . . all that?'

Shaking her head, Kaz turned to give Julia a reassuring smile. Was it necessary to tell her that Glynis's boyfriend Dave had been shot dead by Kaz's brother in order to make Sean the prime suspect for his murder? Probably not. On the other hand, should she warn Glynis that Joey was out of jail? She decided against that too.

Both women were looking at her expectantly. Nothing to do but come out with it:

'Reason we're here, Glyn, is I need a gun.'

'A gun?' Julia yelped. 'We've come here for a gun!'

'You didn't think I was gonna go after this lot empty-handed, did you?'

Her jaw slack with disbelief, Julia turned away, shaking her head with incredulity.

'I ain't got no guns.' Glynis was looking at her dumbfounded.

'What happened to Sean's stash?'

'I dunno.' Glynis's shoulders sagged as the past rose up to engulf her. 'What the fuck you doing back here anyway? Thought you was supposed to be on witness protection.'

'Some things have happened. And a mate of mine is in trouble. Big trouble. I wouldn't be here if it wasn't desperate.

252

Think back, Glyn,' Kaz pleaded. 'I know the Old Bill took this place apart, but did they touch the shed?'

'What, the garden shed?' Glynis frowned. 'They must've searched it.'

'You ain't done nothing to it since?'

She shook her head. 'It's good for the lawnmower and my tools.' Her voice dropped to an agitated whisper. 'I don't want no trouble, Kaz. I try not to think about the past. I don't mix with none of Sean's old mates. I just go to work and do my best to keep everything nice.'

'And it is nice, Glyn.' Kaz touched her arm gently. 'This place is amazing. Isn't it?' She glanced at Julia for support.

Julia was listening to the exchange with the stunned look of a witness hearing of some past atrocity. But she managed to nod her assent.

Looping her arm round Glynis's shoulder, Kaz gave her a squeeze. 'One time – I'm talking years ago – Sean got completely bladdered and he boasted to me about his stash. A stash of guns, said they was buried under the shed. Not even Dad knew. Said he'd got them off some Irish geezer and he was keeping them for a rainy day.'

'Not Mad Mickey? Him and Sean was really tight.' Glynis's face had taken on a haunted look. The ghosts of the past were crowding in on her.

'Probably. Some IRA connection, I dunno.'

Blinking her heavy, mascaraed lashes Glynis peered down the garden. 'Under the shed? You think they're still there?'

Kaz reached for the door handle, took a breath. 'I fuckin' hope so.'

48

Nicci loved the moment when the booze first hit and a warm loosening cheer slid through her veins. It was the only time she felt at ease with herself. For a brief instant the veil lifted and she could see beyond the sorrow that shadowed her waking hours and haunted her dreams.

The problem was it never lasted. The whiff of elation that came with the first drink soon dulled. And by the third or fourth, the anger came seeping back.

She put her wine glass down and smiled at Rory as he topped it up. They were in a small expensive Italian bistro close to Upper Street in Islington. The wine was red and well chosen – Rory's decision, he hadn't sought her opinion. It was the kind of place where the waiters were ageing grey-haired men who took the ritual of service seriously. They seemed to like the fact they were dealing with a gentleman. Or maybe they just expected a bigger tip. Who cared? Despite being cynical about the whole charade, Nicci was enjoying the wine.

After she'd texted Rory he'd picked her up in Mare Street. He was freshly showered and shaved, giving off a faint aroma of something musky and masculine. Nicci felt scruffy by comparison. She'd fallen out of bed with a hangover and had been on the go all day. Persuading Delgado to do the right thing had been taxing. She sank into the soft leather bucket seat of the old Porsche Boxster and was happy to just let go.

They spoke little on the way to the restaurant. As far as Nicci could recall, they'd always harboured a cordial dislike for one another. Then she remembered the debauched office party. Was it him or the other one, Hugo? Hugo was younger and seemed the more likely candidate for a drunken snog, but she'd been so far gone that night she couldn't be sure. For all she knew, Rory was happily married with kids. But then what was he doing driving a natty old Boxster and why had he dressed for a date?

It was Rory who broached the subject of Turnbull.

'So you used to work for our new colleague and you think he's bad news?'

Nicci twisted the stem of her wine glass. 'That's not just my personal opinion. Disciplinary action was taken against him and he was expelled from the Met for gross misconduct.'

Rory considered this. 'Apparently he told Simon he was made a scapegoat.'

'You were in the army. What happens when an officer betrays his own men and sets them up to fail?'

'Worst-case scenario? Someone gets killed.'

'Someone did get killed.' Nicci took a hefty slug of wine. 'A young DC who Turnbull tasked to work undercover.'

'Doesn't necessarily make it his fault. Though any decent officer feels responsible for all his men.' Rory's eyes clouded. 'Those you lose, you never forget.'

A waiter brought their starters, affording Nicci a chance to take a closer look at her companion. There was something almost comic about his storybook soldier manner, as if he'd decided to play the role of an old-fashioned officer and gentleman. He had no discernible accent. He was scrupulously polite but gave the impression he didn't suffer fools gladly.

Nicci wondered about his history. What was behind this carefully managed facade? Maybe nothing. It could be that he was just another emotionally cauterized veteran.

She picked up her fork and eyed the avocado and crab swimming in vinaigrette. 'I went to talk to Hackney CID about a neighbour of mine. An old lady, nearly ninety. She was stabbed last night outside our block. She died.'

'A mugging?'

'No. They've arrested another neighbour, a soldier recently back from Afghanistan.'

That got Rory's attention. 'What regiment?'

'I don't know.' Nicci put a chunk of avocado in her mouth. She hadn't eaten anything quite so healthy in a while. It tasted far better than she'd expected.

Rory rested his cutlery on the sides of his plate and steepled his fingers. 'Well, if I were going to kill an old lady I'd break her neck.'

Nicci stared at him. Was he really such a cold fish or was it all part of the act?

'Easy. Quick.' He raised his hands to cup an imaginary head, then gave it an abrupt twist. 'Part of the training.'

They continued to eat in silence. He seemed comfortable with that.

'I started kickboxing as a kid, then got into mixed martial arts. Used to belong to a club, but I let it go.' Nicci watched him, hoping this might provoke a reaction. Rory didn't seem like the kind of man who'd approve of such unladylike behaviour.

'What made you give up?' To her disappointment, the question was phrased with a bland curiosity.

'I got pregnant.'

They relapsed into silence again. The waiter cleared their

plates. Rory replenished her glass, emptying the bottle. He called for another, then leant his forearms on the table.

'Have you met Duncan Linton?'

'Briefly.'

'You know who he is?'

'Yeah, he's one of our main investors.' Rory's tone, the silences and the wine were all conspiring to make Nicci feel obstreperous. 'I thought we were here to talk about Turnbull.'

'That's what we're doing. It seems to me that Turnbull is Linton's appointment, and Simon feels unable to refuse.'

'That may be so.'

Rory rearranged his napkin. 'I think it most certainly is so. The question is, what can be done about it?'

'You got me there.' Nicci took a large mouthful of wine. She realized she was getting pissed, which had not been the intention. But they were on their second bottle and the main course was a long time coming.

Rory raised his own glass, took a sip. 'When I left the army I thought of teaching. Then a former colleague suggested the security sector. SBA is the third company I've worked for and it's easy to move around because of the rate of expansion.'

'So if you don't get on with Turnbull you can always leave.' Even to herself, Nicci sounded flip bordering on rude.

'I like SBA. I think it has great potential. And so does my brother.'

'Your brother?'

'He works in the financial sector. Now that we're established, he's convinced it should be possible to attract alternative investors to SBA.'

'You mean boot Linton out?'

'I agree with you. The association with a disgraced cop will taint the brand.'

'You want to persuade Simon to look for alternative backers?'

'Exactly. You know the man far better than me. He's got himself in a hole with Linton. The question is, will he take advice and look to bring on board new equity partners?'

Through the warming fug of red wine the evening's real agenda began to dawn on Nicci. Rory was planning his own takeover bid and he was wining and dining her because he wanted her help.

49

Kaz took a crowbar to the narrow boards that formed the floor of the shed. The timber was sturdy and dry, she had to press down with her entire body weight to lever the first one up. It cracked in the centre and she wrenched it free with both hands.

Glynis and Julia stood by the door, both tense and anxious; behind them in a heap were the lawnmower, tools and garden paraphernalia that had been unceremoniously chucked out of the shed.

The second board was slightly easier. But as Kaz ripped it up a shard of broken wood lacerated her hand. She yelped and rocked back on her heels. Her palm started to bleed. Sweating from the effort, heart thumping, a worried glance at her watch told her it was already after seven o'clock. She was running out of time.

Julia stepped into the shed, rested a hand on Kaz's shoulder. 'Let me have a go.' The enterprise still struck her as totally mad, not to mention illegal, but she'd got over her initial shock and now Kaz's fervour was sucking her in.

Kaz gave her a sceptical look but allowed Julia to take the crowbar. As she stood up, clasping her bloody hand, Julia began to attack the floorboards with surprising strength and ferocity. She prised up four boards in quick succession to reveal a sheet of heavy-duty black polythene underneath.

Julia turned to Glynis. 'Have you got a Stanley knife?'

Glynis turned away to rummage in a toolbox. She wasn't happy about her home being invaded in this way, but Kaz had been the one who'd saved her from spending the rest of her life as Sean's punching bag. She owed her.

Julia, crowbar in hand, glanced up at Kaz, who was still clutching her hand. 'You need to stop that bleeding or you won't be able to shoot anyone.'

Was this some attempt at black humour? Kaz really couldn't tell. Her assumption had been that Julia, mousy on the outside, was equally timorous within. Maybe she was wrong. After all, Julia was the one who'd been fighting against the odds for a proper investigation into Helen's death. Kaz pulled a tissue from her pocket to staunch the blood oozing from her palm.

Glynis handed Julia a Stanley knife. Julia knelt down and carved a slash in the plastic, then a second slash at ninety degrees to the first. She pulled back a triangle of sheeting to reveal the end of a dark blue holdall nestling in a shallow depression covered in cobwebs and dust.

The three women peered down into the hole at it.

Glynis turned to Kaz, wide-eyed. 'Bloody hell, you was right.'

Working together, Julia and Kaz rapidly excavated a big enough opening to pull the bag free. It was Julia who hauled it up and out of its hiding place and dumped it down between them. Their eyes met. It was some kind of sports bag, long and narrow, possibly designed for cricket. The zip was partially corroded with rust. Kaz gave it a forceful yank with her good hand and drew it back.

Inside the holdall was a soft plastic bin liner. Whatever was inside was heavy. Kaz needed Julia's help to lift it out of the bag. They brought it to rest on a piece of shed flooring that had remained intact. Kaz reached inside and pulled out a rifle. It was nearly three feet long from stock to barrel, but the top appeared to be missing. The women exchanged incredulous looks.

'A fucking rifle! That is not what I fucking need.' Kaz dived back inside the bin liner and brought out several smaller components and another disassembled rifle.

She threw them down. 'Shit, and it's all in fucking bits!'

'Do you know what kind of gun it is?' Julia frowned.

'Looks like an AK47 to me.' Glynis surprised them both. She shrugged. 'I seen Sean with one. He loved playing around with it. Well, you know Sean.'

Kaz flashed her an angry scowl. 'Oh, so now you remember? You can't tell me he dug a fucking hole under the shed without you noticing.'

A sorrowful look spread over Glynis's face; close to tears, she turned away.

Pressing the tissue to her bleeding palm Kaz exhaled. 'I'm sorry, Glyn. This ain't your fault, none of it is.'

Julia checked her watch. 'We're running out of time here – why don't we just call Nicci?'

Kaz glared at her. 'You think she knows how to assemble an assault rifle?'

'Even if you can put it together, what the fuck are you going to do with it?' Julia shook her head in frustration. 'You're going to stand outside a pub in Tottenham with it? Don't you think that might attract some attention?'

Kaz slumped back on her heels. Her hand was sore, but the real pain was searing through her brain, spinning round her synapses with the image of Yasmin being slowly choked to death. And it was all her fault. She bent double, clasping her arms around her body as if that would somehow help her hold it all together. It didn't. Tipping back her head, she howled with despair.

50

Nicci lay flat on her back staring up at the hairline crack that snaked across her bedroom ceiling. She was definitely pissed. But in the last year she'd cultivated a hard head. A bottle of wine didn't finish her off in the same way it would've done before her bereavement. She wished it had, at least she'd have an excuse.

She could hear his soft breathing though she didn't turn to look at him. Rory was dozing after his exertions. The sex had been fast and furious. He was a passionate lover, which was not what she'd expected, given how buttoned-up and cynically detached he was the rest of the time.

The drive home, the ritual coffee invitation, the mild embarrassment at last night's washing-up – Nicci had observed their courtship dance from some remote part of her own mind. Earlier, when he'd taken her gently by the elbow to shepherd her out of the restaurant, the pheromonal hit had aroused her curiosity as much as anything. What would it be like now? After all that had happened, how would it make her feel? Factoring in the amount of alcohol they'd both consumed it would probably be a washout.

In the event, Nicci had been agreeably surprised. Rory was confident, his desire for her unambiguous but not selfish. Apart from him asking whether this was 'all right', neither of them had spoken. She'd allowed herself to let go.

The sensations that swept through her body seemed to come from a place far away and long ago. She came quite quickly; it wasn't earth-shattering, just a simple sense of pleasure and release.

Resting on her back, her mind meandered down memory lane to her early days with Tim. They'd met at Hendon, though they were on different courses. Back then he'd been a joyous young man, handsome, fun; there'd been plenty of girls after him. She remembered their first sexual encounter. He was extremely nervous, a lad of barely twenty, full of jokes and japes with his mates, but shy of the opposite sex.

Nicci was a year older and more experienced – she'd been to uni, had three boyfriends but no orgasms – apart from the ones she'd given herself. Still, she knew how to put him at his ease, stroke his ego, and they'd learnt together. They'd laughed a lot, played a lot; in the bubble of their romance it felt as though dreams could come true.

Coming out of Hendon near the top of her class, Nicci was always headed for CID. Tim was a complete petrolhead. Being a traffic cop, out on the open road, suited his temperament. They were a carefree couple, until the unplanned birth of their daughter.

Nicci never found it that much of a problem juggling motherhood and a career. She had plenty of energy and optimism, she adored Sophie and they muddled along. However, encouraged by his father, Tim got it into his head that having a wife and child meant it was time for him to stop mucking about, step up to his responsibilities and be a man. Which would have been fine except that in Tim's mind that translated into him being the one with the career and Nicci being a full-time mother.

Tim's parents were traditional people. Nicci managed to

get on with them but had never considered how their narrow views might have shaped their son. As her happy-go-lucky husband gradually morphed into a clone of his father, the rows began. Sophie was five when Nicci finally threw in the towel, picked up her daughter and left.

Under family pressure she'd gone along with various attempts at mediation. But a lecture from the Armstrongs' family priest had been the last straw. She went out and shagged a young DC from Fraud, who'd been temporarily seconded to her unit. She kept the relationship going just long enough to give Tim grounds for divorce. His family reluctantly acquiesced in the belief that she was a scarlet woman who'd entrapped their naive son.

In the years that followed, contrary to what her former in-laws liked to believe, she'd lived a largely celibate life. It was just her and Sophie, and life as a working single parent had not been easy. Still, compared to now it was a time of bliss.

Glancing across the pillow at Rory she tried to recall the last man she'd actually slept with. It must've been a holiday in Cornwall that she and Sophie had taken with her parents. Late at night in the hotel bar she'd fallen into conversation with a local fisherman. He wooed her with tales of his valour as a member of the volunteer lifeboat crew. She knew it was probably a chat-up line he used regularly on the tourists. But they'd had several nights of summer sex and dawn walks on the beach. She thought his name was Steve – or was it Sam?

Rory opened his eyes, raised himself on one elbow, smiled and kissed her forehead. 'I need the bathroom.'

As he got out of bed and retrieved his discarded condom from the floor, she surveyed his naked back. He had a thin white scar following the curve of his torso from the spine round to the front of his ribs. He padded down the hallway and she sat up wondering whether to have a cigarette. He clearly didn't smoke, but she had a pack in the bedside drawer and it was her flat.

She was weighing the pros and cons when she noticed the screen of her phone light up. She'd put it on silent back in the restaurant. Sighing, she reached over and clicked it on – she had twenty missed calls and five texts, all from Julia Hadley.

51

Julia sat in her car, phone in hand. She was parked in a side street in an area of north-east London that was unfamiliar to her. The houses seemed ordinary, if a little scruffy, but according to Kaz the one they'd pulled up outside was a brothel.

The return trip to London had been at breakneck speed. Traffic cameras flashed and they were lucky not to be stopped. Julia had been scared stiff but at the same time, she had to admit, exhilarated. Despite her best efforts, it had proved impossible to get to Tottenham by eight o'clock.

At Julia's suggestion, Glynis had produced a laptop and they'd gone on the Net for instructions on how to reassemble the assault rifle. It turned out to be surprisingly straightforward.

The same couldn't be said for the unspoken bond that linked Kaz and Glynis – that remained impossible to fathom. Glynis seemed a nervous and meek woman, the polar opposite of Kaz, yet she'd been ready to do anything Kaz asked of her. She had even offered them the loan of her dog.

Buster, the Staffie, looked mean in his studded collar but was actually quite a benign beast. He was sitting in the tiny back seat of the Figaro now, occasionally licking his chops and drooling.

Julia glanced at the dog and wondered what the hell she

was doing parked outside a brothel with an AK47 in her boot, waiting for a convicted criminal.

Kaz had rung the doorbell a few minutes ago and disappeared inside the house. Julia had phoned Nicci Armstrong for the umpteenth time, but she still wasn't picking up. She'd given up the idea of calling the police – it was too late for that. Innocent concerned citizens didn't drive around with guns in their cars and consort with criminals.

An image of Helen's sardonic smile flashed into her mind. Julia's predicament certainly would've amused her. On one occasion Helen had coldly accused her of being the straightest lesbian she'd ever met. If straight meant upright and honest, she hoped she was certainly that. She'd never broken any laws to her knowledge, although she was feeling extremely uncomfortable about the rifle.

Kaz had slotted a loaded magazine into the barrel, as per the instructions, and as far as Julia could see the gun was ready to be fired. Was she about to become an accessory to murder? The situation would've been surreal if it wasn't so frightening.

The front door of the house opened and Kaz came out.

She jogged towards the car and jumped into the passenger seat. 'Okay. I got a possible address.'

'What do you mean "possible"?'

'Just fucking drive, Julia. Bottom of the street, turn left.'

The tone of voice didn't brook any argument. Julia started the car and did as she was told. They navigated several backstreets until they hit a main road. Brow furrowed, Kaz glanced up and down. She had a calmness and concentration about her, even though both fists were clenched.

The road contained a range of shops and fast-food outlets. Drinkers enjoying the summer evening spilled out of a pub on the corner. Kaz scanned the shopfronts and her eye came to rest on a kebab shop next to a Turkish grocery.

She seemed to waver but only for a second. 'Turn right. Then take that side road down there on the left.'

'What are you going to do?' Julia's palms were sweating.

There was a darkness in Kaz's eye, a steeliness that scared Julia.

Kaz simply smiled. 'I'm gonna get a kebab.'

52

A concreted alleyway leading to a line of lock-up garages ran behind the parade of shops. It was barely wide enough for a car to squeeze past the row of overflowing dumpsters.

Kaz moved cautiously, keeping to the shadows, but she was pretty well concealed. In the summer twilight the alley was already quite dark and lights were on in the back windows of the flats and offices above the shops.

She'd left a nervous Julia parked in the adjacent side street with instructions to set the dog on anyone who hassled her. Julia had stared at her mutely, but Kaz had to admit the woman had some bottle. She'd expected her to simply bail after they'd dug up the guns. However, Julia'd shown no sign of that, although she did keep bleating on about Nicci.

There'd been no time for niceties during Kaz's visit to the brothel. She'd seized Hanna by the throat, held her against a wall and demanded to know where she could find Mr Kemal. Before leaving, she took the precaution of trashing the girl's phone. Hanna had been surly. The kidnapping of Yasmin obviously meant a promotion for her and Kaz didn't think it would take her long to find another phone to alert the boss.

The back door to the kebab shop was ajar and the smell of meat and hot fat wafted from the bright interior into the yard behind. Kaz gently eased the door open a few more inches and peered inside. There was a stairway on the right, then a corridor that appeared to lead to the kitchen. Two men in chefs' whites could be glimpsed moving back and forth. The kebab shop was doing steady business.

Kaz had the gun resting against her right shoulder, muzzle tilted down, safety catch on, hand grasping the pistol grip. She drew a breath to steady herself then stepped through the doorway, turned to the right and crept slowly up the stairs. Under duress, Hanna had told her that Mr Kemal had an office above the kebab shop. She reached the top of the stairs and found herself on a landing facing two doors. Light was seeping from under both. She hesitated. She had a fifty per cent chance of being right. Assuming he was here in the first place.

The decision was taken out of her hands as one of the doors opened.

At the sight of her, Sadik Kemal froze in the doorway. His lips twisted into an amused sneer. 'What the fuck?'

Kaz flicked the safety catch off and pointed the rifle. 'Don't think I won't shoot. I'll fucking cut you in half. You won't be the first bloke I've killed. So back up! Nice and slowly.'

Sadik raised his palms. 'You're one fucking crazy bitch.'

'Yeah. I am. So do it.'

He edged back through the open door into the room behind. The office wasn't large but it was smartly furnished. Several filing cabinets, two newish desktop computers, a couple of high-back, leather swivel chairs. Seated in one of them, a grey-haired man was staring straight up at Kaz over half-moon glasses.

Sadik mumbled something in Turkish, but the other man seemed unfazed by the invasion. He looked much older than

Sadik. He wore a polo shirt and a diamond-patterned cash-mere sweater as if he'd just stepped off a golf course.

Wearily he removed his glasses. 'Miss Phelps, I presume.' The Turkish accent was still there, but less pronounced than Sadik's.

Kaz took up a position in the corner of the room away from the door, back against the filing cabinets. 'Where's Yasmin?'

'Doing business, I should hope.'

'You need to call your scumbag of a son and get him to bring Yasmin here now. And if she's dead, you're going to be joining her.'

Mr Kemal leant back in his chair. He spoke in Turkish to his brother. The tone was one of mild annoyance. Sadik's reply was accompanied by a shrug.

'There seems to have been a misunderstanding.' Mr Kemal waved his hand dismissively. 'But I'm sure we can sort it out.'

Kaz found that her breathing was remarkably steady; the adrenaline was pumping, but nevertheless she felt sharp. The gun rested lightly in her hands, tucked snugly against her shoulder. She had no real idea what the outcome would be if she pulled the trigger. She presumed it would be messy and that gave her confidence.

She directed her gaze at Kemal. 'Just call him.'

The man behind the desk sighed and picked up his phone. Kaz knew she was on dangerous ground. He could be calling anyone. Half a dozen armed meatheads could come storming up those stairs. The conversation was short, but the tone sounded very like an exasperated father lecturing his son.

He clicked the phone off and smiled. 'He's on his way.'

Sadik flopped down in the other chair, the sneer never leaving his lips. Mr Kemal picked up a pack of cigarettes from the table, took one out and lit it. Then the brothers both stared at her. Presumably they were hoping to unnerve her, but their attitude only fuelled her anger and her resolve.

'Y'know, it should never have come to this.' Mr Kemal drew on his cigarette, smiled at her through the smoke. 'My son is young and sometimes foolish. But I'm a businessman. I've seen your product. It's very good.'

Kaz met his eye. 'What fucking product?'

He flicked ash from his cigarette into a small ceramic ashtray. '"The best weed in London" – isn't that your slogan?'

'I'm not here to do business. I don't do business with people who kidnap my friends.'

'And what about Sean? Maybe I should be talking to him.'

Sean again? What was that all about? Perhaps he was being used as a front to continue Joey's cannabis business. If so, who the hell was running things? Questions flashed through her mind. Too many questions.

She brushed them aside, forced herself to concentrate. She knew Kemal's purpose was to distract her.

'Right now I've got the gun. So you're talking to me.'

The two men exchanged looks. If one of them made a move, Kaz expected it to be Sadik.

'You ever shoot one of those things?' he smirked. 'It's a big gun for a woman.'

Kaz returned his gaze with her own piercing stare. 'The advantage is you don't have to be a particularly good shot. I can tear your balls off and rip your stomach open with one short burst. At this range, I can hardly miss.'

That wiped the smile off his face. He mumbled something in his own language. It sounded like a curse.

They remained in silence for the next five minutes. Kaz didn't let her eyes waver and they gave up trying to stare her down. Finally a car could be heard pulling up outside in the alley. Mr Kemal sat with his back to the open window, smiling to himself. Kaz knew he was waiting for her to make a mistake.

Footsteps in the downstairs hallway were followed by a voice floating up the stairs. 'Baba?'

Mr Kemal turned his palm upwards. He had the same hooded eyes as his brother. 'You want him, he's here.'

Kaz adjusted her position so the gun was pointing straight at Kemal. 'Call him. Just Yasmin and him. No one else.'

Sadik shouted something in Turkish. He was getting fidgety, which made him dangerous.

The boy downstairs replied, but only briefly. He could be heard retreating down the hall and into the alley. The car door opened and that's when Kaz heard Yasmin's voice drift up through the window. She was alive.

And she was begging: 'Nah, please! I call her. I do what you want. She'll come if I call. She will.' The tone was desperate, punctuated with sobs.

Mr Kemal turned his head slowly towards Kaz. He gave her a sardonic smile. 'Friends, eh? Sell you down the river every time.'

Kaz eyeballed him. 'Only 'cause that scumbag son of yours tortured her.'

Heavy thumping footfalls could be heard as Tevfik propelled Yasmin up the stairs. As he thrust her through the door she was crying and pleading. Tevfik saw Kaz first and his arm went round Yasmin's throat.

His face crumpled into a scowl of pure rage. 'I fucking break her neck, you fucking bitch!'

Mr Kemal sighed. 'Let her go.'

Tevfik replied angrily in Turkish.

Kemal shook his head wearily. 'How is it I am cursed with such a stupid son?'

Giving his father a petulant look Tevfik released her. Yasmin simply stared at Kaz. Relief and fear mingled in her battered and bleeding face.

Kaz took a breath. 'Now I want everyone to listen carefully to my instructions. 'Cause if you wanna stay alive, you follow them.'

53

Taking the Kemals by surprise was one thing, but Kaz had known from the outset that getting out of there unscathed with Yasmin would be another matter entirely. And Yasmin was a trembling wreck. One eye was closed up completely and she was limping. She had problems just standing upright.

She continued to cry and mumble. 'I'm sorry, Mr Kemal. I'm really sorry.'

Kemal glanced at Kaz and shrugged. 'You see? She has the mentality of a whore. What can you do?'

His total disdain infuriated Kaz. In spite of the golfer's get-up and the neat office, he still exuded the hypocrisy of a pimp.

'Get up,' she ordered.

He rose slowly to his feet. 'Okay, I give you fair warning. This is where you make a choice. You leave here now, alone, I'll let this go. You pursue this course, you'll end up getting yourself killed for an ungrateful whore.'

Kaz jabbed the barrel of the gun into the side of his neck. 'Or maybe it's you who gets killed?'

He raised both palms. With her free hand she grasped the soft cashmere sleeve of his jumper and pulled him round the desk. Sadik and Tevfik stood glaring at her, less than a couple of metres away – two mad dogs wired and ready to spring.

She glanced at Yasmin. 'You go in front. Down the stairs, out into the alley.' Yasmin didn't move, she was shaking and crying. 'Trust me, Yas, it's the only way you're gonna live.'

Lip trembling, she met Kaz's gaze. Holding on to the filing cabinet for support, she staggered towards the door. Once she was through it, Kaz backed out of the room after her. She towed Kemal behind her, the barrel of the gun pressed against his neck.

She knew once she was out of the office Sadik would go for any weapons that might be stashed in the filing cabinet or a desk drawer. Then the shooting would start.

Yasmin's progress down the stairs was painfully slow. She stumbled several times and fell once. Kaz used Kemal as a shield and remained at the top of the stairs, staring through into the office.

She could see Sadik edging forward. 'Don't you two fucking move, or I'll blow his fucking head off.'

Mr Kemal spoke curtly in Turkish.

Sadik raised his hands. 'Hey, no sweat.'

Once Yasmin had reached the downstairs hall, Kaz changed her grip from Kemal's sleeve to his collar. 'I'm going down first and you're coming slowly after me. Backwards. One step at a time.'

Kemal didn't speak. He obeyed Kaz's instructions. In the office beyond she could hear Sadik and Tevfik having a whispered conversation. Drawers and the filing cabinets were being opened. They were searching. Kaz reckoned she had maybe thirty seconds to get out into the alley.

Yasmin was already outside, her breath coming in gasps, leaning against the wall. A four-by-four was parked beyond the yard gate; the driver standing beside it was young, one of Tevfik's mates. Unsure how to react, he was glaring at them.

Kaz yanked Kemal's collar. 'Tell him to come in the yard. Over there, where I can see him.'

Kemal spoke in Turkish. The young driver complied. It gave Kaz some satisfaction to see that the Turk had begun to sweat. She could feel his tension, smell his fear; it was contained, but it was there.

Then Yasmin gave a hoarse shout. 'Kaz! The window.'

Her eyes flew up and she saw Sadik framed in the open window above them, brandishing a handgun. He took aim. Kaz yanked Kemal round to cover herself.

Panic erupted in him. 'Sadik, no!'

Sadik cursed, lowered his arm and disappeared.

Kaz turned to Yasmin. 'Down the alley, to the right!'

With Yasmin limping ahead of her, Kaz dragged Kemal out into the alley. It was now completely dark, the surface uneven. This was the part of the plan that Kaz hadn't thought through in any detail. In truth, she hadn't ever really expected to get this far. Then at the end of the alleyway, standing with her back to the lighted street, she saw Julia. She was simply standing there, hanging on to Buster. The dog started to bark.

Kaz nearly flipped. 'Get in the fucking car!' The car was parked across the road. Kaz's panic rose – how the hell would they get to it and escape before Sadik started shooting? 'Now, Julia!' But Julia didn't move.

As Kaz tried to propel Kemal along in front of her, he twisted round and made a grab for the gun. He wasn't a large man, but he was wiry and fit for his age. He wrenched it from her grasp and shouted out in Turkish.

Suddenly from the dark maw of the alley a fist flew out and struck Kemal squarely under the jaw. He reeled back and collapsed, the gun clattering from his grip. Kaz froze in surprise, but only for a second. She was stooping to retrieve it when two figures emerged from the shadows. Kaz didn't recognize the man; she assumed his fist had felled Kemal. But she did recognize Nicci Armstrong.

The man grasped her arm urgently. 'Give me the gun.'

Nicci was beside him. 'It's okay. Just do it.'

Kaz let him take it. He spun round, checked it, pointed it upwards and sprayed a hail of bullets into the air above the alley, then fired a volley into the back of the four-by-four and the wall of the yard behind the kebab shop.

The shots pinged and cracked and ricocheted off car and wall. Shattered brick and wood flew upwards in an eruption of smoke and dust.

Nicci caught hold of Yasmin, hauled an arm round her shoulder. 'Right, let's get out of here, before my former colleagues arrive.'

54

Kaz sat on a chair in the waiting room at Whipps Cross A&E. She felt drained but curiously calm. It was approaching eleven and the place was filling up with the casualties of a night on the lash. Nicci was speaking to the charge nurse. Yasmin had been stretchered away into the treatment area.

The man, Rory, had driven Kaz with a petrified Yasmin crammed on her knee in the passenger seat of his old Porsche. Nicci and Julia had followed in the Figaro. He hadn't spoken during the journey. His manner was detached and alert. Kaz wondered who the hell he was. Once he'd deposited them at the hospital, he'd driven off. Julia went in search of a parking space whilst Kaz and Nicci had practically carried Yasmin into the department.

Kaz watched Nicci. She still dealt with situations as if she were a cop. And the charge nurse was responding accordingly. It crossed Kaz's mind that she should get up and out of there while she could. Nicci had no power to detain her. But she and the bloke had the gun – definitely incriminating evidence.

Having given the nurse a nod of thanks, Nicci walked over.

It was hard to read the look she gave Kaz – pissed off, certainly. 'She's gone to X-ray, but she's been badly punched about. Several fractured ribs, internal bleeding. Bones of the cheek could be fractured too. She'll be admitted.'

Kaz managed a thin smile. 'Thanks.'

Nicci shook her head fiercely as if she were trying to erase the whole event. 'Fucking hell, Karen! What did you think you were playing at?'

Ignoring this, Kaz exhaled. 'What if the Kemals come after her?'

'I'll talk to the local CID. They'll want her as a witness, so she'll be protected.'

'What will you say to them?'

Nicci had no answer for this. What the hell would she say? The delicacy of her position hadn't escaped her. On the phone she'd provided the police with the sketchiest outline of events, posing as a concerned passer-by.

'Y'know, a stunt like this, by rights you should be headed straight back to jail.'

Kaz dipped her head, stared down at the tough cord carpeting. She didn't speak. Was there any point trying to explain? Cop or no cop, Nicci lived on the other side of the fence. She would never get it.

Folding her arms, Nicci positioned herself right in front of Kaz. Her tone was one of sarcastic belligerence. 'I don't know what it is about you, but Julia's got you pegged as some kind of hero. And you know and I know that you were shagging her partner behind her back. So how does that come about, eh?'

Kaz's gaze rose defiantly to meet hers. 'If you're gonna dob me in, do it. But I don't have to justify myself to you.'

'It would serve you right if I did. Where the hell did you get a gun like that?'

'Ah yeah, the gun.' Kaz gave a wry smile. 'I just borrowed it to scare them. It was your mate who sprayed bullets all over the shop like he was in some fucking back alley in Baghdad.

You might have a bit of a problem explaining that to the Old Bill, don't you think?'

Nicci scanned the room. They were attracting curious glances from the restless gaggle of druggies, drunks and walking wounded waiting their turn to be seen.

Lowering her voice, she moved in closer. 'You are one ungrateful bitch, y'know that?'

'Yeah, well, that's pretty much my mum's opinion too.'

The two women glared at one another. Nicci was frustrated and furious in equal measure. How on earth had she landed in this mess? Didn't she have enough problems?

When they'd arrived on the scene and heard Julia's garbled summary of events, she'd called the police. But Rory had simply crossed the road and headed straight into the alley behind the kebab shop. Nicci was completely taken aback. She had no idea what he planned to do, so she'd followed. It was only then that she'd realized how crazy he was. The buttoned-up major was just a facade. He was a combat soldier and this was what he craved – the danger, the adrenaline rush. Gangsters or insurgents, they were all the same to him. He loved conflict because like her he had a creature of his own hidden inside and it needed feeding.

'You want gratitude?' Kaz curled her lip. 'Okay, I'm grateful.' She kowtowed. 'Thank you. Thank you.'

The automatic doors opened with a swish, bringing a cool rush of night air as Julia stepped into A&E.

She hurried over to join them with an anxious frown. 'Will she be all right?'

'Hopefully.' Nicci sighed and turned away.

Julia met Kaz's eye with an apologetic look. 'I didn't know what else to do. I'm sorry if, well . . .'

Kaz gave her a rueful smile. 'You did the right thing.' Julia still looked sceptical. 'Really. You did. Thank you.'

They both turned to face the ex-cop. Nicci had her back to them, arms clutched around her torso. She appeared to be brooding.

Julia reached out tentatively. 'You okay, Nicci?'

She spun round. 'No, I'm not fucking okay!' Glancing round, she brought her voice down to a whisper. 'Now unless you two want to spend the night in a police interview room explaining to a bunch of not very sympathetic cops what the hell you thought you were doing, you need to get out of here.'

Julia gave her a pleading look. 'I'm really sorry for involving you, but I—'

'Shut up, Julia. Just listen and do what I say. That way we'll maybe all avoid getting arrested.'

'Sorry.' Julia dropped her eyes like a scolded child. But Kaz met the ex-cop's fierce gaze with a jut of her chin.

Nicci raised her index finger and eyeballed Kaz. 'You owe me. So tomorrow morning, ten a.m., be at my office. 'Cause you are going to give us a complete and detailed account of your relationship with Helen Warner, including the meeting in Glasgow. You don't turn up, I'll make sure the relevant authorities know you're in breach of your licence and that a warrant is issued for your arrest.'

She produced a business card from her pocket and thrust it at Kaz. 'I'm serious. Be there.'

Kaz took the card. There was still intransigence in her demeanour, but her tone was less confrontational now. 'Yeah. Okay. All this stuff today was . . . well, the result of a stupid mistake. I came down here to find out what happened to Helen.' Her gaze floated over to Julia's tense face. 'We all want the same thing. The truth. And I got nothing to hide.'

Nicci couldn't help noticing the soppy expression on Julia's face when Kaz looked at her. Had grief made her stupid? She was being taken in, maybe even seduced. Kaz Phelps had always been smooth, the lies seamless. Would she even turn up tomorrow? Nicci doubted it.

Realizing she was in danger of losing it with them completely, she waved them toward the door. 'Just go home. Now. We'll talk tomorrow.'

Julia nodded. She and Kaz headed for the exit and Nicci watched them disappear through the automatic doors.

Being alone finally was a relief. She had a toxic headache brought on by red wine and stress. Pulling some change out of her pocket, she walked over to the vending machine. What she longed for was a stiff drink and a cigarette, but a liquid sugar-hit would have to do. As she fed the coins into the machine she reflected on the sheer madness of the evening.

She'd got drunk and had sex with a man she hardly knew then watched him shoot up an alley in North London. Had anyone actually been hit? She hoped not. And to top it all off, she was now protecting a convicted criminal who should be sent back to jail.

The vending machine dumped a plastic bottle of orange fizz in its tray. Nicci lifted it out, cracked it open and took a long draught. Ethel Huxtable's murder, the Helen Warner case . . . the thoughts kept on and on, spiralling round in her brain. She had to get a grip.

Having downed half the bottle she noticed an unmarked car with a blue flashing light drawing up outside. It was time to make herself scarce. She screwed the top back on to the bottle and headed off down a side corridor in search of an alternative way out.

55

The meeting had been called for nine thirty and Fiona Calder presented herself in good time, in fact several minutes early. However, when she entered the Commissioner's office, Phil Slattery was already there, comfortably ensconced, with a half-drunk cup of coffee on the table in front of him. The boys, it seemed, had been having a cosy chat. As a female officer she was used to finding herself out of the loop. Much lip service was paid to ridding the organization of institutional racism, but institutional sexism was simply ignored.

She painted on her best smile; she wasn't taking any prisoners. 'Morning, sir. Sorry if I'm a little late.'

The Commissioner gave her a vague smile. 'Not a problem. Phil has been bringing me up to speed. Help yourself to coffee.'

'Thank you, sir.' She picked up the silver thermos jug from the side table. 'Can I get anyone a refill?'

Both men declined. Slattery watched her, a sour and vengeful look flickering over his features. He'd had a bad twenty-four hours trying to shovel up the shit she'd dumped on him. Now the smug bitch was making them wait as she poured herself a coffee and settled at the conference table.

Calder could feel the resentment pulsing off him. He was on a short fuse, which could play to her advantage. She took a sip of her drink and waited.

The Commissioner removed his glasses and pinched the flesh between his eyebrows. 'I think the decision to pull the plug on the inquest was essentially sound. The problem is, where do we go with it now?'

Slattery fidgeted in his seat. 'I really don't see how a week's adjournment helps us. The investigation is complete. The woman committed suicide. All it's succeeded in doing is stirring up media speculation and making things worse for the family.'

The Commissioner gave Calder a quizzical glance. She remained silent.

He sighed. 'To be fair, Phil, I think this is a question of erring on the side of caution. If the family reject the suicide verdict, we don't want to appear negligent in any way.'

'It's not the family, it's her bloody partner.' Slattery was having a real problem holding on to his temper; Calder's calm presence was winding him up even more. 'Julia Hadley's the one who hired Simon Blake and his crew.' He shot Calder an accusing glance.

She made a conscious effort to relax into her chair. He was spoiling for a row but there was no way she'd let herself be drawn in. What would be the point?

It was obvious the Commissioner was starting to get impatient with Slattery. He rose from his chair and strolled to the window. 'Phil, I think you'd better tell Fiona about your conversation with Hollister.'

The Detective Superintendent looked surprised. 'That really was only for your ears, sir.'

Calder smiled to herself. Bingo! Slattery was relying on boys' club rules, but anger had got the better of him. He'd openly criticized the Commissioner's decision and now he was being slapped down for it.

The boss met his aggrieved eye. 'I appreciate what you're trying to do here, Phil. But when it comes to politics, I rely on Fiona's judgement.'

Slattery picked up his coffee cup and drained it. He'd ballsed this up completely and he knew it.

Calder decided it was time to give him a helping hand: 'Of course, I'm not familiar with the details of the case, but Robert Hollister is an old family friend of the Warners, isn't he?'

Slattery aimed a baleful look at her. 'It seems he'd become more than that. He and Helen Warner had apparently been involved in an affair for some time.'

'I thought she was a lesbian. Surely her partner's a woman.'

Slattery shrugged. 'Beats me. I'm just telling you what Hollister said. They'd been having this affair. She was pretty smitten with him. He decided to end it. She was very upset, begged him to reconsider. He refused, admits he was pretty harsh with her. A week later she took her own life.'

Calder leant forward. 'Has he made a statement to this effect?'

An uncomfortable look of complicity passed between Slattery and the Commissioner.

It was the Commissioner who picked up the baton. 'This only came out in a confidential conversation yesterday after the inquest was adjourned. It certainly corroborates all the other evidence that Phil has gathered.'

'Is there some reluctance on Hollister's part to make a formal statement?'

Slattery jumped in. 'I think he's a decent man trying to do the right thing. But obviously the political repercussions of this could be huge for him. You know what the media are like. They'd tear him to shreds.'

Calder tilted her head towards the Commissioner. 'So we're not asking him to make a statement?'

'The thing is, Fiona, do we have to?'

'If he's asserting that Helen Warner killed herself over him, then I think the Coroner and his jury need to hear that assertion tested in open court.'

'And what bloody good's that going to do anyone?' Slattery was glaring straight at her.

'So we believe him?' She raised her eyebrows. 'I'm just asking the question, Phil.'

His face had crumpled into a scowl. 'Robert Hollister's putting his career on the line here.' He drummed his index finger on the smooth, oak-veneered table to emphasize the point. 'Given the circumstances, why the hell would he lie? He didn't have to speak out.'

She pursed her lips. 'A private word with you is hardly speaking out.'

'Fiona, the stupid woman killed herself. Tragic, but there it is. All the evidence points to it.'

The Commissioner returned to his chair and settled back into it, resting his palms on the soft leather arms. Fixing his officers with a pensive smile, he prepared to wrap the discussion up. 'These are difficult times. The spectre of privatization is not going to go away. It's corroding the organization inside and out. You know this better than anyone, Fiona.'

'Yes, sir, I do.' Her mind skittered back to Alan Turnbull and his blatant attempt to set her up for a charge of misconduct in a public office – an attempt which had damn near succeeded.

'We need our allies,' intoned the Commissioner. 'And Robert Hollister's commitment to the public service ethic is solid. We get a change of government, he'll become Home

Secretary – that could help us a lot. A hell of a lot. So I'm asking myself the question: how is justice best served here?'

Calder already knew his answer – protecting Hollister was about to become the Met's priority. A thorough and proper investigation of Helen Warner's death might put him in jeopardy, so that must be blocked.

She glanced across at Slattery, saw the relief on his face. Did his 'confidential conversation' with Hollister really only take place yesterday? Or had he been in cahoots with the politician all along? She strongly suspected the latter. What was clear to her was that she'd reached an impasse. But the Commissioner wasn't the only one weighing the interests of justice in his mind. Fiona Calder had asked herself the same question. And come up with a radically different answer.

56

Starting the day with paracetamol, a cigarette and strong coffee was becoming an unfortunate habit of Nicci's. She'd tried to call Rory but he wasn't picking up. It was hardly likely that he'd tell anyone what had happened, but she wanted to make sure they had their stories straight in case the police traced her 999 call. And then of course there was the victim herself, Yasmin. What would she say? Nicci had rung the hospital and left a message asking the charge nurse to remind the police that Yasmin would need protection. More than that she'd resolved to keep a low profile. It wasn't her mess; she wasn't carrying the can.

On her way into the office she'd received a text from Delgado asking her to call him. Presumably he'd been following up her lead on Ethel's murder. Or maybe not. Tottenham was close enough to his patch. Could he have heard anything? She knew she was being paranoid. Why would he? And why would he connect it with her? She reined in her unruly thoughts. It was just another day and she was going to work.

As she stepped out of the lifts into SBA's reception area the first person she saw was Alan Turnbull. He was chatting to Alicia, the receptionist, who was laughing and obviously enjoying his attentions. Nicci was hoping to slip by without being noticed, but Alicia put paid to that.

'Morning, Nicci.'

Nicci gave a nod and carried on walking, but Turnbull had already swivelled round and was beaming at her.

He fell into step beside her. 'I'm glad you're bright and early. I was hoping for a private word.'

Nicci's mind was already whirling forward to the complications that could ensue if Kaz Phelps did indeed turn up at ten, as arranged, and bumped into Turnbull. Any inclination she might have to help Nicci would disappear like a fart in the wind.

She glanced at him. 'Haven't got a lot of time right now. I'm late for an appointment.'

He stopped in his tracks. 'Listen, Nicci . . .' His tone was friendly but emphatic enough to force her to stop too. 'I think we need to lay a few ghosts to rest.'

The smug bastard was just standing there, expecting her to listen to his bullshit. It was too much, her fragile temper snapped. 'Ghosts? Mal Bradley you mean? His ghost should certainly haunt you.'

'I was speaking figuratively, Nicci.' He seemed impervious to her obvious disgust. He shook his head sadly. 'No one regrets DC Bradley's death more than me. It's on my conscience, if that's what you want to hear. I made an error of judgement. A serious error. But believe me, I've paid the price. All I'm asking for now is for us to put the past behind us. You were one of the best officers in my team.'

Nicci looked him up and down. He hadn't changed a bit. Expensive tailored suit, silk tie, diamond-studded tiepin. Turnbull had a rich man's tastes; perhaps that had always been his problem – it's not easy to dress like that, to live the life he led, on a police officer's salary. And he still thought he was a charmer. Was that his strategy now? To bewitch the SBA staff one by one, starting on the front desk with Alicia?

She fixed him with an unremitting stare. 'You hypocritical scumbag. You set us up. You set us all up. And you got Bradley killed.' She took a step closer. 'Put the past behind us? I'm fucked if I will.'

As she strode off his voice floated after her: 'Don't make an enemy of me, Nicci. That would be foolish.'

She spun round and gave him her middle finger.

57

Eddie Lunt had had a few memorable nights out in Glasgow over the years but he wasn't really a drinking man. He enjoyed the odd jar. What interested him was food – haute cuisine or a burger, he wasn't fussy. Didn't matter what crap life threw at you, sitting down to a hearty feast always made you feel better. And breakfast was his favourite meal of the day.

He'd found a place on Albion Street and had ordered the full Scottish – Stornoway black pudding, bacon, beef sausages, potato scone, mushrooms and two fried eggs. Plus toast and a large cappuccino.

Since he'd arrived in Glasgow the previous evening he'd been busy. A meet-up with Alistair, his contact on the *Herald*, had put the wheels in motion. Back in his phone-hacking days he and Alistair had had an informal arrangement. But when the shit hit the fan and the police came knocking, he'd omitted to mention it. So Alistair owed him – big time.

On the way up on the train he'd made a few calls. He'd confirmed that Helen Warner did spend the night at Malmaison. He'd got a copy of her mobile phone records for the period of her visit, and her credit-card receipts. Checking the receipts against the hotel's website and room tariffs he'd come to the conclusion that she must've eaten there too. The hotel boasted a cosy-looking brasserie. A good place for an intimate dinner?

If he could get a breakdown of the hotel bill, that would tell him whether she'd dined alone.

He'd decided to leave it to Alistair to dig up a copy. Asking one of his tame hackers to trawl for it might've been quicker, but Nicci's instructions had been to keep a handle on expenses and the extra cost wasn't really justified. He usually billed such items under miscellaneous. The accounts manager never questioned them and Simon Blake always signed them off. However, given Nicci's hostility towards him, he had a point to prove – he wanted to show her he could get results, quickly and on a budget.

Proving himself to Nicci wasn't the only thing that had him galvanized. The apparent suicide of old Ray, his mate at the Labour Party, had made this whole thing personal. Eddie had worked in the underbelly of Fleet Street and Wapping for enough years to identify the whiff of skulduggery. And the Warner case stank of it.

He'd spent some time trying to work out what information Ray could've had in his possession, more than common gossip, that might've got him killed. But Ray was a backroom boy. Eddie could find no specific link between him and Helen Warner.

He was already tucking into his breakfast when Alistair arrived. The Scot shook his hand and sat down opposite.

'What'll it be, mate?' Eddie beamed at him. 'The full monty?'

Alistair shook his head. 'Just a coffee, thanks.' He was straight down to business, lifting a laptop out of his bag and clearing a space for it on the table.

'You sure? This is ace.'

The reporter's resigned look turned to one of abject

misery. 'The wife's got me on muesli and fruit. She says she doesn't want me keeling over at fifty with a heart attack.'

Eddie shrugged. They were both in their middle forties but he had to admit that, apart from his shaved, balding pate, Alistair was a lot fitter and slimmer than when they'd last met.

He puffed out his cheeks, took a slurp of coffee. 'I figure when your number's up, your number's up. Anyway, what you got for me?'

Alistair was booting up his computer. 'This girl that you think she met – middle twenties?'

Mouth full of egg and toast, Eddie gave him a nod.

'Well, I got CCTV from the hotel that shows Warner and another woman having a meal. But you take a look yourself, this woman's older. Older than Warner, I'd say.'

Loading QuickTime Player, Alistair found his first video clip and pressed play. 'I've edited it down to the relevant bits.'

Both men peered at the screen. The brasserie wasn't particularly full. A waiter appeared, escorting Helen Warner and her companion to a corner table. They settled in their seats and were handed menus.

Alistair pointed at the screen. 'Now it's coming up. You get a good view of the other one's face. I don't think it can be your girl.'

Eddie leant forward, a forkful of sausage frozen mid-way between plate and open mouth. It took him a moment to recover enough to respond. 'No, you're right – it isn't.'

'Any idea who she is?'

Eddie put his loaded fork down. 'Yeah. Her name's Paige Hollister.'

58

Kaz Phelps had never felt comfortable with dogs. The guard dogs her father had kept during her childhood had been brutal beasts. She and Joey had gone in fear of them and her little sister Natalie had been bitten when she was only a toddler.

However, Buster was an amiable creature. He ambled around the enclosed garden in the middle of the square, took a dump, scratched up a patch of turf and did a circuit of the bushes, nose down, tail wagging.

Julia had driven Kaz and the dog back to Onslow Square from the hospital in the early hours. Mike had opened the door to them with visible relief.

Kaz had apologized although she didn't explain. His face was more ashen than usual. She'd felt a pang of guilt for causing him worry.

But he'd simply smiled and rubbed his stubbled chin. 'Thought you'd done a bunk.'

He had made her beans on toast and opened a can of cat food for Buster. They'd both crashed out on the sofa.

With the warm body of the animal nestled beside her, Kaz had sunk into a heavy, dreamless sleep.

The morning sun had long been seeping through the curtains when she was woken by the phone vibrating in her pocket with an incoming text from Nicci. The message was brief – their meeting was rearranged for noon at Julia's house. There was no explanation, just an injunction to be there.

Taking her phone out into the garden, Kaz had sat in the small arbour at the end and called the hospital. She was passed from pillar to post until she'd finally located the ward Yasmin was in.

The voice that had come on the line was barely a whisper. 'Yeah?'

'Yasmin, it's Kaz. You okay?'

'As if you give a fuck.' The tone was sour. Kaz put it down to shock and pain.

'I'll come and see you later. We can talk.'

'Nah, stay away. I got cops crawling all over, asking fucking questions. And if Mr Kemal gets wind, I'm dead meat.'

Kaz sighed, she felt more than responsible. 'We'll think of something, just—'

'Nah, soon as I can, I'm outta here. Got a mate in Manchester.'

'Will you be safe there?'

Yasmin coughed, a dry painful rasp. 'Whadda you care? Such a sweet deal I had 'til you come along. Try to do a mate a favour and this is how it ends up.'

'I'm sorry, Yas.'

'Not as fuckin' sorry as me.'

The phone went dead. Yasmin had hung up. Kaz had sat for a while trying to process her friend's anger and self-pity. It was understandable, the product of fear. Still she felt indignant. The real source of Yasmin's problems was her connection to the Kemals, but maybe it was naive to think she'd ever acknowledge that.

It wasn't until Mike had come out and suggested that Buster might be in need of an airing in the square that she'd

managed to corral the conflicting feelings of guilt and griev-
ance spinning round in her head. He'd handed her the pass
key and a plastic bag. While she was gone he was going to
prepare them a slap-up breakfast.

It was a perfect summer morning – the day was set to be a
scorcher – heat was already rising off the flagstone pavements. But the high leafy canopy of plane trees transformed
the gardens into a cool oasis. Kaz wandered, clad only in
T-shirt and jeans. She'd dutifully scooped up Buster's poop
with the plastic bag and deposited it in the designated bin.
Then she slipped off her trainers and walked barefoot across
the soft springy turf.

A fellow dog-walker gave her a friendly nod. The simple
acceptance of her right to be there, in this enclave of the rich,
struck Kaz as faintly ironical. They were of a similar age. The
young woman wore shorts with high-heeled sandals and was
towing a small Tibetan Spaniel.

Whilst the two dogs sniffed and pirouetted round each
other, the woman smiled. 'Good idea. So hot for shoe.' Leaning
her hand on the mottled bark of one of the great trees she
pulled off her sandals and wiggled her toes in the grass. Her
accent was definitely foreign, Middle Eastern maybe. Kaz
couldn't be sure.

'Yeah,' she agreed. 'It's gonna be a lovely day.'

'You live here?' The enquiry seemed casual enough. The
woman flicked back her silky chestnut mane. She was sizing
Kaz up, a definite flirtatiousness in her eye.

'Staying with a friend.'

The woman exhaled with pleasure, running her tongue
over her lip. 'Such a good place London. I like so much. So
elegant.'

Kaz gave her a rueful smile. It was certainly true of this

part of London. The graceful Victorian terraces exuded style and wealth. Kaz wondered if she'd ever ventured further afield, beyond the designer shops and posh restaurants. It was doubtful. She looked the girl up and down – pretty enough in a pert, pop-princess way. But did she want to play games with some bored bi-curious rich kid? Not really. She had neither the time nor inclination.

'See you around.' Tilting an amused look in the girl's direction, she strolled off after Buster.

The dog was having a fine time darting in and out of the shrubbery. The notion that he could've been used to scare the Kemals seemed faintly absurd now. In retrospect, here in the quiet dappled shade of the gardens, the whole escapade felt vaguely unreal.

Yasmin might be wishing that Kaz had never come knocking at her door, but the feeling was mutual. She just wanted to escape, return to her secure and ordinary art student life and become Clare O'Keeffe again. Her excursion back into the old world had scared her. The rage that had driven it had been so consuming. She'd been out of it, completely reckless and mental, like the old Kaz. Now that it had subsided, she felt exposed and jittery. And without the prop of booze or drugs she didn't know how to come down. She took a deep breath and focused on the greenery. She needed to relax and let it all go.

For the time being the Kemals would have enough on their plate dealing with the Old Bill. Would Yasmin tell the cops what they'd done to her? Pretty unlikely. They were serious organized criminals with a wide reach and a long memory. And sooner or later they'd be looking for Kaz.

The decision to come to London had been rash and impulsive, born of shock and grief. If anyone could solve the conundrum of Helen's death Nicci Armstrong might. So maybe she should just return the dog to Glynis then head back to her anonymous life north of the border? That would be the sensible course.

But then her restless thoughts homed in on Tevfik Kemal. She couldn't help it. The arrogant scrote reckoned he could hurt Yasmin, or any woman for that matter, as if it were his God-given right. Not in Kaz's book. No way. As her indignation rose again she began to feel pleased about what she'd done. Okay, she'd stuck her neck out, maybe a bit too far, but she'd taught that piece of shit a lesson he wouldn't forget in a hurry. Him and his slimy father.

The discordant emotions swirled in her brain and she couldn't seem to make them stop. Deciding what to do next felt impossible. She had to force herself to calm down. Resolving to take one step at a time, she clipped the leash back on to Buster's collar. The next step was breakfast.

She stroked the dog's head; the creature gazed up at her with its big sappy eyes. She could see why Glynis liked it; why, after all the mean and useless blokes she'd encountered in her life, she'd settled for Buster.

Kaz was amusing herself with this thought as she opened the gate to leave the gardens. She didn't immediately notice the man standing just outside the railings. He had a beard, wore a baseball cap over straggly hair and aviator shades.

As the voice drifted in her direction the blood froze in Kaz's veins.

'Fuck me! I never thought I'd see you with a dog. You was always shit-scared of 'em.'

Her eyes flew up to his face. He took off the glasses, though there was no need. Smiling at her nonchalantly from under the brim of his cap was her brother Joey.

59

Nicci Armstrong sat at her desk, jittery from too much caffeine, staring at her laptop screen. She was on a Skype call with Eddie Lunt in Glasgow. His sweaty face was slightly pixelated, the connection wasn't that good.

He took a slurp of coffee and his staccato voice came through the speaker out of synch with his lips. 'I got a series of edited clips.'

'From the hotel CCTV?'

There was a couple of seconds delay. 'Yeah.'

A puzzled frown settled on Nicci's brow. 'Paige Hollister? No one else?'

Eddie leant forward, his forehead and wiry eyebrows filled the screen. 'I'm emailing you them now. See what you think, boss. Cosy dinner, very intimate, then next morning, in the hotel foyer, they had words.'

'What d'you mean words?' Her tone was tetchy, she found Skype calls frustrating.

'Looks like a row to me. Warner's trying to keep it down, but Hollister's having a right old strop. Walks out on her.'

Nicci sighed. 'No sign of Kaz Phelps?'

The image on the screen fractured into rectangles for a moment then rearranged itself in the form of Eddie's smiling features. 'Nope. Unless Warner met her somewhere else.'

'That's possible.'

Eddie rocked forward. 'Come again?'

'Did Warner go out for any length of time?'

'Arrived about four in the afternoon. Had dinner in the brasserie at half seven. She and Paige Hollister checked out at ten the next morning. Didn't have breakfast.'

'Did Paige stay in the same room?'

'Looks like it. I know I said I thought Robert Hollister was giving her one. But maybe that's wrong. Maybe it was Warner and the wife?'

The email icon on Nicci's dock pinged with an incoming message. 'Your email's just arrived. Thanks, Eddie.'

'No probs.'

She hesitated for a second. 'Oh, and well done.'

His impish features broke into a broad grin. 'Thanks, boss. Should be back mid-afternoon. You need anything else, give us a bell. Oh, hang on, nearly forgot the other thing. I was trying to tell you yesterday before I came up here—'

'Yeah, okay, get on with it.' Much as she wanted to, Nicci couldn't rein in her impatience.

The eyes on the screen blinked at her. 'Ray – my mate who went under the train – I finally got his wife on the phone. Poor woman's gutted. Delicate situation, obviously. She told me that just before he died he talked about – guess who – Helen Warner. He was helping her out.'

'Doing what?'

'He never said. But thing is, Nic, he never mentioned that to me. And I asked him. So he was keeping it secret. Even after Warner's death. What does that tell us?'

Nicci was getting irritated. Was he being deliberately obtuse? 'Well, what does it tell us?'

'There was still something to hide. Tina – that's Ray's wife – she couldn't tell me any more and I didn't wanna press her.'

Nicci stroked the soft skin between her brow and lids, it felt sticky and sore. It was all rolling round in her head, this new information. But somehow she couldn't make it compute.

She realized Eddie was staring at her and waiting.

'Okay, Eddie, thanks. See you when you get back.'

'Cheers, I'll—'

She clicked off the call, interrupting him in mid-flow and turned to the blank page of her notebook. Surely she'd been making notes? No, she'd been about to. Then – then what? Something had distracted her. Rubbing her temples with her fingertips she took some deep breaths. It was as if the hangovers were starting to become seamless. What with that and the constant jumble of skittering thoughts, she couldn't think straight. Maybe she should just go home and crash out? Later. She'd have to wait until later. There was too much to do.

Paige Hollister? An affair with Paige Hollister? It was definitely plausible. Did Julia Hadley know? She checked her watch. She'd be heading over to Hadley's place later for the meeting with Phelps, having rearranged the time and venue in order to avoid Turnbull. She got up and glanced round the room. No sign of him at the moment. He was probably bitching to Simon Blake about her behaviour and trying to get her fired. She'd resolved to ignore him and get on with her day.

What she did see was Rory heading for his desk. They hadn't spoken since the previous evening outside Whipps Cross Hospital, though she'd tried to call him several times. He shot an aloof glance in her direction, their eyes met and immediately he looked away and went to talk to Hugo, his number two in the security department.

Nicci sat down and took a breath. Great. A crap morning

had just got worse. The dull ache in her head, the vague feeling of nausea, if only those annoyances would abate maybe she could get back on track. She took a long drink from a litre plastic bottle of water. Should she go over and confront Rory? Probably not. What she needed to do was focus on the job in hand.

She spun her chair round in Pascale's direction. 'You got a minute?'

Pascale gave her a warm smile.

'Okay. I want you to focus on Robert Hollister's wife, Paige Hollister. Everything you can get: biog, what the gossip mags say about her – everything that's out there.'

As the researcher got down to work, Nicci picked up her phone. She still needed to call Delgado before she headed over to Julia's. But as she scrolled through her address book for the Hackney cop's number, the phone buzzed with an incoming call. It was a mobile number and came up as unknown. Nicci stared at it for a moment.

The curiosity of a cop was still her default setting so she immediately answered the call. 'Nicci Armstrong.'

There was a brief lacuna of silence. 'Nicci, it's Fiona Calder.' The tone was clipped and confident. 'I think our meeting the other day was . . . well, unfortunate in its outcome. I'd very much like to see you again.'

This threw Nicci. She took a breath, then thought, fuck it, do I need to be polite? 'See me? Why?'

'Believe it or not, I would still like to be of use to you.' There was a hesitation. 'In fact, I think we might help each other.'

Nicci's brain was scrambling to play catch up. Help each other? An innocuous enough phrase yet freighted with possible meanings. And the Assistant Commissioner was calling from a mobile, which, as far as Nicci knew, was not her usual number.

Nicci decided to test the water. She adopted a casual tone. 'Okay, well, I'm a bit busy right now. I could come over to your office, I don't know, some time in the next couple of days.'

'No, not the office.' Calder's voice took on a tone that assumed authority. 'Let's meet for coffee. I've got a window in my diary this morning at eleven. That is, assuming you can make it.'

60

Kaz's first instinct was to take her chances and run for it. There were people about. If Joey chased her and tried to grab her he'd risk drawing attention to himself. And if she hollered and screamed surely someone would call the police.

As if he'd read her mind, Joey grinned at her and pointed across the street. Standing at the top of the steps leading down to Mike's basement flat was a familiar figure, sleeve tattoos emerging from his tight black T-shirt.

Joey put the aviator shades back on. 'You remember Tolya.'

The Russian raised three fingers in mock salute and smiled. He and his elder brother had been Joey's enforcers before he went down.

Letting the threat sink in, Joey slipped his hands in his pockets. 'We been having a chat with Mike. He's making pancakes. I told him to put a few more on 'cause I'm starving. Well, y'know yourself, babes, the food in the nick is crap.'

'Don't hurt him, Joey. He's an old man and he's not well.'

'I ain't planning to hurt anyone. All I want is a quiet chat.' His face was all innocence, but the dark glasses concealed his eyes.

'Why don't I believe you?' She stared at her own reflection in the mirrored lens.

'Believe what you like. Me, I'm gonna go and sample some of old Mike's pancakes. You coming?'

Kaz knew that once she was off the street and out of the public gaze she'd be at his mercy. He probably had a gun somewhere. Easy enough to conceal, tucked in the back of his jeans under the loose polo shirt. On the other hand if she ran away, Mike would be left unprotected. Joey wouldn't take any chances, he'd just kill him.

She tugged on Buster's leash. It was a pity he wasn't some vicious, half-starved attack dog. She crossed the road in Joey's wake, one question burning through her brain – how the hell had he found her? Glynis? That seemed unlikely, since he was surprised by the dog. But then who else had her number? Putting a trace on her mobile would've been no problem. If he had Tolya back on board then he'd have other resources as well.

In one sense she admired his nerve. Anyone else who'd just escaped from jail would've been out of the country, heading for a safe bolthole. Not Joey. He was wandering around as bold as brass with a baseball cap, a beard and a pair of sunglasses as his only disguise.

As they neared the steps to the flat she turned to him. 'How d'you track me down?'

He smiled. 'You pissed a few people off last night, you and your mates.'

'What d'you mean?'

'I've had Sadik Kemal on the blower, threatening me with all sorts of bollocks. I calmed him down.'

'How the fuck d'you know him?'

'We've never actually met. But I been negotiating with them for a couple of months. I had a warehouse full of top-quality weed and no one to distribute it.'

'Did they know you was in jail?'

This prompted a dry laugh. 'Nah, course not. But then

they think I'm Sean.' He took off his shades and looked at her. 'I must admit, when you shot that miserable fucker I never realized how useful he was gonna turn out to be. He's the perfect cover.'

Kaz stared straight into the piercing baby-blue eyes. 'You gonna kill me here or somewhere else? I'll go with you now if you leave Mike out of it.'

Joey shook his head wearily. 'For fuck's sake, babes, you're my sister.' There was an edge to his voice, but the irritation was born of fatigue. He had an uncharacteristic lassitude about him. She wondered if he was on something.

'I testified against you. Mum hates my guts. I reckon you do too.'

'Mum's . . . well, y'know what she's like. All them drugs she took over the years – silly cow lost the plot. She don't really understand the world the way you and me do.'

'What's that's supposed to mean?'

He leant on the railings. 'I ain't gonna hurt you, okay. I just want a chat. But first of all I could murder one of them pancakes.' A wry smile lifted the corner of his mouth. 'Sorry, bad choice of words.'

Kaz scanned his face. The handsome boyish features had become almost gaunt. The beard and the hair made him look older. Jail time had hardened him. And it touched her. She could still feel the connection, the childhood bond, dragging her back. But was he just playing with her? Was this part of his revenge – persuading her to trust him again, drawing her into his web so that he could pull the trigger? She had no way of knowing.

61

His face was pale and baggy-eyed, but then Simon Blake had had two sleepless nights wondering how the hell he was going to get his business back. Moneymen, they were all the same. They used you up and spat you out. There was no integrity. They looked for where the most profit was to be made then they cashed in their chips.

Across the desk from him Alan Turnbull was lounging in a chair, one leg loosely crossed over the other as he dished up his spiel. A concierge service. A fucking concierge service! That was his big idea. He wanted SBA to buy out some two-bit company that specialized in running around wiping the arses of rich foreigners. Or high-net-worth-individuals, as Turnbull called them. Blake felt like grabbing him by the lapels and asking 'What the fuck happened to you? What turned a respected senior police officer into Duncan Linton's lackey?'

But then, if he was honest, he already knew the answer.

They weren't so very different, him and Turnbull. They'd both seen the kind of money that was swilling about in the City, the million-quid bonuses and share options handed out to men with no more talent or brains than them. Envy had seeped into their consciousness and they'd decided they wanted their share. The difference was, Blake was determined to operate in an ethical fashion. Security and investigations

309

– areas in which he had serious expertise – that was his core business, expanding into cybercrime, which was where the future lay.

He'd thought standing up to Linton would be a piece of piss. Now he was wallowing in the backwash of his own naivety.

He'd sat up most of the night trawling the Net – obscure financial websites, arcane blogs read only by the cognoscenti. He'd been a good detective once, meticulous, thorough. The devil's often hidden in the detail – he'd learnt that from his first boss in CID, an old sweat who used to walk around in a trilby hat. What he'd discovered was that Duncan Linton had a business plan of his own.

He was investing in new UK businesses based on a high degree of technical skill or professional know-how. Usually they'd been set up by individuals who'd got their training in the public sector – in universities, in hospitals, in organizations like the police. Linton gave them his backing, pushed them to expand, then a couple of years down the road, when they were really taking off, he'd force them to sell. The sale was usually to investors from abroad – the last two or three had been to the Chinese. Each time, Linton had recouped a sizeable return on his investment while his hapless victims, individuals like Blake who'd simply wanted to run their own show, ended up making a fraction of what they should have and answering to a new boss.

Now that he'd figured out Linton's game, Blake was sure of one thing – he wasn't going down without a fight.

He continued to listen to Turnbull with half an ear as he waffled on about building a brand. Blake wasn't daft, he'd read the books. He already knew his brand – ex-coppers and ex-military – professional, reliable, solid, people you could really trust. Part of him almost felt sorry for Turnbull. He'd been suckered by Linton too, forced into a foolish ploy which had totally failed. The result was he'd become a pariah to his old colleagues and friends. He had no choice now but to dance to Linton's tune and he'd been slotted into SBA for the sole purpose of acting as Linton's informant.

Blake knew he'd been stupid, but he wasn't about to compound it by turning soft. Turnbull could go to hell. Glancing through the glass door of his office he noticed Nicci Armstrong walking across the reception area towards the lifts. For some odd reason the very sight of her filled him with hope.

He raised his hand, cutting Turnbull off mid-sentence. 'Sorry, Alan, we'll have to continue this later.'

Jumping up from his desk he headed out of the door without a second glance at Turnbull. He caught up with Nicci as she pressed the call button for the lift.

She jerked her head in the direction of his office, where Turnbull was still sitting. 'Is he trying to persuade you to sack me?'

'We need to talk. This has all been a stupid distraction. What matters is the Warner case.'

Nicci sighed. 'I'll take that as a yes, shall I?'

'Actually, he hasn't mentioned you.'

'He will,' she smirked. 'I told him to go fuck himself this morning.'

'That was diplomatic.' He couldn't help smiling. One of the many things he admired about Nicci was her fearlessness. Grief seemed to have liberated her from the usual social constraints. She'd face down anybody. She had no time for bullshit.

'I'm not working with him.'

'I'm not asking you to.' He lowered his voice. 'Listen, Nic, this is a complicated situation. I need you to bear with me.'

Nicci was studying his face. They'd worked some difficult cases together and she'd seen him looking like shit before. What she'd never seen was this nervy tension pulsating off him. Though struggling to conceal it, he was radiating uncertainty. She wondered idly which of them was in worse shape, him or her. Probably her.

She gave him a quizzical look. 'Can't you find other investors? 'Cause Linton's got you by the balls, hasn't he?'

He shot a nervy glance back across the office to where Turnbull was chatting amiably to one of Bharat's computer guys. 'What I need is to crack the Warner case. A big, headline-grabbing result to really raise our profile and make us serious contenders. That would give me some leverage.'

'Then you need to stop pissing about and give me some help. Because at the moment it's a fully resourced squad of detectives versus me, Eddie Lunt and his dodgy contacts, plus a couple of researchers. And I have to tell you, Simon, it's an uphill struggle.'

'I know. And I appreciate your efforts. I really do.'

He was giving her that look again. She shifted uncomfortably. 'What about the guy from the transport police? Has he come up with anything?'

'Ken Sturridge? He's getting back to me.'

'Hassle him.'

'I will.'

The lift announced its arrival with a ding. The doors slid open. Nicci just wanted to escape – from the office, from Blake, from the complications of her own folly. But he put his hand against the door sensor to hold it.

'I know how fucked up this must look to you.'

Nicci stared at him wide-eyed: the F word was not a normal part of Blake's vocabulary. 'No, I get it. I know what Turnbull's capable of. As for Linton, I can only guess. Be careful, Simon, that's all I'm saying.'

'Thanks, Nic.' His hand brushed her sleeve – a gentle, comradely gesture – it was in no way intrusive. 'Thanks for your support. I'm going to sort this mess out, believe me.'

Nicci returned his smile. 'I do.'

62

Tolya demolished four pancakes, drenched in butter and maple syrup. Joey, for all his protestations about being starving, struggled with two. Keeping a wary eye on his guests, Mike tidied the counter, picking up the discarded eggshells and dropping them in the bin. He shot a concerned look at Kaz. Joey had come knocking at his door with all the smiling insouciance of a casual caller. By the time Mike had twigged who he was it was too late. He'd been catapulted into a world where normal rules didn't apply.

Kaz sat across the table from her brother, watching and waiting. Buster was at her feet wide-eyed and hopeful. Joey fed his last half-pancake to the drooling dog, then put down his knife and fork.

'I gotta say, Mike, that was wicked. My mum tried to make pancakes once – remember, Kaz? Stuck to the pan like fucking glue. She went mental, chucked the frying pan at Kaz and the batter at me.' He grinned and pointed in his sister's direction. 'You was quick, you ducked. Me, I ended up with the stuff in my hair, eyes, up my nose.' His face twisted into a sour smile. 'Funny now. It weren't at the time.'

Mike gave Kaz a surreptitious glance then smiled at Joey. 'Glad you enjoyed them.'

Joey eased back in his chair but there was a tension, a rigidity to his movements. Kaz had noticed the care he took when he first sat down. His eyes seemed over-bright and when he removed the cap his forehead was plastered with sweat. He was toughing it out, being jokey. But she knew him. Something wasn't right.

Now that her panic had subsided a few notches a new question was dominating her thoughts – if he wasn't here to kill her then what did he want? Or was this all just an elaborate tease? Did he want the power trip of fooling her? Did he need to prove how clever he was before he could take his revenge? If there was one thing she'd learnt about Joey, it was that he was capable of anything.

He reached into his jeans pocket and pulled out a silver blister pack of tablets. 'You got some water, Mike?'

As Mike went to the tap and filled a glass, Joey snapped three tablets out of the pack.

Kaz watched in silence. Joey liked to be the centre of attention, so the best way to get him to open up was to say nothing.

He popped the first pill into his mouth. 'Ain't you gonna ask what it is?'

She tilted her head. 'None of my business.'

'Diclofenac. Painkiller.'

He pulled up the front of his polo shirt to reveal a white adhesive dressing about fifteen centimetres square on the left side of his torso just below the ribs.

'Set up a knife fight, that's how I got out. Smart, eh?'

She met his gaze but said nothing.

His face crumpled into a brittle grin. 'Bastard was only supposed to nick me. Fucking hurts, I'll tell you that much.' For a brief instant she was reminded of little Joey, the needy child he'd once been.

'Well, it would.' Her face remained impassive, but there

was a lump in her throat. Stab wounds could be nasty. And the sight of him in pain, her little brother, her precious Joey, it hit her on a visceral level in spite of herself. She'd spent her entire childhood and adolescence loving him, protecting him, and she couldn't switch those feelings off, however much she wanted to.

The startling blue eyes zoned in on her. 'Ended up in Basildon Hospital.' He chuckled. 'We been there a few times over the years, you and me, in't we? They sorted me out.'

How he'd managed that while on the run, his face plastered all over the media, was a mystery to Kaz. But she wasn't about to pander to his vanity by asking the question. Then there was Tolya. How had Joey managed to hook up with the Russians again? The last she knew, they'd walked away from Joey and been happy to do so.

He raked back his tangled hair. 'I'll be glad to get a haircut, I can tell you. And all this face fuzz makes me feel like a fucking tramp. I've never trusted blokes with beards, have you?'

Another tease? With Joey it was impossible to tell.

She tossed her head defiantly; she feared him, that was only sensible, but she was damned if she'd show it. 'What you playing at Joey? What is this? What do you want?'

He finished popping the painkillers, washing them down with several large gulps of water. Then his brow puckered. 'You done what you had to. I get it. In your shoes, I'd've probably done the same. Things had got out of hand. I've had time to think and I can see that now. You was right, the Old Bill was on my case. They weren't gonna give up. I should've stuck to business like you said.' He gave a nod in Tolya's direction. 'They knew it too, that's why they buggered off. You're a smart girl, I should've listened to you.'

The face was mature but the eyes carried the innocent,

angelic look of the little Joey. His tone was apologetic. No doubt about it, he was trying to hook her.

He smiled wistfully. 'Before, when we was teenagers and I fucked up, you went down. You took the fall for both of us. Okay, so I fucked up again. This time it was my turn, I took the fall. Far as I'm concerned, we're square.'

Her eyes met his. Did he really think he could sucker her like this? Lying was second nature to him. Maybe he even believed it himself. For as long as it suited his purpose.

There was a heavy silence in the room. Mike stood by the kitchen sink, watching the discussion unfold with an eagle eye. Tolya sat at the table; it was hard to tell if his English had improved sufficiently for him to understand. But he was a huge, potentially threatening presence. He understood enough to follow his boss's orders.

'You still ain't answered my question. What the fuck d'you want? My help? My advice?' Kaz swept her hair back from her forehead. 'Here's my advice: if you don't wanna go back to jail, get out of the country now.'

'I plan to. Gonna run the business from Amsterdam.'

'So what's stopping you?'

He dipped his head, peering up through the sandy lashes. 'I've missed you, y'know.' He glanced at Tolya. 'He's here 'cause there's a hundred-grand bonus waiting for him and his brother once they get me away and set up with a new identity. But who the fuck do I talk to? You're right, I should just go. But I'm putting myself on the line here. I need you, Kaz. I don't mean you no harm.' His smile was magnetic. 'When I say we're square, I mean it. Lot's happened since Dad died. I seen the inside of a nick and I learnt my lesson.'

She pulled out her phone and plonked it on the table between them. He wasn't the only one who could play games.

'What if I call the Old Bill right now, tell them where you are? You gonna stop me? You'll have to hurt me to do it.'

He raised his palms in mock surrender. 'Look, I know I've taken you by surprise and I can see why you don't trust me. So let's make a deal. You like deals.'

She shook her head wearily. 'This is fucked, Joey.'

'Doesn't have to be. I got this special private doctor I need to see. Harley Street. Practically round the corner. He's gonna check me over, make sure I'm fit to travel. Day or so, I'll be out of your way.'

'You can't stay here.' She shot him a challenging look. 'No fucking way.'

He winced as he turned in his chair towards Mike. 'Play cards do you, Mike? Poker maybe?'

Mike raised his eyebrows. 'Poker?'

Joey turned back to his sister. 'See, what I'm thinking is, I could stay here and rest up and Mike could keep me company. Just 'til the doc signs me off and I get my passport sorted.'

'What? You're holding us hostage?' Kaz huffed.

'Nah, course not. If you go out, Mike stays here with me. Just a little bit of insurance. Given your record, you can see why, babes. Just 'til we can trust one another again.'

Kaz glanced at Mike, one of the few people in her life who'd treated her with kindness and decency and she'd visited this on him. Whether it was out of guilt or anger or both, a sudden fury engulfed her.

Grabbing the phone, she jumped up, kicked back her chair, and started to punch in the digits. 'Fuck you, little brother!'

Tolya was out of his seat in a flash. For a large bloke he had lightning reactions. He seized her wrist and flipped the phone out of her hand. It clattered to the floor.

Joey simply grinned and turned to his host. 'You gotta hand it to her, Mike. She's got balls, my sister. It's what I love about her.'

63

Nicci slumped back in the seat of the taxi. The tube would've finished her off – she'd've puked – and the bus wouldn't have been much better. So she was putting this on expenses. Blake owed her that much.

As she gazed out of the window watching the belching traffic, the scramble and scurry of London sliding by, she wondered if she'd become an alcoholic. But surely addiction wasn't just something you acquired through bad habits. Addiction was about the brain, defects in the hedonic neural systems, she'd read that somewhere. It was more than a lack of willpower, it was a disease, that had been scientifically proven. Not that people like Tim's parents would agree; with their religious certainty and snap judgements, they'd see it as weakness of character. Nicci wondered if she did lack moral fibre, or was her problem with booze simply the product of grief?

Before she'd lost Sophie, even with all the stresses of divorce and single parenthood, she hadn't been much of a drinker. She'd enjoyed a glass socially, but juggling the job and caring for her daughter she'd needed to keep her wits about her. Since Sophie's death, drink had crept up on her, becoming her stealthy comforter, her reliable and uncritical companion.

Still she had to face facts. An invisible line had been crossed and she was making herself ill. It was the middle of the morning, an ordinary working day, and she wanted desperately to go home to bed. And what was stopping her?

She had the odd sensation that her toes were touching the edge of the precipice. Easy enough to tip forward and let go. If her life was in freefall she wouldn't need to worry any more. She wouldn't have to argue about Turnbull or work out what had happened to Helen Warner; she wouldn't have to feel guilty about Ethel. She wouldn't have to bother with any of it. Eventually she'd hit bottom, crash onto the rocks below. By then oblivion would've engulfed her, booze anaesthetizing the pain.

The irony was she'd been feeling marginally better just prior to Ethel's murder. It was the sight of the old lady bleeding out on the pavement that had catapulted her back towards the abyss. She'd felt responsible and impotent. What could she do to bring the culprit to justice? Hope that Delgado would do his job?

Giving up and giving in took many forms. She considered the possibility that straight suicide might be the braver option. A clear decision followed by decisive action. Maybe that's what Helen Warner had opted for. If she'd got involved in a silly affair with a politician's wife that would end up hurting those she cared about and most likely ruin her career, maybe she had chosen to simply exit the scene. Her text message to Julia was certainly full of guilt.

Nicci wondered about guilt. Was it a corrosive enough feeling to drive a person to suicide? In some people it could be. Her thoughts drifted back to her own situation. If she were going to kill herself, she didn't think jumping in the river was a particularly easy way to go. How long would it take to drown? She'd been on a course once where they reckoned two to three minutes to unconsciousness, around five minutes to death. That was too scary, that amount of time, fighting the body's own reflexes as they struggled to stop water flooding the lungs. It was much easier to just drink yourself to death.

The taxi pulled up outside a branch of Patisserie Valerie on Marylebone High Street. Nicci got out and paid the cabbie. Checking her watch, she saw she was ten minutes late. Did she care? She decided she didn't.

Inside she threaded her way through a smattering of customers – middle-aged lady shoppers, bags embossed with designer logos heaped at their feet, a party of rowdy Chinese tourists – towards the back of the cafe where Fiona Calder was sitting. It was the seat Nicci would've chosen herself, tucked away, but a good view of all the comings and goings.

As Nicci walked round the tables towards her old boss she felt the tension taking hold in her stomach, gripping it, twisting it. Calder looked up and smiled. It all appeared quite casual, but Nicci knew full well Calder would've clocked her as soon as she got out of the cab.

Though she was loath to admit it, Calder still made her nervous – it was a reflex action.

She just about managed a smile. 'Sorry I'm a bit late. Traffic.'

'Not a problem. I'm afraid I've been indulging myself. The treacle tart was just too tempting.' Calder's tone was breezy, as if they were simply friends meeting for coffee and a gossip. 'What can I get you?'

Nicci settled into the chair opposite. 'Just a cup of tea.'

'Builder's brew, herbal?'

'Actually, camomile'd be nice.' Not so much nice as a way of calming her nausea.

Calder summoned the waitress and placed the order, then sat back and cast an eye over Nicci.

Nicci shifted in her chair, her hungover state would be unlikely to escape Calder's alert eye. Struggling for an air of normality, she slipped off her jacket and slotted it over the back of her chair.

'I owe you an apology.'

Nicci looked up sharply. 'Really? Why?'

'I had no idea you worked for Simon Blake. When we last met . . .' She hesitated. 'Well, let's just say it wrong-footed me.'

Nicci had already decided that she wasn't making herself a hostage to fortune again. 'You had every right to be pissed off. Blake knew you wouldn't see him. He sent me in the hope we could exploit your sympathy.'

Calder smiled ruefully. 'Well some might call it a smart move.'

Nicci was on a roll. Now she just wanted to get it all out. 'He's also hired Alan Turnbull.'

The Assistant Commissioner's brow darkened. 'I thought he was in Abu Dhabi.'

'He's back. It wasn't Simon's choice; the main investor in the firm forced his hand.'

'Let me guess: Duncan Linton.'

Nicci nodded. Her stress was subsiding now that she had nothing else to lie about.

'And what are your feelings about Turnbull?'

The waitress arrived and set down a small pot together with a cup and saucer.

It gave Nicci a chance to consider her answer. 'I need the job. Obviously. But I've told Simon I won't work with Turnbull. Sounds as if I won't have to – he's supposed to be doing some strategic-planning bollocks.'

'Will he have any involvement with the Warner investigation?' A sharp unease had crept into Calder's voice. Nicci shot her a look, was she really going to open up about the Warner case?

'Not if I have anything to do with it. And to be fair to Simon, he's not Turnbull's biggest fan. He was railroaded. If he can, I think he'll keep Turnbull well away from investigations.'

The Assistant Commissioner stared into space and pondered. Finally her gaze travelled back to Nicci. 'This is complicated. Originally I thought there'd be a way to deal with this whole situation.'

'We are talking about the death of Helen Warner?'

'Yes. I suggested to Julia Hadley that she go to a private investigator because I realized there might need to be a plan B.'

Nicci poured her tea but her eyes were on Calder's face. This in itself was a major admission. She was taking quite a risk, talking to Nicci in this way.

'Why SBA?'

'I respect Blake. He was a good officer and a particularly good detective. It was the politics that defeated him.' Her expression turned doleful. 'Which can easily happen in an organization like the Met.'

Nicci waited, knowing it was important to let the Assistant Commissioner do this at her own pace.

'Okay.' Calder sat forward, as if she'd come to a decision. Her tone was now resolute, all hesitation gone. 'I became acquainted with Helen Warner through various policy discussions instituted by the Home Office on the subject of drugs. Several months ago she came to see me to seek my advice on another matter. A more personal matter. This meeting was private and confidential – as far as I know.'

Calder took a sip of her coffee. Behind the professional facade the strain was beginning to show. Nicci noticed the weariness in her eyes, the web of fine lines either side of her mouth.

She dabbed her lips with a napkin. 'I've been backed into a corner, Nicci. I think it extremely unlikely that Helen Warner took her own life. Some sort of bizarre accident?' She shook her head. 'Also unlikely.'

'You think she was killed?'

Calder fixed her with an intent stare. 'If I tell you what I know, what will you do?'

'Depends what you tell me. What do you expect me to do?'

The Assistant Commissioner sighed. 'Life hasn't been kind to you, I know that. In different circumstances I would've expected you to become a senior detective, probably chief superintendent by the time you were forty.'

Was this flattery, Nicci wondered, or a poke at the mess she'd ended up in? 'Have I fucked myself in the head with booze? Is that what you're asking? Can I still cut it as a detective?'

'I'm asking whether you and Simon Blake have the will to follow this investigation through and bring Helen Warner's murderers to justice?'

Nicci opened her palms. 'Tell me what you know and we'll find out, won't we?'

64

Even after her angry outburst, Kaz had found it surprisingly easy to strike a bargain with Joey. Turning up as he had at Mike's, minder in tow, appeared at first to be threatening; yet his manner bordered on the conciliatory. What did he really want? She was all too familiar with his mercurial temper and its dark undertow. Joey had been made a criminal by circumstance, but he was a killer by inclination. It would be foolhardy to regard him with anything less than total suspicion. All the same, she couldn't help wondering whether the stab wound had shaken his confidence. Or maybe it was the jail time, facing the harsh reality of being a lifer?

He was working hard to keep it under wraps but she knew him well enough to get a whiff of his underlying desolation. It reminded her of how he'd been as a boy after their father had given him a thrashing. Emotionally and physically battered, he'd always run to her for comfort. Was that habit, that default setting, just too hard for him to resist? In spite of the fact she'd testified against him, maybe there really was no one else. Could it be that deep down he was simply lost and lonely?

Seeing his potential weakness, Kaz had seized the initiative. She'd announced without preamble that there was an appointment she really had to keep. She furnished him with the skimpiest explanation – Helen Warner had committed suicide and Kaz had arranged to go and offer her condolences to Warner's bereaved partner.

Joey had lounged on one of Mike's large squidgy sofas, scratching his beard in puzzlement. 'The lawyer? Weren't you and her, y'know, shagging? In't that what you told me?'

Kaz didn't miss a beat. 'Nah, you was right all along. I was lying when I told you that. Helen was a bender, but not me.'

Since their reunion as adults, Joey had kept his affections brotherly and satisfied his sexual needs with a string of casual girlfriends. The secret incestuous bond of their teenage years had slipped into the shadows of the past; neither ever mentioned it. But Kaz knew full well that it mattered to him to believe she was attracted to men. It kept the door open, if only a crack.

He'd grinned and wagged a finger at her. 'You're a little tinker, in't you? I knew you was fibbing. Think you can pull the wool over my eyes.'

Kaz was banking on the fact she could. Leaving him in the flat with Mike was a calculated risk. But she worried that Nicci Armstrong would be as good as her word. If she didn't turn up to the meeting as arranged, Nicci might be pissed enough to turn her in. Once a cop always a cop. In any event, it was a gamble she couldn't afford to take. Escaping from the flat might also present some kind of opportunity she hadn't yet fathomed to get Joey off her back.

'Ain't a problem so far as I'm concerned, babes.' He gave her a breezy smile. 'Tolya can drive you.'

The big shouty four-by-four with tinted windows, which had been Joey's vehicle of choice before he went down, had been replaced by a grey and anonymous second-hand Ford Focus. Tolya took the satnav out of the boot and fixed it to the windscreen with a suction pad. He let Kaz tap in Julia's address as he drew on his leather driving gloves, then they set off.

Mike had assured her both verbally and with a pointed look that he would be fine. He'd turned to Joey and asked if he'd ever had his portrait painted. Appealing to Joey's vanity proved an astute move and as Kaz and Tolya had left, Mike was setting up his easel.

Kaz gave her driver a sideways glance. During his time on Joey's payroll he'd seen her abused by her cousin, hysterical, and stark naked with a gun in her hand. It didn't make them friends, but they were certainly more than acquaintances.

She adopted a casual tone. 'How's your brother?'

'Yevgeny? He good.' His eyes remained on the road.

She relaxed into the seat. 'What you guys been up to then? You been away?'

'We make a little trip back home, see family. But we come back. London is best place. Plenty Russian friends, but free. Good work. No hassle.'

'I must say, Tol, your English has improved.'

'Yeah?' He grinned broadly and shot her a glance. 'You really think?'

'Definitely.'

'I study. Lessons two time a week. Yev still much better than me. I catch up.'

'So what's Yev doing?'

'Y'know. Business. We should have drink. He like you. He always say you smart lady.'

'I like him.'

'My sister, she come back with us. Aaah, she love London.'

'Yeah?'

For a mile or two they travelled in silence. Through

Fulham and then along the King's Road. Kaz let her gaze drift over the procession of swanky boutiques and upmarket design shops. London was a great place to be rich. The fact that she had no money made her feel like an outcast in the city where she was born.

An excited look came into Tolya's eye.

He raised a gloved finger from the steering wheel and pointed. 'Road there. Very good restaurant. My cousin boyfriend. Chef. One star Michelin.'

'Really. D'you get any free grub?'

'Grub?'

'Food.'

'Sometimes.' He hesitated, as if searching for the right words. 'Joey go away. Amsterdam maybe. Keep low . . . er . . .'

'Low profile?'

He grinned. 'Yeah. Low profile. Good word. So maybe you run things for him now?'

Kaz gave a disbelieving hoot. 'I don't think Joey would be happy with that.'

The Russian shrugged. 'Why not?'

'I testified against him, Tol. Grassed him up. He's not about to trust me, is he?'

He brushed this aside with a wave of his gloved hand. 'He don't blame you.'

'Not much.'

'I am four brothers. Me youngest. We all go to army. Nicolai, Yuri, dead in Chechnya. Two son my mother lost. For what? For motherland? For greedy fucking politicians in dachas with fat wives? Fuck them all. Family is blood. Yev I trust. Sometime we argue. Still, Yev I trust.'

This was the most Kaz had ever heard him say. She wondered about the extent of his loyalty to Joey. Did it stretch beyond the next payday? Probably not. Yet Joey was forced to rely on these guns for hire. He was an escaped convict on the run. It was his offshore bank accounts that paid for their protection. But what if Kaz could renegotiate the deal?

The brothers' only allegiance was to each other. Was there some way she could persuade them to favour her over Joey? She'd managed to come to an understanding with Yevgeny before. Could she do it again? Could they provide the escape route she was searching for?

They turned south down Wandsworth Bridge Road and headed for the river. The tide was low and sluggish, a dog-walker wandered the muddy foreshore, her canine companion scattering the gulls.

As they drove over the bridge, past the tiered ranks of upscale apartments rising up from the riverbank, she glanced at Tolya. 'What's she called, your sister?'

'Irina.'

'Nice name.'

'She work for hairdresser.' He added a dismissive frown. 'For now. She loads ambition. Her English . . .' He grimaced. 'Not so good. She study hard.'

'She could become a stylist.'

He puzzled over the word. 'Maybe . . .'

'Someone who does the whole look – y'know, hair, clothes. For models and actors. It's all about taste. You can earn loads. Someone I knew at art college got into that.'

He was listening intently, processing it all despite his shaky grasp of the language. 'She like art. She very pretty. Not like me and Yev.' He laughed. Kaz joined in.

It was becoming clear to her that she'd stumbled on an angle that might just play. It was certainly worth a punt.

She adopted an offhand tone. 'I'd like to meet her.'

'Yeah?' He beamed with genuine pleasure. 'She want very much make English friend.'

'Maybe we should all get together? Have a night out? You, me, Yev, Irina? Course, you'd have to persuade Joey.'

Tolya dismissed this with an abrupt shake of the head. 'I tell him. He don't mind.'

65

Nicci had sent texts to both Julia and Karen Phelps to let them know she'd be late. She was still feeling like death warmed up, but her mood had changed completely. The meeting with Calder was a game changer. Blake had insisted that the Assistant Commissioner held the key to the investigation and he'd been proved right.

Having dosed herself with paracetamol, Nicci took a taxi to Wandsworth. She sat in the back of the cab with a notebook balanced on her knee, making sure she'd got all the main points down. Swigging from a bottle of water she reviewed her conversation with Calder. She'd been *backed into a corner*, that was the phrase her old boss had used. Nicci wondered to what extent this was true. In her view the more accurate explanation was probably that Calder didn't want to jeopardize her position in the hierarchy and her chance of the top job.

Still, the conflict between Calder's guilty conscience and her reluctance to stick her head above the parapet had yielded the breakthrough that Nicci needed.

She paid the cabbie and walked up the path to Julia's front door with something approaching a spring in her step. She would knock the booze on the head and show those bastards. A write-off, discharged as medically unfit? She was a bloody good detective, Calder was right about that. Now she was going to prove it.

She found Julia and Karen sitting at the kitchen table nursing mugs of coffee. The atmosphere was freighted with tension and a postcard sat on the table between them. As Julia bustled around making a fresh cafetiere, Karen picked up the card. The image on the front was a painting of a nun by Gwen John.

She offered it to Nicci. 'I've just been telling Julia about this. Came to me via witness protection.'

Nicci took the card and turned it over. The handwriting was tight and neat, in blue fountain pen.

Saw this and thought of you. I hope you're leading a virtuous life now. I thought the pain of missing you would go away eventually. It hasn't. My life is busy, but full of lies and complications. You know my number. I wish you'd bring some light into my dismal existence by calling it. H xx

Nicci shot a look across the kitchen at Julia. She was waiting for the kettle to boil, fidgeting with the mugs and keeping it together – just.

The ex-cop's gaze travelled back to Karen. 'When did you get this?'

'April. Witness protection gave it to my probation officer. It was in an envelope. They'd maybe had it a couple of weeks. I dunno.'

'Did you call her?'

Kaz pinched the end of her nose, her eyes were welling up. 'No. I wish the fuck I had.' She folded her arms tightly, her chin jutted. She was determined to hold it together too. 'I don't know why she was in Glasgow. She had no way of knowing I was there. You know the rules.' She stared defiantly at Nicci. 'I never got in touch with her. And I never met her. I swear.'

Unfastening the straps on her bag, Nicci lifted out her notebook and laptop. 'I know you didn't.'

Julia flashed a look of surprise at Nicci.

She set the laptop on the table and opened it. 'I had someone check it out. And we've got CCTV footage from the hotel of the person it seems she did go there to meet: Paige Hollister.'

Kaz frowned. 'Who?'

Scrolling through her emails, Nicci clicked on the message Eddie had sent her. 'She's—'

Her reply hung in the air, incomplete, as Julia picked up one of the delicate white porcelain mugs with a silver band around the rim and hurled it at the wall.

66

Kaz found a dustpan and brush in the cupboard under the stairs. The mug had shattered into smithereens, which were spread liberally across the kitchen floor together with some flakes of plaster that had been gouged from the wall on impact.

She returned to the kitchen and started to sweep up. Julia was slumped in a chair, face in her hands. Nicci poured boiling water into the cafetiere and carried it to the table with fresh mugs. She gave Kaz a neutral smile.

If she'd noticed Tolya parked across the road in a residents-only bay, she didn't say. Kaz was glad not to have to deploy a lie to cover it. The unvarnished truth about Helen's last communication with her was painful. It left her full of self-reproach. Yet there was a relief in being honest and apparently believed. Especially when Kaz had been expecting accusations and argument.

Julia raised her head and wiped her face with the back of her hand. 'Paige is Scottish, though you wouldn't know it from the accent. I think her father was an oil exec for BP. When he retired, her parents moved to Rothesay. It's nice; we took Charles to visit them one time.'

Nicci poured fresh coffee into the three mugs. 'That's not far from Glasgow?'

Julia nodded, pulled out a tissue and blew her nose. She

glanced at Kaz, then looked away. 'I don't understand why she couldn't talk to me. Lies and complications? Secret meetings with Paige?' Her face began to dissolve and the tears started to flow again.

As the laptop loaded the CCTV clip Nicci reached across the table to pat Julia's hand. 'Listen to me, the first thing you need to know is that Helen was most probably trying to protect you.'

'From what?' Julia's face crumpled with anger. 'She fell in love with Paige when she was fourteen. Paige was the fucking babysitter! Her first love. I knew all about that.'

'What about Paige's husband?'

'You mean Robert? He was one of Charles's students at Oxford. Paige was his girlfriend.'

'She was a student too?'

'Yeah. Helen's parents were a bit old-fashioned. Even though Helen was fourteen, they didn't think she and her brothers should be left alone, so they hired a babysitter.' Her tone sharpened. 'They might've thought twice if they'd realized it would help turn their daughter into a dyke.'

Kaz emptied the shards of porcelain into the bin and joined the others at the table. She'd always known the fragile connection she and Julia had made would likely be torpedoed by Helen's card. Yet keeping it secret, she'd decided, was a fool's option. She wanted the truth as much as Julia did.

She sat down and Julia gave her an aggrieved look. 'First Paige, then you. Was it because you both rejected her? She wanted what she couldn't have.'

Kaz met her eye. 'I told you, she could've had me, but she chose you.'

'Okay, I know this is difficult.' Nicci decided it was time to play peacemaker. 'But let's stick with Paige and Robert. They were students at Oxford and Helen was fourteen when she met them. So what else do you know about them and their relationship with Helen's family?'

Julia exhaled. 'They became family friends. Robert Hollister was Charles's star student. He and Paige got married after they graduated, Helen was a bridesmaid at the wedding.'

Nicci popped a sugar lump in her coffee. 'A bridesmaid? That must've been tough for Helen.'

'It was a crush, an adolescent crush. I don't think anything ever came of it.' Julia seemed rattled as she pushed away the unwanted images invading her head.

'You sure about that?'

Julia sighed wearily. 'I don't know. In recent years Paige has been unhappy. Her kids are grown-up, Robert's affairs are pretty much common knowledge. Helen stayed friends with the Hollisters for her father's sake. Charles thinks that Robert's the dog's bollocks.'

Nicci nodded. 'Well, his protégé could be in government soon, that's quite flattering. And presumably the Hollister connection helped Helen's political career?'

'She hated all that. The nepotism.' Julia took a mouthful of fresh coffee. 'She went out of her way to avoid Robert's help.'

Idly brushing flecks of dust from the computer screen, Nicci turned to Kaz. 'Did she ever talk to you about the Hollisters?'

'Once we talked about first love. She said hers betrayed her.'

That was putting it mildly, thought Nicci. Telling them what she'd discovered from Calder would not be easy. The fact neither seemed to have an inkling meant it was going to come as a major shock. Kaz would cope, she wasn't so sure about Julia.

'Okay, well, a former colleague of mine has given me some information.'

Julia jumped in, immediately suspicious. 'A police officer? I knew there was a cover-up!'

'Helen went to see this . . . person for advice. She explained that as a teenager she'd fallen in love with a girl who was a few years older than her. She was besotted and would've done anything for this girl. The girl told her that they could have sex, but only if she allowed the girl's boyfriend to watch.'

Julia's hand grasped her mug, the knuckles whitening with tension. Kaz merely shook her head and sighed.

Nicci ploughed on. 'Helen was fourteen. The first few times they had sex the boyfriend watched, then he joined in. Then he took over. Reflecting on this as an adult, Helen realized it was probably the plan all along. She was afraid to tell her parents, the girl told her she wouldn't be believed. So she continued to acquiesce for the next couple of years.'

Scraping back her chair, Julia got up, a restless fury taking possession of her. She paced up and down the room a couple of times. Nicci waited.

Julia turned. 'Is that it?'

'That's only the beginning.'

Julia and Kaz exchanged glances.

Kaz's brow was darkening. 'The *beginning*?'

Nicci fortified herself with a mouthful of coffee. 'In her early twenties, Helen did her best to avoid the couple. But as we know, they were family friends. On one occasion she tried to speak to her mother, who got extremely upset and made her promise never to mention it to her father.'

'Or anyone else, presumably?' Kaz huffed. 'Why didn't Hollister just find himself a hooker? There's loads who'll play the lesbo game for a john.'

'Apparently he took the view that he and Helen were simply having an affair and his now wife understood. On a number of occasions he trapped or forced Helen into situations where they had sex. Finally, she confronted him, insisted it had to stop. He agreed, then reneged on that agreement.'

Julia slapped her palm on the table. 'Why the fuck haven't the police arrested Hollister?'

'Helen didn't name him specifically. She wanted to know the chances of a prosecution being successful. All she would say was that he was a high-profile politician. My colleague told her that it would be tricky – historical allegations of child abuse, her word against his? She needed corroboration from the wife. Or other evidence.'

Kaz pushed back in her chair. 'D'you think that's what she was trying to get from Paige?'

'Maybe.' Nicci glanced at Julia. 'A week before she died, Helen called my colleague. She'd been on a trip to Brussels about a month earlier. Remember it?'

Julia was pacing, hugging her own torso in a vain attempt to contain the pain. 'Yeah, some EU thing. A summit on drugs policy.'

'So Hollister was there?'

The reply was a terse nod.

'Well, she told my colleague that she was raped by Hollister in a hotel bedroom. However, guessing he might try this, she'd set up a camera in the room and filmed it.'

Kaz and Julia exchanged incredulous looks.

It was Kaz who spoke, a rising tide of rage in her voice. 'You saying that bastard had her killed?'

Nicci raised both hands. 'One step at a time. I'm saying that if such an incriminating film exists, and he knew about it, it's a motive for murder.'

67

The wardrobe doors were wide open. Julia was frantically pulling out drawers from the bottom. She handed them to Kaz, who emptied them onto the bed. Nicci sorted through the piles of underwear, tights, socks and pyjamas. The process was brisk, all three women on a mission.

Removing the last drawer, Julia stepped back, sweating and frustrated. 'I don't know where else she might've put it.'

Nicci frowned. 'You saw it when she first got it?'

'She ordered it off the Net. I opened the door to the postman. I did wonder; she only ever took the odd photo with her phone. She said it was a present for her brother to fix on his bike. He does lots of road races.'

Kaz picked up a handful of lacy lingerie; white – Helen only ever wore white underwear. In deference to Julia, she tried to remain nonchalant, but it gave her butterflies; it felt almost sacrilegious to be rummaging through her dead lover's things like this.

She made herself focus. 'Let's be clear what we're looking for here. A GoPro comes with mounts, accessories. The crucial thing is the memory card. If this is what she used, I don't think she'd leave it in the camera.'

Nicci turned to her. 'How big's the memory card?'

Kaz held her thumb and index finger barely a centimetre apart. 'Tiny. Like a phone SIM. I know this girl on my course who uses a GoPro. You can put them in all sorts of places. Even underwater. She controls it with an app on her phone.'

Julia cast about her distractedly; she seemed ready to tear the whole house apart. 'It must be here somewhere.'

Brow deeply furrowed, Nicci's gaze roved the room from ceiling to skirting board, assessing, analysing.

She shot a concerned look at Julia. 'Okay, I don't think this is getting us anywhere. Is there a local pub? I suggest we go and sit down quietly and think this through.'

'I don't want to go the fucking pub!' Julia exploded. 'Jesus wept! We have to find this camera.'

In contrast with Julia, Nicci was pensive and calm. It reminded Kaz of their previous encounters. Nicci was back in cop mode and she was in charge, which Kaz found surprisingly reassuring.

The detective put a tentative hand on Julia's arm. 'I need to contact my office. And we're going to have some of our security people come over here and sweep the whole house. You understand what I'm saying?'

The objections died on Julia's lips. Her jaw slackened, she nodded, eyes darting around the room.

Her home, her private haven had suddenly morphed into an alien place. 'You think—'

Nicci didn't let her finish. 'Probably not. It's just a precaution. In the circumstances.' She pulled out her phone and turned away. Mentally she was making a list – planning, organizing. She needed them out of the way so she could do her job.

Kaz weighed up her next move. The details Nicci had given them were burning through her psyche. It was a major head-fuck and then some. In the meantime she had a delicate juggling act to perform. With Tolya waiting for her outside, things might get complicated. Could she have a word with him without Nicci noticing?

She took a step towards the bedroom door. 'Come on, Julia. Let's you and me go down the pub. Nicci can meet us there.'

Julia stood marooned in the middle of the room. She was clutching a handful of socks and tights. She dumped them on the bed.

'Come on, mate.' Kaz gave her an encouraging smile. 'We've both had a fucking shock.'

She glanced at Nicci. The ex-cop was intent on writing a text. 'Okay, Nicci?'

'Yeah, good idea.' She looked up with a frown. 'Which pub exactly?'

68

The text Simon Blake received from Nicci was at the same time cryptic and precise:

Call me. Now. On a landline.

He picked up the desk phone and keyed in her number. 'Nic?'

'I think we may have a situation.' Her tone was neutral yet it conveyed volumes.

'Okay. What do you need?'

'A sweep. Some help from Bharat. And when's Eddie back?'

'I'll check.'

There was a moment of silence. A sweep meant she suspected surveillance. But where and of whom? Blake's brain shifted into overdrive – Nicci had discovered something major, that much was clear. And the phone line wasn't secure. Since they'd spoken in the morning Blake had noticed she'd remained out of the office. Though he didn't keep tabs. Nicci did things her own way, which had been the arrangement since she'd joined SBA.

His office door was open, he beckoned urgently to Alicia. 'Where shall I meet you?'

'There's a pub next to Wandsworth Common, the Hope.'

He checked his watch. 'Forty minutes?'

'Right.' Nicci's tone softened. 'By the way, you were right.'

The line went dead. Alicia was hovering in the doorway. Right about what?

Hooking his jacket off the back of his chair, he turned to Alicia. 'Is Rory around?'

'Out on a job, I think.'

'Find him. And tell Bharat I need him.'

As Alicia hurried back to her desk, Blake strode across the room to the investigations section. 'Pascale?' The researcher swivelled her chair and met the boss's eye. 'What's Nicci doing in Wandsworth?'

'She had a meeting with Julia Hadley I think.'

He frowned. Was Hadley the surveillance target? 'You got her address?'

The urgency in his tone was signal enough.

'Is Nicci okay?' Pascale's fingers hovered over her keyboard.

'She just needs some backup. Did she have anything else planned this morning apart from Hadley?'

Pascale glanced across at Liam, the other researcher, then back to Blake. 'Perhaps. She got a call just before she went out.'

Liam chipped in. 'I ordered her a taxi. Someone she had to meet and that was going to make her late for Hadley.'

'Did she say who?'

They both shook their heads.

'Think.' Blake was standing with hands on hips. At six foot two he was imperious. 'Or take a guess.'

Liam could only open his palms and say, 'Sorry, boss.'

Pascale pondered for a moment. 'I wasn't really listening to the call. But she was a bit annoyed. I'm not sure but . . . I think it could have been Fiona Calder.'

A laconic smile crept over Blake's features. That made sense. *Right about what?* Calder of course! Calder held the key to the investigation. Had Nicci finally cracked her? But surveillance? That worried him. Was the Security Service targeting Hadley, and if so, why?

There was nothing random about Warner's murder, it had been a planned, professional hit. That had been his opinion from the outset. Now they were getting under the skin of the case. He'd always loved this moment, when the pieces of the puzzle started to make sense, like pixels on a screen rearranging themselves to produce a discernible image.

Bharat wandered across the office towards him. He was an extremely bright lad, but lived on another planet. Was he a little autistic? Blake suspected this might be the case. Bharat blinked at him with liquid dark eyes – he didn't speak or even smile, he simply waited.

Blake patted him on the shoulder; he usually found the paternal approach worked best with Bharat. 'Right, mate, get your box of tricks. Nicci needs some help.'

'Should I bring a dongle?'

'Definitely.'

69

All eyes were on Bharat, which didn't help his nerves. He took a sip of his beer. 'Okay, well, erm—'

Blake gave him a genial smile. 'Just keep it simple. No cyber jargon.'

The afternoon had turned overcast; there was a freshening breeze and a threat of rain in the scudding clouds. Apart from a lone smoker, a large bloke with tattoos, they were the only ones occupying the wooden picnic benches fringing the pavement outside the pub.

Nicci, Julia and Karen sat looking out across the road to the green acres of Wandsworth Common beyond. Blake and Bharat faced them across the table.

Nicci had met the two men when they'd arrived in a taxi and brought them up to speed. Rory and a surveillance techie had turned up ten minutes later in a Range Rover. Julia had given them her house keys.

Bharat held up a rectangular sliver of plastic. 'So er, well, the SD card would be like this. Sixty-four gig, plenty of space. From the camera it can be downloaded to various devices: phone, tablet, any computer really. Or uploaded to the Net. We could start by checking the apps on her phone.'

Wired on Red Bull and painkillers, Nicci was impatient to move things on. 'Okay, say she emailed the clip to someone from her phone – how secure would that be?'

'Very insecure. It was video, so there'd be the size of the file to consider. But really any random hacker could pick it up.'

Blake cleared his throat; they were entering murky waters, he knew that. Still it didn't bother him.

The breakthrough had filled him with optimism. 'The police would've forensically examined all her computers, checked her internet history. And if they were doing the job properly, they'd have gone through all the deleted files too. That would include any photo files.'

'Maybe they did.' Kaz glared at him. 'Maybe they found it and that's why she got whacked.'

Blake gave her a faintly disdainful look. 'You're jumping to a lot of conclusions.'

Blake's whole attitude, oozing the cop mentality, grated on Kaz. He'd turned up and now he was taking over. Added to that, he seemed so fucking pleased with himself.

She slammed her palm on the table. 'There's only one question here, are you going after this fucker or not?'

'Karen, I know you're angry—'

'You arrogant twat, you know fuck all! You don't give a toss about Helen – this is just another job for you.'

Blake couldn't understand why Nicci had insisted on involving Kaz Phelps in the mix. It seemed unnecessary and unhelpful. He shook his head wearily and glanced at Nicci for support.

'Okay, this isn't getting us anywhere.' Nicci eyeballed Kaz. 'What d'you want here, Karen? 'Cause what I'm looking for is the truth – who killed Helen Warner and why? You go jumping in and making assumptions, chances are you will get it wrong.'

'Are you stupid or what? The cops are protecting Hollister.'

Nicci met the wrathful look. 'Probably. But that doesn't tell us who killed her, does it?'

A keening sob rose from Julia. Her small frame was wedged between Kaz and Nicci on the bench and she began to shudder and weep.

Kaz looped an arm round her shoulder and squeezed her. 'This is so fucked! Can't you lot see that?'

'Listen to me, both of you.' Nicci twisted in her seat. 'The only thing that will nail Hollister, and Helen's killer or killers, is evidence. That's what she was trying to do – get evidence.'

Blake pulled a laundered handkerchief from his jacket pocket and offered it to Julia.

She glanced up at him and took it. 'All this arguing, it's just – it's a waste of time and energy.' Her face disappeared into the white linen hankie.

'You're right. And I should apologize to Karen. It is a job.' Blake met her eye. 'But every job matters. This one certainly does.'

Kaz's face remained impassive. He was a slick bastard, she'd give him that.

Nicci turned to Bharat. 'So we're clear that sending or uploading the clip wouldn't have been secure?'

'Unless it was encrypted. There are various ways—'

Blake cut him short, focusing on Julia. 'Presumably Helen was savvy enough to realize that her communications could be monitored?'

Julia dabbed her nose. 'She wasn't stupid.'

'No, of course not. But we're all continually playing catch-up with the technology.' He gave her a reassuring smile. 'Maybe there was someone she'd have gone to for advice? An IT specialist of some sort?'

Nicci scribbled a note on her pad: *Ray?*

'I can't think of anyone.' The truth was, Julia couldn't think, period. She was too busy asking herself why Helen hadn't trusted her. What had she done wrong? And how could she have remained so oblivious to what was going on?

On social occasions with the Hollisters there had always been an awkwardness. Julia's private belief was that Helen still carried a torch for Paige. Helen had told her that Paige had suffered with depression for years, and Julia had pitied her. Now all she wanted was to wring the stupid bitch's neck.

Tapping her pen on the pad, Nicci swept her gaze round the table. 'Okay, let's not ignore the obvious. Something so small, this little SD thingy, would be easy to hide. Right?'

Bharat glanced at her, he was feeling annoyed and that fuelled his confidence. He resented the fact that he'd been dragged out of the office just to have his theories and expertise ignored. Encryption would have been the obvious course for the professional, though he accepted that Helen Warner might not have managed that on her own.

He reached into the pocket of his chinos and brought out a bunch of keys. Door keys, car keys, all fastened together on a large steel ring; it was a sizeable collection. Attached to the ring and acting as a fob was a short fat plastic penguin.

Grabbing the penguin's head he pulled it off to reveal a USB stick. 'If you're thinking easy, the simplest thing would be to transfer the data onto a memory stick like this one. I carry this round with me all the time in case I'm out and about and need to back stuff up.'

Blake and the three women all stared at the decapitated penguin with its rectangular metal neck.

A grin spread across Nicci's features. 'I think you've put

your finger on it, Bharat. It's what most people would use, and they'd make several copies for safety. This is what we're looking for: a memory stick.'

70

By the time Nicci got back to the office it was mid-afternoon. She'd left Blake to sort out Julia Hadley. Her parents lived in Blackheath and he'd ordered a car to take her there. Floundering in the backwash of emotional shock she'd become monosyllabic; separating her from Karen Phelps also seemed a sensible precaution. Phelps continued to be belligerent and confrontational. Her volatility concerned Blake. Though if Nicci was honest with herself she knew she might've had a similar reaction.

A complete forensic search of the house would take some hours. Blake had called up a retired SOCO, who helped them out from time to time. Rory and his surveillance expert were carrying out a systematic sweep to ensure the place was thoroughly debugged. However, Nicci doubted they'd find the SD card or any memory sticks. Helen Warner had not been acting impulsively. Setting a trap for Hollister, in which she was the bait, took guts and determination. She'd planned it carefully and that would've included a secure hiding place for the footage.

Nicci had begun a list: a safe deposit box was the obvious choice. But Helen had probably given herself several options. She must've also realized that she might be putting herself in danger. So who would she have trusted to be the custodian of her secret in the event of her demise? And if there was such a person, why hadn't they come forward?

Keeping Julia out of the loop had been done to protect her. The forethought to do this, plus the whole tenor of her approach to Fiona Calder, suggested Warner was not naive about the forces that could end up ranged against her. And yet the card she'd sent to Karen Phelps, attempting to rekindle that relationship, suggested a woman who felt beleaguered.

She had family: two brothers. Would she have trusted either of them? Nicci hadn't noticed them at the aborted inquest. As for the elderly father, his relationship with Robert Hollister would've precluded taking him into her confidence.

Nicci crossed the room and dumped a small paper carrier on her desk. She'd picked up supplies en route, which comprised her personal hangover cure.

As she unpacked them, Pascale turned round to greet her. 'You cracked Calder then?'

Nicci nodded, then downed half a bottle of superjuice. Dark green, laced with vitamins and ginseng, it had the appearance and consistency of pond slime. She followed this immediately with half a bottle of Coke. Belching, she clutched her stomach and grimaced as the acid reflux stung her oesophagus.

Pascale gave her a sympathetic smile. 'You need paracetamol?'

'Already had three.' Another eruption of sugary gas rose in her gullet; she placed her palm over her mouth, burped and settled in her chair.

'Remind me, Pascale, what do we know about Helen Warner's family? Particularly the brothers.'

The researcher swivelled to face her computer screen and

with a couple of rapid mouse-clicks brought up the relevant document.

She scrolled through it. 'Charles Junior, two years younger. He's an economist like his papa. Works for Nomura as an analyst. Currently based in Tokyo. Has a Japanese wife.'

Nicci unwrapped a Mars Duo and took a pensive bite. This would explain why he hadn't attended the inquest. Would Helen have been close to him? Impossible to guess. Nicci pulled the notebook from her bag and scribbled a reminder to herself: *Ask J if H saw C anytime just prior to death.*

Munching her way through claggy chocolate and nougat she felt the sugar hit starting to work its magic and loosen what felt like an iron bridle encasing her skull. 'And the other brother?'

'Adam. Much younger. Eight years. He's a . . . sculptor.' Pascale's French accent made this sound wildly exotic.

Nicci devoured the rest of the chocolate bar as she considered the Warner siblings: Helen, the big sister, responsible, high-powered, a woman who wanted to change the world; Charles, a clone of the old man; and Adam, the typical baby brother, determined to be different.

She licked the corners of her mouth; a hint of nausea rose in her stomach, but she decided to ignore it. 'Where's he live?'

'Still studying. At the San Francisco Art Institute.'

Leaning back in her chair, Nicci reflected on the privileged education available to the moneyed; not so much billionaires, but that upper-middle-class strata who were comfortably rich. Nicci had worked her way through uni, received a bit of help from her parents, but had still embarked on her working life as a police officer with a pile of debt. Juggling the payments on three or four credit cards was simply a way of life.

Buying Sophie a bike one Christmas then a mini iPad the next had only been achieved by jacking up the amount owed.

Helen Warner's affluent background had provided her with every advantage, yet she'd made the choice and the political commitment to campaign for the underdog. Nicci appreciated that. Moreover, the respectable strait-jacket of her family and the injunction not to upset her distinguished father had exposed her to abuse. And she'd decided to fight that too. Embarking on such a parlous course without any obvious support was courageous, even foolhardy some might say.

Nicci's time as a homicide detective had involved some of the most challenging work of her police career. She'd been on several different murder teams, providing rapid response and also taking part in any number of in-depth investigations. She'd learnt to hold her empathy for the victims in check. Sometimes that was tough. Cases involving murdered kids particularly had the potential to crack open even the most experienced and hard-bitten officers.

In her own mind, Nicci had come to divide victimhood into different categories. There were the complete innocents – victims of malign fate who found themselves in the wrong place at the wrong time. Then there were those who'd spiralled to a violent end through broken lives peppered by bad decisions. This category trickled over into the out-and-out villains, those who'd chosen to get their living on the wrong side of the law.

But there was another category, rarely encountered and set apart, in Nicci's mind, from the rest. These were individuals who'd taken a moral stand and risked their own neck to do the right thing. Nicci's dead colleague, DC Mal Bradley, fitted into this group. And, in her opinion, so did Helen Warner.

Although all murder victims deserved justice, there was an added imperative in these instances. Someone had to pick up the baton, if only to affirm that civilized values must triumph and that making the choice of right over wrong continued to matter.

Nicci was debating whether to start on the family-size bag of Maltesers when Liam came across the office carrying two takeaway coffees.

His face broke into a boyish grin at the sight of her. 'What did Calder say? Does she know who killed Warner?' He had none of Pascale's style or restraint.

Catching the arch look Pascale was giving him, he changed tack. 'Want a coffee? You can have mine. Salted Caramel Mocha.'

Nicci smiled grimly. 'Thanks for the offer, but any more liquid, I'll probably puke.'

Both researchers continued to gaze at her expectantly.

She rubbed the back of her neck and embarked on a succinct summary of Fiona Calder's revelations. The Assistant Commissioner hadn't been told specifically that the politician in question was Robert Hollister. But when the circumstances of Helen's teenage years were factored in, it could only be him.

Pascale pursed her lips and shook her head in disgust.

Liam, as usual, tended more to the crass. 'Well that shortens the odds on his chances of becoming the next but one Labour Prime Minister.'

Nicci smiled; Liam's laddish bravado reminded her of the black humour of the murder teams. It was an attempt to restore normality, ring-fence the unacceptable in order to get on. All the same, she was about to issue a teasing rebuke when her attention was drawn to an altercation in the reception area.

'Just tell me where she is!' The raised voice belonged to DI Tim Armstrong and he was holding his warrant card several inches from the end of Alicia's nose.

'What the fuck?' Nicci got up and glared at him.

Catching sight of her, he flipped his ID shut and strode towards her. They met in the middle of the office.

He looked hot; his collar was unbuttoned, tie askew, his face sweaty and ugly with rage. 'You're just out to fuck me up, aren't you?'

'I don't know what you're talking about.'

Flinging his arms out, he encompassed the room. 'Look at this, bunch of fucking con artists and gravy-trainers! You are not the police.' He jabbed his index finger in Nicci's face. 'When you gonna realize that? You're the fucking rejects.'

Liam came up behind Nicci. 'Want me to call security?'

Tim rounded on him. 'Yeah, call fucking security, you streak of piss. And I'll nick you all for obstruction.'

Curious eyes were peering above screens in the computer section; Alicia was speaking rapidly on the phone. Hugo got up from behind his desk and put his hands on his hips.

Nicci fixed her ex-husband with a penetrating look. 'Whatever it is you're here to say, would you like to come in the conference room and say it?'

Her composure seemed to rile him all the more. He was gearing up for another explosion when Nicci turned her back, walked towards the corner meeting room and held the door open for him.

He had no choice but to stomp after her.

She shut the door behind him with a gentle click. 'So what's rattled your cage?'

'You think I'm stupid, don't you?' His eyes narrowed to peevish slits. 'The case was solved. We were going to the CPS for the go-ahead to charge. Then you stuck your oar in. Now Delgado's running round every fucking school in Hackney, looking for some kid. You tell me that's not you trying to fuck me up?'

A smile spread over Nicci's features. Delgado was following the lead she'd given him, bringing the arrest of Ethel Huxtable's murderer a step closer.

She folded her arms. 'I know you're going to find this hard to believe, Tim, but this is not about you.'

'You think you're a better detective than me, don't you? You always did.'

'It's not about you. It's not about us.' She shook her head wearily.

Shoulders hunched, his lip twisted into a sour curl, part smile and part grimace, he leaned towards her. 'Amy's having a baby. Is that why?'

Nicci raised her eyebrows. She felt curiously detached from any connection she might've once had to this man. The fact she'd loved him was a poisoned memory. He stood before her like an aggrieved adolescent.

'One kid dies, you replace it with another? You really think that's going to work?'

Face flushed, he took a step towards her. 'You Godless bitch! If you'd been a proper mother, it would never have happened. My daughter would be alive.'

She met his fury with an icy stare. 'I had no idea Amy was pregnant. How would I know? As for Sophie's death, you think I don't feel guilt? It's torn my life to shreds, no question of that. But it was an accident and a tragedy – I have no need for revenge.' She took a breath and exhaled a sigh. 'What I hadn't appreciated until this moment is just how unhinged it's made you. Look at yourself, Tim. You're so fucked up, you can't even see it.'

He raised his clenched fist and for an instant it seemed it might be coming her way. He swayed on the balls of his feet and she saw his eyes were glassy with tears. Then, giving her a wide berth, he dived at the door and wrenched it open.

'Stay the fuck out of police inquiries!' he shouted over his shoulder.

On the threshold he almost collided with Alan Turnbull, who stepped back to let him pass.

Turnbull gave her a quizzical smile. 'Everything all right?'

71

Kaz had remained at the pub with Julia. She knew that Simon Blake wanted to get shot of her, but that suited her fine. Julia was in shock. The realization she'd probably been kept in ignorance by Helen to protect her gave her no consolation.

One question consumed Kaz: was Helen looking for help, someone to share her secret, when she tried to get in touch via witness protection? The niggling guilt that Kaz had been feeling since she first learnt of her former lover's death had now ballooned into devouring self-reproach. At the time of receiving it, Helen's card had merely fuelled her anger. Kaz had tossed it to one side; she was fucked if she was going to dance to Helen Warner's tune again. She'd been led on before, only to be dumped when their liaison no longer suited the lawyer's convenience.

Now, with the benefit of hindsight, Kaz was eaten up with regret. Could she have saved Helen? It was a question that would never be answered. The fact remained, Helen had saved her. When she first walked into the visitors' pen at Styal, Kaz had been just another teenage junkie whose life was caught in a downward spiral. Falling in love with her lawyer had been the catalyst that helped Kaz turn her life around. Her decision to go straight had been self-interested rather than moral. She'd wanted Helen Warner, it had been as simple as that.

Glancing at Julia – poor, respectable, broken Julia – Kaz understood why Helen hadn't confided in her. Julia was part of the politician's image, the most acceptable face she could put on her lesbianism. With Julia at her side, there was no danger of frightening the horses. But when it came to dealing with her life's more unsavoury aspects, with the skulduggery festering below the surface, she'd needed someone tougher. Kaz knew she'd let Helen down when she was still alive and she vowed to make up for that now.

Nicci Armstrong had come up with crucial information, but how zealously would she pursue it? Kaz wasn't impressed with her boss, Blake. Though they'd been hired by Julia, they were cops in all but name. They talked and acted like cops; for them it was all about evidence. They were following a process. But as far as Kaz was concerned, that was all too fucking slow.

Tolya had been sitting at an end table on the pub's pavement terrace throughout the round-table discussion. He'd smoked and slowly ploughed his way through a copy of the *Sun* with the aid of the dictionary on his phone. None of these brilliant detectives had given him a second glance.

Far from seeing him as an encumbrance, foisted on her by her brother, Kaz was beginning to think that she might turn the situation to her advantage in her quest to find Helen's killers. Tolya and his elder brother, Yevgeny, were guns for hire; Joey had used them and relied upon them increasingly in his business because they were more than thugs. Much more. They were resourceful and smart. However, their loyalty came with a price tag – a hefty price tag. That was the problem.

A minicab pulled up at the main entrance to the pub and Blake, who'd been making phone calls, shepherded Julia

towards it. With the back door of the cab open, Julia hesitated. She looked in Kaz's direction, face pale, frowning.

In all the weeks since Helen's death she'd remained tough,
insisting her partner did not commit suicide, demanding that
someone find her the truth. But now, with the revelations
about the Hollisters, she'd hit a wall. The relationship she'd
thought she had with Helen was a sham. Helen had excluded
her from the real emotional issues in her life. Julia, with her
PR woman's confidence and her arty friends, was simply
Helen's mask. The bombshell for Julia was the realization she
hadn't known her partner at all. Now all the fight had left her.
What seemed to her Helen's total lack of integrity was the
ultimate betrayal. It destroyed everything.

Kaz gave her a nod. 'I'll call you, Julia.'

The reply was a ghostly smile. Julia got into the cab and
was gone.

Blake turned briskly to Kaz and offered her his hand. 'We
will of course keep you posted, Karen. Nicci has your
number?'

Her hand wasn't large but she returned the dry, masculine
grip with some force. 'She has.'

His smile was shrewd, he knew she didn't like him. 'Are
you headed back up north?'

'Yeah.'

'We'll be in touch.'

Kaz could tell he was lying to her as much as she was lying
to him. She watched him and his computer geek cross the
road and head off on foot in the direction of Julia's house.

Tolya folded his newspaper and gave her a grin. 'She very
sad your friend.'

Kaz sighed. 'Yeah, she is.'

'We go now?'

'If it's all the same to you Tol, I'd like to make a detour. Only if you think Joey wouldn't mind . . .'

The Russian shrugged, but Kaz could see he was intrigued. Acting as a minder must get boring at times, she figured a bit of variety might appeal to him.

He got up. 'Okay. Where we go?'

'To see a man about a memory stick.'

72

Eddie Lunt stepped off the train at Euston and walked up the ramped platform to find Nicci Armstrong waiting – arms folded, scowl on her face – the other side of the barrier.

She greeted him with a curt dip of the head. 'Did you talk to her?'

'Left a couple of messages, finally she picked up. She's not in a good way.'

'But she's agreed to see us?'

'Half five.'

A brief smile of acknowledgement spread across her features as she started to walk off. Pale, pouchy-eyed, he'd seen her look better. She had a fondness for the sauce that was apparent. He hoisted his bag on his shoulder and followed.

Stopping abruptly outside one of the station's coffee franchises, she turned. 'We got time for a coffee?'

'Yeah, she's out at North Finchley. Allow half-hour on the tube to Woodside Park, ten-minute walk.'

Nicci veered off into the cafe. 'What you having?'

Eddie shook his head, gave her a sunny smile. 'You sit down, boss. My treat.'

Typical of Eddie to insist on playing the gentleman. Nicci asked for a double-shot espresso and plonked herself down at a corner table. She pulled out her notebook and flicked through the pages. Escaping the office and Alan Turnbull's mocking eye had been her first priority. Witnessing her rowing with her ex-husband must've afforded him some amusement.

Nicci dismissed him from her mind. She had a job to do. Her task now was to move things on. Following leads, asking questions, this was the process she knew. The Assistant Commissioner had handed her the end of a delicate thread. If she could just track it through the labyrinth of lies and obfuscations without breaking it, the identity of Helen Warner's killer would be revealed.

She gazed out on to the station concourse at the ebb and flow of travellers passing by. A welter of busy lives and private concerns swirling round each other, maybe touching for an instant before sweeping on. Crowded places bothered her more than they used to. Back in her uniformed days she'd done her share of public order policing; from moshes to football mobs, she'd been in the thick of it, holding the line. Maybe she was developing some kind of creeping agoraphobia? Or perhaps it was just that London and its torrent of passing strangers made her feel all the more alone.

Eddie beamed as he set down a tray on the table and unloaded two cups of coffee, then held up a plate containing two chocolate muffins.

'Can I tempt you?'

His impish grin still annoyed her, but Nicci managed a smile. 'Cheers.'

Her blood sugar level was probably bordering on the diabetic, but her brain was back in gear and the headache was fading. She peeled the paper wrapper off the muffin and took a bite. The chocolate filling oozed and she caught a drip with her tongue.

'Good, innit?' Eddie smiled. 'My old mum reckons I'm a

chocoholic.' He patted his ample girth and sighed. 'But what you gonna do? You only live once. You gotta enjoy life, else what's the point?'

Brushing crumbs from her mouth, Nicci realized that, aside from his criminal past, she knew next to nothing about Eddie Lunt.

'You married, Eddie?'

'Divorced.' He chuckled. 'Well, who'd stay married to me, eh? I live back with Ma now. She's getting on. Means I can keep an eye on her.' He nodded, partly to reassure himself.

Nicci watched him thinking of his mother, the tightening of the jaw, the bobbing of the Adam's apple as he swallowed his emotions; a son caring for an elderly parent didn't quite accord with her image of him.

She sipped her coffee. 'You know what you said about Helen Warner – you thought Hollister was "giving her one", to use your elegant turn of phrase. Turns out you were more than right. He'd been abusing her since she was fourteen.'

'Stone the crows.' Eddie's cup stalled between saucer and mouth. 'Didn't have him pegged as one of them.'

'She decided to try and turn the tables on him. So on some political beano to Brussels she set up a camera in her hotel bedroom and waited for him to pounce. She got it all on film – him raping her.'

He frowned as he digested the information. 'Where d'you hear all this? The girlfriend?'

Nicci shook her head. 'She had no idea. Warner visited a former colleague of mine for advice.'

'She was planning to go public?'

'More than that. She wanted to know what would be needed for a successful prosecution.'

A low whistle issued from Eddie. 'That would've set the

cat among the pigeons. Specially since some of the top brass in the Met are looking to Hollister to save their bacon.'

'And Helen would've known that, obviously. So she must've had some plan to go to the media if the Met blocked an investigation.'

Eddie nodded enthusiastically. 'And you're thinking that's what she was up to with old Ray?'

'Well, what do you think?'

'Ideal choice. His press connections were mint, that's why the Labour Party hired him.'

'But when she died, he did nothing. Several weeks went past.' She opened her palms. 'What was he waiting for?'

'Either he didn't know the full story or he didn't have the evidence.' The chocolate muffin sat uneaten on his plate.

Nicci raised a finger. 'You and him meet up, and a few hours later he's dead under a tube train.'

Eddie puffed his cheeks, a sorrowful look in his eye. 'Yeah, tell me about it.'

She laid a hand on his arm. 'No one can blame you, Eddie. What I'm saying is, after he saw you, he did something.'

'You think he was being watched?'

'Yeah. He made a move that someone had been waiting for. Or that caused them to panic.'

'And he gets shoved under a train?'

She nodded and drummed her clenched fist on the table. 'Those last couple of hours, what was he up to? Where did he go? What did he do?'

'All he said to me was: "Catch you later, mate." Like he didn't have a care in the world.'

73

Kaz stared at the palm tree. She remembered the first time she'd seen it – an indoor palm tree, the odd but magnificent centrepiece of the building's airy atrium. She'd run her fingers across the bark to check it was real.

The day she got out of jail, paying a call on Helen Warner had been top of her list. She'd felt ridiculously nervous. Taking Helen by surprise was maybe not a good strategy. But the lawyer had greeted her with warmth and a skittishness that told Kaz the sexual frisson between them wasn't just in her imagination. That had been the beginning of the affair. It seemed like a lifetime ago now.

Helen had given up the law for politics. However, her old firm, Crowley Sheridan Moore, still had their offices on the fifth floor of this smart block off Cheapside. Kaz stood beside the reception desk as the young woman behind it spoke on the phone.

Returning the receiver to its base, she smiled at Kaz. Her shirt was blue and tailored with small epaulettes on the shoulder, a uniform designed by the security company that employed her to convey an unthreatening sense of impregnability.

'Mr Moore is only able to see clients by appointment. If you email his assistant, she'll arrange this for you. You can find their address on the website.'

Kaz sighed. 'You told them my name?'

The young woman's smile didn't waiver, the eyes were fixed, staring through Kaz. 'Yes, of course.'

'Did the assistant actually speak to him?'

'I'm sure if you email they'll get back to you.' There was no impatience in the young woman's manner. This was what she spent her days doing – getting rid of dubious-looking casual callers, politely.

Kaz swivelled on her heel. Tolya was standing a few yards away, arms folded. Their eyes met, he tilted his head indicating she should follow him. Kaz glanced back coldly at the young woman. She wasn't about to thank her, she knew the helpful smile was fake.

Tolya exited via the revolving doors.

When Kaz joined him on the pavement he was rubbing his bare arms. 'So fucking air-con freezing they make it. I don't know why.' He stood for a moment soaking up a brief burst of afternoon sun. Kaz paced in a small frustrated circle.

In addition to being Helen's erstwhile boss, Neville Moore remained Joey's lawyer. Crowley Sheridan Moore, in its earlier incarnation, had been an East End firm of villains' briefs. They'd represented the Phelps family since the very early days of Terry Phelps' 'trouble' with the law.

With the demise of Fred Sheridan, Neville Moore had moved the firm upmarket and to its current City location. He'd diversified the client base and sanitized its image with pro bono work and a dash of radical campaigning. But Moore knew that the shrinking legal aid budget couldn't be relied on, whereas organized crime could. He trod a fine line between defending his clients and aiding and abetting them in their criminal careers. Kaz reckoned that if Helen Warner had been looking for a confidante as slippery and shrewd as her opponents, she might well have chosen her old boss.

The problem, it seemed, was getting to see him. Tolya was peering at her over his aviator shades and she noticed he was grinning.

Catching her eye he laughed. 'Don't look so worried. You wanna go inside? We use back door.'

She followed him as he wandered round the corner and down a narrow side lane leading to the flank of the building. Hardly more than a snicket dating back to the warren of streets that underpinned the old City, it was painted with double yellow lines that filled nearly half the road. They walked along beside twenty-foot high concrete walls and finally came to a gap. Only just high enough to accommodate a Luton van, the opening led down a short ramp to an underground car park. Access was controlled by a red-and-white chequered automatic barrier and two snub-nosed black security cameras pointing downwards from brackets on either wall.

Tolya scanned the entrance and smiled. 'I prefer back door.' Turning to her he placed his palm over his left cheek, eye and his nose. 'You do like this.'

With his hand concealing half his face he strolled past the cameras and ducked under the barrier. She followed suit. They descended the ramp into the low-ceilinged vault, which was divided into slots for a couple of dozen cars. It was relatively empty – a Bentley Continental, several high-end BMWs – only the cream of the building's tenants got a parking space.

In the far corner there was a plain grey door with a keypad beside it. Tolya headed for it, glancing round as he went. The only other camera was fixed above the door and angled downwards. For a man well over six feet tall he hardly needed to stretch to reach the camera from underneath. He gave it a couple of sharp nudges until the lens was pointing upwards.

He turned to the keypad. Kaz watched him with fascination. Each move was carefully considered but there was no urgency. He remained totally relaxed.

Rubbing his chin he pondered. 'Okay . . .'

'How d'you know what number?'

He smiled. 'Most people got no imagination.'

He keyed in 1234. The small light at the top of the device remained stubbornly red. He tried 1939. Still no dice. He sighed. His gaze roved round the dingy basement for inspiration and alighted on an Aston Martin DB5 in ace condition at the end of a row. With a grin he tapped 0007 into the keypad, the light turned green and the door clicked open.

Kaz chuckled in admiration. 'Piece of piss!'

Puzzled, he held open the door for her. 'Piss? You mean like . . . toilet?'

'Nah, it's a saying. Means easy. Clever boy, aren't you, Tol?'

He accepted the compliment with a smile.

A service lift carried them to the fifth floor and, taking a leaf out of Tolya's book, Kaz strolled past the law firm's protesting receptionist and down the corridor to Neville Moore's office. She had a rough idea of its location, which was a couple of doors down from Helen's old office.

Sauntering up to the PA's desk, she tapped her index finger on the top of the shocked woman's VDU. 'Now you gonna tell him I'm here?'

The PA lurched back in her chair. 'I'm sorry, you can't just walk in here like this. I'll have to call security.'

'Your choice. Your job.' Kaz gave her a thin smile. 'I think you'll find my brother, Joey Phelps, is one of Neville's . . . well, more lucrative clients. He's gonna want to see me.'

Hand poised above the phone, the PA dithered. This tall young woman, eyes as dark as her leather jacket, was definitely intimidating. Also she knew who Joey Phelps was.

Kaz tilted her head. 'Make up your mind time.'

Ignoring both of them, Tolya wandered round the PA's desk towards the inner sanctum. *Neville Moore LL.B* was engraved on the glass panel running along the side of the door. The Russian didn't hesitate; he grasped the handle, depressed it and pushed the door open. The office was empty.

'As you can see, he's really not—' The PA's annoyance turned to panic as Tolya crossed the threshold. 'Urm, you really can't go in there.'

It was too late. Kaz joined him. For a lawyer's office, it was curiously pristine. The desk was completely bare, no files, no phone, no computer. A shelf of immaculately arranged law tomes and some bland ornaments were the only other objects in the room.

The PA hovered in the doorway. 'Mr Moore is away on sabbatical.'

Kaz glared at her. 'Since when?'

'For the last month.' Raising her chin she gave the intruders a sniffy and triumphant look. 'He's visiting family and friends in Australia. They're currently on an island in the Great Barrier Reef.'

Kaz plonked herself down on the leather sofa. 'Well, that's kinda weird. 'Cause I bumped into him just yesterday morning – in London.'

74

The house was a white-fronted, three-bedroomed semi in a street calmed by speed bumps and shaded with trees. The curtains in the downstairs bay window were almost closed and a child's tricycle stood abandoned by the side gate.

Eddie raised his eyebrows, glanced at Nicci and pressed the doorbell. Its sing-song chime echoed through the quiet house beyond and after a couple of minutes the door was opened by a brisk woman in her thirties.

'You must be Eddie. I'm Tina's sister.'

'This is my colleague, Nicci Armstrong.' He stood aside to let her go first.

Nicci had done enough 'bad news' calls to know the drill. The sister escorted them through to the conservatory at the back of the house. Tina was curled up on the sofa cradling a blonde-haired toddler in her arms. The doors opened onto the garden where two slightly older boys were kicking a football to each other.

Nicci was struck by the gruff but heartfelt sincerity of Eddie's manner as he greeted the widow. If he was playing a role, he was very good at it. She expressed her condolences, tea was made by the sister and they sat in silence for a few minutes, waiting for Tina to adjust to their presence.

Hair pulled back in a pink scrunchie, her face was puffy from crying. She edged the small girl off her knee and stroked back the child's fine blonde hair. It brought a lump to Nicci's throat.

Tina straightened her daughter's dress. 'Go on, lovey, go and play in the garden with the boys.'

The sister took the child's hand. 'Come on, Ruby. What's happened to your bike? Let's go and find it, shall we?'

The mother watched as Ruby was led out into the garden. Her eyes followed the child, reluctant to let her go, fearful of yet more loss.

Nicci cleared her throat. 'It's very good of you to agree to speak to us.'

Tina's gaze travelled back grudgingly from the three children on the lawn to Nicci.

'If you know what he was up to, I want to know about it.'

Nicci opened her palms. 'We're trying to piece it together.'

An angry frown gathered on Tina's brow. 'Fucking police – I told them. My husband would not've . . .' She had to swallow hard. 'They treated me like some kind of airhead who couldn't face the truth. Suggested I "get something from the doctor".'

Eddie leant forward, rapping the glass of the low coffee table to make his point. 'I told Nic soon as I heard, I've known Ray a good few years and there's no way he'd've topped himself.'

Tina nodded fiercely and sniffed back a tear.

Giving her time to compose herself, Nicci pulled a notebook out of her bag and opened it at a fresh page. 'We think Ray's death and Helen Warner's might possibly be connected.'

Tina compressed her lips. 'Eddie said, on the phone.'

'So let's begin with anything he said to you about working with her.'

Tina closed her eyes, ordering her thoughts. 'He first met

her a few months back. New MP, smarter than most of them – everyone recognized that. He'd been working on the drugs brief for some time, testing the water for a more rational policy, that was the idea. Robert Hollister wanted Helen Warner to front it.'

Nicci made a note. 'Do you know how Ray viewed Warner's relationship with Hollister?'

Tina gave a dry laugh. 'Jesus wept, he wasn't knocking her off too, was he?'

'What did Ray think?'

A sad smile spread over Tina's face. 'Ray was . . . well, y'know, gossip was why he got out of the newspaper business. It drives the agenda on all the red-tops. He came to hate all that. He wanted to tackle the serious issues of the day. He reckoned people's private lives should remain private.'

Nicci tilted her head. 'What if their behaviour in private was immoral or even illegal?'

'He knew of plenty who were popping pills and shoving coke up their noses but still publicly backing the war on drugs, if that's what you mean. He hated hypocrisy.'

'What was his response to Helen Warner's death?'

'We heard about it on the radio at breakfast time. He always listened to the *Today* programme on Radio Four. He was . . . really angry.'

'Angry? He didn't think it was suicide?'

'He usually drops the boys off at school. He went stomping out the house that day, left me to take them.'

'Did he talk about why he was angry?'

'Came home very late that night, so we never really got a chance. Then of course next day we had the burglary.'

Nicci and Eddie exchanged looks.

Eddie frowned. 'He never told me you'd been burgled.'

'They didn't take anything much. Not even the telly. Just made a hell of a mess. He said it was probably kids. But that pissed him off too. He went out and spent about five hundred quid on alarms and security cameras.'

Nicci twizzled the pen between thumb and index finger. 'Did you have an alarm before?'

'Well yeah. Truth was, when I went out with the kids, sorting out the buggy and all that, I sometimes forgot to put it on. That must've been what happened that day.'

Eddie laced his fingers and smiled reassuringly. 'Easily done.' He and Nicci were deliberately avoiding eye contact.

After she finished scribbling a note in her book, Nicci looked up. 'The day of his death, were you in touch at all once he'd gone to work?'

'He texted me about four thirty. Said he had a meeting with the lawyers, he might be late. The thing I don't get is what was he doing at Bond Street?' She rubbed her forehead as if physical pressure could solve this conundrum for her.

Nicci scanned her troubled face. 'Going to this meeting?'

'The lawyers were just downstairs from him.'

'In Labour HQ at Brewers Green?'

'Yeah. If the meeting had finished, he'd just be coming home, wouldn't he? Nearest tube was St James's Park. But he always walked to Victoria because it was easier. Only one change if he took the Victoria Line to Euston then got on the Northern Line.'

Eddie sighed. 'Problems on the tube that day?'

'Why go via Bond Street?' Tina's expression darkened. 'I have wondered if he was seeing someone. I don't think so. But it's crossed my mind. I asked the police about CCTV. They said the platform was so crowded they couldn't see him, much less what happened.'

Nicci had been peering at her notes. 'Are you sure he meant the Labour Party's lawyers? Could there be some other lawyers he might need to see?'

'I don't know. I just assumed. Do you think it was a lie and he was carrying on with some woman, taking her shopping maybe?'

Eddie shook his head firmly. 'No.'

Tina gave him a grateful smile. Then she took out her phone. The tears welled up and she found her husband's last text. As she read it, a puzzled look came into her eye. 'Actually, he wrote "lawyer".' She held up the phone for Nicci to see. 'No "s". Probably just a typo though.'

Nicci peered at the phone. She didn't reply, she simply smiled and nodded.

75

It had taken three security guards to escort Tolya and Kaz from the offices of Crowley Sheridan Moore. A huge, muscular Russian covered in tats, gazing at them sardonically from behind mirrored shades, had produced a jittery response and threats to call the police unless they left quietly.

Neville Moore's PA had continued to insist he was in Australia, and though Kaz herself didn't believe it, she could see that the PA probably did.

They had returned to Mike's flat to find her brother dozing on the sofa, the dog, Buster, curled up beside him and Mike putting the finishing touches to a bright acrylic portrait of Joey, in the style of the cubists. A face of flat multi-faceted planes, punctured by two iridescent blue eyes side by side, succeeded in conveying a sense of him, whilst remaining totally unrecognizable.

Kaz admired the painting. 'Yeah, it's . . .'

'Amusing?' Mike gave her an ironic grin. 'Cubism tends to look dated to the modern eye, but I think it was a cunning way for the likes of Braque and Picasso not to upset their girlfriends.'

She grinned and scanned his face anxiously. 'So everything's been all right?'

He shrugged. 'Yeah.'

Joey opened his eyes and sat up. Smiling at the sight of his sister, he stretched his arms above his head only to wince. 'Aaww, fuck me. Time for more painkillers, I reckon. All right, Kaz?'

Kaz went to the tap and poured him a glass of water. She was mulling over her next move. He was still dangerous, no question, but there was also a fragility about him, a neediness. The younger Joey had suffered enough physical beatings from their father, but he'd never let on how he felt. Acting tough was not just a product of his macho upbringing, it was an issue of personal pride with him. So something had definitely shifted in her brother's psyche.

He gave her a sleepy smile as she handed him the water. 'How'd it go then?'

'Okay.'

He glanced at Tolya. 'She been a good girl? Behaved herself?'

The Russian simply nodded.

Easing himself into a more upright position, Joey grinned. 'Just kidding, babes.' He drifted off for a moment. 'You know what I really missed inside: proper fish and chips. They got their own version, but it's shit.' He turned to Mike. 'You got a decent chippie round here?'

'There's a good one I use down on Fulham Road.'

Joey gave Tolya a speculative glance.

The big man shrugged. 'You want me get some?'

'Aaw, cheers, mate. Get some for all of us. And some mushy peas.' He shot Mike a look. 'Maybe you could show him where it is?'

Mike wondered about the advisability of leaving brother and sister alone together. He could see that was what Joey was angling for. He tried to catch Kaz's eye, but her face was as inscrutable as her brother's. Having his desolate life invaded had been invigorating at the start, but now Mike was feeling weary. He wanted to help Kaz, but he hadn't bargained for all this. Still he smiled. 'I'll get my jacket.'

As Tolya and Mike left, Joey popped a couple of pills from the blister pack.

'When I was at Frankland, I had this shrink called Dr Fishburn. Bit of a twat in some ways. But he got me thinking. Mainly about the old man.'

Kaz settled in a chair. 'Bet that was fun.'

Joey tossed a pill into his mouth and downed it with a swallow of water. 'Mike, he's a funny old bugger, but I like him.'

'So do I.'

A giggle erupted from her brother. 'Imagine if you put a gun in his hand – he could frighten the living daylights out of anyone! You should've set him on the Kemals.'

Kaz had to smile. 'Don't hurt him, Joey. Whatever he looks like, he's not a villain. He's not tough.'

'I ain't planning to hurt him.' A wistful look crept into his eye. 'You ever wonder how we'd've turned out if we'd had different parents?'

'Yeah, it's crossed my mind.'

Joey had always been surprising, but the tone of regret and doubt in his voice was not something she'd encountered before. It pained Kaz to hear it.

Rubbing the scratchy beard he continued to ponder. 'What would it've been like to have a dad like Mike? A normal dad, who made you go to school and all that stuff?'

'Says he don't get on with his own son.'

'You and me, babes, we drew the short fucking straw and no mistake.' He swallowed the second pill, drained his glass and set it down with a snap.

She could sense the insidious feeling rising within her. It seemed her brother's anguish still had the power to upset her. Though she resisted, she could feel her gut tightening. Shifting abruptly, she tried to shake off the tension. It made her sound tetchy. 'What you gonna do, Joey?'

'Stay out of jail.' He flopped back against the cushions of the sofa. 'Y'know I really do wish I'd listened to you before. Being banged up, I never realized how bad it would be. You done the time, you knew what you was talking about.'

The blue eyes appealed to her, as unnerving and unpredictable as they'd always been. She got up, the pressure inside was turning to annoyance. He was drawing her in, she could feel it.

'I got a bit stashed away, but what I need is serious money. Once I sort out some decent product, I can sell it on the Net. Then get back to building a property portfolio. Don't much fancy living abroad, but needs must.'

'You gonna use Sean's identity?'

He patted the sleepy dog beside him. 'It's been useful while I was inside. But, nah, I think maybe we should give Sean and the dog back to Glynis.'

She met his gaze. Had he said 'we' deliberately?

It was another hook, but she wasn't biting. She moved into the kitchen area. 'Fancy a cup of tea?'

He gave her a wry smile. 'Okay, let me ask you a question. What the fuck's going on? What really happened to Helen?'

Kettle in hand, she turned to look at him.

'Suicide?' He shrugged. 'Really?'

Filling the kettle, she couldn't help smiling to herself. This was Joey, sharp as a hypodermic.

'Well, something's up, babes. You turf up here at Mike's. Why? You practically got steam coming out your ears.'

Kaz felt a rush of gratitude. Here was someone who would understand proper anger, her fury at what had been done to Helen. Not an ex-cop going through the motions, not someone as uptight as Julia or as moral and decent as Mike. The desire to confide in him was overwhelming.

Slotting the kettle on its base and flicking the switch, she sighed. 'Okay, yeah. I'm here 'cause I think Helen was murdered.'

'You know who done it?'

'Not exactly, though I got a line on why.'

There was a gleam in Joey's eye, although he sounded casual enough. 'You want help?'

A cascade of emotions tumbled through her mind. Course she wanted help. But 'help' from her brother was a double-edged sword; she'd be a fool to trust him.

'Yeah. If you know where I can find Neville Moore.'

'Neville? He's mixed up in this? How come?'

'I think he might've been trying to help her.'

76

As Nicci let herself into her flat she couldn't help noticing the police crime-scene tape still sealing the door to number five, where Ethel Huxtable had lived. She retreated rapidly into her own bolthole and in that moment the weariness that she'd been holding at bay for hours engulfed her.

Flopping on the sofa, she let the last warming shafts of evening sun ripple over her. The next thing she was aware of was opening her eyes to darkness and a ringing doorbell. She clicked her phone on to check the time and found two missed calls from Jack Delgado, the Hackney DS.

Muzzy-headed with sleep, she struggled to her feet and meandered down the hall to the intercom. She pressed the button and a blurred image of forehead and heavy eyebrows filled the tiny screen. It took her several seconds to realize it was Rory McLaren.

She hesitated. What the hell did he want? Too tired to figure it out, she hit the open button, unlatched the door and leaving it ajar wandered back to the main room. As she turned on the standard lamp in the corner and closed the blinds, she heard footsteps, the front door shut and a moment later he appeared, unhooking a backpack from his shoulders.

'Evening.'

She gave him a nod and waited. What do you say to a

stranger you've had sex with but who'd studiously avoided you ever since? The ball was in his court, she decided.

His smile was formal and a little chilly. 'Simon thought you might want to know what we found at the house.'

She frowned. It couldn't wait until the morning?

Unzipping the backpack he pulled out a bottle of red wine. 'And I thought you might fancy a drink?'

'I'd prefer a cup of tea.' She wandered over to the kitchen area. A drink, not to mention another disengaged sexual encounter, was the last thing she wanted.

He shrugged. 'Well, whatever. Tea's fine with me.'

Going from the hysterical rage of her ex-husband to the awkward froideur of a casual lover struck Nicci as too taxing for her present mood. She concentrated on making a pot of tea and ignored him.

Rory hovered in the doorway for a moment. When no invitation to sit was forthcoming, he moved over to the sofa, perched on the edge and started to unload items from his backpack onto the coffee table.

Nicci turned to find an array of plugs, a smoke alarm and several more deconstructed electronic gizmos spread out on the table.

Surprise overcame languor. 'You got all this out of Julia's house?'

'This is just a selection. Every room was wired for sound and vision – motion-activated, remote monitoring – a serious surveillance operation. What puzzles me is why the police didn't find it.'

His tone carried a hint of a challenge. Maybe he expected her to defend her former colleagues.

She merely shrugged. 'I suppose they could've put it there themselves.'

'Very unlikely. This is high-spec kit. Way beyond any police budget. Well concealed, too.'

'What about the Security Service?'

He was sorting through the items on the table. 'That's what Simon said and it's possible. I've seen some of these devices before.' Holding up what looked like a simple domestic wall socket in his hand, he offered it to her. 'This little chap is something the CIA developed to eavesdrop on our lot.'

Nicci took the socket – a common-or-garden item available in any DIY chainstore. 'The CIA?'

'Well, I say the CIA. But it mainly gets farmed out to private contractors.' He took the socket from her. 'The clever thing about this is you'd never suspect it. Even an electrician. You can buy plenty of stuff on the Net and it's obvious you've got a listening device shoved in a socket. But this – this is high-end kit, the real deal.'

An astounded Nicci plonked down on the sofa beside him. 'You think the CIA bugged Helen Warner's house?'

'No, probably not. The contractors who make stuff for the CIA also sell it. But we're talking about the defence industry here. They don't sell to just anyone. And it's expensive.'

Nicci's fatigue had evaporated. 'If they were as professional as you say, then presumably no prints?'

Rory shook his head. 'Simon's SOCO had a look at a few bits. Clean as a whistle.'

Nicci stared at the items on the table. 'So everything Warner did, with her camera, whatever other preparations she made to trap Hollister, they would've known about it. Why didn't they just stop her?'

'You're the detective, you tell me.' Nicci met his eye; Eddie Lunt had baited her in exactly the same way. But she saw the hint of a teasing smile.

She smiled back. 'Oh, fuck off, Rory. Who the hell is behind this? Helen Warner gets incriminating evidence, then she gets killed.' Her brows furrowed with concentration. 'So what if someone was just using her? Maybe it's not really about her at all?'

77

The grey Ford Focus cruised sedately through the contra-flow at the roadworks on the A23. The moon sat high and bright in a dark, cloudless sky. Joey dozed in the passenger seat, Tolya drove in backless leather gloves, window down an inch to admit the fresh summer breeze. Kaz was curled, legs up, on the back seat. The journey had given her time for reflection. Her conclusion? She was probably making a massive mistake.

Joey had sent a text and ten minutes later he'd received a phone call with instructions. Trusting him was at best a gamble. She still found herself wondering if she was about to end up in some remote downland field with a gun to her head.

The anonymous grey car slid into Brighton shortly before ten o'clock and headed for the front. The summer evening was full of revellers, fires dotted the steep pebble beach and gaggles of drunks sashayed along the promenade. Tolya found a parking space near the skeletal hulk of the ruined West Pier and they walked back a few hundred metres to the hotel.

The only concession Joey made to the possibility of being recognized was to pull his baseball cap firmly down over his eyes. He swept through the revolving doors, up the several steps and into the opulent foyer of the Grand with an air of

386

confidence and entitlement. Ignoring the concierge desk, he turned immediately left into the bar. Tolya and Kaz followed in his wake.

In the furthermost corner of the grand high-ceilinged salon, with a good view of all comers, Neville Moore had installed himself in a large wing armchair. Kaz had only ever seen him puffed up in his expensive business suits, so the nondescript bloke in faded jeans, T-shirt and hoodie seemed like an impostor. Only closer inspection of the foxy features confirmed it was indeed him.

At the sight of Kaz, he scowled, his eyes zeroing in on Joey. 'What the hell's going on?'

Joey sat down on the sofa opposite. 'Chill, Nev. You remember my sister. Now, what's everyone having to drink?'

Joining her brother on the sofa Kaz shook her head. 'Nothing for me.' She met the lawyer's tense gaze and smiled. 'All right, Nev.'

Joey ordered a beer from a hovering waiter. Tolya positioned himself on an adjacent bar stool and began to graze thoughtfully on the bar snacks.

'I thought we had an agreement.' Neville glowered at Joey.

'Yeah, and I thought you'd be tucked up at home in Godalming. Or, as your PA told Kaz, on holiday down under. What's going on, Nev?'

The lawyer fixed his client with a glacial stare. 'I shouldn't even be meeting you. You need to be on your way. I thought it was all arranged.'

'You seen my mugshot in the paper?' Joey adjusted the brim of his cap. 'I look like I'm about twelve. Only me mum'd recognize me.' He grinned. 'Anyway, Kaz wanted a word.'

Neville Moore's lizard-eyed stare glided over to Kaz.

Behind the tough carapace she could detect a definite whiff of fear.

'Your PA insists you're in Australia.'

'I had some matters to tie up for a client. My wife went ahead with the children. I'm joining them next week.'

'I thought maybe you'd stayed for the inquest?'

The lawyer dipped his head and frowned. 'It was . . . a consideration. Tragic business. I would've liked to have seen it resolved.'

'Resolved? I'll tell you what I think, Nev. I think she was murdered and I wanna know why.' Kaz noticed a hint of unease in his composed features. 'Yesterday, when we bumped into each other, what was it you said about Helen? You enjoyed her confidence on a number of matters?'

'It was simply a turn of phrase.'

'You must've meant something.'

He gave her a rueful look. 'I suppose I was just boasting. I wanted you to think – oh, I don't know.' He flicked his hand dismissively.

'That she trusted you? I think maybe she did. Before she died, did she give you something to look after? Something like a memory stick?'

Neville Moore's eyes flew to her face with a look of alarm. It was a reflex action, which he immediately suppressed.

'It was an idle boast. Helen no longer worked for me. We both had busy lives. I hadn't seen her for . . . oh, several months.'

'She made a film of Hollister raping her. Did you know that?'

The lawyer blinked at her several times. On the table in front of him was a tumbler of whisky and ice. He picked it up and drained it, the melting ice clinked in the bottom.

Joey took the empty glass from him and held it up for the waiter. 'Oi, mate. Over here. Large Scotch.'

Moore leant forward and put his face in his hands. He was a man who'd spent his whole career walking a tightrope, but the events surrounding his former employee's death had led him to the edge of a much scarier precipice.

Finally he raised his head; the light had drained from his eyes. 'Look at me – in a hotel because I daren't go home. My wife and kids are on the other side of the world. Doesn't that tell you something?'

Kaz met his eye. 'She did tell you about Hollister and what she was trying to do then?'

He shook his head wearily. 'Helen made herself a hostage to fortune. I told her to leave well alone. In fact I begged her.'

Kaz frowned. 'Why?'

The waiter placed a paper coaster on the table in front of Neville Moore, followed by his Scotch. Joey took a slug of beer, he was watching the lawyer with curiosity.

Once the waiter had withdrawn from earshot, Moore glanced across at his client. 'You think of yourself as a villain, Joey. But you're not. You're a criminal. Criminals break the law, the police chase them, the courts process them. That's where I come in.'

Joey grinned. 'And some wriggle through the net.'

A ghostly smile crossed the lawyer's face. 'Indeed they do.' He took a sip of his drink. 'But a true villain, a serious villain, that's something else. True villains make the law to suit their own purposes. They control the levers of power. The police are rarely involved, no courts. Morality, any notion of right and wrong, is simply by-passed.'

'What's this got to do with Helen?' An impatience had edged into Kaz's voice.

Moore hesitated. Now that events had spiralled out of control, all he wanted was to get out.

'Helen was killed by villains. Her colleague at the Labour Party, he had copies of the footage she made of Hollister. He wanted to get it admitted in evidence at the inquest, make a big splash in the papers. Two days before, he went under a tube train. They knew every move before he made it.'

Joey scratched his cheek, a glint had crept into his eye. 'These villains got names?'

The lawyer shook his head. 'Don't even think about it, Joey. These people are out of your league. You both need to do what I'm going to do – make yourselves scarce.' He took another swallow of whisky. 'I don't want them to get the wrong impression and think I'm involved. So I'm taking my family on an extended holiday. And I'm letting sleeping dogs lie. You should do the same.'

Kaz smiled. 'I'm sure that's good advice, Nev.'

'It is. You're not going to take it though, are you?'

Joey turned the innocent baby-blue eyes on his brief. 'Don't worry about us, Nev. We ain't too bad at taking care of ourselves. So I'm gonna ask you again – these villains got a name?'

Neville Moore met his gaze. Joey Phelps was a cocky young man, violent but smart. He was also an escaped convict. The lawyer had taken every precaution in setting up this meeting, but he could still end up severely compromised. He'd warned them, that was all he could do. Whatever happened now was out of his hands.

He held out his palms. 'Okay, you win. Viktor Pudovkin. You've probably never heard of him.'

Joey shrugged. 'Can't say I have.'

Tolya's hand froze between the crisp dish and his mouth as he shot a glance in Moore's direction.

The lawyer returned the look with a thin smile. 'But he has.'

78

Kaz awoke with a start. What time was it? After midnight certainly. The car was cruising steadily north along a dark tract of the M23 motorway. Traffic was light and a waxing gibbous moon cast an eerie glow over the woodland fringing the carriageway.

She yawned. Joey was fast asleep in the back seat. She envied his capacity to switch off no matter what. Stress didn't appear to affect him that much.

They'd left Brighton, and Neville Moore, with more questions than answers. Joey had reflected that he'd never seen the lawyer so rattled.

On the subject of Pudovkin, Tolya was obtuse, taking cover behind his language difficulties. 'Me, don't know nothing. Ask Yevgeny.'

Kaz wondered about the Labour Party bloke, who'd ended up dead under a train. Did Nicci Armstrong know about him? And what had happened to the evidence he had?

Her boss, Blake, was determined to keep Kaz out of the loop. But Nicci herself might be amenable to an exchange of information. And then there was Julia. Perhaps Kaz still had some influence with her.

As to the lawyer's dire warnings to leave well alone, Kaz dismissed them. Helen had asked for his help but he didn't have the bottle. It was all about him trying not to look bad.

A bunch of Hollister's mates, led by this Pudovkin, had got together to protect the pervert. Maybe there were a few bent cops in the mix too. They were villains all right and Kaz didn't underestimate them. But now she had a line on them, she wasn't about to run away and hide. Quite the opposite.

The footage Helen shot was out there somewhere – on memory sticks, on a computer, locked away, hidden away. Sooner or later Kaz would find it. And she'd stick it on the Net and blow Hollister out of the water.

It should've been her that Helen confided in, not a skanky lawyer, or some random bloke from the Labour Party. But when she'd tried to get in touch, Kaz had ignored her. She'd let her lover down and that fact was tearing at her insides. The very least she could do now was make that bastard pay.

As they passed the Gatwick turn-off, a vehicle glided down the slip road to slot in behind them. Kaz glanced across as the driver turned his head towards them. Caught in the moon's chilly spectral light his features seemed menacing. Kaz felt an involuntary shiver travel up her spine.

She looked over her shoulder into the back seat at her sleeping brother. The night drive to Brighton and back had left her feeling detached and wary. She and Joey had arrived at what? An understanding? She'd wanted to talk to Neville Moore; he'd been as good as his word and arranged it. But that didn't mean he could be trusted.

Tolya's hands rested easily on the wheel. He seemed relaxed but alert. Kaz wondered once again how exactly Joey had persuaded his Russian minders back on-board. Money was certainly part of it, but was there more?

She was starting to doze off again when she realized the steady hum of the car's engine had been joined by another far more intrusive clattering sound. And it was coming from above. Tolya leant forward and peered up through the top of the windscreen just as a crisp beam of light danced across the road in front of them and pulled back to graze the bonnet of the car.

The Russian cursed under his breath. 'Joe. We got company.' His tone was urgent.

Joey's eyes opened, he was awake in a flash. 'Behind?'

'Up.'

Kaz peered out and up. She could see very little.

'Don't look up!' Joey growled. 'They got cameras.'

She turned to glare at him. 'A fucking helicopter? What? Is it following us?'

Joey's grin was just visible in the car's shadowy interior. 'C'mon, babes, soon as we walked out the door, you think old Mike wasn't gonna call the cops?'

Kaz was stunned. The thought hadn't entered her head. Mike was her friend, the one person she could trust.

Joey chuckled, he seemed pleased. 'Canny old bugger, in't he? He must've given them the car reg.'

'Mike wouldn't . . .' The words died on her lips. Of course he would. She'd been so focused on tracking down Neville Moore that she'd never considered what he might do. They'd eaten their fish and chips and left, Joey raising no objection to leaving Mike alone. But Mike was on her side – he'd proved as much with the stolen briefcase – so why had he done it? Maybe he thought it was the best way to help her.

The rhythmic thwack of the blades became louder and suddenly they saw the helicopter itself as it swooped round in front of them, like some malevolent bird of prey, dark blue underbelly with a yellow crest.

Joey put a hand over his face as he gazed up at it. 'It's the Old Bill all right. Looks like the Met.'

Kaz could feel the muscles in the back of her neck go taut. Her mouth was dry. This was another one of her brother's neat little traps and she'd stepped right into it. How the hell could she have been so gullible?

A hand came to rest on her shoulder, she felt his warm breath close to her ear. 'Don't blame him, babes. In his world, it's what you do.'

'You fucking knew, Joey!' Rage flooded her veins.

'You'd've known too if you hadn't got yourself all confused and forgot who you are and which side of the fence you're on.'

'Oh fuck off! Stop the car, Tol. I wanna get out.'

Joey tried to rub her shoulder. 'C'mon – on the motorway, in the middle of nowhere? Where you gonna run?'

She shoved him off. 'I don't need you, Joey.'

'Yeah you do. You know the system. You get picked up tonight, you can try telling them you was kidnapped. But they ain't gonna listen. They'll revoke your licence and you'll be straight back in the nick.'

The pit of her stomach felt hollow. He was right of course.

Tolya's gaze was firmly fixed on the road. The car's engine screamed as he accelerated hard up a short incline. They swept under a high-arched bridge then roared down the hill towards the junction with the M25. The helicopter bobbed up over the bridge and dived down after them; nose tipped slightly forward, rotors chopping the night air. It seemed to be holding them in its tractor beam.

Kaz concentrated on her breathing, calming her wrath, getting her brain back in gear. Had Joey deliberately wrong-footed her or was it just her own stupidity? Returning to prison was her nightmare. And the nightmare was about to come true.

The car sped down the left-hand lane and Tolya held it firm round the tight bend, which merged into the M25 heading west.

Joey scanned the column of traffic they were joining. 'Still moving along okay. Means they ain't got intercepts on the ground yet, so I reckon we could make it to the services.'

Tolya raised a gloved hand to point up at the gantry they were speeding under. 'Loads of cameras. Maybe turn off before?'

'Nah, mate, not enough cover. The chopper'll track us wherever. Get stuck on some side road, they'll just roll out a stinger.'

Joey was sitting bolt upright in the back seat. The lassitude of recent days had lifted. He seemed energized; for him the chase was exhilarating.

'You fucker! You're enjoying this.' Kaz was feeling decidedly sick.

'Bit of adrenaline, always a buzz,' he giggled.

'We're both gonna end up back in jail.'

'Don't be so pessimistic. They ain't got us yet.' He leant forward between the two front seats. 'Y'know, I'm curious, babes. What upsets you more? Fear of getting nicked or the fact that someone you trusted has let you down.'

The helicopter was directly above them, blades thrashing, pinning them to the road.

Kaz craned her neck to look at him. 'You'd risk going back to jail, just to teach me a fucking lesson? You're mental.'

She was sweating, every nerve in her body was tense. But Joey was perfectly calm.

He seemed to be smiling. 'We trust people, but 'til push comes to shove, you don't know their agenda.'

'Mike hasn't let me down. He just thinks I'll be safer with you behind bars.'

'Have I ever hurt you?' Light from the oncoming traffic flooded Joey's pupils, turning them milky white like an albino. 'Go on, can you think of a single instance?'

She stared at the road ahead. 'No.'

'No. I ain't saying that you grassing didn't piss me off. It did. Royally. I thought about whacking you. Can't say I didn't. But in the end, where'd that get me?'

'Revenge ain't sensible.'

'Leaves me with Mum and Natalie. Though who knows where the fuck she is – holed up somewhere smoking crack, probably.'

She swung round to face him again. 'If you don't want revenge, then why d'you come looking for me? What the fuck do you want, Joey?'

'I want my sister back.' His face was in deep shadow now, she couldn't see the eyes. 'You and me, Kaz, in the end all we got is each other.'

The dark road stretched ahead of them, just a smattering of vehicles. They were travelling in the outside lane, engine at full throttle, being pursued by the police. Kaz hunkered down in her seat. She felt powerless. Maybe freedom, the notion she could turn her life around, had always been an illusion.

Joey was a consummate liar, but something in the timbre of his voice rang true. She thought about the months she'd spent in Glasgow, living her new life with a false identity, a faked history, a handful of so-called friends she could never confide in. If she was honest with herself, it had been desolate, as desolate probably as her brother's life in jail. Perhaps he was right. With Helen dead the only connection that came close to touching her was her little brother.

They drove on in silence, the helicopter stalking them. Sooner or later, Kaz thought, there'll be a roadblock and that will be it. The inevitability of it all somehow calmed her, her mind became blank.

She didn't even notice the road signs and it wasn't until Tolya veered over into the slow lane that she realized they'd reached Cobham services.

Joey's palm brushed her shoulder. 'Listen, babe, you wanna bail, take your chances, it's up to you. It's me they'll be after.'

'What the fuck you gonna do?' She imagined some dramatic shoot-out with armed police, her brother choosing suicide by cop instead of a life sentence in jail.

He shrugged. 'Boost another car, whad'you think?'

The Ford Focus zigzagged across the car park and pulled up sharply next to a large white Transit.

Tolya pointed across at the next bank of parked cars – a weary, middle-aged bloke was climbing out of a newish 5 Series Beemer. 'Him?'

Joey chuckled. 'You and your fucking Beemers.'

They got out of the car, Kaz followed suit. Turning up the collar of her jacket to hide her face, she glanced skywards – the helicopter was circling.

The bloke eased the belt round his paunch, pulled on his suit jacket, clicked the car lock and wandered towards the main building. Tolya and Joey, hands slotted in pockets, sauntered after him.

Inside the vast hangar most of the food franchises were closed due to the lateness of the hour. Only McDonald's and KFC remained open, each with a few customers.

The bloke stopped for a moment to consider the

McDonald's menu, took off his glasses, rubbed his weary eyes and continued in the direction of the toilets.

Joey flashed his sister a grin. 'Looks like we're in business. Wait here.'

Kaz didn't know what to do. She watched her brother and Tolya disappear into the Gents. Then a flashing blue light caught her eye. She moved forward into the closed Starbucks franchise to peer through the plate-glass wall at the car park beyond.

A police car had pulled up next to the Focus. Two officers in Kevlar vests jumped out and began shining a torch into the vehicle.

Kaz turned on her heel and hurried back towards the toilets. She met Tolya coming out. He was wearing a suit jacket – sleeves way too short, but covering his tattoos – and heavy-framed glasses.

He dangled a set of car keys from his index finger and smiled. 'You coming?'

'They're out front.'

'Then we make like a nice couple.' He held out his hand.

She hesitated, but only for a second. His confidence was reassuring. She placed her palm in his. He scooped up a discarded carton of fries from a table. 'Hungry?'

She shot him an anxious look. 'Where's Joey?'

'We pick him up.'

As they approached the double doors, the two cops were coming straight at them. Tolya simply held the door open for them. They gave him a quick, appraising glance. He re-adjusted his spectacles and smiled. Their eyes shifted to Kaz. She ignored them and thrust her hand into the carton of fries Tolya was holding. She stuffed her mouth with cold chips, but the cops had already moved on into the building.

They set off across the car park towards the Beemer. Tolya set the pace, which was hardly more than a stroll. A second unmarked police vehicle had pulled up behind the Ford Focus. Three officers were swarming round it.

Tolya clicked the key fob in his hand, dumped the fries in a bin and got into the driver's seat of the Beemer. Kaz climbed into the passenger seat next to him. As he slowly backed the car out of its parking space, the three cops trotted across the tarmac behind them, heading for the main building. All in vests, one was cradling an MP7 submachine gun.

Kaz glanced across at Tolya. 'Shit! What's Joey gonna do?'

'Don't worry. He be fine.'

The Beemer swung sedately out of the car park and along the access road. At the mini roundabout it turned left into the petrol station. When they reached the forecourt it drew up at the air and water pump. Tolya got out, walked round the bonnet and peered down at the front tyre.

Kaz remained in her seat, anxiously craning her neck to look back at the car park and the main service area. She could see very little. Her thoughts were in a whirl. Was Joey trapped in there, cornered by the cops? Had he sacrificed himself so they could escape? That wasn't very Joey.

There were only a couple of vehicles filling up at the pumps under the bright orange glow that drenched the whole forecourt. But because she was looking the other way, Kaz didn't see him slip out of the shadows behind the service station shop. Tolya opened the rear door and Joey dived across the back seat and lay down flat.

The Russian returned quickly to the driving seat, pressed the ignition and the turbo-charged engine purred to life. Rolling over onto his back, Joey gazed up at his sister and laughed. 'Wow! What a blast! Just like the old days, innit? You and me, babes, legging it from the law.'

Kaz didn't trust herself to reply. She was relieved and angry in equal parts.

The Beemer cruised down the slip road onto the motorway, Tolya put his foot down and it surged forward, heading westwards into the darkness and safety beyond.

79

Rory McLaren had spent most of his teenage years wondering how to talk to girls. Then a pal of his older brother, who at twenty seemed impossibly wise and mature, advised him to ask questions. Ask them loads of questions and listen patiently to the answers. It was a technique that had carried Rory through two marriages and a string of affairs. He rarely answered questions himself, unless of a purely practical nature. Feelings remained a private matter, he couldn't stand blokes who whined.

The two wives eventually threw in the towel; his grown-up daughters, whom he rarely saw, treated him more like a distant uncle. It wasn't in his nature to analyse what had gone wrong. When his parents had dumped him at the prep school gate, aged eight, his father had explained that success in life depended on getting on with the job in hand. Rory followed his father into the army and the job did seem pretty straightforward – until Iraq.

Fighting insurgents in the vast southern deserts, Rory came to the conclusion that most of what he'd been brought up to believe in was rubbish, including his country's foreign policy. Still, the army was what he knew and he went on to serve a number of gruelling tours in Helmand, finally leaving with the rank of major.

He had no idea whether Nicci Armstrong liked him; he

rather suspected she didn't like anyone that much. Blake had mentioned the dead child, so he'd steered clear of the twenty-questions technique with her. The ramifications of grief were something he knew about. He'd stood beside enough flag-draped coffins and watched premature widows struggling to bring meaning to their loss. His personal conclusion was that there was no meaning – to any of it. This nihilism had crept up on him over the years and he'd found it oddly liberating.

Gazing at Nicci across the pillow he wondered if he should just get up and leave. She'd probably prefer it. Her sleep was restless, she muttered and ground her teeth. But when her features were in repose, minus the usual scowl, she was a beautiful woman. Did she know this? He doubted it.

He'd never seen her in make-up and her eyes were often bloodshot and pouchy with fatigue. But she had what his mother would've called bone structure. In looks she reminded him of his first wife – symmetrical face, Greek nose, curvy lips. He liked the fact she seemed to be without vanity.

Slipping out of bed and into his boxers, he wandered into the open-plan sitting room and kitchen. The sink was piled with dirty dishes, the worktop littered with the detritus of several different takeaways. He found a pair of rubber gloves and some washing-up liquid and set to work. Having lived in some wild and hostile places, he understood the comfort and reassurance of orderly kit and a clean billet. Also he enjoyed the cleansing and tidying process. His younger brother, a spoilt banker, had once visited his flat and accused him of living like a damned faggot.

Having completed the washing-up and bleached the sink, Rory was carrying a black PVC sack of rubbish down the hall, when there was a rap at the door. Peering through the spy-hole all he could discern was a tall figure in a dark suit. He opened the door.

The caller did a double-take. A half-naked man in boxer shorts and rubber gloves was not what he'd been expecting. His gaze shot to the door to check the flat number.

Reaching into his inside pocket he brought out a warrant card. 'Erm . . . is Nicci at home? I'm DS Delgado.'

A sleepy Nicci emerged from the bedroom clutching a towelling bathrobe round her.

She glanced at the two large men confronting each other over the threshold and beckoned. 'Come in, Jack.'

Stepping back to admit the cop, Rory stripped off the gloves. 'I'll . . . get dressed.'

Delgado hunched his shoulders and followed Nicci down the hall into the main room. If she was feeling any embarrassment she gave no indication of it.

He gave her a sheepish look. 'Sorry, it's a bit early.'

Nicci crinkled her nose, distracted by the pristine kitchen and the overwhelming smell of bleach. Rory had disappeared into the bedroom.

She turned and smiled. 'I was going to call you this morning.'

He shifted awkwardly from foot to foot. 'Well, I think I've tracked down this kid of yours. This Leon.'

'Well done.'

Nicci watched him fumbling with his phone. He seemed more than a little disconcerted, which puzzled her. The Hackney DS must've seen most things. Why would it bother him that she had a lover, albeit one who wore rubber gloves?

Scrolling through images he finally found what he was looking for. 'Yeah, here we go. Is this him?'

He held the phone out for her to see.

She peered at the tiny screen. 'Yep, that's Leon.'

'Definitely?'

'Yes.'

Delgado sighed. 'Well, we've had a word. Sorry to say he's got an alibi for the evening of Ethel Huxtable's murder.'

'You sure?'

'There's a beat boxing class at one of the youth centres. He says he was there. I know the guys that run the centre. Good blokes, not the sort that'd lie. I phoned them. They confirmed he was there.'

Nicci shrugged. 'Oh well.'

'I will double-check. Make sure it's watertight.'

She ran her fingers through her hair, it needed washing. Had she convinced herself of Leon's guilt merely to assuage her own? She'd always been critical of the old-school coppers who operated on gut feelings, usually based on prejudice, just because they couldn't be arsed to collate the evidence properly. All the same it niggled her; a random mugging felt like too much of a coincidence. But however counter-intuitive they were to the human mind, coincidences happened.

Rory appeared in the doorway, fully dressed. The two men looked each other up and down.

The place suddenly felt very overcrowded to Nicci. This was why she lived alone. She didn't want the burden of other people's needs and expectations. She wished she could boot them both out, step into the shower and let the water rinse away her guilt: for Ethel, for Sophie.

Delgado seemed to sense her discomfort. 'We're handing over to the murder team anyway. No real evidence against the soldier at number six.' He moved towards the door. 'Back to square one, I guess.'

She met his eye, two cops who understood the system and its shortcomings. 'Thanks anyway, Jack.'

He gave her a wistful look, followed by a curt nod, and was gone.

80

Kaz looked out of the bedroom window, drawn by the chatter of children and the bounce and slap of a ball being booted around on the neighbouring driveway. It was the summer holidays, a balmy morning and the world was at play.

The house was brand new, spacious, a detached executive home on a corner plot in an exclusive cul-de-sac. The developers had preserved a huge spreading oak as the centrepiece for the half-dozen premier homes that filled the site.

When Tolya had dropped them off in the early hours the whispering tree had filled Kaz with foreboding. But in the brilliant morning sun its wide limbs provided a benign shade.

Tolya had driven away to some wasteland and torched the Beemer. No forensics. No trail.

They were home free, on the outskirts of Reading. Kaz had no real idea where. Having left the M4 they'd travelled another few miles west towards the fringes of the Berkshire Downs. Tolya's sleepy brother had greeted them on the doorstep.

Yevgeny and Tolya were itinerant former soldiers who'd never bothered much about where they lived. But the arrival of their sister Irina had changed all that. Yevgeny wanted the family to settle and had hopes of persuading their mother to join them too.

A comfy bed had been provided for Kaz and when she'd

stepped out of the steaming shower Irina had been laying out some of her own clean clothes for Kaz to borrow.

Nearly matching her brothers in height, Irina was willowy and blonde. Full of easy laughter she resorted to facial contortions and flapping hands to get over her difficulties with the English language. Kaz found it impossible not to like her and even harder not to fancy her.

Irina held up a black lacy bra, scrunched her features into an exaggerated frown and looked speculatively at Kaz's upper torso, which was just about covered by a towel.

'It . . . yeah, good I think. You think?' She giggled.

'I think it'll fit, yeah. Thank you.'

Irina gestured at the knickers, jeans and T-shirt all laid out neatly on the bed. 'You try, you take. Yeah?'

'Yeah. Thanks.' Clutching her towel, Kaz felt absurdly shy. The two women stared at each other awkwardly for a moment. Then the Russian laughed.

She pointed at the door. 'Breakfast? Yeah?'

Kaz nodded, holding on pertly to the towel until her hostess disappeared out of the room.

Bra and jeans were both slightly too snug. But with her own stuff abandoned at Mike's all she possessed were the clothes she'd arrived in. However, when she strolled into the kitchen, it was immediately apparent from the reactions of the three men, that her new figure-hugging threads were a hit.

Joey sat drinking coffee at the large farmhouse table. Yevgeny stood at the hob frying bacon and eggs. Tolya was checking his phone. But all eyes turned to scrutinize her.

'All right, babes?' Joey beamed. Their narrow escape from the police the night before seemed to have revitalized him. In spite of his injury, the energy and spark of the old Joey had returned.

She couldn't help smiling at him. 'Yeah. I'm good.'

'Yev, he does an ace breakfast. Full English, all the trimmings. No fucking idea where he learnt it.'

Yevgeny was larger, older, more solid than his brother. He had a tea-towel tucked neatly into his belt.

Spatula in hand, he turned to face them. 'I learn recipes. Live like an Englishman, eat like an Englishman, this is my aim now.'

Kaz met his eye. Their complicated history skittered through her mind – on the night her brother had been arrested she'd persuaded him to walk away and spare the cop, Mal Bradley. She'd never been sure why he'd agreed.

'Really nice place you got here, Yev.'

He dipped his head formally to accept the compliment. 'Thank you. Please take a seat.'

Irina joined them and breakfast was served. Yevgeny certainly lived up to the rep Joey had given him. The plates were large and loaded, with copious amounts of toast and coffee on the side. Irina was anxious to practise her rudimentary English and the conversation darted in and out of Russian as her brothers helped out with some translation.

Kaz was surprised to learn that Yevgeny also spoke German and the basics of Arabic. He'd worked in many countries, but all three siblings agreed that they preferred the UK.

Joey was rueful. Facing a life in exile made him see London in a different light. He missed the pubs and clubs, his riverside flat with its panoramic view of the City.

As he turned to Kaz, she noticed him blink away the moistness in his eye. 'I am one dumb-fuck. Didn't realize what I had. Took stupid risks. I shoulda listened to you, babes.'

Yevgeny patted his arm cheerfully. 'You go Brazil, get new face. I seen guys, their own mother don't recognize them.'

There was laughter round the table.

Irina threw Joey a vampish look. 'No! No cut! He pretty!'

Leaning back in her chair, Kaz watched and listened. Did Irina flirting with Joey make her envious? If she was honest, it did. It wasn't just that the Russian was gorgeous; she exuded verve and spirit. She possessed the same energetic aura of self-belief that had first drawn Kaz to Helen. It was something that Kaz had been missing in her Glasgow life, though she hadn't realized it until this moment.

Scanning the two brothers – Joey's minders, his employees – Kaz wondered again about their agenda. They were undoubtedly being paid well for their current services. But the nomadic, globetrotting life of guns for hire didn't exactly fit with a posh new gaffe in the leafy Royal County of Berkshire, just a spit down the road from Windsor Castle and the Queen. Were they still illegals, living beneath the radar? It didn't look much like that to Kaz.

The breakfast dishes were cleared away and Kaz's attempts to offer help resisted. Tolya and Irina shared the chores. Yevgeny pulled out a pack of cigarettes and suggested Kaz and Joey join him in the garden.

The lawn still had the ridged and lumpy appearance of new-laid turf. There was a terrace with recently planted pots and a small bower with a low wicker, glass-topped table and four easy chairs.

Yevgeny invited them to sit. He sparked up, leant his head back and blew a fine plume of smoke towards a cloudless cerulean sky.

Joey rested his left ankle on his right knee. 'Okay, let's talk business. After all, you come looking for me, Yev.'

This was news to Kaz. She'd presumed her brother had somehow got in touch with the Russians. Now it seemed they must've learned of his escape from the media and decided it was an opportunity for them. An opportunity for what though?

Joey rubbed his beard. 'The fee for getting me out the country, a hundred grand, that's already agreed. But that's not all you're after, is it?'

The Russian opened his palms and smiled. 'My sister come now, even I hope my mother too. Time we make a proper home. England such a good place. Good for business too.'

'You got leave to remain?'

'Temporary. But with cash, business interests we make things permanent.'

'You're settling, I'm leaving.' Joey grinned. 'Funny old world, innit?'

The Russian inclined his head. 'We get the three cannabis factories back to full production, we take a controlling interest of fifty-one per cent. Your man, he agree?'

'Quan's flexible. His end's always been twenty per cent.'

'Leaves you twenty-nine.'

'I can live with that. But the Kemals are your problem.'

Yevgeny grinned. 'I take Kaz along to frighten them.'

Joey chuckled. Kaz's gaze was travelling back and forth between the two men. So the price of her brother's freedom was a takeover of the firm – all amicable enough on the surface – but a takeover none the less.

Joey sighed. 'The Ibiza end of the business is a mess, all kinds of hooligans have tried to muscle in while I been away. But I'll sort that out.'

'We can maybe help.'

'Cool.' Joey laced his fingers. 'But that would have to be a sixty–forty partnership. I still gotta make a living.'

The Russian shrugged. 'Partnership yes. But fifty–fifty I think.'

They both knew Joey was in no position to press the point. Again he laughed. 'You're a hard bastard, but okay, agreed. Provided you do one more thing for me, Yev. I want you to help my sister out.'

Kaz looked at him in surprise, but he was focused on the Russian.

Taking a heavy pull on his cigarette, Yevgeny frowned. 'Pudovkin?'

'Is it doable?'

The big man shot a glance at Kaz. 'Depends what you want.'

She returned the look. 'I've been told he had my friend killed. First up, I wanna find out if that's true.'

Yevgeny gave a dry laugh. 'You know who he is?'

'No idea.'

He ground the half-smoked cigarette underfoot. 'He's maybe not a man you should upset.'

Joey gave him an inquisitive look. 'He a friend of yours then, Yev?'

The Russian snorted with derision. 'Fuck me, no! I hate siloviki.'

Joey threw his sister a cheeky glance. 'That's all right then.'

Kaz understood this was a big ask. If Neville Moore was right – a murder organized to protect a politician – he wasn't likely to be an ordinary thug.

'What's silo . . .viki? Sounds like vodka.'

'Aww, you disappoint me, Kaz,' Yevgeny teased. 'Any Russian word, don't matter, English people think it some kind of vodka.'

She chuckled. 'Okay so I'm just a stupid English bint.' Keeping it light and friendly was all she could do. Joey had no leverage, that was apparent. The Russian didn't need to help, he'd already got what he wanted.

'Siloviki is – well, Putin is siloviki. Ex-FSB.'

Joey chipped in: 'The lot that took over from the KGB?'

Yevgeny nodded. 'Many was KGB before too, or military.'

'You were in the army. Why don't you like them?' Kaz frowned.

He shook his head wearily. 'Me, my brothers, we proper soldiers. Not fucking officers. We fight, get shot, blown to fucking bits. They stay in barracks.' His lip curled with a sneer. 'Drink vodka.'

'I get it. So this Pudovkin, he's rich?'

'Rich, oh yes.'

'One of these oligarchs?'

'No, oligarchs – siloviki, not the same thing. Pudovkin is businessman. But really, Kremlin sends him here to watch oligarchs. Kremlin use him to control oligarchs. And for politics.'

Joey was looking impressed. 'Fuck me, Yev. How d'you know all this?'

He puffed out his cheeks. 'Many Russians in London got money, like to party. Pudovkin, he pretend to be friends with everyone. But we know who he is, why they send him here.'

Kaz was pretty sure that Nicci Armstrong knew none of this. But how did Hollister come to be mates with some kind of Russian spook?

Yevgeny gave her a speculative grin. 'Okay, I got a deal for you. I have invitation. You put on sexy dress and big smile, be my date, I take you to meet Viktor Pudovkin.'

81

Eddie Lunt sat at his desk ruminating on how to break the news to Nicci. She disapproved of his methodology, he was well aware of that. He'd encountered a number of ex-cops in his colourful career and, in his experience, most couldn't give a monkey's about the legal niceties. But Nicci was different. She was a stickler.

In Eddie's world it had always been payment by results. The technology was there, if you didn't use it they'd soon find someone else who would. That made any moral line decidedly shaky. You had to be a pragmatist to survive and prosper.

As soon as Eddie had seen the CCTV footage of Paige Hollister arguing with Warner in Glasgow he knew he was on the scent of something. Putting tabs on her wasn't that difficult once he'd got hold of her mobile number.

A hacker of his acquaintance specialized in collecting data on politicians' spouses, partners and random lovers. He wanted to charge Eddie two fifty for Paige Hollister's number; Eddie thought that was cheeky and knocked him down to a grand and a half.

Before he left Glasgow, Eddie was on to Denzil, his contact at the UK's largest mobile phone operator. Thanks to his careful cultivation of the lad, Denzil didn't muck about. He started to track Paige Hollister's phone straight away. And the three-hourly updates he sent Eddie had made interesting reading.

Eddie could see Nicci was at her desk. He knew he'd probably get a bollocking, but that was par for the course with her. No matter what she thought of him, he knew the value of his achievements. And the fact he had a job meant that Simon Blake did too.

As he strolled across the room in her direction he noticed she looked quite perky. She didn't seem hungover, which was a bonus, and she appeared to be sipping something that looked alarmingly like green tea.

He hovered tactfully – she was chatting to Pascale – until she turned and smiled at him.

'Morning, Eddie.'

'All right, girls?' He included Pascale, though she swivelled back to her computer and ignored him.

He took a breath – in for a penny, in for a pound. 'Thing is, boss, I thought it might be an idea to keep an eye on Paige Hollister.'

Nicci leant back in her chair. 'We've just been talking about her. Pascale's been doing some digging too.'

Eddie was certain that the very proper ferreting about and collating of all the information in the public domain that the researcher would have done was unlikely to have produced the nugget he had to offer. He was quietly competitive in his own way, but had the good sense not to show it.

'Well, it seems yesterday afternoon Paige Hollister took a trip down to Surrey. Paid a visit to a lawyer named Neville Moore. I checked him out – Sheridan Crowley Moore – he used to be Helen Warner's boss before she went into politics.'

Nicci was frowning with concentration. 'A lawyer?'

'That's what I thought. Old Ray was off to see a lawyer the afternoon he bought it. So what if it's the same bloke?'

She nodded. 'Makes sense if he was someone that Warner knew and trusted.'

Surprised to have got this far without controversy, Eddie decided to busk it. 'Say this lawyer had been holding a memory stick for Warner. He gives it to Ray, Ray gets whacked.'

Nicci shook her head. 'No. Ray goes under a tube train, how would his assailants recover it from his body? Too complicated for them. More likely that it was Ray who had the memory stick and he passed it on to the lawyer. He gets eliminated. No loose ends.'

'So Paige Hollister visits him to try and get it?' This was going far better than Eddie had expected.

Nicci tapped the desk with her finger. 'We need to talk to this lawyer.'

'Here's the odd thing, his office insist he's in Australia.'

'Hang on, you said she went to see him.' Nicci turned to glare at him.

'Well, she went to his house, in Godalming. Stayed half an hour, left. I don't actually know who she saw. But it must've been him.'

'I presume you've been tracking her phone?'

Eddie had a feeling shit and fan were about to connect. 'I would've followed her, done it the proper old-fashioned way. But I was on a train coming back from Glasgow. Can't be in two places at once, boss.'

Nicci raised her eyebrows, then she chuckled. 'Simon says you're a resourceful bloke. And I guess he's got a point. You do deliver.'

He gave her an impish grin. 'No IPCC looking over your shoulder now, boss.'

'That doesn't make it right. But – what the hell? Just stop calling me boss, okay.'

'No probs.'

She steepled her fingers and pondered. 'So, if this Neville Moore was actually holding the evidence Helen Warner gathered against Hollister, it's no wonder he wants people to think he's in Australia. Suggests he's scared.'

'What if he gets it from Ray, jumps on a plane to Oz, takes it with him?'

'Then why did Paige Hollister spend half an hour at his house?' She shook her head. 'No, you're right, he must've been there. Question is, did he give it to her?'

'And how did she know he had it?'

They exchanged looks.

She smiled. 'Know where she is now?'

'Last update, she was at a hairdressers in Covent Garden.'

'Probably getting ready for tonight. Some big charity bash.' She twisted her chair. 'What is it she's up to, Pascale?'

The researcher turned from her screen to face them. 'She's like a . . . what is it, helper of this charity?'

'You mean a patron?'

'Yeah, a patron. They dig wells. All over Africa. Some celebrity photographer has been taking pictures of them.' Her voice dripped sarcasm. 'Y'know the style – happy little black people with buckets on their heads. There's an exhibition and a big launch. Get all the rich people pissed so they open their wallets. She's been tweeting about it. It's tonight.'

Nicci twizzled in her chair. 'I've got a mind to gatecrash. Might manage to ask Paige Hollister some questions before they throw me out. Her old man too, if he's there.'

Eddie scratched his beard. 'Maybe I can help. Old contact of mine is a big gossip columnist on one of the tabloids. She owes me a favour or two. I'll see if I can scare you up a proper invite.'

'You're incorrigible, Eddie, you know that.' Nicci gave him a rueful smile.

'Just doing the job, boss.' He grimaced. 'Sorry.'

82

It wasn't the dress that bothered Kaz so much as the shoes. They were in Irina's room rifling through her large closet. Stripping down to her bra and pants had caused Kaz some awkwardness to start with. But she decided she was just being adolescent. If she hadn't fancied the Russian, it wouldn't have been a problem.

Prison life and communal showers had cured her of any pretensions to modesty. It was more that she felt at a disadvantage – she was exposed, Irina was not. And although the Russian had been flirtatious enough with Joey, shut up alone in a bedroom together, Kaz could feel a definite sexual frisson. She knew she wasn't imagining it.

Irina's dress collection was sizeable, mostly new and full of designer labels. But she was blonde whereas Kaz was dark, so quite a few colour combinations were considered and discarded. Finally they hit upon a silver sheath dress. Kaz put it on. The neckline was square, revealing only a hint of cleavage, it grazed the knee – elegant but in no way vulgar.

Kaz stared at herself in the full-length mirror. Standing slightly behind her, Irina brought the tip of her index finger to rest on Kaz's bare arm. It sent a shiver straight through her.

The Russian tilted her head coyly. 'Prada. You like?'

Kaz turned to face her. Irina's eyes were grey – just like Helen's. She liked their seductive look way more than the dress. Her perfume was light enough not to mask the smell of her skin. The temptation to move in, to touch, maybe even to taste, was almost overwhelming. And Kaz could sense that the Russian wouldn't say no. But she hesitated. She wanted this; the tension in her lower belly was telling her to go for it. Still the voice in her head counselled caution. It would be all too easy to get teased and used.

She grinned and stepped back. 'Shoes? I hate wearing heels. You can't bloody walk. You certainly can't run.'

Irina giggled and turned to the cupboard. Reaching down to the neat stack of shoe boxes, she opened one and lifted out a four-inch black patent stiletto.

Kaz pulled a face. 'You want me to break my fucking neck?'

After some experimenting they settled for a strappy pair of sandals, also silver, with a more manageable heel and Kaz set off on the perilous journey down the stairs.

The boys were lounging in front of the sixty-inch plasma screen watching American football on catch-up. But Kaz's entrance produced a stunned silence. Yevgeny clicked off the TV, Tolya gave a low whistle and Joey gawped.

Yevgeny stood up, his brother followed suit. They seemed to do it without thinking.

Joey put his head to one side. 'Blimey, if Mum saw you in that, I think maybe even she'd be impressed.'

'I doubt it.' Kaz was concentrating on keeping her balance in the heels.

A dark, mischievous look crept into her brother's eye. 'Not exactly the kind of gear Clare O'Keeffe'd be caught dead in, is it?'

Kaz's heart missed a beat. 'What?'

He leant one arm along the sofa back and beamed.

'Glasgow, too. How d'you find it? Bit chilly, I reckon, especially in winter.'

Her chin jutted. 'Who told you this? Mike?'

'Mike?' He laughed. 'Poor old Mike. Nah, it weren't him.'

Fear suddenly gripped her. Was this it? Was this Joey's endgame? String her along, dress her up like a fucking doll, then strike. She glanced at Yevgeny, Tolya and the smiling Irina. Was she in on the act too?

Reaching down, she wrenched off the shoes, she wasn't going down without a fight.

Joey laced his fingers. 'Don't look so worried, babes. I known since before the trial. Soon as you went on witness protection.'

'What d'you mean?'

'Wonderful thing, computers. All that data stashed away. And you know the Old Bill, they have to keep a record of everything.'

'You hacked the police computer?'

'Not me personally. I was worried about you. Wanted to know you was okay.'

Kaz stared at him in disbelief. 'Then why didn't you . . .' She sighed, none of it made sense.

'Send someone after you? Stop you testifying? I thought about it. Then Yev come to see me in the nick, while I was on remand.'

She shot a glance at the Russian, he'd adopted his habitual stance – tattooed forearms folded, an inscrutable look on his face.

Joey smiled wistfully. 'He told me what an arrogant little prick I was. You'd offered me the chance to stop being a petty villain and move up. But I didn't trust you, I tried to control you. Told me a bunch of other stuff too, didn't you, Yev?'

Yevgeny's eyes were flint hard, he didn't smile. 'You got the bloodlust, Joey. I seen it on the battlefield. You like too much to kill. She knew that. She try to save you from yourself.'

Joey rubbed the back of his fist across his nose. 'I realized he was right. You was the one person in my whole sorry fucking life who really loved me and tried to help me.' He sniffed and she saw the baby-blue eyes were brimming with tears. 'So I had to just let it all play out until I could find a way back. This is my way back. Don't give up on me, big sister. Give me another chance. I'll make things right. I promise.'

83

She'd had enough experience of her brother's mercurial temper and manipulative nature not to take any emotional outburst at face value. Joey lied much as he breathed – it wasn't something he ever had to think about. But his apparent change of heart and desire to win her trust presented Kaz with an opportunity she wasn't about to pass up.

With Tolya as her driver and escort she headed back into town and to Onslow Square. It seemed peaceful and normal in the afternoon sunshine. The builders were still renovating the house down the street. A traffic warden was ticketing cars that didn't have a resident's permit. If the police had got Mike's place staked out, it wasn't in any way obvious. Nevertheless Tolya was cautious, he cruised round the square, parked up at a safe distance and they waited.

A UPS van delivered a massive parcel to the house next door; two nannies pushing buggies wandered by chattering away in Spanish. Tolya had headphones on, listening to Kylie, which struck Kaz as an odd choice for a Russian gangster. But his eyes monitored every movement on the street.

'Can't I just go and knock at the door?'

Tolya pulled one of his earphones out and Kaz had to repeat her question. He shook his head.

Shortly after three a stooped figure appeared, climbing slowly up the basement steps. His ratted locks were pulled back in a ponytail, he wore his old hoodie, it was definitely Mike. Kaz's heart soared, she was about to jump out of the car when Tolya put a restraining hand on her arm.

'Not yet.'

They watched him meander down the street with his hessian shopping bag. He stopped to stroke a cat in a neighbour's doorway. Once he'd turned the corner, Tolya started the engine and they stalked him discreetly to a parade of shops on Fulham Road.

Tolya glanced up and down the busy thoroughfare, gave Kaz the nod.

She got out of the four-by-four and followed Mike into a small mini-market. The aisles were narrow and stacked from floor to ceiling. He was leaning into a chiller cabinet to extract a plastic bottle of milk when she came up behind him.

'Hello, Mike.'

He turned to stare at her and his chin quivered. 'Never thought I'd see you again.'

'I'm sorry.'

'You're sorry? I only wanted to help you. That's why I called them.'

'I know that. But if they'd caught me with Joey they'd have revoked my licence and sent me back to prison.'

He gave her an apologetic look. 'I thought that was preferable to being killed.'

'You're probably right.'

'You're okay then?' He gazed at her for a moment, his eyes as sharp and penetrating as ever.

'Yeah, me and Joey have come to an arrangement.'

'You trust him?'

'No. But I know him.'

Mike leant on the side of the vast freezer, piled high with

frozen vegetables and oven chips. He shook his head wearily. 'You stick with him, he'll bring you down.'

'Don't worry, it's a very temporary arrangement.'

Scratching his brow, he gave her a tentative smile. 'Let's go outside, hail a cab and put you on the next train to Glasgow. That's where your life is now. Just walk away, Karen. You did it before, do it again.'

She met his eye. 'I think I know who killed Helen.'

'Leave it to the police, to that private detective. Nicci whatever-her-name-is?'

'I can't.'

Tilting his head, he sighed. 'They said if you came back, I should call them.'

'Will you?'

'Course not. Will you leave me a number where I can contact you?'

He was gazing at her earnestly, his dark eyes feverish and over-bright. It probably wouldn't be long now before he checked into the hospice. Stretching out his bony claw he grasped her arm; the grip was surprisingly firm.

'Karen, you've got a wonderful talent. Don't waste it.'

'I have to do this first, Mike. And I can't give you my number. It's not that I don't trust you—'

'But you don't trust me.' His vulpine features twisted into a grin. 'And you'd be right. If going back to prison is the only thing that's going to save your life – and there's a good chance it is – I'd make that call.'

'I can take care of myself. You need to do the same. I just wanted to say goodbye.'

Wrapping her arms round his skeletal shoulders, his angel wings, she pulled him into a hug. He didn't resist. He had a musky old man's smell mixed with oil paint. Patting her shoulder gently, he waited for her to release him.

She turned sharply on her heel and headed for the door; she didn't want him to see the tears in her eyes.

84

The hotel was in Park Lane. Nicci Armstrong arrived in a taxi and, armed with the invitation Eddie Lunt had procured for her, was directed to the ballroom on the first floor.

The evening sun flooded in over Hyde Park burnishing the cherry-wood panelled walls and the gold fittings. A concertina of a dozen photo display boards bisected the room, tables were dotted round the edge, each with a white damask cloth, a floral centrepiece and several chairs.

Nicci presented her invitation, received a flute of champagne from a white-gloved waiter and wandered over to inspect the photographic exhibits. Large glossy prints, in warm sumptuous colours, were tastefully displayed two to a board. Nicci let her gaze meander over them. Pascale had got it about right – lots of cute black kids and smiling women with buckets on their heads or splashing each other with water and looking generally happy and grateful.

The photographer was standing by one of the boards with an attentive group around him. He was tall, rakishly thin with a mane of iron-grey hair swept back from his forehead. He wore khaki combats and a somewhat crumpled linen jacket. This made Nicci feel better, since everyone else was dressed up to the nines – several men in dinner jackets, the women in a colourful and competitive array of cocktail dresses.

And at the photographer's side, with a pleased and proprietorial look on her face, was Paige Hollister. Nicci had been staring at her image from grainy CCTV to slick PR shots for a couple of days. She'd glimpsed her only once in the flesh, at the inquest, when Hollister had looked zoned out. But this evening she was all sparkle. She was a slight figure, her outfit less gaudy than the women around her. Her dress was taupe, her jewellery elegant and understated.

Nicci sipped her champagne and watched from the side-lines. She had to admit that Paige Hollister was a class act. Her easy manner was polished but egalitarian enough to play anywhere. Nicci speculated she wouldn't be that different drinking tea in a day centre of OAPs.

Hollister's voice carried the faintest hint of a Scottish dialect. 'When Gavin agreed to do it, well, we couldn't believe our luck.' She placed her hand on the photographer's forearm and chuckled. He looked at her as Nicci imagined many middle-aged men did: with the secret lustful hope that she might favour him with more than her public charm.

The room was filling up. Quite a few of the guests seemed to know each other. Nicci scanned them: a chat-show host, a couple of actors, what she took to be a gaggle of politicians. But there was no sign of Robert Hollister.

There was also a smattering of different languages, particularly among the contingent in dinner jackets. These were the real targets of the bash. High-net-worth individuals, who'd made London their home and liked to mix social networking with philanthropy.

Nicci noticed a jovial, barrel-chested man at the centre of one such group. He had a booming laugh and the crowd clustered round him seemed to appreciate his humour. Paige went over to join them, he put his arm round her shoulder and switching to English repeated the joke. Nicci edged closer to eavesdrop.

The noise in the room had increased several decibels and it took a moment before a slight altercation at the door drew Nicci's attention. It caught Paige Hollister's eye an instant later. Both women turned to see the dishevelled figure of Julia Hadley arguing with the security man.

Paige swooped immediately. 'Julia!' She dismissed the security man's concern over the lack of an invitation with a flick of her head.

Homing in on Julia, she hooked her by the arm. 'This is so lovely. I never dreamt you'd feel up to coming or I'd've—'

She didn't get a chance to finish.

Julia wrenched her arm free and glared. 'I wanna talk to you. And Robert.' The slur in her speech suggested a considerable amount of alcohol. Paige's expression went from feigned delight to genuine panic. Nicci was near enough to hear.

The possibility of a drunken Julia blowing it with a premature public accusation, not to mention potentially placing herself in danger, gave Nicci no option but to intervene.

Julia was swaying slightly. Her expression suggested she'd like to deck Paige.

Nicci moved in and caught her by the arm. 'Oh, Julia, you know what the doctor said.' She glanced at a confused Paige. 'Nicci Armstrong – I'm a friend.' She shook her head wearily. 'My God, it's been such a terrible time . . .'

Paige gave her a tepid smile.

'. . . the stress of the inquest being adjourned – well, you can imagine. The medication they put her on is terribly strong. And it really shouldn't be mixed with alcohol.'

Regaining her composure, Paige painted on a look of concern. 'I was there myself, I'm sure we all found it frustrating.'

Julia blinked several times as she tried to focus on the person who had hold of her. 'Nicci? Whad'you doing—'

'I'm here to take care of you.' She grasped Julia firmly.

The fact they knew each other seemed to absolve Paige of further responsibility.

Flapping her hand airily, she frowned. 'You're clearly far better equipped . . . but if there's anything I can do? Anything at all.'

'Oh, absolutely. Don't worry, I'll make sure she's okay.'

'Thank you so much.' With a gracious smile, Paige turned and escaped into the crowd.

Nicci started to guide her charge out into the foyer. The smell of alcohol coming off Julia was overpowering. It was amazing she'd even managed to get herself there.

Julia's head was lolling and she was mumbling: 'Fuckers! Hypocrites and fuckers, all of them!'

Nicci shepherded her towards the Ladies. 'I know. But this is not the way to deal with it.'

As they rounded the corner to enter the toilets, Julia staggered and lurched against Nicci, who had to grab her round the waist to keep her upright. They both nearly toppled over. Suddenly a helping hand reached out to steady Nicci from a woman, who'd just emerged from the cloakroom.

Turning to thank her, Nicci did a double-take. She was tall and stunning in a silver sheath dress, her lustrous crimson lips parted in a smile. Nicci really did have to look twice to confirm it was Karen Phelps.

85

They sat Julia down on the lavatory seat in one of the cubicles. She slammed her fist against the flimsy partition and howled.

'Fuck 'em! Fuck the lot of 'em! Rapists!'

Irina and the Filipina cloakroom attendant, responding to her distress rather than any comprehension of what she was saying, fussed over her in competing versions of broken English.

Having checked all the other cubicles were empty, Nicci turned to Kaz. 'Did you know she was planning to come here and confront the Hollisters?'

'The Hollisters? They're here?'

'She's the patron of the fucking charity, Karen.'

Kaz whistled. 'I had no idea.'

The ex-cop looked her up and down suspiciously. 'What? You just fancied a night out?'

'I'm here because of Pudovkin.'

'Who?'

'Viktor Pudovkin?'

Nicci was seething. Between them, Julia and Kaz had managed yet again to complicate her life when they should've left well alone. Her plan had been simple – to corner Paige Hollister and ask her what she'd been arguing about with Helen Warner at the hotel in Glasgow. She and Blake had discussed it and agreed that leaning on the fragrant Mrs Hollister was the way forward.

'Never heard of him.' She shrugged in irritation.

Kaz lowered her voice to a confidential whisper. 'Me neither. Till I was told that he's the scumbag behind Helen's murder.'

Nicci's scowl morphed into a look of astonished disbelief. 'Says who?'

'Helen's old boss.'

It took a few seconds for Nicci to absorb this. 'Neville Moore? You talked to him?'

'Last night.'

'How did that come about?'

Kaz didn't want to sound too evasive. 'I knew him from when Helen was my lawyer. He turned up at the inquest. Struck me that he was someone she could've confided in.'

Nicci huffed. 'Might've been useful if you'd shared that thought.'

'You mean like you told me about the bloke at the Labour Party?'

They glared at one another. Julia could be heard retching in the toilet.

The outer door to the cloakroom swung open and two laughing girls sailed in, chattering in Arabic. Early twenties, dripping jewellery, one disappeared into a cubicle, the other positioned herself right between Nicci and Kaz, directly in front of the mirror and began to touch up her make-up. She cast a disdainful glance in Nicci's direction. Nicci stared back until she broke eye contact.

Kaz sighed. 'Okay, listen. We need to talk. Properly.'

The ex-cop was still eyeing the interloper. 'Agreed. First I'll have to get Julia home. Make sure she's safe. I mean, if they get any inkling she knows . . .'

'Yeah, obviously. So let's meet later. Where?'

'How about I text you my address?'

'Fine.'

The young woman seemed to resent the fact that this conversation was taking place across her. She huffed and emptied a compact and lipstick out of her gold lamé clutch bag, then she turned and clicked her fingers at the Filipina cloakroom attendant. 'Get me a towel!'

Nicci and Kaz exchanged looks. For Nicci it was the last straw.

'We're having a conversation here.' She clicked her fingers in the astounded girl's face. 'And you need to learn to get your own fucking towel, sweetheart.'

86

Kaz and Irina rejoined their escorts in the foyer. Yevgeny wore a tuxedo, his younger and cooler brother favoured a dark lounge suit with a collarless black shirt. Yevgeny offered Kaz his arm, they handed in their invitations at the door and strolled into the ballroom.

Kaz surveyed the room; she recognized Paige Hollister from the inquest. According to Nicci she was the patron of the charity, but Pudovkin was the one bankrolling the event. Yevgeny had explained that this was what he did. He provided generous financial backing for a number of worthy causes and this in turn earned him social prestige and a network of connections among the great and good, not to mention all the ambitious wannabes scuttling at their heels.

The man himself stood in a small circle of acolytes. His confident booming laugh singled him out and Kaz took a long hard look at her dead lover's nemesis.

Close-cropped grey hair, lively features, he was large and solid but not fat. Kaz guessed he was around sixty, though the immaculate sylphlike blonde at his elbow was a good quarter-century younger.

Tolya and Irina had turned aside to get drinks, but Yevgeny pressed forward to join the group surrounding Pudovkin. Kaz watched as the big man's gaze slid round and came to rest on Yevgeny. The eyes were narrow and shrewd, dark as wet slate.

He stuck out a meaty, hirsute paw and the two men shook hands, exchanging greetings in Russian. The tone was formal, the body language wary; they were not friends, that much was immediately apparent to Kaz.

As Yevgeny drew her forward he switched to English. 'And this is Karen.'

Pudovkin's eyes flitted over her, his smile was bland, impossible to read. 'Always happy to meet a friend of Yevgeny.'

His English was precise, only mildly accented, he dipped his head politely. Kaz had a cascade of questions she wanted to ask. Who the fuck did he think he was! That was fairly near the top of her list.

She painted on a smile. 'D'you dig many wells then?' The hint of sarcasm in the tone was slight enough to be ambiguous.

A glint came into his eye and he chuckled. 'Not personally.'

Kaz had the odd feeling that if she'd asked: *Do you kill many people then?* She'd have received exactly the same reply.

A flurry in the vicinity of the door signalled Robert Hollister's arrival. He entered, flanked by two aides. Kaz noticed his wife studiously ignoring him as she listened earnestly to a tall West African in a Senegalese kaftan and a kufi.

Hollister worked his way across the room, shaking hands, sharing a quip and a laugh. Pudovkin didn't move. He'd taken up his position, he was the real nucleus and guests flowed naturally round and towards him.

Yevgeny turned to Kaz. 'Champagne?'

'Nah, just a juice or water.'

He nodded and headed for the bar.

Kaz let her eyes rest on Robert Hollister. He was gradually moving her way and she allowed a space to open up around her. She stood still and waited. This wasn't something she'd tried lately, but she had confidence in her powers of attraction. It took several minutes before she caught his eye. He turned and noticed a dazzling woman in a silver dress staring right at him.

Curiosity piqued, he inclined his head and came over. 'Robert Hollister –' he extended his hand '– I don't believe we've had the pleasure.'

She slid her palm into his. 'Karen.'

The heat of his hand was surprising, but it was dry and soft, not clammy.

He held on a few seconds longer than necessary and gave her a knowing smile. 'I agree, surnames are so boring. And I prefer a woman of mystery.'

'I'm not mysterious.'

'You disappoint me.'

She ran her index finger through her hair; he was absurdly easy to hook. 'Depends what you're looking for?'

His smile widened, he narrowed his eyes and peered at her. 'Me, I'm always looking. So what interests you most here – digging wells in Africa or photography?'

'The wells, obviously.'

He chuckled. 'Now I think you're mocking me.'

'Maybe I'm mocking your wife.'

His lip curled into a sardonic smile. 'Paige is very serious about her charity work. But she's also a woman of great good sense, one of life's pragmatists.'

'That's useful.'

'It certainly is. So can I ask for your number?' The look he gave her was one of undisguised lust. Kaz wondered if this approach usually worked with women. Presumably it did. He was a powerful man, handsome, he simply expected to get what he wanted.

'What if I tell you I have a boyfriend?'

He shrugged. 'I'm open-minded. I could take you to dinner and we could take it from there. Your boyfriend need never know.'

'So I give you my number and wait for a gap in your busy schedule? I've got a better idea, you give me your number.' She gave him a sultry pout, her eyes half closed. It sealed the deal.

He reached in his pocket, pulled out a business card. 'The bottom one's my private number. Send me a text. You'll be glad you did.'

She took the card just as Yevgeny joined them, a glass of champagne in one hand, orange juice in the other. Hollister smirked and beat a hasty retreat.

The Russian handed her the juice. 'You want me to scare him off?'

'No. But maybe you've got a nice compact, untraceable handgun that I could borrow?'

He nodded thoughtfully. 'I find you one.'

87

With some discreet assistance from the hotel security staff Nicci got Julia Hadley into a cab and they headed across town to her parents' house in Blackheath. Julia slept for most of the journey, her head slumped on Nicci's shoulder.

Nicci texted the address of her flat to Phelps, as promised, then made two phone calls. The first was to Blake.

He answered on the second ring. 'Nic? Did you get to speak to Paige Hollister?'

'No. Events overtook me a bit.' She went on to explain about Julia.

She heard him sigh. 'Understandable I guess. The poor woman's been under considerable stress. Realizing her house had been bugged probably tipped her over the edge.'

'Well I think I might've got a line on that.' Nicci paused. She'd already decided not to reveal Karen Phelps' involvement. That would be likely to produce a negative reaction. 'At Paige Hollister's charity beano there was a Russian called Viktor Pudovkin. Ever heard of him?'

'Nope.'

'Well, we need to do some urgent digging because he could be a significant player in all this.'

'Who do we think he is?'

'No idea really. I was going to get Eddie on it. But given all that surveillance kit in the house and the fact Hollister is a politician, I'm wondering – well, you know what I'm wondering.'

Silence. She could hear a television in the background. Sounded like cricket. Blake and his sons were avid Twenty20 fans.

When he came back on the line his tone was brisk. 'Right. I'm going to talk to some people. You ring Eddie. Cover all bases. I'll see you at the office first thing.'

'Okay.'

He rang off. Nicci glanced at her sleeping companion. Julia's face was damp and heavy and her eyelids twitched as though she was caught in some private dream, or nightmare.

The conversation with Eddie Lunt was brief. He didn't seem at all bothered to have been called at home and his evening disrupted.

A rhythmic munching underpinned his response. 'Couple of reporters I know specialize in doing stuff on rich Ruskies – y'know the form – more money than taste, billionaires whose wives wanna be pop stars. I'll see if he's on their radar.'

Nicci thanked him and hung up. The traffic had thinned and the cab cruised through Deptford and the edge of Greenwich to Shooters Hill Road and up on to the dark expanse of the heath.

Julia awoke with a start and a gasp. She blinked several times and rubbed her face, clearly confused about where she was. Nicci had ridden out enough hangovers in her time to know exactly that feeling of panic as the effects of the drug subsided and reality kicked back in.

She pulled a plastic bottle of water from her bag and unscrewed the top. 'Here, have a drink.'

'Where are we?' Julia took the bottle.

'Just going over the heath, I'm taking you back to your mum and dad's.'

'What did I do?'

'Not a lot. We got hold of you in time.'

Julia frowned as memory came flooding back. 'Oh fuck, now I remember. I went to Paige's charity thing.'

'What exactly did you have in mind?'

'I wanted to make them confess.'

Nicci smiled. 'A nice idea in principle.'

Sighing deeply, Julia took a long draught of water. 'It's just that I've been thinking about the recording Helen made. Of him and . . . well, I know it's important evidence.'

'Would be if we could find it.'

The cab was passing through Blackheath Village and the streetlights threw Julia's face into garish relief. Nicci realized she was crying. She took her hand and squeezed it.

'It's the thought of it being played, in court, on the Net.' She choked down a sob. Whatever Helen had done, in spite of the lack of trust, Julia still loved her. 'Everyone seeing what that bastard did to Helen. And seeing Helen . . . like that.'

'That's presumably what she planned to do to nail him.'

'I know. But now she's dead. Once it's out there, that's how she'll be remembered. Sweaty perverts getting off on it. Her memory will be defiled. I don't want that, Nicci. I don't want people to see her degraded like that, turned into cheap porn.'

Nicci sighed. 'I guess we hadn't really thought of that aspect.'

She could just about see Julia's eyes, and the look in them was desperate. 'Promise me you'll protect her. Protect her memory. 'Cause that's all that's left of her now.'

88

Nicci asked the cabbie to drop her at the edge of Newington Green so she could visit her favourite Indian takeaway. Julia had been deposited safely into the care of her concerned and bemused parents.

The ride home had taken the best part of three-quarters of an hour and afforded Nicci some quiet thinking time in which to try and piece together the bits of the puzzle.

Karen Phelps had known Warner well enough to take a better guess than anyone else at who she might've trusted. Or if not trusted, who she might've involved in her plan. Neville Moore, the lawyer, may well have received the vital evidence from Ray. And Ray, like Moore, was a colleague, part of Warner's professional world.

Gazing out of the cab at the night-time hustle of the streets, Nicci had begun to sense a window opening up on the dead woman's thinking and the emotional struggle behind it. It was about the separation of personal and professional, the division of her life into private and public.

The years of abuse that the Hollisters had visited on Helen had been messy and clandestine, a secret so private she shared it with no one. But when she entered politics and tried to make her relationship with Robert Hollister purely professional, he kept dragging her back into the personal realm. She realized that the only way to stop him was to make the whole thing public, and she deliberately chose the allies to help her do that from the professional sphere. Nicci could see why that detachment helped her. It was because she refused to be cowed. She wanted it to be clear in her own mind and everyone else's that the shame was on him, not on her.

Nicci sat next to the window in Sea of Spice nursing a beer while she waited for her order. It was a regular haunt of hers and she chatted to Sanjay, the proprietor, as he watched his team, Arsenal, battling it out in a pre-season friendly on the television screen above the bar. It was a relief to escape even for a short while into his rollercoaster world of outrageous tackles and missed penalties. As she left the restaurant with her dinner in a paper carrier, he was shaking his fist at the referee's incompetence.

She walked the few hundred yards down the street and crossed the road towards her block. Her mind was on the aroma and heat wafting up from the bag – she hadn't eaten since lunch – and she didn't immediately notice the figures bunched in the shadows by the door. Her key was in her hand and as she reached out to insert it in the lock she was barged sideways.

Regaining her balance, she spun round to face her assailant. He seemed to hesitate.

Then a low female voice behind him growled. 'Fuckin' do 'er, Leon!'

Nicci saw light flash on a blade and she swung her carrier bag at it. The knife clattered to the floor. Leon froze. Nicci lurched sideways to make a run for it. But her way was blocked as three more bodies moved in to back him up.

'Wot? I 'ave to fuckin' do this for yer 'n'all?' She was large in all senses, feral eyes framed by an outsized baggy hoodie, she raised her pudgy fist and pointed a steel-bladed sheath knife at Nicci. 'Now we gonna teach you some fuckin' respect, bitch!'

Nicci kicked out, went for the kneecap and the howl from the fat girl told her she'd hit the target. Then they rushed her.

Throwing up her forearm to parry the thrust of the blade, Nicci felt a sharp sting as it sliced into her arm. A fist rammed the side of her head and she felt herself spinning downward into a yawning chasm. Her brain scrabbled to hold on but it was useless. The darkness rose up to swallow her, she was falling into the void and it was pitch-black.

89

The voice seemed to be coming from a vast distance away. Someone was holding her, cradling her head and shoulders. Nicci managed to open her eyes and peer up.

Kaz Phelps looked down at her. 'It's okay. You're gonna be okay.'

Was it really her? She remembered – they'd arranged to meet up. Her right arm was extremely sore and sticky with blood. Kaz appeared to be trying to hold it straight as someone else – was it Sanjay? – wrapped some kind of cloth around it.

Nicci felt woozy and slightly sick. She drifted off.

When she woke again there were bright lights. She was on a trolley in A&E. Her right forearm felt heavy and stiff; it was bandaged from palm to elbow.

The pale-blue curtain was pulled back and a nurse appeared. She was small, twinkling dark eyes and a sunny smile. She stroked back Nicci's hair and gave her some water. She spoke but Nicci couldn't quite seem to latch on to the words.

Nicci dozed. They came and moved her trolley. Her eyes were heavy and she fell back into the same languid slumber.

She dreamt of wandering through a derelict house. The rooms were dusty and dilapidated, old bits of broken furniture littered about. She opened doors and was surprised to find another shut-up room and then another. She wrenched open a shutter, the wood was rotten and splintered in her hand. But light flooded in through the window and dust motes danced around the room.

A noise in the adjacent cubicle woke her – a dropped metal dish clanged as it hit the floor. She opened her eyes; her mouth was very dry but her head felt clear. She sat up and examined the tube bandage on her arm. The arm was sore but not too painful. The left side of her jaw and ear felt tender to the touch. She remembered the blow – the girl's pudgy fist socking into the side of her head.

The curtain was drawn back and another nurse appeared, taller and brisker than the first. 'Good morning. How are you feeling?'

'Thirsty.'

'I'll get you some fresh water.'

'Thank you. Where am I?'

'A&E at Homerton. The doctor wanted to keep you under observation overnight because of the concussion. She'll come and speak to you in a bit. Oh, and there's a policeman wants to talk to you, if you feel up to it.'

'Yeah, okay.'

'I'll send him in.'

Nicci sank back into the pillows. It was morning, normality had returned, she was safe. And from her clinical refuge she could let her mind travel into the darkness.

It was Leon, the boy from the bus stop, the boy she'd suspected of Ethel's murder. It was definitely Leon. But with three others. A girl – huge, close on six feet tall and overweight – she'd egged him on. Nicci had managed to disarm him, but the girl had been her main attacker.

The nurse returned with a jug of water and in her wake

came Jack Delgado, shoulders hunched, hands in trouser pockets.

He gave her a sheepish smile. 'How you doing?'

'Surviving.'

Taking the jug from the nurse, he poured her a glass of water. 'You'll be pleased to know we nicked all four of the little bastards.'

Nicci sipped the water. 'I'm impressed.'

'Don't be. They'd been rounded up for us and locked in the walk-in freezer in the Indian restaurant across the road.'

This immediately broke for Nicci the memory that had been niggling the edge of her consciousness. Kaz Phelps. When Nicci had first come round, Kaz Phelps had been there.

'Who intervened and why, we don't know. A gunshot was reported. That brought Sanjay out of the restaurant. I think you know him.'

'Yeah. I remember him helping me.'

Delgado puffed out his cheeks. 'And my boss said to tell you we owe you an apology.'

'How come?'

'We should've taken a closer look at Leon before.'

'He wasn't the main assailant. He was being egged on by this girl.'

The cop nodded wearily. 'Nearly tall as me but three times as wide?'

'Yeah.'

'That's Buchi. The reason we owe you an apology is we didn't realize she's Leon's stepsister. Different surnames. My fault, I should've checked it out.'

'She's known to you then?'

'Oh yeah. Only sixteen, but she's a complete headbanger. Antisocial personality disorder is what it says on her file.

Runs this girl gang. They're twice as vicious and vengeful as the lads.'

'You think she could've killed Ethel?'

'That's what Leon's saying. Poor little sod's scared stiff of her. He's been blurting it all out. Apparently word got round of your encounter with him at the bus stop. Buchi took it very personally. You'd made a fool of her brother and that reflected badly on her.'

'I'm so stupid.' Nicci's bandaged arm was beginning to throb. 'I should never have gotten into all that.'

Delgado smiled sympathetically. 'She's a complete nutter. It wasn't your fault. She forced Leon to identify you and Ethel. Apparently, her backup plan was to burn down the flats.'

'You got any forensics that can link her to Ethel?'

'We're hopeful. She wears this outsized hoodie, with a Slipknot logo on the back. Idolizes the band, never takes it off. It's got fresh blood on the sleeve, probably yours. But there are some older stains too. It's gone to the lab. And her knife with it.'

'Otherwise her word against Leon's?'

He jangled the change in his pocket. 'She's a piece of work, Nicci. And once word gets out that she's going down I think we might get a few others willing to testify about all sorts.'

She smiled. 'Good luck with that.'

'Well, I'd best get on. Oh and I think your boyfriend's waiting.'

Nicci gawped at him. 'I don't have a boyfriend.'

Delgado stared down at his scuffed shoes, gave her his hangdog smile. 'Whatever. It's none of my business.'

'You don't mean Rory?' She chuckled. 'When the place gets really messy I just get him round to clean up.'

The cop grinned and met her eye. It was only then that it dawned on Nicci that his interest in her was not purely professional. His long lugubrious face didn't give much away, but the look in his eye was boyish and hopeful.

'Okay, you reckon you owe me an apology? You can buy me dinner. But make it somewhere posh, Delgado. None of your rubbish.'

He beamed and pulled back his shoulders; she'd obviously made his day. 'I'll do some research, find somewhere special and give you a bell.'

He slipped out through the curtain, leaving Nicci to ponder. The lonely months of isolation since her daughter's death had been like living in a time warp. The pain of that loss would always be there, she'd never stop thinking of Sophie. It was like her bandaged arm, sore but not agonizing, a wound that was maybe starting to heal. And now there appeared to be two men interested in her.

She was smiling to herself at this ironic turn of events, when Simon Blake pulled back the curtain. Somehow he seemed much more like a policeman than Delgado.

He was trying to look tough and professional, but at the sight of her his voice cracked. 'Bloody hell, Nic. Why didn't you tell me about this other thing? This neighbour who got murdered?'

His face was fierce, his jaw clenched against any display of emotion. And standing just behind his left shoulder was Rory.

'Sorry, I didn't realize it was going to turn into something . . .'

As she spoke Rory stepped round Blake, took her hand, lifted it gently to his lips and kissed it. 'You okay?'

Blake did a double-take. He shot a look at her then glared at his Head of Security.

Feeling decidedly uncomfortable, Nicci withdrew her hand. 'I'm fine.'

The last thing she wanted was for her and Rory to be seen as an item. Especially by Blake.

He painted on a tight smile, now his tone was brisk. 'Doc says you're okay. Once she's checked you over, we can take you home.' He gave the other man a tepid glance. 'I've decided to bring Rory in on this to handle our security, because I've been doing some digging on Viktor Pudovkin.'

Nicci frowned. 'Oh yeah.' She'd completely forgotten about him. But getting back to business did seem the best way to escape the awkwardness of the moment. 'What did you find out?'

'My contact at Vauxhall was very interested in what he might be up to. He's ostensibly a businessman – oil and gas – but his background is the security service, FSB and before that KGB. He hails from St Petersburg – him and Putin go way back, apparently.'

'How come he knows the Hollisters?'

Blake folded his arms, he was ignoring Rory completely. 'He makes a point of getting to know anyone who might be in a position of political influence. He comes over like just another rich businessman living the high life in London. That's just the day job. Basically he's a spook.'

'Wow! Murky waters.'

'Indeed. Explains all the surveillance kit in Warner's house. And it tells us we need to tread very carefully. We need to be very aware of our own security.'

Nicci eased back into her pillows. She just wanted them to go and leave her in peace to recover. However, the two men seemed to be vying to be her protector. Well, it was a bit bloody late for that.

'So what are we talking about here? A Russian spy might be implicated in the murder of a British MP?' She frowned. 'What the hell do we do with that?'

'I'm not sure. I'm going to see if anyone at the Met will actually talk to me. Meanwhile Rory'll take care of you.'

'Simon, I don't need a minder.' She avoided Rory's eye.

'You do. Just until I get the lie of the land. I don't want any more trips to A&E.'

Before she could argue, he gave Rory a brusque nod and he was gone.

90

Kaz Phelps strode across the paved concourse, under the glass canopy and into the soaring cathedral vault of Terminal Three at Heathrow. Tolya had dropped her off and gone to park. The Saturday-morning traffic on the M4 had been slow and tortuous. Would she be in time? Kaz broke into a trot, weaving round gaggles of passengers with their loaded baggage trolleys. She checked her watch – already half eight – she was cutting it very fine.

After the complications of the evening she'd fallen into bed exhausted. Her encounter with Robert Hollister had left her wound up. She found her anger with him all too palpable. The enigmatic Pudovkin, who'd been the intended object of the outing, remained a spectral presence in her mind. Hollister was the one she wanted to kill.

They'd left the hotel before ten; Yev and Irina had gone to a club to join some friends, while Tolya had driven Kaz up to North London to see Nicci Armstrong.

Pulling up outside Nicci's flat they'd found her under attack by a gang of local hooligans, which provided a surprising outlet for Kaz's seething discontent. In spite of the fact she was wearing a tight designer frock and four-inch heels she waded into the melee. Things might not have turned out so well though if Tolya hadn't produced a pump-action shotgun from the boot of his car, fired a shot in the air, then corralled the dumbfounded kids. Having called an ambulance for Nicci, they'd left before the cops arrived.

The landside area of the Departures Hall was choked with lumbering check-in queues – a July weekend, it was peaktime for holiday getaways. Kaz zigzagged around them, her gaze darting about in search of the coffee franchise.

She'd been heavily asleep when Joey had woken her shortly before seven. He'd just received the call from Neville Moore, who was at the airport. Moore's message was cryptic – he'd had time to consider the situation and was prepared to discuss the matter further with Kaz, if she could meet up with him before he boarded his plane.

There were two branches of the coffee shop Moore had specified and Kaz finally found him in the second. He was almost unrecognizable. The smooth English lawyer had been replaced by the tourist. He looked like a preppy American on a world tour, which was perhaps the intention.

He removed his dark glasses and gave Kaz his lizard-eyed smile. 'I was beginning to think you wouldn't make it.'

She sank into the chair opposite him. 'So was I.'

He checked his watch. 'This'll have to be brief. I should've gone through into the departures lounge by now.'

'You're headed for Australia presumably?'

'Dubai first. Just a short stop-over. Did Joey tell you the deal?'

Kaz frowned. 'What deal?'

A thin, sardonic smile spread over the lawyer's features. 'Very Joey. Oh well. That's up to the two of you to sort out.'

He reached into the pocket of his chinos and produced a short stubby cylinder of grey plastic. He held it in his palm.

'It had been my intention to ask for this to be admitted in evidence at the inquest.'

Kaz stared, her heart lurched. She could hardly believe it. Was it a memory stick? It certainly looked like it.

'You got this from Helen?'

'From a colleague of hers.'

Kaz picked it up between thumb and forefinger. 'Have you looked at what's on it?'

He sighed. 'No, I was just an intermediary. My task was to place it in the hands of the Coroner. I planned to do that then make myself scarce. However, after the adjournment I was . . . made aware, shall we say, of how detrimental that might prove for myself and my family.'

'This toerag Pudovkin threatened you?'

A low rumbling laugh shook his shoulders. 'No no. I've never met the man.'

'So how do you know he's behind this? That he's protecting Hollister?'

'As I said, I received a visitor who clarified the situation for me.' He glanced up at the Departures Board. 'Now I really must go.' Rising to his feet he slipped on his varsity jacket. It had Yale emblazoned across the chest and looked like the genuine article not some knockoff.

Kaz got up too, tucking the memory stick safely away in her jeans pocket. 'How come you changed your mind?'

A weary, almost bitter look slid into his eye. 'I haven't, in one way. But Helen was a colleague and a friend. I don't think these people should be allowed to dispose of her like so much excess baggage. It offends me.'

He hoisted a small backpack on to one shoulder. 'Men like Pudovkin, to them London is like some kind of free port, an open city, where money buys them everything they want. That offends me too.' The lizard eyes zoned in on her. 'So when Joey phoned, I thought, well, maybe it does take a villain to catch a villain.'

She gave him a quizzical frown. 'I thought you called Joey?'

He put the sunglasses back on and picked up his baseball cap from the table. She could no longer see his expression behind the dark polarized lens. 'No, he called me. About six this morning.'

As he turned to walk away he raised two fingers in mock salute. 'Take care of yourself, Karen.'

Then he melted into the crowd.

91

Kaz thought for some time about whether she wanted to be alone when she viewed the footage on the memory stick. It was likely to be upsetting, she was expecting that. Still she needed a device to watch it on. Her own laptop had been abandoned at Mike's. The last thing she wanted was to return to Reading with Tolya and have Joey looking over her shoulder.

Joey had lied. He'd called Neville Moore, not the other way round, and this was bothering her. Was it just a small thing, a slip of the tongue on his part? She didn't think so. The end result had undoubtedly helped her, but he was still up to something. He was always up to something. All this 'give me another chance' bollocks, she knew from bitter experience that Joey had an agenda. The problem was now she had the memory stick burning a hole in her pocket and she hadn't got time to be second-guessing her brother.

In the end she decided to go with her gut. She sent a text to Nicci Armstrong: 'Got something to show you.' She didn't know how Nicci was or even where. Was she still in hospital? Either she'd understand what Kaz was on about or she wouldn't.

Ten minutes later she got a text back: 'Meet you at the office 11.30.' There followed an address off Gray's Inn Road.

Kaz left Tolya at the airport and took the tube into town.

456

The side streets around the building where SBA's office was located were comparatively quiet. The weekday scramble had been replaced by Saturday strollers and tourists taking advantage of the sunshine. Many of the cafes and sandwich shops were closed, although pavement drinkers sat languidly outside the pubs.

The foyer of the building was occupied by a solitary security man, who looked rather bored. He seemed unsurprised to see Kaz and asked her to wait while he made a call.

A few minutes later the lift doors opened and Rory emerged. The last time Kaz had seen him, he'd dumped her at Whipps Cross Hospital having sprayed bullets at the Kemals in a back alley in Tottenham with a gun he then purloined.

'Morning. Nicci's upstairs.'

His manner was a little starchy as he escorted her through the security barrier and into the lift. As it ascended, Kaz shot him a sidelong glance. 'She okay?'

He nodded, avoiding her eye. 'Yes.' End of conversation.

They walked through the deserted office to a glass-walled boardroom. Nicci was seated at the table, her right arm resting in a padded sling. She was pale, but apart from that she seemed to be functioning. Simon Blake stood behind her chair, arms folded.

Nicci got up from the table a little stiffly, stepped forward and pulled Kaz into a one-armed hug. 'Thanks.'

Kaz shrugged. 'Now we're even.'

'I'm still grateful.'

Blake watched the two women. Involving an ex-con like this was against his better judgement. But Nicci was fairly convinced that Phelps had obtained vital evidence. He'd decided to go with the flow.

'We'll leave you to it then.' He gave their guest a thin smile and sauntered out to join Rory in the main office.

Nicci offered her guest a chair. 'I'm hoping they'll bring us a coffee. But that might be a bridge too far.'

Kaz lounged back in her seat, affecting nonchalance. 'I don't think he likes me, your boss.'

'He's worried.' Nicci adjusted her sling. 'He has contacts in MI5 and they're telling us that this Viktor Pudovkin is a fully fledged spook.'

Maybe it was because she was grateful, but Nicci's tone of voice was amicable and her whole manner seemed open in a way Kaz had never experienced with her before.

'So now you've decided to trust me?' She gave Nicci an oblique look.

'I think you want to see Helen Warner's killers brought to justice as much as anyone. So yeah, I've decided to trust you.'

Kaz met the ex-cop's gaze; it was steady, neither intimidating nor conciliatory. There was a candour about Nicci Armstrong that Kaz had always been aware of, but the layer of cop-caution that had previously covered it seemed to have been peeled back.

Slipping a hand in her pocket she brought out the memory stick and set it on the table. 'Well, there it is.'

Nicci studied it. 'How did you come by it?'

'From Neville Moore. Who got it from the Labour Party bloke. He says he was going to give it to the Coroner. Then he got warned off.'

Picking up the stick, Nicci rotated it between her fingers. 'He say by who?'

'No. But I think that was when he found out Pudovkin was behind it.'

Nicci placed the stick back on the table as she pondered. 'Guess who went to Moore's house to see him on Thursday? Paige Hollister.'

Kaz frowned. 'When on Thursday?'

'Afternoon I think. Why?'

'Thursday night, poor old Neville was holed up in a hotel in Brighton shitting bricks. That's when he pointed the finger at Pudovkin.'

Nicci pursed her lips. 'So it probably was her that warned him off. Can you get him to admit that, do you think?'

'Not right now. He's on a plane to Dubai.'

Cradling her injured arm, Nicci sighed. 'Okay.' She glanced towards the memory stick. 'Have you looked at what's on it?'

'Not yet.' Kaz opened her mouth to say more, then hesitated.

The ex-cop gave her a sympathetic look. 'I'm sure it's not going to be how you want to remember Helen.'

'I just wanna nail that bastard. So let's do it.'

There was a laptop on the table. Nicci opened it up. Kaz uncapped the memory stick for her and she slotted it into the USB port. Kaz dragged her chair next to Nicci's and the two women sat side by side to watch.

The footage opened in what was obviously a hotel room. It was upmarket, modern and minimalist in design. The camera position was high up, wide-angled and it looked down on a neatly made king-sized bed. The door to the en suite appeared to be to one side of the bed. It was ajar with the light on.

After a moment or two a figure emerged from the bathroom. Kaz felt her stomach lurch. It was Helen in a pair of brushed cotton check pyjamas. She walked round the bed and raked her fingers through her hair in characteristic fashion. It was a small, habitual gesture and it tore Kaz up like a high-velocity bullet. She gasped.

Nicci glanced at her. 'Want me to stop it?'

Kaz swallowed hard and shook her head.

On screen Helen was completing a circuit of the room and adjusting the lighting. It was subdued, but bright enough for the camera. She disappeared from view momentarily then returned, dragging a chair. Stepping up onto it her whole face loomed into the camera lens. She was checking it over. She seemed satisfied. Her head bobbed out of view and the chair was moved away.

The sequence then cut abruptly to a new scene. Two people on the now rumpled bed – Helen was naked, face down, her cheek pressed hard against the mattress, struggling to breathe. He was on top of her, his right hand gripping the back of her neck, forcing her down as he entered her from behind.

Distraught, Kaz shoved back her chair, got up and walked over to the window. Nicci stayed where she was, eyes glued to the screen.

From the glimpses of the man's profile it certainly looked like Robert Hollister. But the view was mainly of the back of his head. Nicci knew she'd have to watch all the way through to be certain.

She pressed pause and turned to Kaz, who was staring out of the window. 'Go and get a coffee. There's no reason for you to look at this.'

'Is it him?'

'Yeah, I think so.'

'Promise me that fucker is going down.' Her voice was hoarse and menacing.

Nicci sighed. 'Get Rory to make you a coffee and ask Simon to come in.'

Kaz's face was tight with rage, she was fighting back the tears. But she followed Nicci's suggestion.

Putting the video on fast forward, Nicci ran through to the end of the sex. She slowed it and got the full face ID of Hollister that she needed. She listened. There was a brief conversation. Hollister seemed to be talking in a matter-of-fact way about the conference they were attending as he removed his condom. Helen said virtually nothing. She certainly looked battered and abused as she gathered up her pyjamas and put them back on. Then the screen went black.

Blake pushed open the door. 'She seems pretty upset. I presume we've got him.'

Nicci shook her head. 'I don't think so. It's not a continuous sequence, the footage has been edited. We've got Warner setting up the camera, then it cuts to about five minutes of rough sex. We need to check all the dialogue carefully to see if she actually says anything. But as it stands, there's no evidence here that she refused consent.'

92

'It's not rape? What the fuck d'you mean? I saw what that bastard was doing to her.' Kaz was slumped on the low leather sofa in the reception area. She had a mug of coffee in one hand, which she dumped down with some ferocity on the floor. Coffee slopped out and onto the carpet.

Nicci was standing in front of her, cradling her injured arm. Blake scooted the receptionist's chair from behind the desk so she could sit down. Rory picked up a box of tissues and mopped up the coffee.

Easing herself down onto the chair, Nicci sighed. 'You saw two people having rough, quite violent sex. But to be rape there has to be a lack of consent. The bit that's missing is her refusing her consent – saying no, I don't want this, get off, whatever. She has to object.'

Kaz scowled across the room at her. 'You can see she was hating it! She could hardly breathe.' She glared at Blake. 'Couldn't you see it? It didn't look like just normal sex to me.' Her tone became bitter. 'But then, maybe it's me, I'm the abnormal one, that's the trouble, innit?'

Blake met her eye. 'For what it's worth, Karen, I agree with you. It's not normal sex. Our problem is the footage has been tampered with.'

'What do you mean?'

Nicci picked up the baton. 'It starts with her checking the

camera. You saw that bit. The intention was clearly to let the thing run, record whatever happened. But it cuts from that straight into the sex. Where's him arriving? What happened before the actual intercourse?'

Kaz's expression remained surly. 'You saying you think she agreed?'

'No. Just the opposite. She wanted proof of an offence. So I'm sure she did object, argue, try to fight him off. She knew the law. I'm saying that it's been edited out of the footage. The crucial bit, in terms of evidence, has been deliberately removed.'

Kaz was clenching and unclenching her fists, just about holding it together. 'It don't make sense. Why would she take it out?'

Blake's phone buzzed with an incoming text. He glanced at it surreptitiously: Detective Superintendent Phil Slattery.

Turning back to Kaz, he gave her a quizzical smile. 'Maybe she didn't. The footage has passed through various hands. We'll get it forensically examined, see if that tells us anything.'

His eye strayed back to the phone and the text message. So his efforts were finally bearing fruit. Channels were opening up, Thames House had informed the Yard of Pudovkin's possible involvement and now Slattery wanted to talk to him. About bloody time!

Kaz glared at him, she wasn't about to let go. 'Why would Neville Moore want to change it? Or the bloke from the Labour Party.'

'That I can't answer.'

Nicci was watching him. He was fidgeting and she could see from the glint in his eye that the message he'd just received was important. The video clip had carried them two steps forward and one step back. The significant thing it confirmed was that Paige Hollister had played a key role in events that led to Helen Warner's murder.

Glancing up at Blake, she gave him a speculative smile. 'If you need to deal with . . . that other matter.'

He met her eye and grinned. Even injured or half-cut, Nicci never missed a trick.

'If you're sure.' He shot a glance at Rory, then back to her. 'But you stay safe.'

She sighed, raised her bandaged arm. 'It was a gang of local kids, not the Russian mafia.'

'Even so.' A curt nod to Rory, a tepid smile in Kaz's direction and he was gone.

Nicci got up from her chair and moved over to the sofa to sit beside Kaz. 'You all right?'

'Yeah. Peachy.'

Instinct told Nicci not to prod any more. She shifted sideways to give Kaz some space.

'Okay, let's think this through. Helen had a plan. She'd asked advice from a police officer about mounting a successful prosecution against Hollister. She went to some lengths to gather evidence. Then what?'

Kaz picked up her mug of coffee, her face sullen. 'It's back to the camera, innit? What happened to it? Did she hide it or did it get nicked with the SD card in it?'

'You're right. If it got nicked, that would have alerted her to the fact someone knew what she was doing.'

'Unless she told someone.'

'Paige.' A smile spread over Nicci's features. Suddenly it all made sense. 'Helen goes to Brussels, makes the film. Comes back, sees Paige in Glasgow. They have dinner, spend the night in the same room – so we could speculate that they were close.' She gave Kaz a sideways glance. No reaction.

'What was that meeting about? Maybe Paige was fed up with her husband and how he'd treated her? Helen could've thought Paige would support what she was doing.'

'Well, she got that wrong, 'cause Paige ended up putting the frighteners on Nev.'

'Perhaps that's what the argument was about: Helen thought Paige was an ally. Turns out she wasn't . . .'

Rory admired the careful way Nicci was coaxing Kaz, keeping her in the loop. The girl was a bit of a loose cannon, he agreed with Blake on that. And it was Blake who'd asked him to get involved.

He cleared his throat. 'What about all the surveillance equipment in her house?'

Nicci shot him a look. 'Could she have discovered it?'

'Your former colleagues searched the place and they missed it.'

Kaz turned to Nicci. 'What? Her place was bugged?'

'Extensively.'

Rory scratched his chin. 'What if the camera was stolen and the house bugged at the same time?'

Nicci nodded. 'And it happened after Glasgow. Helen's left with one copy of the footage on a memory stick. Her house is bugged, her movements were probably being tracked via her phone. She might not have known for sure, but, if the camera disappeared from inside the house, she'd have certainly suspected. Surely her behaviour would've changed at this point?'

Kaz took a slug of coffee, the knot of rage in her stomach growing. Nicci was a detective, this was how they operated, working it all out step by step. For Kaz it was frustratingly slow. 'Still doesn't tell us who nobbled the footage.'

Nicci frowned. 'Neville Moore. It has to be.'

'Why? Why bother? Why not just chuck it in the bin?'

'It's a gesture.' Rory inclined his head, thinking aloud. 'He's taking out insurance.'

'What the fuck is that supposed to mean?' Kaz glared at him.

'It's not for us. He's telling Pudovkin, "Don't worry about me, I get the message. I'm on side."' An enigmatic smile crept across Rory's features. 'I would suggest we need to change our perspective on this. Our starting point is Helen Warner, but is it really about her?'

'Yeah, it's about this fucker Pudovkin trying to protect Hollister.' Kaz spat the politician's name.

Nicci turned to Rory. 'Okay, you're saying let's look at it from Pudovkin's point of view rather than Warner's.'

Rory slotted his hands in his pockets. 'A businessman connected to the security service? What's in it for him? Why go to such lengths to protect Hollister? Because they're friends?' He dismissed this with a shake of the head. 'My guess is he's collecting assets.'

Nicci relaxed back into the sofa; this was Rory's world more than hers – strategic thinking, the military mind. Part of her was reluctant to go there, and his superior attitude didn't help. Nevertheless, he'd made an important point. 'So you're saying this isn't about protecting Robert Hollister, it's about trapping him?'

'I think it's a premise worth exploring. Pudovkin saw the opportunity and took it.'

Kaz watched the two of them, debating, analysing. As they riffed off one another there was a definite sexual vibe. But Helen's life and death didn't matter to them, it was just a problem to be solved, a conundrum to unravel. That was what excited them. They were both smart and he wanted to impress her. Kaz was merely an outsider. And that was okay with her. Even if the memory stick wasn't enough to nail Hollister, Nicci was like a dog with a bone now. She was determined to put all the pieces of the puzzle together. This was who she was and what she did. All Kaz had to do was stick with her, sooner or later they'd get a result. Kaz could decide then what she wanted to do with it.

93

Rory drove them over to Blackheath in the SBA company Range Rover. Julia's parents lived down a gated private road in a substantial detached Georgian house covered with ivy.

Kaz had assumed her background was posh, but it wasn't until she followed Nicci through the elegant rooms to the back garden that she realized just how posh. The Hadleys were respectable and rich and charming. Kaz felt envious – parents and a home straight out of a movie fantasy. It seemed to her the dice had always been loaded and her rival for Helen's affections had always had the drop on her. But in an odd way, that didn't matter now as much as it had.

The object of the expedition was to ask more questions and to re-examine the text Helen had sent to Julia just before she died. Nicci was annoyed with herself for not taking a proper note of it when she'd seen it before. On the journey over to Blackheath she'd been pensive, mainly silent. It had given Kaz a chance to try and wash the image of Helen and Hollister out of her mind.

While Rory chatted amiably with Mr Hadley about cricket, Nicci and Kaz joined Julia in the garden. She was on a sun lounger, looking miserable. Nicci had suggested en route that it was unnecessary for Julia to view the content of the memory stick. Kaz had agreed. Why upset her more than she already was?

But for Kaz there was also pride involved. Julia had many advantages; what she lacked was the guts and resolution to face up to the truth behind Helen's death. She may have started the ball rolling with the investigation, but pushing it to the endgame? Kaz had decided to reserve that role for herself.

After polite enquiries about Nicci's injured arm and the offer of tea from Mrs Hadley, Julia went into the house and brought out the phone.

In a sombre voice she read the text:

Hey babe – don't think badly of me. I never wanted to hurt you. Politics, what a shit-show! I really thought I understood the game and was smart enough to play it. How dumb am I? Love you always.

Nicci had a notebook on her lap and struggled to write with her bandaged hand. Kaz offered to do it for her and Julia repeated the message in a monotone so Kaz could take it down.

A tension hung in the air; the unspoken rivalry lingered. Julia clicked the phone off and placed it on the wrought-iron garden table. Kaz handed the notebook back to Nicci.

She looked down at the unexpectedly neat handwriting. 'Okay: "I really thought I understood the game and was smart enough to play it."' Her gaze homed in on Julia. 'Was that how she usually talked? Politics as a game?'

'Not really. She talked more about wanting to make a difference.'

'So this was cynical for her?'

'I suppose.'

'As if she'd lost her faith in the whole set-up?'

Julia frowned. 'I don't know. Look, I don't see what you're getting at here.'

'I'm wondering if she suddenly realized that she was being used.'

Julia blinked several times like a startled rabbit. 'Used to do what?'

'Helen was trying to collect evidence for a prosecution against Hollister, but it could've also been used to blackmail him.'

'Helen would never have stooped to that.' Julia visibly stiffened.

'I'm not saying she would.' Nicci gave her a reassuring smile. 'Think back to just before Helen died. Was her behaviour in any way unusual?'

'I can't really remember. It's all just got . . .' She sniffed and wiped a palm across her nose. Her eyes were dull and medicated.

'Confused, I understand. Did she ever talk about the GoPro camera? It could well have been stolen when the house was bugged. Possibly a couple of weeks before she died.'

Julia's face remained blank for a few moments, then a light seemed to dawn. 'Well, I was out at work. The cleaner let them in. I'd arranged it over the phone. The electricity company wanted to change the meters to these new smart meters.'

Nicci nodded. 'Where are the meters?'

'In the cellar. I discussed it with Helen. She thought it was a good idea. More green, and all that.'

'When was this?'

Julia seemed to be dredging her memory. 'I'm not sure. But, yeah, I think it was a couple of weeks before she died?'

'So the day they came to do it, when you got home and Helen got home, did anything happen?'

'I was home first. I was cooking supper when Helen came in. She went to her study. I think possibly ten minutes later she came down, said she was going for a run. In fact we had words, because the food was ready.' The recollection produced a resentful look. 'I was pissed off with her.'

'She went out anyway?'

'So you're saying I helped them break in and bug our house?' Julia looked up at Nicci, tears in her eyes.

'Maybe. But you weren't to know.' Nicci patted her hand.

Kaz sat back in her chair watching. All the fight seemed to have gone out of Julia. Sitting in the sunshine in the lush and leafy walled garden, she remained locked in her own personal hell.

'I phoned Charles this morning – Helen's father. Just wanted to check he was okay. You know what he told me? Paige and Robert are getting a divorce. Robert told him in confidence. They're trying to keep it out of the papers for as long as possible. What do you make of that?'

94

Eddie Lunt was not a man who liked exercise, particularly on a Sunday. Sunday was a day of rest and reflection on the sofa with a bowl of popcorn and a DVD. He was a sci-fi fan – not the silly stuff full of lovesick vampires and zombies – he preferred hard-core techno, where the robots were far smarter than the humans. Most weekends he watched with his brother David. It was their special time together. David didn't always manage to follow the entire plot, but he liked loads of guns and action.

Nicci Armstrong had called him Saturday teatime; keeping tabs on Paige Hollister had become top of the agenda. She wanted full details of the GPS phone tracking, she also wanted boots-on-the-ground surveillance. What she was looking for was a window of opportunity – the chance to doorstep Paige and catch her off guard.

Eddie had decided to take David with him in his motorized wheelchair. It was a fine day, David loved to get out and about and Eddie knew that the world tended to look away when it saw a buggy containing a thirty-year-old bloke with cerebral palsy and learning difficulties. The carer of such a person also became invisible, so on an open-air surveillance David was the perfect cover.

The Hollisters' London base was a three-storey, yellow-brick Victorian terrace in Victoria Park Road. The house was expensive and substantial. Still Robert Hollister had managed to play this down with a tale, repeated in a number of interviews, of how he'd bought the house because he'd looked out of the front window overlooking the park and imagined the Chartists rallying in 1848 in that same spot, demanding radical reform. Living there reminded him of what mattered, he said.

What had mattered to Paige was ripping out half the rear wall and replacing it with plate glass to bring light into the totally remodelled open-plan kitchen and downstairs living area.

Eddie and David positioned themselves across the road from the Hollisters' house, the other side of the park railings. They strolled up and down a bit, they took their ease under the shady canopy of London planes, they chatted to passing dogs and their walkers. All the comings and goings at the house were completely visible and Eddie had a bit of extra kit – a directional rifle mike – stashed under the wheelchair, which helped him monitor any conversations on the doorstep.

They'd been in place most of the morning by the time Nicci turned up. She had her arm in a sling and Karen Phelps in tow. Eddie introduced his brother and they all peered as inconspicuously as they could across the road at the Hollisters' glossy black front door.

'I seen a couple of paps I know cruise by, so I don't know if any of the news desks have got wind of the divorce yet.' Eddie pointed in the direction of the pub on the corner. 'They're in there, probably waiting for instructions. Means we should probably get a move on.'

Nicci nodded. 'So is she on her own?'

'I think so. He arrived at half ten, picked up the kids.

Looks like he's definitely moved out. She came to the door with a glass in her hand. Bit early, some might say. I picked up a few snippets of their conversation with the rifle mike. All a bit let's be nice in front of the kids. She sounded half-cut, or on something, or both.'

Turning to her companion, Nicci raised her eyebrows. 'Want to give it a go?'

Phelps interested Eddie; ex-con, tall and quite a looker, but with a slightly don't-fuck-with-me dykey air about her. He couldn't figure out why Nicci had brought her along though. To unnerve the cool Mrs Hollister, tip her over the edge? It amused him that his oh-so-straight boss wasn't shy of playing a few tricks of her own. Or maybe working on the outside was teaching her to improvise.

He watched the women follow the park railings along to the gate and cross the road towards the house. He pulled a thermos from the backpack slung on the back of the wheel-chair.

Smiling at his brother, he unscrewed the top. 'Fancy a bevy, mate?'

David gave him a grin. 'Cheers.' His speech was slow and breathy, but easy enough to decipher. 'All the stuff you done for her, why don't she say thanks?'

Eddie poured the tea. 'Very good question, David. But that's bosses for you. Heads up their arses most the time. I do the job as best I can and I don't let it get to me. You fancy a Jaffa Cake?'

95

As she walked across the road to the Hollisters' house with Kaz, Nicci felt vaguely disgruntled. Eddie Lunt seemed to have a talent for wrong-footing her. Was this some kind of elaborate ploy on his part to win her over? Living with his elderly mother was bad enough, now he'd conjured up a disabled brother.

Kaz glanced at her and smiled. 'Smart bloke. He's certainly got his finger on the pulse.'

Nicci gave her a baleful look. 'He's been in prison for phone hacking.'

'No kidding?' The chuckle was provocative. 'Perhaps I should get to know him better.'

They paused on the Hollisters' doorstep, Nicci raised her eyebrows, Kaz replied with a reassuring nod. Nicci pressed the bell.

It took several minutes for a figure to appear behind the tall rectangle of frosted glass. The door opened a crack. Nicci could smell the booze.

She had her business card ready and she held it up in much the same way she used to hold her warrant card. 'Mrs Hollister? I'm Nicci Armstrong from Simon Blake Associates. We're private investigators retained by Julia Hadley to inquire into the death of Helen Warner. We'd like to talk to you.'

The eyes visible through the crack were glassy pinpricks,

the voice throaty with nicotine. 'I really don't think I'm able to help you.'

Nicci stepped forward and blocked the door with her good shoulder. 'We have CCTV footage of you arguing with Helen Warner in a Glasgow hotel a month before she died. I'm sure you'd prefer to explain that in private rather than in public.'

There was a moment of hesitation then the door swung open.

Paige Hollister stood in the hall, small and sinewy in lycra running tights and a tank top, with a smouldering cigarette between her fingers. 'You'd better come in.'

Nicci stepped over the threshold with Kaz in her wake. 'This is Karen Phelps. She was a friend of Helen's.'

Paige blinked up at Kaz and a sour look of realization spread over her features. 'My God! You're her little jailbird, aren't you? She was completely obsessed with you.'

Without waiting for a response she turned on her bare heel and padded down the hall to the kitchen at the back of the house. Nicci gave Kaz a shrug and followed.

The kitchen was ultra modern, the folding doors onto the garden partly open. A pink plastic kiddie car with fat rubber wheels sat half in and half out of the doorway.

Paige tossed the half-smoked cigarette in the sink, where it landed with a hiss. She opened the fridge, drew out a bottle of white wine and refilled the glass on the counter.

She held the bottle up. 'Drink?'

Nicci shook her head. 'We're fine, thank you.'

Paige gave a sardonic smile. 'Well, lucky old you.' Then she took a large swallow of wine. 'I've got a very good doctor who prescribes me Xanax. Of course he says I shouldn't drink. But then they all say that, don't they? Personally, I find it's a good combination.'

Placing her notebook down on the wide granite counter, Nicci perched on one of the high stools. 'So tell us what you and Helen were doing in Glasgow then?'

Paige tipped back her head and laughed. 'Glasgow? Fucking Glasgow? I saved his bacon. Do you realize that? And now he thinks he can just dump me flat. Well, he's going to find that I've got friends who'll have something to say about that.'

Nicci gave her an amiable smile. 'Friends like Viktor?'

Paige seemed to drift off as she leant against the counter. 'I have many friends. Numerous friends.'

'Including Viktor Pudovkin?'

Turning towards her, Paige wagged a finger. 'Robert is very lucky.'

'Why's he lucky, Paige?' Nicci gave her a patient smile.

'That bitch was planning to bring him down. I mean, seriously?'

'Helen Warner? Is that who you're talking about?'

Paige took a slug of wine. 'Fifteen years I've been married to him. Three fucking kids. He expects me to step aside so he can trade up to a newer model with a tighter arse and a PhD.'

Kaz wandered round the counter and folded her arms. 'Well, they're all bastards in the end, aren't they?'

Paige narrowed her eyes and peered at Kaz with disdain. 'Hard to fathom what she saw in you. She said you were creative, good at art.'

'I try my best.'

'Were you a good fuck? Tried your best at that too?'

Kaz met her gaze with a piercing stare. 'Helen never complained.'

Nicci watched the stand-off. Kaz seemed to be doing an excellent job of getting under Paige Hollister's skin.

But Paige just laughed. 'All men are bastards? Is that your line too? So if we girlies just stick together we'll beat them in the end?' She chuckled and took another mouthful of wine. 'Do you have any idea how to succeed in politics?'

'I'm sure you're gonna tell me.'

'Identify the winning team and join it.' Paige picked up the bottle of wine. 'Women are not the winning team. In case you haven't noticed.' She topped up her glass. 'Sure you don't fancy a tipple?' Her lip curled. 'Hang on, though, weren't you some kind of alchy and drug addict? Took the pledge for love of Helen. She really got off on that particular ego trip, I can tell you. Brings new meaning to the whole concept of a bit of rough.'

Kaz was standing stock-still like a panther coiled and ready to spring. Nicci could feel how dangerous she was even if Paige was too zoned out to notice.

Sliding off her stool, Nicci stepped between them. 'Let me get this clear – Helen wanted you to join with her and help bring your husband down?'

Paige giggled. 'Can you believe it? Stupid woman.'

'Must've been really tough though, when she showed you the footage she'd shot of her and Robert?'

Paige's lips compressed and then twisted. 'Porn is porn. If he'd seen it, he'd have probably enjoyed it.'

Nicci glanced at Kaz, caught her eye. Kaz inhaled, took a step back.

'What did you do?' Nicci kept her tone neutral. 'Once you discovered what Helen was up to you wanted to protect your husband. When you came back to London, what did you do?'

'I may be drunk, but I'm not naive. I'm not prepared to discuss this any further. You'll have to take the matter up with my lawyers.'

Kaz shot a look at her. 'That wouldn't be Neville Moore by any chance? Helen's old boss.'

Panic rippled momentarily across Paige's features. 'Who?'

Nicci joined in. 'You went to see him. Thursday afternoon. I'm guessing Viktor Pudovkin sent you? You suspected Moore had the memory stick. Wasn't it your job to get it or warn him off?'

Paige picked up a packet of cigarettes from the counter and fumbled to light one. She had to spark the lighter several times.

Nicci pressed on, confident that now they were getting to the heart of it. 'What did Robert say when he found out you'd asked Viktor for his help? He went apeshit, didn't he?'

As she drew on the cigarette her hand shook. 'I think you should leave now.'

Nicci merely smiled. 'And I think you should tell us the truth, Paige. Your husband's cutting you loose because you've served him up on a silver platter to Viktor Pudovkin and the FSB. And Robert's mad as hell, isn't he? You thought Viktor was just a "concerned friend" with the power to help, didn't you? You thought it'd be business as usual – you carry on ignoring Robert's little peccadilloes, even facilitate them, you'll wake up in Downing Street one day. Trouble is, you underestimated Viktor.'

Grasping her right wrist with her left hand, Paige struggled to steady her shaking arm. 'I've no idea what you're talking about. Viktor is simply a social acquaintance. He's a businessman and a philanthropist.'

Nicci shook her head sorrowfully, like a wise teacher chiding a wayward child. 'Now you are being naive. You really think that? You made a monumental error asking for his help. You must've realized that. And you know why Robert's cutting you out of the loop? Because if he needs a fall guy, you're it. Divorce is not the worst thing that could happen here. You think that Robert's not going to try and save his own skin? You could go to jail as an accessory to Helen Warner's murder.'

Fighting back the tears, Paige ground out the cigarette savagely in a plate on the kitchen counter. Kaz refused to pity her. This woman had betrayed Helen's youthful trust in the most fundamental way, and she'd carried on doing it for years.

Arms wrapped tightly around herself, Paige's voice came out almost as a sob. 'Okay, I had no idea they would kill her! No idea. I swear. It was just a matter of breaking into her house and getting this wretched film.'

Nicci stepped forward and gently placed her hand on the weeping woman's shoulder. 'Listen to me, Paige, I used to be a police officer. The people who murdered Helen are professional killers. Totally ruthless. They will tidy up the loose ends. And that's what you've become.'

Shoving Nicci away, Paige straightened up. 'No, I've been given assurances. Robert won't divorce me, you know. He's just huffing and puffing. He'll come back, he'll have to.'

'You believe that?' Nicci glanced at Kaz, who stood watching with folded arms.

Paige picked up the wine bottle and topped up her glass. 'I'm not saying any more. I admit nothing. Now go.'

96

It was Monday morning, warm, overcast and smoggy. Blake sat behind his desk, shirt sleeves rolled up, listening to the recording on Nicci's phone. Paige Hollister's posh, strangulated, faintly Scottish voice was clearly audible: *I'm not saying any more. I admit nothing. Now go.*

Nicci clicked the recording off and picked the phone up. 'I'll download it and get it transcribed.'

Blake beamed at her. 'Nice piece of work, Nic. She certainly incriminates herself, so Slattery'll have to take her in and interview her.' The smile collapsed into a frown. 'Problem is, what have we actually got? Hollister's estranged wife, jealous of his affair with the younger, more attractive Helen Warner? He could still walk away.'

'He's setting his wife up to take the fall, isn't he?'

Blake chuckled and nodded. 'Not what you'd call the most loving husband.'

'Did you talk to Slattery?' Nicci adjusted her sling. 'What does he say?'

'Met him in a pub in Barnes yesterday lunchtime. He's trying to keep it all under wraps and chummy. He reckons Hollister and Warner had a long-term affair. Hollister dumped her, she was distraught, topped herself. That's the Met's story and they're sticking to it.'

'And the video we've got does nothing to contradict that.'

Nicci sighed. 'I've got the researchers and Eddie digging around for any other politicians who might've got into bother recently and accepted a helping hand from Pudovkin.'

He leant back in his chair. 'That's only ever going to be circumstantial until we crack Hollister. He's battening down the hatches. What we need is to find a weak spot and prod it. But it's not going to be easy.'

'I know that.' She gave him a belligerent look.

He replied with a wave of his hand. 'Sorry. I know you know. I suppose I'm missing the power. I'd like to just march in and nick both the Hollisters and sit them in an interview room until somebody blinks.'

'So would I. But we're on the outside now. We have to find new strategies.'

He gave her an appraising look. 'You've changed your tune.' It occurred to him she was looking almost jaunty, the colour had returned to her cheeks. The haunted look behind the eyes seemed to have faded.

'Adapt or die, boss.' There was an arch glint in her eye. 'So, if we can find a way to put the screws on Hollister, you'll go along with it?'

He gave her a sardonic look. 'Depends what you've got in mind?'

'Not sure yet. But I'll get back to you.'

She sailed out and across the office. Blake watched her go. Mourning the death of her daughter had been a long and gruelling process. Blake knew it wasn't over. By no means. But it had moved into the background, she was functioning, she was living from day to day and doing the job.

He became aware of Alan Turnbull hovering outside his door. He groaned inwardly. It had turned into a daily battle, trying to keep Turnbull at arm's length while he tried to come up with a plausible plan to turf the cuckoo out of the nest.

Turnbull opened the door. 'Have you got a minute?'

'Of course. Come in, Alan.'

'I think you should come out here and take a look for yourself.' Turnbull continued to hold the glass door open.

Reluctantly Blake got up from behind his desk and joined Turnbull in the doorway.

Turnbull pointed across the office. 'We appear to have acquired a new staff member.'

Blake's gaze travelled across the room to the Investigations Section. Pascale and Liam were in place. Nicci had scooted the chair away from her desk and was chatting animatedly to Karen Phelps. He wasn't thrilled. This was possibly taking new strategies too far. Still that was between him and Nicci.

'You realize who she is?' Turnbull smirked.

Blake returned to his desk. 'I believe she's a friend of Helen Warner. I think possibly Nicci may be getting a witness statement from her.'

'She's been here all morning. According to Liam, she's helping Nicci. Did you authorize this?'

Blake was annoyed and uncomfortable in equal parts, but that didn't mean he'd tolerate Turnbull's tone.

He fixed him with a gimlet eye. 'Alan, Nicci knows what she's doing and she has my full confidence.'

Turnbull slipped his hands in his trouser pockets; the suit was, as ever, immaculate. 'Her name's Karen Phelps. She's an armed robber, released on licence. A week ago her brother murdered a prison officer and escaped from jail.'

Blake settled back in his chair. 'And your point is?'

'You forget, Nicci Armstrong used to work for me. She was never the most careful or compliant officer.'

Blake steepled his fingers. 'That's good, because I'm not looking for compliant.'

'The profile of this firm, Simon, its public image—'

'Will depend on results. That's what the investors want to see and that's what I intend to give them.' Blake loosened his tie. He was well aware that in comparison to Turnbull he looked scruffy. Turnbull was probably the sort of bloke who got a manicure.

Almost as though he'd read Blake's mind, his tormentor's lips formed a contemptuous sneer. 'Image is important. You're not a down-at-heel policeman any more, Simon. Investigations is a minor and very subsidiary part of this firm. We're in the security business. That's what makes money. Corporate clients and protecting high-net-worth individuals, their property and assets.'

'Really? I'm glad you've clarified that for me, Alan. And you know what, I don't think our business philosophies are gelling that well. Do you?'

'Duncan and I—'

'Can go fuck yourselves.' Blake was on his feet. 'Tell him I'm in discussions with a couple of new equity funds who'll be happy to buy him out.' He came round the desk and eyeballed Turnbull. 'Now get out of my office, Alan. Because we're done.'

Turnbull exhaled; he seemed no more than mildly put out. 'You talk a good game, Blake. Lots of bluff and swagger. I wonder if you can follow through. I guess we'll see.'

Blake watched the back of the elegantly cut suit as it disappeared out of the door. He took a breath and considered what he'd just done. It was impulsive, certainly, but what the hell? Sometimes when you were standing on the edge of a precipice the only thing left to do was leap – and it wasn't nearly as scary as he'd expected.

97

It was just getting dark as Kaz approached the mansion block on the edge of Belgravia. She got out of the taxi at the end of the street and walked the last few hundred yards to make sure that she felt the part and could manage the shoes.

Irina had volunteered to be her stylist again. The outfit that they'd come up with was deliberately understated – a tight pencil skirt, not too short, a silk top and some discreet jewellery. Yevgeny and Tolya had given it their seal of approval.

Joey had stood in front of his sister holding both her hands. A wistful look came into his eye. The doctor had called earlier in the day – a Syrian refugee with poor English but plenty of experience treating the results of violence – he'd given Joey more antibiotics and signed him off.

His hair had been trimmed and the beard sculpted. With coloured contacts to turn his baby-blue eyes brown, the passport photos had been done. Heavy-rimmed spectacles made him look older and rather scholarly. He'd awarded himself a PhD and that completed his new identity as a travelling academic.

He grinned at his sister. 'You gonna be back in time before I go?'

'Yeah, I hope so.'

Kaz's feelings remained extremely mixed. It had crossed her mind that she might use Nicci Armstrong as a conduit to inform the police of Joey's whereabouts. But that would have involved implicating Yevgeny, Tolya and Irina, and they weren't just Joey's people any more. She'd come to regard them as her friends, especially Irina.

Kaz was only too well aware that the lines had become dangerously blurred in her own mind as much as anywhere. Who was she now? What was she doing? The old Kaz Phelps was dead. But should the art student she'd been for the past two years really be strolling through one of the wealthiest parts of London, looking like a model with several thousand pounds' worth of designer threads on her back?

She paused outside the mansion block. Most of the flats were dark. Simon Blake Associates had the security contract for the building. The owners were mainly from South-East Asia or China; their flats were rarely used. There was a Greek couple who lived on the second floor and two Chinese students, studying at the LSE, who occupied one of the top flats. The rest of the building was in effect empty.

Following instructions, Kaz walked confidently up to the front door. She didn't need to ring the bell, the doorman saw her through the glass and sprang forward to open it.

Dressed in smart uniform and moving with a military bearing, he dipped his head as he held the door open for her. 'Good evening, miss.'

Kaz smiled awkwardly, her stomach was becoming decidedly jumpy.

Waving her through with an outstretched palm, he informed her, 'The lift is on your right, miss.'

She managed a more confident smile. 'Thank you.'

Kaz took the lift to the third floor and walked down the softly carpeted corridor to number six. Taking the key she'd been given from her handbag, she unlocked the door.

The smell that assailed her was a mixture of wax polish from the honey-coloured oak floor and fresh flowers from the bouquet on the hall table. She slipped off her shoes and carrying them in one hand started to explore.

There were two bedrooms with en suite bathrooms, a sitting room with bay windows overlooking the street, which opened into the dining room and a gleaming white kitchen. All the rooms were high-ceilinged and generously proportioned, the whole apartment resembled something out of the pages of an interior design magazine. Polished wood, plush carpets, abstract paintings, low leather sofas.

However, the place had been carefully dressed to appear lived in – some books and magazines, box sets of DVDs, a bowl of fresh fruit on the table. In the kitchen there were glasses and an ice bucket; a saucer of olives and champagne in the fridge.

Kaz wandered round the sitting room and dining area, checked all the drawers and cupboards, rearranged the cushions on the sofa to create a little nest for herself. Taking her phone out of her bag, she placed it on the glass coffee table. Then she picked up the remote handset and clicked the television on. She went to the kitchen, poured herself a glass of water. Finally she settled down to wait.

Shortly after nine o'clock the doorbell rang. Kaz muted the television – she'd found a documentary on an obscure channel about kids growing up in Ramallah. It had turned out to be far more interesting than she'd expected.

She took her time answering the door. Robert Hollister stood on the threshold, tieless and with his jacket slung rakishly over one shoulder.

She gave him what she hoped was a mysterious smile. 'I didn't know whether you'd come.'

'I never like to disappoint a lady.' He was carrying a bottle wrapped in tissue paper. He offered it to her. 'This might need chilling a little.'

'Thank you. I'll pop it in the fridge.' She lowered her eyes coyly and he followed her into the flat.

'Nice place.'

'Make yourself at home.'

She took the bottle to the kitchen. It turned out to be a cheap Cava. She deposited it in the fridge and brought out the Dom Perignon that was already there.

Carrying the ice bucket, bottle and glasses on a tray she joined him in the sitting room.

He had the television remote in his hand, the sound was back on. 'What are you watching?'

'Oh, just a documentary. I like to keep abreast of what's going on in the world.'

He gave her a thoughtful look. 'I've been to Ramallah you know. Fact-finding trip.'

'And did you find many interesting facts?'

He laughed. 'Yeah, one or two.'

She indicated the bottle. 'Perhaps you'd do the honours.'

He switched the television off, lifted the champagne from the ice bucket and cracked open the foil. 'So does your boyfriend mind you entertaining guests? I presume he foots the bill for all this.'

She gave him a roguish look. 'Why do you assume I have a boyfriend? I could be an independent woman.'

'Are you?' He looked her up and down. 'I'm even more impressed.'

'I was married briefly. My ex left me quite well off.'

Holding on to the bottle, he extracted the cork with a muffled pop.

She leant her head to one side and smiled. 'Good technique.'

He poured the champagne into two flutes. 'Oh, I think you'll find I'm quite expert at a lot of things.' He handed her a glass. 'What shall we drink to?'

'What do you suggest?'

'Clever girls.' He half closed his eyes and gazed at her. 'I like clever girls.'

They clinked and drank. He took a large swallow of champagne, Kaz managed to barely wet her lips. She sat down on the sofa and he plonked himself beside her.

Two more mouthfuls and he'd emptied his glass; he flicked the ends of her hair with his fingers. 'You're an intriguing one, aren't you?'

'Am I? I've always thought of myself as pretty ordinary.' She reached over and refilled his glass. 'You look like you've had a busy day.'

He accepted the replenished glass. 'Tell me about it! My life is a little complicated just at the moment.'

'Complicated in what way?'

Taking another drink, he sighed. 'Politics can be tedious at times. I wouldn't want to bore you.'

'You think I'm some sort of airhead who wouldn't understand.'

He gave her a sidelong look. 'Not at all. I told you, I prefer clever girls. I like my women feisty, someone who puts up a bit of a fight. If you know what I mean.'

'What sort of fight?'

A teasing smile played round his mouth. 'Oh, come, don't play the ingénue.'

She got up from the sofa and wandered round to the other side of the coffee table, glass still in hand. 'Is that what you liked about Helen? She was a clever girl and she put up a fight?'

He stared at her blankly for a moment. 'Helen who?'

Kaz fixed him with a glacial stare. 'Helen Warner. She was a friend of mine.'

Hollister's jaw literally dropped.

Kaz put her glass down, walked over to the sideboard, opened the drawer and brought out an iPad. 'I've got something here I'd like to show you.' She clicked through the functions rapidly. 'This is just a clip. A little taster.'

She held the tablet up directly in front of him.

He glared at her. 'Who the fuck are you?'

'I told you, a friend of Helen Warner.' She pressed play and an image from the video footage of Helen and Hollister appeared on the screen.

He jumped to his feet and grabbed the device from her. The clip lasted no more than thirty seconds.

Kaz took a step back; she could feel the rage pulsing off him. 'Helen made more than one copy and she sent one to me. You didn't know that, did you?'

His eyes scoped the room and alighted on her phone on the coffee table. 'What the fuck do you want? A pay-off?'

'I'd prefer an explanation.'

With a hollow laugh he plucked the phone off the table. He clicked it on and the icon for recording sound popped up.

He chuckled. 'You're recording this on your phone! I think I'm going to have to revise my opinion. You're not a very clever girl at all, are you?'

He strode out of the room and into the bathroom. She heard a splash as the phone hit the toilet bowl, followed by water flushing.

Returning, he paused on the threshold, hands on hips.

'Any other little tricks up your sleeve?' He scanned the room, made a circuit, opening drawers, peering in corners, looking under the lampshades. Once he was satisfied, he came round the coffee table to face her. 'No, not very bright. Now, I think you and I need to have a serious conversation.'

Kaz edged backwards towards the corner; she picked up a heavy ceramic vase. 'Don't come any closer.'

He laughed. 'You stupid bitch. You really think you can set me up?'

'I'll scream.'

'Will you now? Where's the rest of the film?'

Kaz took another step back. 'Somewhere safe.'

'Okay, let's have a little reality check here. You're going to get it and return it to me.'

'It's not yours, it's Helen's. Proof you raped her.'

Shaking his head wearily, he put his hands in his pockets. 'Rape? That's a loaded word.'

'It's also a crime.'

'I never raped Helen Warner. I just gave her what she really wanted.'

Kaz could feel the bile rising in her throat. 'You're not what she wanted.'

'Oh, I get it.' He grinned. 'You were one of her little sweethearts, were you? You think she wanted you? Sexuality is a complex thing. But nature doesn't change. Girls don't always know what they want, they need guidance.'

'She wasn't a girl, she was a woman.'

He laughed again, his tone was peevish yet proud. 'She was a girl when I first found her. I was her education.'

'I don't believe you.'

'Her father was my tutor at Oxford. She was fourteen.

Quite the little Lolita. She tried to tease me, but I had her in the end.'

'When she was fourteen?'

'Oh yes. Sadly we've become very puritanical about these matters in recent years. Some countries girls are married at fourteen. So you will give me that film.' His eyes were bright and hard, he took a step towards her.

As she edged sideways to try and put the sofa between them she felt the constraint of her tight skirt.

Dressing up like this had been stupid, it gave her no room for manoeuvre. 'What if I refuse?'

'What if you refuse? Let's think about that, shall we?'

He didn't look particularly athletic, but when he moved he was fast, crossing the room to her in a couple of strides. His right hand flew at her throat and grasped her by the windpipe. She felt the full force of his fury as he slammed her against the wall.

The impact knocked the wind out of her.

She gasped for breath. 'You're . . . choking . . . me.'

His tone was detached and matter-of-fact. 'You're choking yourself. By resisting. Try to relax.' With his left hand he ripped open the front of her silk blouse. 'You just need to be a good girl. Let it happen. Then you won't be hurt.'

Without loosening the hold on her throat, his other hand reached down to pull up her skirt. It was the opportunity she needed. Once the skirt was halfway up her thighs she jerked her leg sharply upwards and kneed him in the balls. As the hand on her throat slackened, her forehead shot forwards and cracked into his nose.

He staggered backwards. 'Aargh! Fuck! You are one vicious bitch!'

Spinning round to the sideboard drawer, she yanked it

open, reached into the canteen of cutlery and pulled out a steak knife. 'Yeah, I am. That's exactly what I am. Now get the fuck out of here!'

Blood trickled from his nose over his top lip; he wiped it with his hand. 'This isn't over. Some friends of mine are going to be keeping an eye on you. So don't think of doing anything stupid. They'll be round to collect the film.'

She brandished the knife. 'You think I'm frightened of them? Who the fuck are they anyway?'

He drew a handkerchief from his trouser pocket and dabbed his nose. 'Oh you should be.' Picking up his jacket, he headed for the door. Then he turned. 'Think about what happened to Helen. Believe me, it was no accident.'

Kaz waited until he was gone then sank down on the sofa. She put the knife on the table and gingerly fingered her bruised neck. It was sore.

A figure appeared in the doorway.

Nicci Armstrong frowned. 'Are you okay? I think maybe we let that run on a bit too far.'

Kaz glanced up at her. 'Yeah but did you get it all?'

'Oh yes. Sound and vision. You sure you're all right?'

Kaz slapped the coffee table. 'No. I fucked it up. I didn't get him to name Pudovkin.'

The ex-cop came and sat beside her. 'You did brilliantly, Kaz. Believe me, Robert Hollister is going down.'

98

The early morning sun leached through the blinds, crept across the wooden floor, up and across Kaz's face, finally waking her. She was curled up on Nicci's wide brown sofa. Rolling over, she dozed for a bit longer until she heard Nicci pad into the kitchen, fill the kettle at the tap and put it to boil.

She sat up slowly and rubbed her face.

Nicci was standing there in her dressing gown. 'Sleep okay?'

'Yeah, it's pretty comfortable.'

'How's the neck?'

'Feels a bit bruised.'

Nicci came and perched on the arm of the vast sofa, her brow knit with concern. 'What you did was, well, extremely brave. Do you know that?'

Kaz gave her a thin smile. 'You lot were in the flat next door, so it wasn't that brave.'

'I've worked undercover. I was always shit scared. When you're trying to hook a violent offender you can never really tell which way they'll jump.'

Sitting up, Kaz wrapped the duvet round herself. 'Have we really got enough to nail him?'

Nicci shrugged. 'I talked to Blake. He's been in touch with the Met. They're coming to the office at nine to see the footage. They'll take Hollister in for questioning, they'll have to.'

'You don't sound as confident as you did last night.'

'It'll be down to the police and the CPS to make the case. Once Hollister gets lawyered up, they'll tell him to say nothing and argue inadmissibility. But we've got a few tricks up our sleeve.'

'What about Pudovkin?'

'Well, as Hollister left the flat, he made a call. We got the number, but we couldn't trace it. The police will though. Half an hour later two thugs turned up.'

'Looking for me?'

'Oh yeah. They trashed the flat. Rory still had all the surveillance gear in place, so he filmed them doing it. It's circumstantial in terms of Hollister. But it'll add to the pressure that can be put on him.'

Kaz sank back into the soft folds of the sofa. 'Still too many ways that bastard can wriggle out of this, aren't there?'

'We're in the hands of the legal process now. You've been on the other side of the fence, Karen. You know how the game's played.'

Kaz smiled wryly. 'Yeah.'

Nicci got up. 'I need to take a shower and get going. Do you want to make some tea? Or there's coffee, if you'd prefer.' She frowned. 'I think there's some instant somewhere.'

Kaz had already deduced from the spartan nature of the flat that domestic organization was not Nicci Armstrong's priority.

'I'll make tea.' She gave her hostess a reassuring grin.

Nicci glanced at Kaz's discarded clothes. 'Want me to lend you some jeans or something?'

'That would be great.'

'Might be a bit short in the leg.'

'I'll cope.'

With a smile and a nod Nicci disappeared. Kaz could see that having a house-guest wasn't totally comfortable for her. She seemed a solitary and secret soul. Kaz knew nothing of her history; things like family and relationships had never come up.

Wrapping herself in her torn blouse, she wandered into the kitchen area. The kettle had boiled. She searched in vain for a teapot and ended up dunking a teabag in a mug.

Her sequin-studded handbag from the night before lay on the table. It began to vibrate. Her own phone had remained in the bag all along; presumably one of Rory's people had fished the plant out of the toilet. Kaz opened the bag and extracted the ringing phone. The caller ID read: Joey.

Kaz stared at it for a moment, sighed and answered. 'Morning.'

'You sound a bit stiff and starchy, babes. Didn't it go to plan?'

'I'm at Nicci's.'

'Oh. Right. I'll keep it short then.'

'Good idea.'

'I'm getting the Eurostar from St Pancras at half twelve. Was hoping maybe you'd come and see me off.'

Kaz hesitated. 'Is that a good idea?'

'I got a surprise for you. Little going-away present.'

A cascade of scenarios flooded her mind – none of them pleasant. On the other hand, what could he do in the middle of one of London's major railway stations?

'I'm not that keen on surprises.'

His tone was impish. 'Trust me, babes. You're gonna love this. Meet me at the champagne bar, it's sort of up on the walkway. You can't miss it.'

'What time?'

'Midday. You won't be disappointed, I promise.'

He hung up. Kaz held the phone in her hand and a dark fatalistic feeling rose up inside her. She brushed it aside and focused on dragging the soggy teabag from her mug.

99

Simon Blake stood at the head of the table in the boardroom watching Rory and Liam set up a screen and projector. His mood was airy; he'd spent his morning commute gazing out of the carriage window at swathes of sunlit woods and pasture. In his long police career he'd had his fair share of ups and downs. Now he was operating in new territory, a place where the old rules and privileges didn't apply, but for the first time he felt at home. The Warner case had done that for him. It had silenced his niggling conscience and proved, if only to himself, that being a private investigator was a reputable calling. He wasn't just in it for the money, as some envious former colleagues believed.

He awaited his guests from the MPS with refreshing equanimity. This was in spite of the fact he'd had Duncan Linton on the phone, issuing veiled threats to put him out of business. Blake's reply had been, 'Fine, bring it on.' He'd had a late-night visit from two absurdly young Thames House spooks demanding to know what he'd got on Robert Hollister; he'd fobbed them off with lies. He'd also received a surprise early morning call from Fiona Calder, fishing for information. He'd been courteous enough but had pointed out that she wasn't the only one who knew how to manipulate the media.

Alicia was arranging mineral water and glasses on the

table when Nicci arrived. Blake scrutinized her: no red-rimmed baggy eyes, which made a change. Her arm was still resting in a sling, but she was wearing a smartish suit and a shirt, which had been ironed. Rory glanced across the room at her with the hint of a smile. But she ignored him entirely and headed for Blake. He knew she was probably just being tactical, still somewhere deep inside there lurked a suppressed adolescent fantasy that if circumstances had been different – but they weren't.

Nicci checked her watch. 'My guess is they'll be ten minutes late.'

Blake grinned. 'Slattery's a cocky bastard, so I'm going to say fifteen.'

They both turned out to be wrong. Pascale escorted the Detective Superintendent and his three sidekicks from the lift to the office suite at nine on the dot. Introductions and handshakes were exchanged. Slattery declined the offer of coffee and pastries, but that was the only outward sign of his peevishness. He was playing the upstanding public official, refusing to sully himself by accepting anything, even hospitality, from the grubby realms of commerce.

He settled in a chair and immediately cut to the chase. 'So Robert Hollister has been telling us he had a straightforward affair with Helen Warner and you're going to tell me he's lying?'

Blake was not about to be baited. 'I'm going to show you some surveillance footage, Phil, and let you draw your own conclusions.'

'Was this footage obtained legally?'

'Shot in a private mansion-block flat, with the permission of the owner. My company provides security for the whole building.'

Slattery inhaled. 'That's convenient.'

His entourage comprised a DI and two DS's. The DI was known to Blake, solid enough, but a bit of a plodder. His value to Slattery was he'd never be a threat. The other two were young and fierce-looking, brought along purely as ballast. The female of the pair eyed Nicci aggressively. Nicci sipped the coffee Alicia had poured for her and waited. Slattery might be stupid enough to think that this was his show. In reality it was Blake's.

Taking a chair at the back of the room away from the table, Blake gave Rory a nod. The blinds had already been adjusted to cut out the morning glare. He switched on the projector and all eyes swivelled towards the screen.

The footage from the Belgravia flat had been edited down to a short continuous sequence. It began with Karen Phelps getting up from the sofa and wandering round to the other side of the coffee table.

Slattery folded his arms. 'Who's the girl?'

Blake could feel the tension pulsing off his former colleague. 'She's about to tell you. She's a friend of Helen Warner.'

Right on cue, Kaz said exactly that. For the rest of the sequence Slattery remained silent. Robert Hollister's admission that he began having a sexual relationship with Helen when she was only fourteen caused the policeman to blink several times. Apart from that he displayed no reaction whatsoever. The clip ended with Hollister dabbing a bloody nose and informing his audience that what happened to Helen Warner was no accident.

Rory reached over to switch the projector off. Liam opened the blinds. They both left the room.

Blake leant forward in his chair; he didn't want to gloat. 'Sure we can't get you a coffee, Phil?'

Slattery drew in a long breath. 'We will of course require the original and all copies.'

Rising to his feet and slotting his hands in his pockets, Blake strolled over to the window. 'You must think I was born yesterday.'

The Detective Superintendent swung round in his chair. 'If you're suggesting—'

Blake held up his palm. 'Whoa there! I'm not suggesting anything. You will obviously want to examine the original footage and have it forensically checked. Of course we will facilitate that. But Robert Hollister's activities are a matter of legitimate public concern.'

Slattery gave him a surly glare. 'You bastard, you've already given this to the press, haven't you?'

'Several editors have been made aware that the footage exists. I'm going to give you two hours, Phil, to do the right thing.'

The cop shoved his chair back and got to his feet, his crew gathered around him. 'Hollister goes down, you know the effect that'll have on the Met? They'll cut and cut until there's fuck all left. But you don't give a stuff about that, do you?'

'I give a stuff about the abuse of a fourteen-year-old girl, the murder of an MP and the blackmail of a politician to corrupt the democratic process – and so should you.'

'I don't see evidence of corruption here. Or even murder. So Hollister's a paedo? If a court buys that, then he'll go down. But I'm not chasing some bloody conspiracy theory you've dreamt up to generate publicity for Simon Fucking Blake Associates.' He paused for effect but his brow was beaded with sweat. 'I think we're done here.'

Blake opened his palms. 'Thank you for coming over, Phil.'

Slattery turned on his heel and strode towards the door. One of the DS's leapt forward to open it for him.

Hesitating, he glanced over his shoulder. 'A lot of people still respect you, Blake. But that could change. The contacts you rely on, the officers who moonlight for you – that could all dry up.'

He swept out of the boardroom with his cohorts in his wake. The heavy, frosted glass door creaked on its hinges.

Nicci glanced across the room at the boss. 'Well, he's not very happy.'

'He's shitting bricks.' Blake chuckled. 'Once the papers start in on Hollister, the Commissioner may need a fall guy. He's the prime candidate.'

'You think they'll arrest Hollister straight away?'

'They'll have to. We'll package the surveillance footage with your recording of the wife. Leaves the Hollisters with a hell of a lot of explaining to do. My guess is the Commissioner'll give it to someone else. Slattery's tainted.'

Nicci sighed. 'And the murder?'

'Depends what happens once Hollister's lawyers get cracking.' Blake was gazing out of the window but his expression had darkened. 'Put him and his lovely wife in separate interview rooms, play them off against each other. That's what I'd do. That's how you'll get to the truth. Maybe she asked Pudovkin to do it. Or Pudovkin simply saw the opportunity.'

Rising from her chair, Nicci came to stand beside him. 'You wish you were back on the inside and in control?'

'Time's like this, hell yeah.'

'Me too.' She gave him a wistful smile. 'But whatever else, we've succeeded in doing what Helen Warner wanted and that's bring Hollister down.'

Blake jangled the change in his pocket. 'True. You want to call Julia and tell her?'

'Okay.'

Nicci was heading for the door when Blake glanced over his shoulder. 'You made this happen. You're still a bloody good detective, Armstrong. In any kind of just world they'd be lining you up for Slattery's job.'

Her smile was ghostly as she rearranged her arm in the sling. 'Yeah, but it's not a just world, is it? Only a fool thinks that.'

100

Viktor Pudovkin had decided, perhaps a little later in life than most, to dedicate himself to being a family man and spending as much time as possible with his two young children. He had a son of forty with a seat in the Duma and two others from his first marriage, both well placed in the Kremlin. But he'd hardly been involved in their upbringing.

The Soviet Union in the seventies and eighties had been a very different place and he'd worked the kind of hours the youngsters of today would simply balk at. His grown-up children were extremely respectful and he suspected that would've been the case even without his vast wealth. However, there just wasn't the closeness, the emotional bond of father and child, the pleasure of watching a young person grow and blossom that Pudovkin had come to realize was one of life's joys. He was determined to do things differently with Sasha and Mariya. And in any event he'd already achieved more or less everything else he'd set out to do.

The family home was in Holland Park, a large detached mansion with a charming garden and a covered pool, which the children loved. Every day the family breakfasted together in the conservatory and occasionally, when the weather was pleasant enough, on the terrace.

There was a very good nursery for three-year-old Mariya just round the corner, all the shops his wife could wish for and a top prep school within reasonable driving distance for Sasha. Both children were growing up bilingual and Pudovkin had already put his son down for Eton.

Life in London suited Pudovkin; the facilities were excellent, the regime was stable but accommodating and everything that mattered was for sale. He remained loyal to the motherland, but living in Moscow could be taxing. It was easier to deal with the political currents and eddies from a distance. And in London he could be useful to his old allies and comrades.

Democracy was a concept that amused the Russian and in particular the way, in the West, so much lip service was paid to it. Rulers ruled; it had been true in the ancient world and remained the benchmark of any effective social order. Men like Robert Hollister, so called democrats, had such a grandiose notion of their own purpose it made them an easy mark.

There were two ways to turn a western politician into an asset and Pudovkin had perfected both. The first was a simple cash transaction and a surprising number went for that. The main political parties in the UK were also by and large for sale. The second option – and the one that required much more finesse – was blackmail. So far he'd become an indispensable friend to three cabinet ministers and several ambitious members of the opposition. Pudovkin served his masters in the Kremlin well and in return they left him in peace to enjoy his money.

Getting his son to eat a proper breakfast was always a game of patience. The boy was an energetic little sprite, his attention darting hither and thither. Pudovkin reprimanded him in Russian.

The boy tossed his head defiantly. 'Speak English, Papa.'

Pudovkin gave him an indulgent smile. 'Have you finished your breakfast? I have a busy day. I have to get you to school.'

His wife was on her phone gossiping with a friend. He got up from the table, kissed the back of her head, he had calls of his own to make.

Robert Hollister had got himself in a panic over some incident. The politician had been angry and hostile initially, refusing to cooperate, but he'd come to heel. Pudovkin had learnt, back in his days as a KGB officer, that the individuals who regarded themselves as having the highest morals and the loftiest ideals were usually weakest and the quickest to crack.

It was Paige Hollister who'd approached him first with the tale of her husband's infidelities and Pudovkin had listened as any concerned friend would. He undertook to sort the matter out and he'd fulfilled his part of the bargain. But Paige was a neurotic woman and likely to be troublesome unless kept on a tight rein. Hollister himself was simply naive about the world he was living in and his country's place in it. It was an arrogance the British and the Americans shared.

Pudovkin strolled through the house and into the magnificent hallway. The butler was waiting with his jacket and briefcase.

He glanced back over his shoulder. 'Sasha, come on!'

The boy trotted after him and collected his backpack from the butler.

Taking his son's hand, Pudovkin stepped out of the front door and proceeded down the short tiled path to the waiting car.

One of his bodyguards held open the rear door of the Mercedes.

Pudovkin was turning to speak to his son when he caught

sight of a motorcycle out of the corner of his eye. It was approaching at speed and a sixth sense, the product of years of front-line experience, kicked in. Even before the pillion rider had raised his arm, Pudovkin had flung Sasha to the ground, covering the child with his own body.

Shots rang out, pinging off the car's bodywork and the bullet-resistant glass. Scooping the boy up, the Russian made a run for the cover of the garden wall. But the motorcycle had already swerved to a halt and was turning back for a second pass.

101

The spinning back wheel of the Kawasaki Ninja left an arc of burning rubber on the road as it fought for traction. Tolya flung it into the turn and opened up the throttle. Perched high up behind him Joey had his left hand round the Russian's waist to keep his gun hand free.

As the bike roared back towards the Mercedes for a second pass, Joey saw the old man scrabbling to his feet and trying to pick up his kid. Joey held his arm steady, locked out his wrist and went for a headshot. But a dip in the road caused the bike to buck just as the Glock 18 delivered a rapid burst of fire; it narrowly missed Pudovkin's head and took a chunk out of the wall.

Joey cursed under his breath. Carrying out a hit from the back of a bike was his least favourite option. There were always too many factors that could fuck up. But the target lived in a fortress and travelled in a fully armoured car. The opportunities to get a clean shot were few. If Joey'd had the time to arrange it, he'd have gone for a sniper rifle. Plotted up properly, telescopic sight, it would be hard to miss. But he'd wanted to sort this out for Kaz before he left.

His sister still regarded him with suspicion and he could see why. For most people anger was an emotion that usually overrode everything else. However, Joey wasn't like most people. Since he was forced to leave the country he needed someone he could trust to take over the firm. And Kaz was by far the best choice. Once she got over her fear of him they'd be the perfect team. It was what he'd always wanted, ever since they were kids.

As the Kawasaki closed on the impregnable car, Joey craned round in his seat to get a shot past it to where the Russian was cowering beside the wall. His attention zeroed in on the sightline and he remained absolutely focused, nanoseconds ticking by as he waited for the shot to line up.

When the hail of bullets hit them, the front of the bike reared up before flipping on its side and launching Tolya over the handlebars. Joey was tossed up in the air as Pudovkin's driver continued to spray them with a PP-2000 submachine gun.

Joey landed on his back, his left leg twisted beneath him. He managed to roll onto his side. The helmet had protected his head, the vest his torso, but several bullets had ripped open his thigh and the pulse of hot blood down his leg suggested the femoral artery was severed.

He needed to tie it off, if he could only get to the scarf round his neck. Fingers fumbling, he clicked open the release on his chinstrap and with a supreme effort pulled the helmet off.

A single shot rang out just to the left of him. He turned sufficiently to see one of Pudovkin's suited minders standing pointing a smoking handgun at Tolya's inert body. Glancing rapidly around he located the Glock. It had landed maybe a metre to his right. Pulling himself up onto his elbows he started to crawl. As he reached out a hand to grasp the pistol butt, a black leather shoe kicked it away.

Lifting his head to look up at the dark tunnel inside the muzzle of the gun Joey wondered idly if there'd be any pain.

A snatch of memory ricocheted across his synapses – jumping out of a tree to surprise his sister, the two of them rolling over and over on soft, springy turf and Kaz laughing.

Joey Phelps didn't hear the shot, the bullet travelled faster than the sound of the explosion in the chamber.

The bodyguard lowered his arm, spat on the corpse then retreated into the house. It was up to the British police to clean up the mess. He had no intention of sticking around to answer any awkward questions.

102

Kaz Phelps leant on the balustrade beside the champagne bar and gazed down the vaulted iron hangar towards the impressive station clock. It was twenty past twelve and still no sign of Joey. He was going to miss his train.

It was all over the news – Robert Hollister was helping the police with their inquiries. The mainstream media was being cautious, but the Net was rife with rumour – a major child-abuse scandal with possible links to the death of MP Helen Warner. The Labour Party and Hollister's political colleagues were desperately distancing themselves; his wife had been admitted to a private clinic for stress and depression, his in-laws had taken the children.

In a snatched phone conversation Nicci had assured Kaz that it was unlikely the police would want to speak to her – certainly not immediately – about her encounter with Hollister. And all efforts would be made to keep her involvement in the sting and her identity out of the press.

Standing in the ex-cop's jeans and an old sweatshirt, Kaz watched the minutes tick by on the huge clock. She'd called Joey several times and got no reply.

Then she saw a familiar figure at a distance coming towards her along the raised walkway – not Joey, Yevgeny. He approached at a steady pace and as he got nearer she could see a coldness and blankness in his face. Was this it? Would it be Yev, who she really liked? Had he come to deliver Joey's revenge?

He came to a halt a few feet in front of her and Kaz realized he had tears in his eyes.

It took several seconds for him to speak. 'I didn't know what they planned to do. Not 'til the last minute.' He swallowed hard. 'I tried to stop them.'

Kaz gave him a puzzled frown. 'What you talking about, Yev?'

'Joey, he want to surprise you. He knew you was upset that Pudovkin kill your friend. And the cops, they never get a man like Pudovkin. No way. Joey decided to take him out for you.'

She stared at him in disbelief. 'Joey's killed Pudovkin?'

The Russian shook his head sorrowfully. 'They tried. Him and Tolya. Pudovkin's people shot them dead.'

'Dead?' *Her brother dead?* The word seemed to just hang in the air. All motion, everything, including her own heartbeat stopped. She grasped the balustrade for support.

'He love you more than anything, Kaz. He thought if he do this for you, you trust him again.'

His voice seemed to fade, overwhelmed by the rushing in her ears. A howl of raw pain engulfed her. It took her a moment to realize it was coming from her own mouth.

EPILOGUE

Kaz wandered along the path through the dappled shade of the towering London plane trees. She'd agreed to meet Nicci Armstrong in Russell Square – it was public and she wasn't taking any chances. She saw the ex-cop turn in at the gate; the sling was gone and she was looking sharp in a business suit with a new leather briefcase dangling from one shoulder.

As Nicci walked up to her, Kaz smiled. 'How's the arm?'

'Fine thanks. Practically healed.'

They stood for a moment in silence. Kaz's brain was buzzing with questions, but she wasn't about to jump in first.

Nicci heaved a sigh. 'I don't know what the fuck you were thinking of, Karen.'

'For the record, I had no idea what he planned to do.'

There was a bench next to them on the side of the path. Nicci dumped her briefcase on it. 'Okay, say I believe that. You're still guilty of harbouring a convicted felon who'd escaped from jail.'

'I wasn't harbouring him. He came after me, as good as took me hostage. I thought he was gonna kill me.'

'So why did he try and shoot Pudovkin if you didn't ask him to?'

Kaz plonked herself down on the bench. 'It's complicated. I think maybe he just wanted to impress me. Get me back onside.' She knew it was more than that. It was an act of love.

514

as well as an act of violence. It was Joey's attempt to win back the affection of the only person he'd ever cared about.

Nicci exhaled, joined her on the bench. 'If they find out that you were even in touch with him, they'll revoke your licence. You'll be straight back inside.'

'You gonna dob me in then?'

The ex-cop shook her head wearily. 'You've put me in a difficult position.'

'What about Pudovkin? When are the police gonna question him about Helen's murder?'

'They're not.' Nicci met her eye. 'The Met have been instructed to leave Pudovkin alone.'

She waited for the explosion but Kaz simply raked a hand through her hair. 'Why? 'Cause the fucker's rich?'

'Because he's an important back channel to the Kremlin. That's what Blake's contact in MI6 told him. The MPS will, however, be looking into your brother's attempt to kill him. They may well want to interview you about that.'

A bitter chuckle erupted from Kaz. 'Let me get this straight – no one's gonna even ask him about Helen's murder. But me, I could end up back in the nick, if they can prove I've seen Joey since he escaped.'

'That's about the size of it, yeah.'

'And what about Helen?'

'They're sticking with the suicide story. She was a long-standing victim of sexual abuse, she despaired of ever proving it, the shame was eating her up, so she took her own life.'

'What's Julia got to say to that?'

Nicci tilted her head. 'I think the revelation of what the Hollisters did to Helen profoundly shocked her. And the fact she had no idea about it. She seems to be leaning towards the view that it was suicide.'

'It's just total bullshit.' Kaz's eyes bored into her, dark and disturbing. 'You don't believe that.'

'It's possible.'

Jumping up, Kaz towered over her. 'Oh, come on, Nicci! Paige Hollister? Her sleazy perve of a husband, you heard what he said.'

Nicci raised a placatory palm. 'Okay, I think Pudovkin had Helen Warner murdered in order to gain leverage over Robert Hollister. But it's a theory and the chances of finding any evidence to prove it are zilch.'

'I wish Joey had killed the bastard. That would be justice.'

Shaking her head, Nicci rose to her feet. 'That would be revenge.'

Kaz folded her arms. 'We're gonna have to disagree on that one.'

'You think in all the years I was a police officer it didn't stick in my craw, all the villains who got away with murder on a technicality, because they had a smart brief? You of all people should know how flawed the system is. But it's the best we can do. You want to see the alternative, look at the Middle East – militias running round with guns. Anarchy.'

A restless rage pulsed off Kaz, she kicked a cigarette butt across the path. 'Pudovkin gets away with it. He's filthy rich, got political connections so he's untouchable. That's the best you can do?'

'Sadly, yeah.' Nicci tried to meet her eye, but Kaz had turned away. The tension of her anger rippled around them both.

The ex-cop picked up her briefcase and hooked the strap over her shoulder. 'Are you going back to Glasgow?'

'And wait 'til your lot come calling, asking me questions about Joey?'

'You can stonewall them. You're good at that.' Nicci hesitated, but only for a split second. 'For what it's worth, I'm not going to tell them anything.'

Kaz shot her a belligerent glance. 'What about your boss?'

'Blake won't either.'

A curt nod was the best Kaz could manage. 'Thanks.'

'Go back to college, Karen. Get your degree. Get on with your life.'

The two women faced one another in a summery London square, surrounded by tourists, joggers, office workers and vagrants. Nicci smiled and held out her hand, Kaz Phelps took it but her gaze remained unreadable and adamantine.

ACKNOWLEDGEMENTS

I have relied once again on the generous advice and professional expertise of DCI Roy Ledingham and Professor Dave Barclay. I also received invaluable help from Professor Sue Black OBE, Director of the Centre for Anatomy and Human Identification at the University of Dundee. The background information and input provided by my good friend GC was, as always, indispensable.

Second novels are notoriously difficult to get right but I was lucky enough to have the advice and guidance of an excellent editor in Trisha Jackson, ably assisted by Natasha Harding. The team at Pan Macmillan have certainly gone the extra mile to ensure that both *The Mourner* and my first book, *The Informant*, have the best chance in an overcrowded market. James Annal produced fantastic covers. Jodie Mullish and Amy Lines ran a brilliant marketing campaign. Stuart Dwyer and his sales team, Guy Raphael, Lucy Dale-Harris and Rebecca Bader, got the books out there and on the shelves. Sam Eades, in charge of publicity, was a whirlwind of creative ideas and energy. Laura Carr and Anne O'Brien sorted out my grammar, wobbly syntax and repetitive verbal ticks.

My agent, Jane Gregory, was a brilliant champion, as ever. And special thanks once again to my two first readers Sue Kenyon and Jenny Kenyon for their excellent feedback and for telling me the things I didn't want to hear.

extracts reading groups
competitions books new
discounts extracts extracts discounts
competitions events
books
new books
events extracts
new reading groups
extracts books
new titles reading groups
interviews
reading books events extracts extracts events new
books extracts discounts new
discounts new books events interviews new books extracts
events new events
discounts extracts discounts
www.panmacmillan.com
extracts events reading groups
competitions books extracts new